PRAISE

"Nobody writes like Tijan. With addicting storylines and unparalleled prose, she's always an auto-click author for me."

—Rachel Van Dyken, #1 *New York Times* bestselling author

"Tijan knows how to create addictive, fun and exciting stories that you simply cannot put down!"

—Elle Kennedy, *New York Times* bestselling author

"I can always count on Tijan to write an action-packed, intense, emotional story that will have me invested until the very last page."

—Helena Hunting, *New York Times* bestselling author

"Tijan delivers on the fun, edge, and angst. Her books never fail to please!"

—Kylie Scott, *New York Times* bestselling author

"Tijan delivers a power-punch with *Anti-Stepbrother*—angst, tension, and an emotional conclusion that'll have you glued to every page. The characters jump straight from the story and claim your heart. You won't be ready to let go."

—JB Salsbury, *New York Times* and *USA Today* bestselling author

"One of my Tijan faves, with a hero to die for and a heroine you'll want as your best friend."

—Katy Evans, *New York Times* bestselling author, on *Anti-Stepbrother*

"5+ *riveting* stars!!! The chemistry between Dusty and Stone was *off-the-charts electrifying*. I was completely absorbed from the first page to the last. Tijan didn't just get a touchdown with this story—she won the Super Bowl!"

—Beth Flynn, *USA Today* bestselling author, on *Enemies*

"Obsessed from page 1! *The Insiders* is yet another addicting read from Tijan."

—Jennifer L. Armentrout, #1 *New York Times* bestselling author, on *The Insiders*

"A whirlwind of high-stakes suspense."

—*Publishers Weekly* on *The Insiders*

"Hello, book hangover! With captivating, unique characters, this story is so much more than an epic sports romance. Redemption. Friendship. Unconditional love. And that ending! Hands down, my favorite Tijan book!"

—Devney Perry, *USA Today* bestselling author, on *The Not-Outcast*

"Blaise is the perfect rich prick to fall in love with! One of my fave reads in 2020!"

—Ilsa Madden-Mills, *Wall Street Journal* bestselling author, on *Rich Prick*

"Emotionally tumultuous, angsty, and beautiful. *Ryan's Bed* is a new Tijan favorite and a must-read for anyone going through loss!"

—Rachel Van Dyken, #1 *New York Times* bestselling author, on *Ryan's Bed*

A *Captive* SITUATION

OTHER TITLES BY TIJAN

A Dirty Business

Mafia Stand-Alones

Cole
Bennett Mafia
Jonah Bennett
Canary

Fallen Crest / Roussou Universe

Fallen Crest Series
Crew Series
The Boy I Grew Up With (stand-alone)
Rich Prick (stand-alone)
Nate
Aveke
Frisco

Other Series

Broken and Screwed Series (YA/NA)
Jaded Series (YA/NA suspense)
Davy Harwood Series (paranormal)
Carter Reed Series (Mafia)
The Insiders (trilogy)

Sports Romance Stand-Alones

Enemies
Teardrop Shot

Hate To Love You

The Not-Outcast

Young Adult Stand-Alones

Ryan's Bed

A Whole New Crowd

Brady Remington Landed Me in Jail

College Stand-Alones

Anti-Stepbrother

Kian

Contemporary Romances

Bad Boy Brody

Home Tears

Fighter

Rockstar Romance Stand-Alone

Sustain

Paranormal Stand-Alones

Evil

Micaela's Big Bad

More books to come!

A Captive Situation

TIJAN

Montlake

This is a work of fiction. Names, characters, organizations, places, events, and incidents are either products of the author's imagination or are used fictitiously. Otherwise, any resemblance to actual persons, living or dead, is purely coincidental.

Published by Montlake, Seattle

www.apub.com

EU product safety contact:
Amazon Media EU S. à r.l.
38, avenue John F. Kennedy, L-1855 Luxembourg
amazonpublishing-gpsr@amazon.com

ISBN-13: 9781662524851 (paperback)
ISBN-13: 9781662524844 (digital)

Cover design by Caroline Teagle Johnson
Cover image: © Wander Aguiar Photography

Printed in the United States of America

A Captive Situation

CHAPTER ONE

SAWYER

I was riding the subway in New York City for the first time, and a part of me was hoping the passengers around me would start singing *The Lion King*'s "Circle of Life."

Logically, I'm sure that rarely happened, but if there was a chance? I was down for it.

Hear me, Universe. Broadway rendition of any song. I'm not picky.

I waited, looking around. There were some people passed out. A bunch of college students. Other workers. I leaned back, eyeing a group of athletic-looking people. They looked like they could be dancers. Broadway dancers?

I was hoping for it, but then the next stop happened and they got off.

Okay. I deflated.

Maybe not.

The last guy I was holding out for was scowling to himself and was fixated on his phone. He had the build. Broad shoulders. He wasn't slim, or he didn't seem like it as he was sitting, but he had the *looks*. And by that I meant that he was hot. Super hot. He was solidly built. There was no excess weight on him. All muscle. Fierce eyes. A clenched jawline. Leather jacket, black Henley, and jeans. Dark hair that was cut short on the sides and left with enough to grab a hold of on top.

He looked as if he could handle himself in a fight, and in my mind, that meant he was made for Broadway.

His energy was all off, though. He seemed all growly, not as though he was ready to burst into song. Perhaps he was the Beast? Or no . . . Gaston?

No. Gaston didn't seem to fit either. Total Beast.

His phone buzzed and he answered it, turning away. I couldn't make out his words, but his very gravelly and pissed-off clipped tones were now about to segue into the beginning of "Seasons of Love."

I was waiting.

Expecting.

Sigh.

It wasn't going to happen.

My phone buzzed at that moment, too, and I checked my text.

Mom: Hi honey! How is New York? Are you safe? Did you see the Wall Street bull yet? I know you were so excited to check it out.

My mom was under the impression I was here as a tourist. Which I was. I had an entire tourist checklist of things to do: See a Broadway show, go to a museum, maybe go nuts and eat at some fancy restaurant that only New York City seemed to have. I wanted to go to Ellis Island, tour the Statue of Liberty, find out what this Canal Street was all about. Then there was Times Square, though I was a bit iffy on this naked cowboy character.

The other reason I was here in New York and not back home was because of just that, I would *not* be back home. So since I was avoiding anything and everything that reminded me of Montana, I was going to skip seeing this cowboy person, naked or not. We had enough cowboys back home.

Another item I wanted to check off my list was to meet my cousin. I'd met his sisters a few times. They lived a few hours away, but not Graham. That was going to change on this trip. My mom was close to two of my aunts, but there was a rift between the three of them and Graham's mom. I'd asked my mom what the issue was, but she never gave me a great answer. She liked to deflect. So while I was here, I was taking things into my own hands.

I'd cyberstalked Graham and he looked awesome. He was adopted, he and his two sisters. He was an architect. He had a husband. He liked to travel. I could get so many great tips on being the ultimate tourist from him.

I was hoping when I met Graham, and when he fell in awesome cousin love with me, that we could conspire on how to bring the sisters together.

That was the secret mission. That, and the whole "not being at home" because this was also the week that I was supposed to be getting married.

But I wasn't, because Beck dumped me.

Beck, the same guy that I'd been with since college.

The same guy that I helped put through chiropractic school.

The same guy that wanted me to quit the receptionist job I loved to work for him, which I did.

The same guy that I gave almost two decades of my life. We'd been engaged for the last two years, but then he decided to fill me in on a simple thing where he'd been cheating on me for the last three years. And that they were having a child.

He and Manda.

And that person he was cheating on me with—Manda—was my best friend from college.

I was about to lose it. This was what happened when I let myself ruminate.

There were thoughts.

And feelings.

And anger. Lots and lots of anger.

I couldn't let myself think about it, because if I did, then I was going to *lose my mind.*

If that happened, there was a chance I'd start hyperventilating. That could lead to other unhinged hysteria, and then who knew what kind of handcuffs I'd end up in at the end of that adventure?

There was also the possibility that I was having a slight midlife crisis.

I was four years away from turning forty, and yep . . . I could feel the hysteria coming on. Though, the hysteria wasn't about my age, it was about the reason I was *not* in Montana this week.

Which I couldn't focus on at the moment.

The scowly guy, who still hadn't broken into any *Beauty and the Beast* Broadway songs, glanced my way. His mouth was pressed in a tight line as he was eyeing me.

Right. I was breathing pretty loudly and thinking about the ex.

"Woman." It was the scowling guy. He leaned forward. His jacket fell open, showing a gun holstered on his hip. "What the fuck's wrong with you? You need an ambulance or something?"

An ambulance?

I hadn't heard him right. I couldn't have. Leaning toward him, I hissed, "Excuse me?"

His eyelid twitched as he ran his gaze over me, lingering on my legs before dipping back up to my mouth. It jerked up to my gaze, and his scowl just doubled. "You look like you're about to pass out. Are you? If so, I gotta call for an ambo."

I didn't know if I should be flattered at the concern, though he was not coming off like he was in the least bit concerned about me. He seemed irritated, like I was the last thing he wanted to deal with, and at that thought, I straightened in my seat, deciding to be insulted. "You think I'm going to pass out because of why? I'm breathing harshly? I'm so sorry. Did I interrupt your phone call because I was just sitting here, minding my own business? Was I not quiet enough as I was thinking about my—well, it's none of your business what I was thinking about, but was I not quiet enough? You want me to be more silently angry? Sure. Totally. I'll be like a statue as I'm processing my own shit here, or can I not have feelings either? Is there a certain way I'm supposed to breathe while I *feel* things, *sir*?"

A part of me was wincing at my snark, but there was a whole side of me that *did not care*.

I stared at him, hotly.

He glared back, but his dark eyes cooled dramatically. He'd been pissed off before, but now he was downright like ice. "If you need medical assistance, I'm obliged to provide it for you."

Obliged?

I skewered him with a look. I had no idea how to respond to that.

"Ma'am." The train was coming to a stop, and he stood once it did. He clipped out, "Do you need medical help?"

He took one step toward me, looming over me. That scowl hadn't lessened or deepened. I was thinking it was permanently fixed on his face. He had resting scowling face. RSF.

"Why are you so fixated on me? Go away. Focus on someone else." I gestured to a guy who was stretched out and sleeping on the other side of us. "He's passed out. Why aren't you asking him if he needs EMTs or not?"

The sleeping guy opened his eyes and lifted his gaze. His legs had been stretched out, his ankles crossed over one another, and he had his arms crossed over his chest. He looked relaxed. "Huh?" he asked now, frowning.

"Go back to sleep, Miguel." The scowling guy jerked in his direction.

"Oh. Okay." He closed his eyes and laid his head back down.

Great. Lovely. They knew each other.

The doors slid open. People were spilling out.

Now I was scowling, and I stood up. Lifting up my arm, I grabbed the same pole he was holding on to. "I'm fine. No. I do not need medical assistan—"

I cut myself off because he wasn't looking at me anymore. His eyes were trained over my shoulder.

People were coming in, filling up the emptied spots, but suddenly a woman screamed. A guy shouted, and the scowling guy yelled right next to my ear, "Marcus Easter, *stop*!"

He cursed under his breath and shoved past me.

I got whiplash. He moved so fast. Twisting around, I saw a guy run off the train and toward the stairs. Scowling Hot Guy was fast behind him.

They were soon gone from eyesight, and I frowned. That was all . . . I didn't even know what that was.

Miguel was sitting up, yawning.

I asked him, "Does that happen a lot here?"

He snorted before giving me a lopsided grin, scratching his head. "Nah. That's just Shorty. I wonder what he did this time."

I sat down, a little dazed. The train started again, and I groaned.

That'd been my stop.

CHAPTER TWO

SAWYER

"Sawyer. Sweetie. I'm concerned. Why are you still in New York City? It's been another week. I understand that you wanted a change of scenery because of the wedding that hap—but, honey, when are you coming back?"

Never.

That was my automatic response, but I had to stop myself from sharing that. My mom would go ballistic, and I knew she was already worried about me. To give her credit, she had reason. In the two weeks being here, I'd alternated between being a zombie or a tourist, but mostly I was trying to get the courage to see Graham.

Technically, he was family, so it wasn't like I was some random person on the street searching him out, but there *was* that weirdness in the family. I didn't understand the rift between his mom and the rest of the sisters.

My mom and my two aunts were so close. Phyllis, Bess, and Clara.

Phyllis was my mom. Bess and Clara never had children and I didn't have siblings, so the four of us were tight. Maude was their fourth and youngest sister, and she had three children. I'd met her girls a few times, but it wasn't enough. I wanted to be closer to *all* of my cousins.

I wanted to fix it. This was a heartbreak that I could fix. At least, that's where I was funneling most of my energy right now. The tourist bucket list was happening, but I kept finding myself needing to fix *something* in my life.

Family issues, you're up to bat.

Also, the certainty that I was *so* having a midlife crisis had risen to 65 percent. That was the only thing that made sense because as my mom was talking, I knew. I just knew.

I wasn't going back.

I gulped as those words went through my mind, but it was the truth.

Oh my goodness.

"Did you get in touch with Graham? His mother called to complain that you called her a few times asking about him, where he works. I believe he's on that picture app, Instacart or something? He works at Exhibit, that's some fancy architecture business. He's an architect. You'd think that'd be something your aunt would be boasting about. You'll have to keep me informed, let me know how Graham is. But I blame my sister. Maude's never encouraged her kids to have relationships with the rest of us. I don't know what her problem is."

I didn't think there was any big secret to why I hadn't met Graham. I was certain it had to do with our mothers and aunts, but whatever it was, it was going to get dealt with.

She kept grumbling, saying the same narrative she always did when she started ranting about the one sister that wasn't close to the other three. Maude was always the odd sister on the outside. That's how it'd been all my life.

But Mom ranting was normal.

What wasn't normal was what she almost said just now. Logically, she was referring to my supposed wedding, but a different sensation went down my spine. I didn't think she was referring to my wedding. It was in the tone of her voice. There was a lack of familiarity with that word, as if it belonged to someone else. Not to the wedding she was supposed to have helped me with.

Dread lined my insides, and I clenched onto my phone tighter. I was sitting at a pizzeria, enjoying an afternoon beer when my mother called today.

The beer was forgotten now.

"Mom," I said.

She quieted.

I readied myself. "You said 'the wedding that hap—' You cut yourself off." I folded my head. "My wedding didn't happen, so it couldn't be my wedding you're talking about." Fuck. Shit. This hurt. My throat was being scraped from the inside out. "Whose wedding were you referring to?"

"Honey." Her voice dropped. "I can't bring myself to tell you."

Oh, god.

He ended things with us. He did. Beck. He dumped me. I gave up so much for him . . . I couldn't go there. What was she about to say to me?

"Mom?" My voice got quiet.

Her voice was strained. "I have to go. We can talk about it when you come home."

She ended the call.

My mind was spinning. What just happened?

My chest felt like it was caving in on itself. I pressed a hand there, and drew in a breath. Jesus. It hurt.

The beer. The pizzeria. The sounds of the city that surrounded me, all of it faded completely.

I felt so alone.

Later that night, my phone started buzzing.

Aunt Clara: Bess and I got the download from your mother. What do you want to know about your cousin? We're on it.

Aunt Clara: You want us to reach out to him? I can do that. I won't go through Maude for his information. I've got internet friends who can help get his 411.

Aunt Bess: Don't go through your mother anymore for that information. It stresses her out. You know how she is. She likes everyone getting along and Maude is the opposite. She thrives on negativity. We're here for you. We're your pillars. What do you need from us?

My aunts had decided to tag in with me.
That meant my mom handed me off to them.

A day later, my phone buzzed again. More texts.

Aunt Bess: We get you don't want to talk about this right now, but Clara is on a trip. She's going to stink bomb Beck's car and she's rallying some of the neighbors to start keeping an eye on him. A heads up. You know how she is. We may need limits because shit can go sideways real quick with her.

Aunt Clara: I joined the walking club that goes past Manda's house. Tomorrow I'll make friends with the neighbors across the road from her place.

Aunt Clara: Don't listen to anything Bess is saying. She needs to keep her nose out of my business. I've got it handled. We'll set up a way to communicate later on. I'll send the code system tomorrow. Stand by.

What? Code system?

I considered asking. Should I ask them what my mom started to spill? They would tell me. My dad was around, but it was the four of us against the world. It felt that way sometimes. Bess and Clara never hid the truth from me. If I asked, they answered.

I held the phone in my hand, and wavered.

My hand started shaking.

No. That was me. I was shaking.

I put the phone aside.

I wasn't ready to know. Not yet.

It could break me further, and Beck didn't get that option anymore.

I'd ask later.

It was time to hit up a Broadway show.

CHAPTER THREE

SAWYER

Two days later, I was stalking my cousin. That wasn't creepy at all.

I was standing across the street from Exhibit, a very sophisticated-looking building. Lots of glass windows everywhere. The bottom floor was all windows. There was a giant statue in the front lobby. There was a clear view of the receptionist, a beautiful blond woman who hadn't been impressed with me when I went inside for a quick check to see if it was actually where my cousin worked.

His name was on the wall, Graham Matsen, along with his picture. Asian. He was a few years older than me. Trim. He looked like he worked out.

Pride swelled up in me. It wasn't warranted because I had no hand in any of his endeavors, but he was family.

He was an architect in this place. He lived in New York City. He was successful. That was obvious to see. Of course, I knew some of this from following him on Instagram. Him and his husband, Oliver. They were adorable. Maybe I shouldn't judge from what was posted on social media, but there were a few videos posted. He and Oliver loved each other.

So yeah. He was successful. He had a loving partner.

I was proud.

I started blinking away some tears, because good for him.

At least one person in our family seemed happy.

That was good. Good for him.

I bet he never gave up a job he enjoyed to support Oliver. I bet Oliver supported him in going for this dream job of an architect.

I kept blinking.

"Miss," the receptionist had called out, standing behind her desk. Her hand went to the phone. "You'll need to leave unless you have an appointment. We don't offer public restrooms to tourists." Her tone was so chilly.

Right. Yes. That made sense. I should tell her who I was, except when I opened my mouth to do that . . . I couldn't. Nothing was coming out of me.

What was I doing? I was two seconds from losing it, just at seeing my cousin's picture on the wall in this place. I couldn't meet him like this. I'd completely lose it and he'd think I was mentally unstable and well, my mission would go down the drain.

I needed to regroup.

Yes. I nodded to myself, feeling more calm at this change.

Regroup. Come back again when I was not about to lose it because of what a failure I was in life, the total opposite of Graham.

"Ma'am, if you don't have an appointment, you need to leave. If you don't go, I'll call security."

I tried to speak, but a ball of emotions was still there, choking me. "I—" My voice came out hoarse.

She picked up the phone and clipped into it, "I need security down in the—"

No! No. I couldn't have security escort me out. That was a whole new type of low. I wasn't quite there yet.

I didn't think . . .

I'd leave, do my regroup thing, and well, maybe not approach Graham at his job.

I swept out of the lobby and headed down the street.

I didn't totally leave.

I left the building, but I wanted a glimpse of the life my cousin had because he'd made something of himself. Whereas I . . . I'd completely and totally fucked up my life.

My hands began shaking. I could not slide back there, to what brought me here, what *really* brought me here, so I crossed the street at the nearest crosswalk, and got a sandwich from a nearby food truck. After that, I camped out across the road.

Correction. I was munching on a hero. That's what the brochure said they called them here.

So far the receptionist hadn't spotted me, but I was ready to bolt if I needed to. I wasn't normally a mess like this, but my god, half of my life had just been pulled out from under my feet.

Focus.

Focus, Sawyer! New mission. Fix the aunts. Starting with yourself and Graham.

Everything aligned again inside of me. My feet found solid ground. I had a purpose in life again.

Pulling up Graham's Instagram, I focused on the pictures of him and his husband. They enjoyed traveling. Paris. Arizona. Redwoods. Japan. They went all over, and I checked the timestamps. All those places were posted within the last two months. They were big travelers.

It was helping. Some of the madness in my mind was fading.

I lost track of time.

My mouth was almost watering at the thought of all that traveling.

Coming here to New York was the most I'd traveled in my life. My parents weren't adventurous like that. If we traveled at all, it'd be Glacier or hiking. We were big on hiking, or my dad and I were. Mom, not so much. Then Beck was always studying.

He said we didn't have the money for traveling.

So I kept working.

He wanted a house.

So then there were mortgage payments for that as well.

And I kept working.

Pain sliced down my insides, but dammit. I needed to start dealing with what happened.

Swallowing a lump that formed in my throat, images flashed from that time in my life.

I loved college. It'd been fun. I liked going to class. I liked having the dreams of my degree, what kind of job I could do with it. Where I could work, if I wanted to travel with my job.

That's where I met Manda. She was on the same floor in my dorm. And after going to a fraternity party, we met Beck and his friends. It'd been flutters-at-first-sight for me.

God.

Beck. He had charisma. He was good looking. He was charming. When he smiled at me, I melted.

What a fucking joke I turned out to be.

Here I was, still in New York. Still hadn't done what I came here to do.

I was still being a joke.

I had one more night booked at the hotel. The honeymoon funds were running low.

I wasn't rich. Most of my money went to supporting Beck, paying for his school loans, paying for the house. I didn't have enough to get a place here. No way.

Beck emerged from graduate school relatively debt-free, thanks to me. He loved what he did.

My college degree was in marketing, but in Bear Creek, Montana, there wasn't a job market for that degree.

Being a receptionist wasn't the fulfilling part for me. It was in who I worked with and the people that came into the business who I helped. People liked me.

I was way nicer than the one that worked at Graham's architecture firm.

Then Beck wanted me to man his practice and things changed.

I didn't enjoy working for Beck or with the other girls in the office, though I tried telling myself that I did.

That was another farce in my life.

Another place where I'd been deluding myself.

Bitter tears rolled down my face. One fell into the corner of my mouth. It was salty.

"Miss."

I'd been so lost in my thoughts that I hadn't noticed the cop approaching. He had a hand to his radio and spoke into it before looking my way. He glanced across the street.

The receptionist was standing at the door, watching us, a smirk on her face. Businessmen and women were beginning to leave the building. I checked the time, seeing it was after five.

"We got a call that you were loitering here. The receptionist at Exhibit said you tried getting inside earlier. What are you doing here, ma'am? She's concerned for you."

"I . . ." was losing my mind. That was the truth of the situation. The real truth.

"What'd you say, Miss?" The cop stepped closer. His radio was going off.

I glanced back over the street, and stood straighter because my cousin was one of the men leaving for the day. He was carrying a briefcase.

I lifted my hand, and yelled, "Graham! Graham."

He turned the other way, going at a fast clip.

"Graham!" It was a large street. Traffic had picked up so he wouldn't be able to hear me.

I started after him.

The cop got in front of me. "Miss, you need to stay here and talk to me."

I pointed in Graham's direction. "That's my cousin. I was waiting for him."

"Your cousin?" He frowned, looking, but Graham was long gone. He'd melted among the sea of other businessmen and women. "Your cousin works at Exhibit?"

"Yeah." I sat back down, my shoulders slumping.

"Did he know you were waiting for him?"

"He doesn't know me."

"He's your cousin, but he doesn't know you?"

"It's a whole thing with the family. His mom and my mom are distant. I don't like it. I came here to start fixing it. I wanted to meet him."

"Do you have a phone number? Could you call him and see if he wanted to meet that way?"

I frowned. "My mom never gave me his number. My aunts would. Aunt Clara knows people online."

"Knows people online?" The cop wasn't looking impressed with me, pressing his mouth in a tight line. "Ma'am, at this point, I think you need to get going. Find another way to reach out to your cousin. I'm sure there's a way."

I shook my head, so much else spiraling inside of me, all of it going down the drain. "There's no way. He doesn't want me." It was the pattern in my life.

Beck didn't want me.

"Ma'am?"

He wanted someone else.

I said, "He married someone else. He didn't want me anymore."

"Your cousin?" The cop's voice sharpened.

I shook my head, tears pricking at my eyes. God. All of it was blending inside of me.

Beck tossed me to the side. Like garbage. I was trash.

"Ma'am, you either need to leave or I will be removing you myself. It's better for you if you leave of your own accord. Do you understand what I'm saying to you?"

Tears began falling down my cheeks.

He was going to marry someone else, and I was being questioned on the streets across the country, eating a sub that was so cold by now. I was tempted to give it to the rat that was hanging out a few steps away. Him and his buddies were moving around, doing their thing, but the one kept watching me. He knew what was up. He could tell. I was a prime target.

"Miss, are you going to leave or not?" The cop was getting impatient.

Leave? I shook my head. I couldn't leave New York City.

"You're not going to leave?"

"I have no place to go," I mumbled, looking down. More tears were falling, but I wasn't feeling them. I wasn't tasting them either.

I couldn't go back to Montana.

I had things to do here.

Tourist things. I still needed to go to Times Square. Ellis Island too.

I failed at even being a tourist. I'd meant to get a fanny pack on Canal Street, but I never went there. I never got a fanny pack. That was Tourist 101, right?

All the spiraling inside of me took me over.

I was openly sobbing.

I meant to regroup.

I had not regrouped.

"Okay. Miss, you've given me no other option. I'm going to take you in for your safety." A hand touched my wrist and I was jerked backward.

I cried out. My sandwich fell to the sidewalk.

The cop yanked my other arm behind me, and cold metal was slapped around my wrists at the same time I heard the click. "Miss, you are being detained for now."

"Wait. What?"

He ignored me, leading me to his squad car. He put me in the back seat, a hand to the top of my head guiding me inside. When the door shut, reality slapped me in the face.

Well, shit.

Being detained by a New York City cop hadn't been on my tourist bucket list. It was now. Check that off.

I looked out.

The little rat dude ran past the car, my sandwich in his mouth.

CHAPTER FOUR

JAKE

The second I stepped inside the station, there *she* was.

The woman from the subway. The same woman I'd not been able to get out of my head. She was like a fly, buzzing around me, poking at my thoughts. I'd been on the train that day because Shorty was still in town. I knew he was going to get banished. It was inevitable because he was a pain in the ass on his good days. He was never going to change, and Ashton would want Shorty as far away from his woman as possible, but I wanted to make sure I got all the information out of him that I could about my cousin.

Christ.

My cousin. That was all a shit show by itself, but Nicolai was dead. And my fucking family decided to take a vote and appoint me as the new head. It was a farce. The whole thing. I had a shit ton of family members. Some were cops. Some were in the oil business. And then I had a section that was Mafia, except most of those uncles all lived in Maine. They ran the business from there, which was a joke by itself.

I was a cop.

Fuck.

I *had been* a cop. I wasn't anymore, not for two days now. There'd been a short period of time I considered going up to Maine and taking over the business. They gave me the power, but I started thinking about it, really thinking about it.

I hated the idea. Loathed it, in fact.

If I was going up there, it would be to destroy the family from inside. I had no allegiance to them. Not one fucking bit. They'd stood by when my parents died in a car accident. I'd just turned eighteen. Justin wasn't far behind me, and no one stepped up to help us out. No fucking way was I going to let my little brother go into the system. We lived in Maine back then, but I took him on.

I packed him up and we went to the city, where I joined the academy.

Being alive for Justin had been my main purpose for so long. Then he died and for the last six months, I found new purpose in finding his killer. My fucking cousin, Nicolai. That's who killed him. It was another nail in their coffin, as far as I was concerned.

Who else knew about it? I didn't believe that no one else knew. Nicolai might not have been the one who pulled the trigger, but he was the reason behind it. Then there I was. A cop who no longer wanted to be a cop. I'd been forced to walk the line between good and bad, needing to choose the dirty side at times, but fuck's sake. No one knew my world.

Justin was gone.

I'd been finding solace at the bottom of some bourbon bottle, then scraping myself out of whatever one-night stand's bed that I went home with for the night.

I was heading to the bar to do just that when my phone started ringing. Recognizing the number, I contemplated not answering it. It kept ringing, and I cursed, knowing she was just going to keep calling. I greeted her with a growl. "Shit's over between us, Laila. Leave me the fuck alone."

She was silent for a beat before sniping, "Jesus, your ego is inflated. Not calling you because of that, asshole."

I frowned. "Why are you calling?"

Laila was another cop. She and I had tangled naked together enough times over a few months that she started thinking we were in a relationship. Hell. Maybe we were, but that was the time my brother's body was pulled from the water and nothing had been the same again for me. Laila didn't just fall to the sideline. I'd punted her ass across the continent, as far as I was concerned. It'd not been the nicest thing, but my mind frame didn't give a fuck.

"I got one of your cousins here."

"Not interested—" I started to say. Any of my cousins, I didn't give a fuck about them either.

I heard shouting in the background, and Laila cursed on her end. "Jesus Christ. She said she's family. I'm doing you a solid. You can come down and pick her up. We won't charge her if you do."

"Her?" I quieted.

"Yeah. Says her name is Viv—"

Vivianna.

Of all my family members, all the different branches, Vivianna was one of the few that was intertwined with the West and Walden Mafia families. She wasn't a part of the Worthing Mafia family. That was a whole other side, but she knew of them. Some of our uncles went into the oil business. Some went into being professional criminals. Of that side of the family, both did well with money. Vivianna, unfortunately for her, was used to that lifestyle, except she'd also gotten hooked on a fast way of living back in her modeling days. She wasn't modeling anymore but hadn't been able to stop trying to live that fast life.

This wasn't the first call I'd gotten about her, but considering how my own life was going, it might be the last. I sighed into the phone. "Yeah. I'll come down and get her. I'm guessing you won't just release her?"

"Yeah." Laila laughed, harshly. "No. You can get your ass down here. I'll let you take her home, but she needs to go to rehab. Look of her, she's not going to wake up one of these times she puts a needle in her arm." She waited after delivering that stark statement.

I checked my stop and saw the one coming up I'd need if I was going to the station. "I'll be there in twenty."

Twenty-three minutes later, I walked in and boom.

There she was.

Not my ex–booty call.

Not my cousin.

But the woman from the subway who had been plaguing my mind.

I almost turned right around to leave because this woman was trouble. She'd had my dick hard on the train. It's the whole reason I was in her face, grilling her about needing an ambulance. And that mouth.

Christ.

Her fucking mouth.

The way she'd been biting it on the train. When she'd been wringing her hands together, when she didn't even know she was doing it, getting all worked up. I didn't even know the shit going on in her mind but I knew it wasn't good. But she'd been gnawing away at her bottom lip and I had to say something. I got up in her face, downright pushing shit on her that wasn't even the truth, all because I had to say something. If I hadn't, I was a second away from doing something else to her mouth to get her to stop chewing on it. No woman affected me like that. I didn't like it. Goddamn. I didn't have time for a woman like her, and now, seeing her on the same bench where they put people being detained, I stopped in my tracks.

Trouble. Just, fucking trouble.

I was fucking hard for her all over again, and she was back to gnawing on that bottom lip of hers.

Her hands were clenched in her lap, wringing together, just like on the subway, but I was glad to see there weren't handcuffs on her.

I paused just inside the door.

In two seconds, I'd be spotted and my ex–booty call would be notified. I'd turned in my resignation. Those who knew me knew I wasn't a cop anymore. News got around because not only was my own flesh and blood mobbed up, not only was I one of the many dozens of cops who was also on payroll for another Mafia family in this area, a different mob, but the irony of all ironies was that they assigned me to organized crime. Seeing this woman sitting there, feeling the way my body wanted to go over and put a claim on her, fury swept through me. I was not a good man. I wasn't. That was the plain fucking truth. I was all the way bad. Grew up bad. Continued being bad. My reasons might've been good, but there was no way around the fact that I had no place to go over, introduce myself to that woman, and see how she'd feel about putting those lips around my dick instead.

Course, I wouldn't go there first. I'd be respectful. Ask her for a cup of coffee first.

Jesus.

I was going for her without even realizing it myself.

Two steps.

Three.

I was nearing her.

She lifted her gaze.

Clocked me, her eyes widening.

Confusion swirled in their depths.

She frowned a little, and again, sank those teeth down in that lip of hers.

I almost groaned out loud.

"Worthing." A smooth feminine voice—one that I used to love, the rasp from her when I'd been dick-deep in her, but now it grated on my nerves—called out from behind me.

Chatter around the front of the station quieted.

That was because of me. I was assuming more people had heard about my resignation.

The woman from the subway continued to stare at me, her eyes narrowing, and then recognition flared. Her mouth opened, gaping a little. A small bit of panic flashed too.

I winced, not really liking seeing that reaction, but I was forced to turn my head as my ex was walking toward me.

I shifted back a step. "Brant."

Laila's face tightened, slowing in her step just a bit before she steeled herself and continued until she was at my side. She knew how to stand and position herself. Laila Brant could wear an Easter Bunny costume and still come off seductive. I knew how she did, but I wasn't giving her that attention. My eyes stayed on her face, so I caught how her mouth flattened briefly before it kicked up in a slow smile. "Retired life must suit you. You look good."

I narrowed my eyes, cocking my head to the side. "Funny. I don't hear the dulcet tones of my cousin. What? She pass out in a cell back there?"

Laila's smile shifted to a genuine grin before we both heard what I knew was missing.

"—the meaning of this! I know people, you know. Do you know who I am? Who my family is? I can make one call and I'll have your badge. I'll have all of your badges—" Her screech got louder as she was brought out from the back.

I shifted on my feet in time to see my cousin being led through the door that separated the holding cells from this main area. Another cop in uniform was bringing her out, and as soon as he saw Laila, he looked relieved, fitting his key to my cousin's cuffs.

My cousin swung her wild gaze around until her eyes landed on me. They went wide and she almost stumbled over her giant-ass high-heeled boots, trying to get to me. "Jake! Jakie! *Jake!*"

I growled. "Shut the fuck up, Viv."

She did, clamping her mouth shut before her body wavered backward.

Laila shouted, a hand shooting out at the same time.

My cousin started to fall.

The uniformed cop caught her, panic fleeting over his face before he swung that still-panicked gaze toward Laila. "I didn't—she was going to fall on her own."

Laila went over, waving him off. "Don't worry, Officer Porath. You can go back to your other duties. I got her from here."

He eyed my cousin, looking relieved as he could step away. "We're releasing her?"

Laila took Viv's arm, drawing her from him. "We got it handled." She indicated me and his gaze trailed over. Recognition flared over his face, having him snap to his fullest height, his back going straight. "Detective Worthing—err . . ." His frown was fierce.

Laila grinned, bringing my cousin toward me. "It's just Mr. Worthing now, I believe." Her eyes found mine, a hint of something deeper appearing. "Or is it Don?"

The uniform was confused, but Vivianna heard and tipped her chin back, a raucous laugh trailing out of her throat. Jesus. She was all skin and bones, wearing . . . I didn't even know what she was wearing. Leather leggings with some animal-print corset top? And were those feathers wrapped around her like a shawl? I had no idea. She looked ridiculous. But she continued to laugh, annoyingly, before she finished it with, "Not Jakie." She snorted, still laughing. "You're joking, right? Everyone knows that was just a joke. A whole farce—" She cut off, seeing my face. She stammered, the blood draining from her face. "S-sorry, Cuz. I, just—you've always been a cop. I mean . . . though, Justin was the golden boy of the two of you—"

"Shut up."

She flinched, going white again, looking as if I'd slapped her. "Sorry, Jake. I—just—"

I turned my back on her, focusing on Laila. Knowing—feeling—the subway woman watching the whole exchange.

I heard Vivianna add behind me, quietly, "I loved him too."

I cringed, but not the time or day. I asked through gritted teeth, "I'm assuming you have strings attached?"

Laila had been watching me carefully, but her face blanked a moment. "Uh. Yeah." Her forehead wrinkled as she thought. "Rehab."

"What?" Vivianna croaked. "No fucking way—"

I leveled her with another look.

She was my cousin, one of my many cousins, but we were not close. Our relationship consisted of this. Of her getting high, getting arrested, using my name to get out of trouble. I tended to come down and haul her out of here more for favors since she used to be buddies with people that I needed information on sometimes. That was before I turned in my resignation. I didn't need those favors anymore. I was thinking my cousin was forgetting that part of our relationship.

I was here for one reason alone. Because my brother would've wanted me to help her.

I said to Laila, "Not a problem."

"What?" Viv screeched again, her eyes darting around the room, looking for someone else to come in and stop this from happening.

I raised an eyebrow.

Laila was waiting too.

My cousin wasn't seeing anyone else there to help her out, until her gaze fell on the woman from the subway. It stayed there.

I asked, "Unless you want to be charged?"

Laila jumped in, not missing a beat. "They'll send you to rehab too. It'll just cost more."

Viv was still staring at the subway woman, but she snorted again, rolling her eyes. "Money is something we have. Our family is rolling in it." She paused, remembering me. "Or some of us are, if we choose to roll in it."

I'd had enough. Reaching for her arm, I growled, "Let's go."

Vivianna tensed, resisting. "Wait!" Her gaze was still trained on the woman, and I was about to jerk her after me, because I didn't like how she was looking at the subway woman. My cousin could spot a mark a thousand feet away. Our family might've had money, like she said, but I knew Vivianna had been cut off long ago. The money she got was handed to her from the family's lawyer, a lump sum given on the same day every month, and she didn't get any more or any less. It drove her nuts, but it also kept her in check. Otherwise she'd blow millions on drugs as fast as she could snort it without overdosing.

Vivianna jerked her chin toward the bench where she was sitting. "What's her story?" She looked to Laila for the answer. "She's been here the whole time I've been here, but I've been watching. There's no one back there processing her, or even looking like they're going to process her." She looked back, her tone warming. "What are you here for, sugar?" She pulled her arm out of my grip and went over, easing down next to the subway woman.

I didn't want to look, but I couldn't not anymore so, lifting my gaze, I let my eyes fall on her. And fuck. I drew in some air, drinking in the sight of her. I could look all I wanted now. She was like nothing I'd seen before. She made me think of rose petals. Lips that were made just for me. She had eyes deep like the ocean, a heart-shaped face. She was slender, but not too slender. There was strength in her bones. In her eyes. In the way she fucking sat there, thinking whatever fucking thoughts that were going round and round in her mind, but she was above it all.

I didn't know what brought her here.

I didn't know what made her hands wring themselves.

I didn't know what was holding her back, making her chew on her lip, but I knew that I took one look at her and I wanted to sweep it all away.

And that reaction scared the fuck out of me, but when my cousin went to her, sat down, and threw an arm around her shoulders, I thanked what God there was for this small assistance from him.

"Come on, Detective Brant. What's this one here for?"

The subway woman's gaze kept darting from Vivianna, to me, to Laila, to me, to Viv, to me, to Laila, to me. She had no idea what was happening right now.

"I don't know. I can find out—"

I knew. This was the bench they put people when they just wanted to pull them away from a situation. There was nothing to hold them, but for some reason they didn't feel like they could leave them where they were.

Laila was crossing the room. "Hey. Yo." She rapped against the clear plaster between us and the other side. "What's with this one? Who brought her in?"

I spoke. "I got her."

At the same time, Vivianna exclaimed, "She's my friend! I want her to come with me." My cousin linked the subway woman's arm through hers and she looked at me, all serious. "If I'm going to rehab, I'm going to need all the support that I can get. Right, cousin?"

I held her gaze.

I didn't know what my cousin was doing, what game she was playing, but if I was drowning, the universe just threw me a rope. I wasn't stupid. I took hold of that rope and I wasn't going to let it go. "Course, we'll take her." I pivoted on my feet, repeating to Laila, "I got her."

My ex frowned, a little flustered. "I—uh—sure."

I crossed to Laila, lowering my head and voice. "Whoever brought her in is long gone. You know that bench. I know the bench. I'll take her."

Another officer approached us, holding his hands out. "Uh, yeah. Sorry. What he said. Brightman brought her in, but he said to let her know she could take off after a bit. He clocked out forty minutes ago."

"What?"

I snapped to attention. "Right. I got her." I motioned to Viv. "Let's go."

She beamed to me, standing up, her arm still linked with the subway woman's. "Splendid!" She marched them to the door.

I started to follow, but a hand stopped me on my arm.

Laila was frowning at me. Her gaze went to where she was holding me back. She dropped it, but sidled closer to me. "Jake. I—"

My heart tugged.

I saw the look on her face. The way she was looking at me, speaking to me. This was a woman whose heart was involved. For this time, this one time, I needed to say the right words, no matter if they were going to hurt or not.

I ignored whether Vivianna and the other woman had stopped. I didn't know if they were watching this or not, but I couldn't think about them. I cupped the back of Laila's elbow and lowered my voice, softening it. "I'm not the man you think I am."

She stiffened, her gaze jerking up to mine.

My hand tightened on her, holding her firm. I kept my voice soft. "We kept company together for a bit, and it was a good time. I'll admit that I think you got in further than anyone else, but my cousin—she's just a mirror for what's going on inside of me. I am a fucking mess, Laila. Don't wait for me. Go on that family trip to Europe that you do this time of year, but go and let yourself meet some rich European millionaire. Don't give me a second thought, because I promise you, I am not worth it. I have blood on my hands. I was a good cop, but I was dirty at times too. I should be a dead cop. You and me, there's nothing there. There will never be anything there. You deserve a good man. Go and find him. It's not me." The last was said harshly, but for fuck's sake, she needed to hear it. I meant every word. "Don't waste your time on me. I'm not interested, Laila."

The last was meant to hurt, and as I said it, the small bit of hope I saw in her eyes died away. The embers dwindled to nothing.

Good.

I left, walking past Vivianna and the subway woman, ignoring the knowing look on my cousin, and feeling pierced by the stricken look on the other. It didn't matter. None of this mattered. Laila would stop wasting her time on me, and that was good all around.

But as I went past the others, Vivianna dropped to a whisper, taunting me. "Look at you. You know, if you were actually the piece of shit that you think you are, you wouldn't have said a thing to her. You would've kept her on a string and when you decided you might want a taste, you'd reel her in, like you were fishing."

I stopped, rolling my shoulders back and bracing myself. "You got the wrong cousin, Viv. I'm not my brother. *His* body was lifted up with fishing nets. Maybe shut the fuck up with more fishing metaphors, hmmm?"

My comment was mean.

I didn't care.

CHAPTER FIVE

SAWYER

I heard what he said to his cousin.

His brother died? Did I get that right?

My heart hurt for him.

"I'm Vivianna, sweetie. What's your name?" She held her hand out to me, and man, she was so skinny.

I wasn't sure what I was doing with these two, but I also wasn't going to complain. I'd seen the other woman get brought in and we'd locked eyes. She and I weren't in the same league. That was obvious. She looked like a model or had been a model and me, well; then there was me. Sooo not a model. But in that moment when we locked eyes, we shared a connection. Sympathy for the other. That was it before she was hauled to the back area.

When she came out, saw me, I knew she was going to do something.

I had no clue she was going to be the reason I got to leave that police station, but again, I wasn't going to complain about it.

I shook her hand and hoped she couldn't feel how wet my palms were. I was all a mess inside. I think anyone would be if they were hauled to a police station and left to sit. I'd been teetering on the edge, not sure if I was going to be arrested or not. The guy said he wasn't going to charge me, but I wasn't criminal-savvy. Getting a speeding ticket was the furthest I'd been in dealing with the law in that way.

"Sawyer." I had to cough to clear my throat. My voice came out so timid. Jesus. That was embarrassing. I snuck a look at him.

Him.

I couldn't believe it when he walked into the police station. Or more like, stalked into the station. It took a second to hit me, but when I realized this was the same guy from the subway . . . *Floor, open up and swallow me now.*

"What were you in for, Sawyer?" Vivianna was asking me, but she was having a hard time focusing on me. Her eyes were all glassy, and her head kept falling to the seat behind us.

Her cousin was on the other side of her, on his phone, but he growled, "Leave her alone, Viv. You've already pulled her enough into your mess."

That'd been the wrong thing to say to her.

Her glassy eyes flashed, focusing, and she snarled, turning to him. "Just because you're emotionally stunted doesn't mean I am too."

"Except you are," he drawled, still focused on his phone.

"You're an asshole."

"Yes, I am, and you're a drug addict."

Also the wrong thing to say.

She came alive.

I needed to detach from this situation. This was family history, and she began laying into him about things that I did not need to know about. She was talking about someone named Remmi, and now she mentioned someone named Ashton. That name got his attention.

Jakie. That's what she called him.

Jake.

Jake Worthing.

I played with his name in my mind. I liked it. *Detective* Jake Worthing.

It'd been loud in that entryway, but I was able to hear enough that he wasn't a cop anymore. And that other woman. Hot jealousy struck me like lightning. She'd touched him on his arm and he hadn't even noticed.

They'd been intimate.

That was obvious. Painfully.

Were they still intimate? Was that why she called him to take his cousin out of there?

They had a moment, their heads close together, before we left. I tore my gaze away, my stomach shrinking because I didn't want to see any more little lovey-dovey touches between them.

Fuck.

That jealousy still pooled in me, and it was spreading, like poison.

I did not need to lose my mind over *another* guy. Hadn't I learned from Beck?

"What are we doing here? I thought you were taking me to my place." Vivianna stopped in mid rant when the cab pulled up outside of an apartment building.

Jake handed some money to the cabdriver, before meeting my eyes. He nodded to the door behind me. "Get out." He answered his cousin. "Let's go."

"What? But—what?" She got out, glaring at him as the cab took off.

Jake ran cold eyes over her, taking his keys out and going to the door. "You're going to rehab, Viv. I'm not fucking around with that, but I ain't taking you in a cab. I need to grab something from my place." He opened the door, looking to me. "She brought you into this, but you can take off from here if you want. I can call another cab."

"What? No!" Vivianna shrieked, literally throwing her arms down, her hands balled into fists. "She's my friend. I want her with me."

His annoyed eyes locked with hers, heat flaring in them. "Drop the fucking act, Vivianna. She's a pawn to you. You're using her as a buffer between you and me. News flash, I *am* an asshole. If I want to tell you that you're a drug addict and you need help, then I'm going to say it. I don't give a fuck who's around us. You're going to rehab—"

"But my friend. We need to give her a ride to where she's staying—"

"I'll take her *after*," he snarled, looking two seconds away from putting hands on her. He didn't. He kept them at his side, but the threat of violence was real with him. Then again, he'd been a cop so I shouldn't have been surprised. His jaw clenched, he looked my way, and he forced his tone to soften. "Unless you want me to call that cab?"

My tongue weighed heavy in my mouth, and I shook my head.

Maybe I should've, but honestly, I had nothing else going on right now. Plus, I could add this to the tourist bucket list. Taking someone to rehab. I didn't think this was necessarily a New York–tourist type of event, but it was an adventure and that was the premise of my bucket list. Doing things I normally wouldn't. This was one of those things. Also, she was giving me distinct Mafia-princess vibes and that felt a very New York or Jersey-esque type of thing I wouldn't get to do somewhere else.

This guy kinda scared me, but I also wanted to see what all was going to happen. I had tuned her out earlier, but I was tuned all the way in when it came to him. He was like no guy I'd met in my life.

Groan. Bad Sawyer.

Still, I said, "I'm good."

"See!" Viv hissed at him. "She's here for me." She slapped at his chest, or would've. His hand moved like lightning, catching her wrist, and time slowed for a beat. It pulsed around them as the two shared a look. She tried to hit him. He stopped her, and his jaw clenched again, that promise of violence just there, swimming under the surface in him.

She paled again, swallowing thickly before she pulled her hand out of his grip.

I waited to see if she'd apologize, but she sniffed and flounced past him.

His eyes met mine, and that tension was still there. It switched to me, but along with it came some underlying heat. I felt it spear my belly, warming me. My tongue thickened again, but my body moved without me knowing. I stepped toward him. My hand began to reach out.

I wanted to . . . I didn't know. Reassure him? Comfort him?

Just touch him?

I ached with it, but so many thoughts and emotions were swirling inside of me. Compounding on top of each other. I'd never felt this way around Beck. I didn't know *how* to react to this, and because I didn't know, my body acted of its own volition.

My fingers ached to make contact with him, but before they could touch his chest, his hand found my wrist. Just like his cousin. But he wrapped his hand around me gently, holding me tight. Shivers raced through me, heating me up.

His thumb began to shift under my arm, and his eyes were smoldering.

I wanted more of this. More touch. More of him.

That scared me.

I yanked my hand back, a soft hiss on my breath.

His eyes shuttered, a wall coming down over him. I felt him pulling away from me, though neither of us moved a muscle.

I didn't like the distance, but I knew it was because of my reaction.

He said, coolly, "I'll give you a ride wherever you want if you endure my cousin for another couple of hours. The facility isn't far outside of the city, but it's still a drive."

I wrapped my arms around myself, trying to ward off the chill from him.

I'd messed up. I wasn't fully aware of it, but I knew I'd messed up. I'd pulled away from him, and neither of us wanted it, but now he was all the way gone. I wanted him back, but I didn't know him. I didn't know how to bring him back to me.

I was in that between phase where my body was having its own conversation with his, but my mind was still playing catch-up. It was a weird place to be, and my eyebrows furrowed, trying to make sense of all the undercurrents going on.

I said, wincing at how raspy my voice came out, "Yeah. Okay. I got nothing else to do today."

He frowned at my words, but I moved forward. I didn't want him to question me. I might answer him, and I didn't want him to find out how I was just another person on the edge, seriously struggling with my current life because everything I'd known had been swept out from underneath me. If he got even a glimpse at how much of a mess I was, he'd kick me to the curb in a heartbeat.

I ached at that thought, at him leaving me behind.

And again, that left me dumbfounded. Never. I'd never felt such a strong and immediate reaction to anyone in my life.

I paused in the hallway, still hugging myself, my head folded down, because I didn't know where I was going. Vivianna had marched on by herself. Jake cursed under his breath, going past me. He glanced back a few times, making sure I was following him, or seeing if I was still here? Did he want me to leave?

I half snorted to myself, under my breath, because good luck, dude.

I'd been drowning for the last two weeks, and the second he walked inside that police station, I felt the first bubble of oxygen being handed to me. Like a hand that reached down into depths where I was slowly dying and offered me a breathing tube.

I took my first breath, and I was hooked. I wanted to keep breathing.

Suddenly my bucket list wasn't just for something to do, to keep me busy so I wouldn't lose my mind.

I felt the first stirrings of something sizzling in me. The first spark of life again.

He was about to find out that once I latched on, it was going to be difficult to shake me.

Ask my ex. I gave him eighteen years of my life.

CHAPTER SIX

SAWYER

The drive to the facility didn't take long. For me, anyway. Jake was the one driving, and his cousin was in the front seat next to him. She talked the whole time. I kinda wondered if she'd taken another dose of something in his bathroom when we were in his place, because she wasn't making sense with the things she was talking about. He didn't seem to care. He didn't engage at all.

He drove, ignored her, and every now and then, he'd look at me in his rearview mirror.

Me, though. I was enjoying this.

I liked his cousin's chatter. I liked the drive. I liked seeing more of the city and even outside of the city. A part of me wondered if I should be worried. I didn't know these two. They were strangers, but my body overrode any rational hesitation my mind might've thought up. I knew him. That's what my body was telling me, and well, I was going with it.

This was all helping to quiet my own demons. For the first time in weeks, some of the hold my ex had on me lessened. I was able to think about it, and I didn't feel like I was being paralyzed by the thoughts.

Just for that, I'd sign up for a couple rides with Jake and his cousin.

I'd never been the type of girl who longed to get married. Maybe that was why I stayed so long with Beck? I always thought we'd get married, we'd have kids, but I wasn't one of those types that put it on the calendar and crossed out each day until the wedding day or the impregnating day. For me, it'd been about the connection. I liked helping. Getting a degree, then a job had been a dream. That dream switched to helping Beck.

He was the one who kept putting off the engagement. That's how he talked about it. "The Engagement." Like it was an event. Though, I guess it kinda was.

I'd been complacent. I was okay with taking a back seat to Beck. I was okay with—and fill in the blank here—but no. No! I hadn't been okay with it. I made the sacrifices for him because I thought that's what a person did for someone they loved. They did what they could to help the other person.

Beck hadn't done that for me.

When we got to the facility, I held back. I was getting steamed up thinking about Beck. I was with an ex-cop. I was pretty sure he might still have a pair of handcuffs, and I'd just left a police station. I did not need to go back, certainly not to see his ex–lovey dovey whoever she was.

Was she like Manda? Hanging around, being the "best friend"—no!

Stop, Sawyer. Keep a lid on your shit.

I focused back on the reality show happening right in front of me.

Vivianna was dramatic. She huffed all over the place. Was weepy. Emotional. Threatening Jake in one breath, then clinging to him in the next because they'd both lost his brother. I was getting dizzy trying to keep up with her, but after a bit, I accepted it was like a roller-coaster ride. Up and down, and whee, let's go in a circle.

She hugged me seven times before Jake hauled her inside, and once they got in there, I heaved a breath. It took them a bit. Apparently Jake had messaged ahead of time. I was guessing that was part of what he'd been doing on his phone when we were in the cab. They were ready for Vivianna.

Jake came back twenty minutes later, looking all tense.

Jesus.

I raked him up and down. He was tall, and there wasn't one ounce of softness on his body. He was all ripped and built. He wasn't big, but he wasn't lean either. He was right in the middle, all perfectly in the middle and again, I was seeing how tight his shirt stuck to him. I was noting the way his biceps moved and shifted under that shirt, and the dip from under his chest to his very flat stomach.

My mouth watered, tracing down his body, wondering what other muscles he might have under the rest of his clothes.

God.

What was I doing?

I'd just let myself segue down a little Jake rabbit hole and I ended up ready to murder Beck. Now this? I was back here again? Or was it that I was going to jump the first guy that caught my eye?

But even thinking that, I was warring with myself because my body was saying one thing while my mind was saying a totally different thing. I wanted to go to him, press against him, but also I didn't know him. He was a stranger to me.

He had stopped in his tracks, taking in how I was taking him in, and we could do that now because his cousin wasn't acting as a buffer. Joke was on her. She'd pulled me in to be the buffer, but the buffer had actually been her.

I took a deep breath in, cooling some of my hormones down. He eyed me, his gaze heating up, but he closed his eyes, and I felt that same distance landing between us. That was him. He was doing the pull-away thing again. My chest hurt at feeling that.

But also, had I done something? I didn't know what I'd done.

When he spoke, his voice was gruff. "I know of a diner in the city. Want to grab some food? Unless it's too far out of the way of where you're staying?" He nodded to his truck, pulling his keys out. He went around to his side and I got in where his cousin had been. It felt more intimate being up here, being so close.

I folded my hands in my lap and tried to breathe out some of my nerves.

"Is that okay with you? If we stop on the way to—where am I taking you?"

I nodded again, quickly. I told him the name of my hotel. I did not tell him that tonight was my last night there and tomorrow, I didn't know where I'd be going.

"Yeah. No. That sounds good to me." I wrung my hands together the entire way there.

I was thirty-six. I had lived almost the last two decades for someone else, and what was I now? A nervous teenager?

I was going to make everything another item on the bucket list. For that reason alone, sign me up.

Remembering what it felt like to be a teenager again? Check.

A cute neighborhood-style eatery? That could be added to the list. This place was adorable.

We sat in silence until the server brought over our coffee. She put another smaller bowl next to it, filled with creamer. "Anything else, sweetie?" That seductive tone was not intended for me.

I scowled.

"We're good. Thank you." Jake kept his eyes on me as he spoke to her.

"Anything for you, Jacob." Her hand went to his shoulder and lingered. I scowled even more at that move. She had ignored me from the first moment we entered, but her eyes went my way now, narrowing a fraction before she went to another table.

"Come here often? *Jacob?*"

He picked up his own coffee, frowning at me. "She used to fuck my brother a long time ago. She doesn't know shit about me. It's Jake." He continued to watch me and since I didn't know what all to say, I busied myself adding some creamer to my own coffee.

My mind was going a million miles here. So much that I didn't even taste my coffee. I put my mug down, looking back at my lap. At my hands. "Why are we here?"

He'd been heated earlier. Then we drove here and in that time frame, he got chillier and chillier toward me.

Now he was just outright like ice.

His cold appraisal lingered on my face, his own eyes narrowing, before he dismissed me and lifted his coffee back up for a drag. He sat back and shook his head. "For food? Because my cousin needed a pawn to truss up between us, and for whatever reason, you volunteered." His eyes narrowed on me. "Maybe I should be asking you that question. Why are you here, Sawyer?"

My mouth watered, parting. That was the first time he'd said my name.

I liked it. I liked it a lot.

Then I realized he was actually asking. He was waiting for a response, so I leaned back in my seat and shrugged. There was no way I could tell him the truth of what I was doing here, but I could vague it up. "I'm being a tourist." If he knew all of it, he wouldn't want anything to do with me.

"A tourist?"

"Yeah. That's what people who don't live here come here and do. They tourist. It's a verb. Active."

He was looking at me like he didn't believe me.

I raised my chin. "I have a whole list of things to do. Got a third of it marked off."

"Oh yeah?"

"Yeah."

"What's all on your list? Your tourist list."

"Riding the subway. Getting food stolen by a rat. You know, things very New York Cityish. Going to a Broadway show."

"What show did you see?"

Eh . . . "I—I went to the place where you are in a zigzaggy line for the tickets, but next time, I'll book online." Next time.

"Sawyer," he said again, more gently.

My heart folded over at hearing him say my name like that. He could make me preen and purr like a kitty cat. I cleared my throat, because no way could I let him know that either. I scrambled for what else to tell him. "I—uh—I came to meet my cousin."

He frowned again, briefly. "Did you meet her?"

"Him. And, I found him."

"You were looking for your cousin?"

Oh. That hadn't come out how I intended. "Uh. Yeah. Kinda. It's not like a big thing. It's just—there's a family rift." I was back to my hands twisting around each other, and I glanced down, making sure I hadn't drawn blood. I'd done that before. I lifted my chin back. "That's where I was before, you know."

I could feel his gaze on me. It was heavy.

This was embarrassing.

He asked, quietly, "What happened?"

"About the family?"

"About where you were before. That's how you ended up at the station?"

I coughed, shifting on my seat, grateful I didn't need to go into the family dynamics. Suddenly feeling flushed, I tugged at my shirt, but I knew it wasn't the temperature. "I kinda . . . Have you had a moment in your life when you were on a path, and it made sense? Like, you made a decision. You committed to it, and you made all these really stupid decisions to stay on that path, even though after a while, there started to be red flags on the sidelines, but you were on the path and you'd come so far, so . . . It's the path. It's the one you put yourself on."

He was suddenly *really* looking at me. "I have an idea, yeah."

I flushed again. I didn't enjoy the feeling so I turned my head. "Something happened to me before I came here."

"You were on the path and you got shoved off it?"

My gaze jerked back. I leaned forward. Did he understand?

I was feeling a little breathless. "Yeah." Wait. He might not understand. I leaned back. "Anyways, I came here to meet my cousin. He's the one cousin I've not met and since I'm here, I want to meet him. I want to see if he'll help mend this rift in the family."

"That's a long trip you took to find him, meet him, and then end up in a police station." He was back to watching me all intent-like. As if he knew I was bullshitting him.

The back of my neck was getting hot. I shrugged. "I mean, I might've needed to not be home right now. I've always wanted to come here, and he's the cousin who lived the farthest away. So . . ." I trailed off. The math was mathing to me. "You know what I mean?"

A hint of dark amusement flared in his eyes, but the side of his mouth lifted up in a wry grin. "Do you want to explain it to me?"

Another flush from me. I was hot all over. "I'd rather not. I needed to get away. Two stones. One bird. That sort of thing."

"I don't think that's quite right, but okay." The corner of his mouth curved higher up. The chill was totally gone, and his eyes were starting to warm.

They made my heart pitter-patter.

Which made me scowl. My heart didn't need to be doing any pitter-pattering.

He remarked, "What specifically happened to make the officer bring you to the station?"

Cue more squirming from me. Because, embarrassment. "Right. Erm . . . I went to where my cousin worked, and I thought about trying to see him, but there was a receptionist there. I got in my head, got all self-conscious. Shy. She thought I was a stalker. Called the cops."

He immediately scowled.

My heart pitter-pattered again. I liked that look on him. Liked it when it was there for me.

"What the fuck? Why didn't she just ask you to leave?"

I glanced down to my lap. "She might've."

"Sawyer."

I lifted my gaze back up. He was just watching me so intently now. I wanted to fidget, just because I couldn't handle all that attention solely focused on me. At least, in this situation I couldn't. An image of me in bed, of him looming over me, watching me with that same concentration, maybe something of his inside of me—and I was squirming *again.*

"Is it hot in here?" I exclaimed, reaching for my coffee and gulping down a good mouthful. I swallowed it.

His eyes fell to it, his eyebrows furrowing a little. He had that dry grin tugging at his mouth again.

It took a second before I saw the steam coming from my coffee, and I was back to almost hyperventilating. I started to shove out of the booth. "I need to walk."

He reached over, caught my wrist. He held me in place. "Stay."

I groaned, but my ass didn't move. "She asked me to leave. I did. I went to the other side of the street. That's when she called the cop on me, and I was kinda losing my mind when he showed up. I felt stupid. And she was there, judging me."

"Did she say something?"

I shrugged tightly. "You know when someone's judging you. Like she's never dealt with something truly horrible in her life? I bet she hasn't."

His phone buzzed. He ignored it, shooting me a look. "Now you're judging her."

Maybe. I didn't care. "He didn't say he was going to arrest me, but he took me to the station and I never saw him again. Your cousin was brought in an hour later. The rest is history."

His phone began buzzing again.

He ignored it. Again.

I asked, "Are you going to get that?"

"No." His response was immediate and he didn't spare me a look, taking another drag of his coffee. When it quieted and started off again, he sighed, putting his mug down. He hit accept and brought it up to his mouth, and growled into it, "Stop fucking calling me. I'll come when I'm ready."

A voice started to speak from the other end, but he ended the call and silenced it, stuffing it back in his pocket. As he did, he stretched back, and his shirt lifted, showing a corner of his stomach underneath. It was enough. My theory was confirmed. The man was ripped underneath that shirt.

I was also being reminded that it'd been three weeks since anyone had touched me.

Damn. What was it about this guy that was making me react like this? It was frustrating.

Catching my stare, he pushed his shirt back down, moving it over the gun that was holstered on his side. "You got a thing for cops?"

I hadn't even noticed the gun. Funny. That should've been the first thing I noticed.

"Don't get a big head. You're *not* a cop anymore, right? Can you even still wear that thing?"

He grinned, relaxing back in his seat. He picked up his coffee, gesturing to me. "It's all legal, if that's what you're worried about. Wore a gun for too long to not wear one so soon into retirement. Feel naked."

Swoon. I was swooning.

He said naked.

His eyes heated. "You know what I mean?"

I wrinkled my nose at him, more to hide the effect his words were having on me. "Not about that, but yeah. I guess. I used to have sex regularly."

I tasted acid in my mouth. Sex with Beck had never been mind blowing, but it'd been sex. I was able to get off with him, or some of the time. My vibrator was all the way back in my hotel room too.

"How long's it been?"

"Since I had sex?"

He had that hawklike expression on him again. "Since the breakup."

"Oh." He *knew*. Damn. "Three weeks." I began picking at my mug, scratching my nail at the handle. "The day he ended things, he fucked me before he told me he wouldn't be marrying me. He'd been cheating on me, and they are going to have a kid instead." I whispered that last part, but my nails suddenly started trying to rip into my mug.

"Did you want to have a kid with him?"

My eyes jerked to his again, and I held there. Feeling like the way he was looking at me was giving me a lifeline. Another one. "I don't know. I . . . he and I had been together since college. We're *supposed* to have kids. That's what society says, right? Status quo. I never questioned it, but it wasn't on my super-urgent list."

The corner of his mouth curved up. "Not like the tourist list you have?"

I grinned, feeling like he was giving me another oxygen bubble. More air so I could breathe. "I should've taken his golf clubs to his car. He has a certain group of them that are his favorite. I should've taken those. I bought 'em."

That made them mine.

My golf clubs.

My car.

My house . . .

A fresh wave of anger was starting to rise up in me.

"You dodged a bullet."

"What?"

"I don't know the guy, but you're better off. I've seen the worst of the worst. If he's going to do that to you, you don't want to be tied to him for the rest of your life. Whoever got him, he's now her punishment. My guess is that's why you weren't pushing the kid thing with him. A part of you knew having kids with him wouldn't be a good idea. Then again, what do I know?"

I sighed. He was saying smart things. "We had a decent sex life."

He swung his gaze my way, a flash of heat there. "Don't give that guy credit for anything. You never married before?"

I shook my head.

"You're what? Midthirties?"

I frowned. Where was he going with this? "Thirty-six."

"Unless you waited to go to college, you were probably twenty? That's sixteen years together, give or take a year or two. Probability of him marrying you after all those years was low, statistically a zero percent chance. You should've seen the writing on the wall. He was never going to marry you."

Indignation swept through me. I took back all the nice things about him.

"I supported him when he went to graduate school."

His gaze softened. So did his voice when he said, "He let you go. That's a gift he gave you."

My stomach was back to churning into a pit, deep down inside of me.

He was eyeing me, narrowing his gaze. "Don't take him back."

"What?" I was back to being breathless.

"When he realizes how much he messed up, don't take him back."

He sounded so sure. He looked so sure, his eyes falling to my mouth and holding there. His face tightened for a second.

I looked away, my insides suddenly feeling empty. "You wouldn't say that if you knew the full story." If he knew how pathetic I'd been in the relationship. I may as well have chased Beck off, with all the ways I'd failed myself. Who'd be attracted to that?

"You're not a woman a guy leaves. I know that much."

Oh. *Oh!*

That—yeah. Wow.

He was looking at me, but not in a way he was seeing me. It was like he was seeing inside of me, and that made him . . . I couldn't tell, but he grew suddenly sharp, all the way alert. His gaze was *only* focused on me.

That breathless sensation was back.

It wasn't there because of the idea of Beck coming back to me.

CHAPTER SEVEN

JAKE

Once we were done, I tossed enough money on the table and we headed outside.

Her eyes were wet with unshed tears, but she was holding them in. She wasn't letting them fall. Still hugging herself. She'd been holding herself like that most of the time we were in there. It did something to me.

But, fuck.

She was lost and I knew one thing. Lost people didn't belong in this city. They became more lost and became my problem.

Or they *did*.

When I'd been police.

Fuck.

I wasn't a cop anymore.

It was going to take some time for me to adjust. That'd been my identity for so long. Justin's brother. Then a cop. Whether I'd been a good or a dirty one, I'd still been a fucking cop. I tuned in that I was glaring at her as we stood on the sidewalk outside of the diner.

I tried to shove my anger down, and reached for her. "Hey."

"Worthing! You piece of shit."

I heard someone yelling behind me.

The voice was male, aggressive, and ice rushed down my spine. I acted on instinct, the same reflex that's kept me alive this far, and whipping around, I shoved Sawyer behind me, my arm up with my gun already extended. I didn't have time to plant my feet because as I looked, the guy was walking my way. He was on the outside of the sidewalk, a long winter coat open, the ends flopping behind him. He was white, had a dark beard. Grizzled face. Weight at two sixty and not with muscle, and he thought he was a motherfucking gangster.

"You gonna be dead, you pi—"

I shot him.

No hesitation. No thinking.

I had my gun in my hand the second I heard him speak. And I was raising it as I turned to look at him. It was like breathing for me, and as everything slowed down, right as I pulled the trigger, I saw the surprise on his face. He was here to shoot me, but he never thought I'd shoot first.

I'd seen that look time and time again, and never understood it. He was shocked that I would defend myself?

The bullet ripped into him, hitting his shoulder, and his hand jerked up right as he pulled his own trigger. His aim went high, shattering a window, but I was moving at him, tackling him before he could regroup and try again.

He grunted, trying to meet me, and instead of a clean hit, I threw him against the vehicle behind us. The car's alarm started going off, but at that moment, it was just him and me. No other sound penetrated my ears. This was a fight for life. My life, and I hadn't made up my mind what I wanted to do with him, but it took a second hit before I got him down to the ground. He was bleeding everywhere. I heard a crack as his head made contact with the cement sidewalk underneath him, but his eyes were wild. Crazed. He was on something. Adrenaline, and bloodlust.

He still wanted to kill me.

A bloodcurdling scream pierced through the air, sending a new wave of chills down my back. That came from the building behind me, second or third floor.

His bullet must've hit an innocent civilian.

I didn't have time to make a decision about what I wanted to do with him. I reared back and came down with a hit to his face, one that should knock him out. It did. His eyes rolled backward, which I'd seen before, but god, I never enjoyed seeing it. It was unnatural. But he was out, and I needed one second, just one, to take a breath, before I shoved myself up and took stock of the scene around me.

People were outside, watching. Phones were up. They were recording this.

Seeing a teenager coming out of the diner I'd just left, fumbling for his phone, I pointed at him. "Call 911."

When he looked ready to protest because that meant he couldn't get the video he'd need for fucking TikTok, I yelled, "Now!"

People were pressed against the diner's window, staring at me. Some went pale. Wide eyes. Stunned expressions with their mouths hanging open. I ignored them all, reaching for my cuffs, but fuck, I didn't have them on me anymore. That would've been my life three days ago.

Seeing a big guy standing on the sidewalk, I pointed at him next. "You!"

His eyes narrowed. He was one of the few without a phone videoing us. Hostility flashed next. He didn't like cops, I was assuming. "I need you to sit on him."

Confusion came over him, though he took a staggering step toward me, dressed in baggy sweats and a Giants jersey. He was well over six three and he had a little bit of a belly, but I was guessing most of him was solid muscle. Rough-shaven. "What'd you say, man?"

"I need him restrained if he wakes up."

"What? How?"

"Sit on him."

"*Sit* on him? What the fuck?"

More screaming broke out from above, and I whirled around, trying to locate it. My gun was drawn but pointed low and I ran past him, yelling over my shoulder, "Just keep him there until I get back."

He was grumbling, but the diner's waitress was waving for me. I went past Sawyer, a brief glimpse showing me that she was still watching the guy outside. She'd backed up against the wall, clutching her bag to her chest.

"Upstairs!" the waitress yelled, motioning to the back door.

"Stay here," I said tersely to Sawyer.

She jerked her chin up and down a few times.

I touched her arm, just briefly, wanting to say something to put the blood back in her face that had drained away, but there wasn't anything I could say. So, instead, I let myself touch her cheek, cupping it for a second. Her eyes went wide, but it was enough for me.

I ran past her back inside.

"The stairs there. They go up to that floor."

The door was locked. I reared back and kicked it in, hitting the stairs running. As I did, I grabbed my phone and called it in, identifying myself, giving them a location and a brief report of what they should expect. "I'll need multiple ambulances on scene."

The operator was swift, replying, "Multiple 10-54 H en route."

As we were finishing, I got to the second floor and found a child standing in the hallway, covered in blood. He looked nine, staring inside with a dazed expression. The kid was in shock. I slowed, getting to the door, and eyeing him, I moved around him so I could clear the doorway.

A woman was kneeling on the floor inside, screaming, crying, with blood covering her as well. She gasped, seeing me, but I held out a hand. "Miss, I'm—" That's all I managed before she jumped to her feet, backed away, and pointed at the floor where another woman was lying there.

She screamed, her voice breaking, "Help her! Help *her*! I don't know—I don't know what happened." Her hands were flailing around her.

"Is there anyone else here?"

"What?"

I needed to clear the scene, make sure it was safe, and as I stepped over the body, the woman in the kitchen began screaming again. I ignored her, doing a quick sweep, but no one else was in the apartment. After that, I holstered my gun and went to the woman on the floor.

I had two sides to me, and both were operational right now.

My heart was pumping. Adrenaline was racing through my veins, but the other side of me locked down. There was a firm divider inside of me, keeping the anxiety, fear, hunger at bay, and the other part of me was where I grew cold. Detached. I needed to be so I was clearheaded as I went through the motions of what I used to do for a living.

First aid. CPR.

This was a part of the job I did for so fucking long, but I hated it.

I didn't realize it until now, but this part, I hated it. But it's what I signed up to do because I didn't feel I had a choice in the matter. I couldn't let Justin join the family business. I wouldn't let him be turned into a criminal so I went to the academy to be something else, but goddammit. In the end, I became worse than what I was trying to save him from. I just didn't know it until I turned my resignation in.

Fuck. How sad was that?

I kept giving CPR until the first EMT got to me. "We got it, Jake. You can back up."

I looked up, confused, but I knew the paramedic. Recognized her.

Her partner rounded, taking my place and I moved aside, letting them do their job. "Stray bullet." I motioned to the window, but the first paramedic had already clocked it, her glance at the window before straying over to me lingering. "We got it. Go downstairs."

I nodded. That divider wall started to lift. Just a bit. Some of my adrenaline slipped through.

Another paramedic was in the hallway, talking to the child. He looked up, familiarity flaring because he knew me too. We gave each other a nod, but I kept moving, circling through the diner where I saw a couple street cops inside, questioning people. Both looked up, saw me, saw the blood on my shirt.

I reached to show my badge.

Then stopped because there was just air there now.

"Sir?" One stepped toward me.

I held up a hand. "I used to be a cop. OC." Organized crime.

That made him pause. His gaze lingered on my holstered weapon before he motioned to the street. "Manhattan South is on the way. Homicide. They'll want to talk to you."

Homicide.

Shit.

The guy had died.

CHAPTER EIGHT

SAWYER

"You want another coffee?" The server came back, eyeing me, but I saw the strain on her face.

I turned in my booth, my back to the whole posse that had formed outside. The ambulances. The fireman. The police. The paramedics.

I was on my third cup since everything happened. I nudged my mug toward her. "Thanks. Yeah."

This was all new to me.

I was alive.

And sitting in a diner, after a shooting that happened in front of me, *literally*, I was getting a wake-up call. My life was officially fucked up. I needed to unfuck it up.

She let out a sigh and didn't move away from the table. Her gaze was on the commotion outside, and I looked too. Jake was in front of the window, his arms crossed over his chest, so it pulled his shirt tight around him, accentuating his athletic build.

"How do you know him? Have you two been a thing for a while?"

I knew who she meant. "I just met him. He stole me from a police station."

"I—what?" She had to blink a few times, slack-jawed.

I shrugged. "His cousin made him."

"What?"

"She's in rehab now."

She continued to blink at me, her face blank.

The door opened then, the bell jingling. Seeing who was coming in, she dropped her gaze and scurried away.

She'd been flirty with Jake earlier. Then she saw him kill a guy and her attitude changed. I paused, my eyebrows pulling down. Should that have the same effect on me? I checked, eyeing Jake as he walked over to me. He ignored the others that remained in the diner. Most took off after they were questioned, but two older guys who looked as if they had no intention of shaving in this decade were perched at the counter, turned all the way around so they could see outside. Their elbows rested behind them.

They had a front-row seat to the scene happening outside.

Both grunted greetings to Jake, who half raised a hand to them. But his eyes went right back to me, trained on me as he approached.

The stirring was still inside of me.

Nope. That didn't have the same effect on me that it had on the server.

He came to the end of the table, his gaze sliding over me, inspecting every inch. After a bit, his jaw clenched. He asked in a gruff voice, "Ready to go?"

I needed to go back to my hotel. I needed to figure out my steps for tomorrow. I still had my list. Things to do. Activities to cross off, but I opened my mouth and nothing.

I didn't want to leave him.

The thought of going our separate ways made my stomach dip.

But then he said, "I got a hold of your cousin. He said I could bring you to his place."

My mouth snapped shut. "What?"

He went back out the door. He didn't answer me.

I was—what did he say? I scrambled after him. "I never told you my cousin's name. How did you get a hold of him?"

He got to the door, eyeing me before he opened it, and because he did, my momentum brought me close. Real close. Lack-of-personal-space close. I could breathe in all the smells wafting from him. His cologne. The smell of gun—was there a smell for that? There were other traces of smells. I caught myself before slamming into him, but his hand fell to my hip, sinking in. He held me in place, keeping me.

I went still.

I could feel his heat.

As if transfixed, my eyes tracked up, taking in his chest, his throat, his Adam's apple, his very prominent jawline, those lips . . . I gulped, pushing the beat of arousal down inside of me, and I finished the trek, coming to see his eyes, his eyes that had darkened. There was a slight smolder in them before he said, "I asked a friend for a favor. Your social media's wide open. He got me a number within twenty minutes."

Something shrank inside of me. "Oh. What—" I licked my lips.

He tracked the movement, his gaze piercing.

My brain fritzed for a second before I remembered. "What did my cousin say? I mean . . . How did he react when you told him about me?"

His eyes warmed before a wall slammed back down. They went dead and his tone was so flat. "He was surprised to hear about you, but I explained the situation, and he said I could bring you around there."

"What did you all say?" Oh, god. Did my cousin know about *everything*? I wanted to give a good first impression when he saw me in person. My whole family-mending mission relied on that first impression. I didn't want to scare him.

"I told him that you witnessed a shooting and you mentioned you were in town to maybe meet him."

My focus sharpened. "That's all you said?" My mouth parted in surprise.

His eyes flashed, but cooled right after. "That was it. Everything else is up to you." He looked behind me for a moment. "You gave your statement. My cousin is in rehab. Our time together has come to an end. That means you and I are done." He spun away from me, stepping outside. "You ready?"

I frowned, pursing my lips.

We were done.

That made sense.

My mouth went sour.

CHAPTER NINE

SAWYER

I didn't like this. Any of it.

Every cell in my body was protesting the thought that he was going to drop me off at Graham's and I'd never see him again. That was bullshit.

I studied him as he drove.

He was too cool. Too smooth.

There was a tic in his jawline, and his hand tightened on the wheel. He wasn't as unaffected as he was playing it off.

"Are you sure you heard my cousin right? He said you could bring me to his place? He's never met me. Maybe a sit-down somewhere else would be more ideal?"

"No. He said to bring you to his place. Apparently some of your aunts had been calling him?"

My aunts? Bess and Clara. As soon as he said it, of course that made sense. They were going to intervene no matter what.

I folded my arms over my chest. "I don't like this."

He threw me a look. "This is why you came here. To see your cousin."

"No. I meant—" I clamped my mouth shut because what? What was I going to say? The total weirdness I got when I was around him? How I felt like I already knew him when it'd not even been a full day?

I wasn't counting the subway meet because he'd been a dick.

"You meant what?" He was pulling over. Letting the engine run, he moved to face me. His voice went low, as if he knew what I was going to bring up. Which, if he did, then so be it. He felt it too. I'd watched him enough to know he wasn't as cold to me as he was acting.

I ducked my head, because could I really say that? I'd sound like a lunatic.

"You are a lunatic."

I whirled on him. "Excuse me?" Had I said that out loud?

I paled. What else had I said out loud?

He smirked, but his eyes were blazing. "A lot of stuff has happened to you in the last month. Your ex. Whatever else that's attached to that, because I don't feel like you're telling me everything. You were losing your marbles outside of your cousin's place of work, and a cop took you to the station. That's not normal for a lot of people. Plus, dealing with my cousin. That's a shitload of stress that you're handling." He quieted, his jaw clenched again. "You saw a man get shot, right in front of you. You are allowed to have some moments of lunacy right now."

Oh. Well. I sniffed at him. "That doesn't give you a right to call me a lunatic."

"You left with two strangers to take one of them to rehab. You went along for the ride. You *are* a lunatic," he deadpanned.

I scowled at him. "Words hurt."

He laughed softly, relaxing. I almost did a double take because was that the first time I saw him relax?

"All I'm saying is that it makes sense if you're not totally with it right now. Plus, this whole project." He motioned out the door. "You need to feel in control of something."

The corner of my mouth turned down. "You're saying I'm a control freak?"

He snorted, quietly. "No, but you do come off as someone who likes to feel in control—"

"Isn't that everyone?"

"—and like I said, a whole bunch of things happened that were out of your control."

I had to confess, "I do like feeling in control."

Another slight snort from him. "Glad our minds just came together."

Our gazes collided, and held.

And still held.

The air in the truck grew thick.

My body heated, and I couldn't stop the image of other parts of us coming together.

I was lonely. I tried to tell myself that. I was hurt because Beck rejected me, and there was this new guy who turned up a second time and hadn't left and I was attracted to him. That's all this was. It wasn't anything more.

And I was completely lying to myself.

But at least I could admit that I was lying to myself, because every cell in my body was protesting the idea that he was just a guy. He wasn't. He was more. I just didn't know what he was yet.

I bit down on my lip, needing to shove that image and that feeling down.

"Stop that," he said, roughly.

"What?" I let go of my lip, confused.

His eyes were staring at my mouth. Hard.

I chewed on my bottom lip again.

He groaned, his eyes darkening.

My mouth fell open again, surprised.

New hope jumped to my chest, and held there. It was suspended because . . . I didn't know, but what did that mean?

He continued staring, no, glaring at my mouth. That sensation of being pulled toward him was filling me again. An invisible rope that had wound itself around me, and it was tugging me toward him. My eyes grew heavy, my eyelids were starting to fall, but I began to lean toward him—

"We're here."

His gaze was solely trained on my mouth as he said that, his voice raspy and hoarse.

I blinked, realizing he was so close to me.

I didn't care. That thought hit me hard, making me blink a few times, trying to right myself, but it was true. I didn't care what I was about to do because I had to see. I had to know. So with that thought, I began to reach for him.

Suddenly, Jake stiffened.

His eyes snapped to the rearview mirror, and as soon as he did, he exploded into action. "Down!" He wrapped his arms over me, throwing himself on top of me. At the same time, he twisted around, his arm rising.

Pop! Pop! Pop!

The window shattered.

I screamed as the glass fell over us, but Jake was still shielding me.

Someone or something was going past the window, and fast.

Jake jerked upright, aimed, and he shot.

It happened so quickly. A few seconds.

Then he was gone, out the door, and running after something or someone.

I sat upright, my heart in my throat. A part of me didn't want to run after him. I didn't want to see further violence happening in front of me, but that was just a brief thought. The next thought, that came immediately after, was to get out and help.

I hurried out of the truck, choosing to go through his already opened door. Once I stepped down, my knees gave way. I clung to the door, keeping myself upright, but I was transfixed by what I was seeing happening a few yards in front of me.

Jake was wrestling with another man. They were both in dark clothing. The other man was wearing a ski mask, and he had more bulk on him, looking like he outweighed Jake by twenty pounds. Not that it seemed to matter. Jake kicked out the guy's knee, and when he would've screamed, Jake shoved his gun in the guy's mouth.

And—*bang!*

I stumbled backward.

My hand let go of the door handle in shock.

He—killed him. Just like that.

I mean, of course like that.

That guy shot at us first. It made sense Jake would shoot him, but in the mouth . . .

I think I was in shock.

I drew in a breath, wanting to cry. Wanting to scream. I didn't, though. The pop sounds from the other guy's gun. They'd been like soft pops. My vast knowledge accumulated from movies told me that he had used a silencer.

I groaned, my knees buckling, and this time I couldn't hold myself up.

I slid to the ground. My legs splayed out underneath me.

Who would shoot at us with a silencer?

Two men. Two men just shot at us.

I . . . I was trying to have that make sense, but no plausible explanation was coming to me.

Jake knelt down over the guy and looked around. Who was he looking for? His gaze skimmed over me, hardening for a second, before continuing his scan.

There was no one else on the street.

Was that odd? I didn't know. It'd been late when we left the diner. I had no clue what time it was.

Jake rolled him over and pulled off the ski mask.

Then he cursed. It was a fierce whisper, but I heard it and he looked back at me. His eyes were stark.

I started shaking, because I don't know. A bodily reaction? Something else I could control?

I might be verging on some hysterical thinking again.

Jake got up, holstering his gun as he came to me. "Get up." He touched my arm.

I didn't. I kept shaking, hugging my legs to my chest as hard as I could. I did that instead.

Jake bit out a curse, kneeling in front of me. "The game just changed. I need you to come with me."

I shook my head. Nope. I was just fine where I was. If I stayed here, maybe no one would try shooting at me for a third time. I changed my mind about Jake too. I was good. I didn't need any of whatever *that* was between us.

"I'm good here."

"No," he clipped out, now cold again.

Twice.

We'd been shot at twice.

I glared at him. "Who are you?"

I almost died today. Two times.

I kept shaking.

Jake cursed again, standing up. He moved, and he moved fast, so fast I didn't have time to react. He scooped me up and had me in his truck before I could fight him.

"Wha—no!" I tried kicking at him.

He dodged my feet, and I heard a *click click* as something plastic wrapped around my wrists.

Horrified, I looked down. He'd zip-tied my wrists, and as I was processing that, he bent down at my feet.

Zip-zip.

"What? What are you doing?" I tried kicking him. I couldn't because *they were also zip-tied*. "Whatareyoudoing?" I had officially lost it. "You're not a cop. You can't arrest me. Or detain me. This is illega—arghmph."

I belted out a scream, but it was muffled as he wrapped a shirt around me, stuffing it into my mouth. He tightened it again so I couldn't spit it out.

"Yeah, sweetheart. That's the point." He straightened up, checked me over and pushed me so I was lying down. I was struggling by now, squirming around, trying to kick him.

Nothing. All to no avail because as I was doing that, he wrapped seat belts around me, basically hog-tying me in place.

I couldn't move one bit.

He shut the door, disappearing.

A few minutes later, he returned, opened the back, and something was tossed into it.

Something heavy.

My eyes bulged out, and I tried screaming again.

I only needed one guess to figure out what that was. A dead body.

Oh my god.

Oh my god.

I was panicking.

I was starting to hyperventilate.

Everything was all . . . ugh. I had no idea, but as Jake got behind the wheel, started the engine, and drove away, I knew one thing.

He was *kidnapping* me!

CHAPTER TEN

SAWYER

I woke, tied to a bed, and instant anger boiled in me.

I was about to lose my mind. Kidnapped! I was freaking kidnapped. What the hell? I didn't come to New York City for this. To be in a freaking *Taken* storyline.

And I had liked Jake. I'd been attracted to him.

I had legit lost my mind.

Kidnapped. I still couldn't believe it.

"Ahhhh! Let me out of here! You asshole." I struggled, but my wrists were tied to the bedposts. I could talk, and my legs were left free, so yay for that. I could do windmills in the air above me, but that was it. I didn't think he'd climb on top of me so I could . . . There was a thought.

I'd been ready to let loose with another scream, but I quieted, now thinking.

Headlights flashed through the windows. Tires moved over gravel as a vehicle approached the cabin.

I had no idea how long I'd been here. He hadn't said anything to me as we were driving, but I knew we weren't in the city anymore. We pulled up to some cabin. I got a glimpse when he carried me inside. He asked if I needed to go to the bathroom, and yes. Of course. I'd downed three cups of coffee after the shooting and two before the first one. My bladder was screaming, but he wouldn't let me go to the bathroom alone, so I couldn't do anything. When I was done, he tied me to the posts. *Again.*

He took off after that, and eventually I fell asleep.

Every muscle in my body ached, and I needed to go to the bathroom again.

I looked up, wondering if the universe was listening and could help a jilted girl out.

The headlights turned off, and it wasn't long before I heard keys outside the window. I strained to hear him enter the house, but couldn't. The guy was as silent as a cat. That was annoying.

The bedroom door opened, but no lights were turned on. My eyes had adjusted a while ago so I could see him come straight for me, moving lithely, so quiet, like a ghost. He stopped in front of me.

I glared at him, *so* wishing for the power for murder by vision.

Alas, it wasn't working.

I couldn't make out his face, so I couldn't get a read on what he was thinking, but I was hurting, and before I knew it, a whimper left me.

He let out a small sigh and squatted by the bed, moving a little bit into the moonlight so I could see him. Jesus. There was a burning in his gaze, and his jaw was clenched so tight. Whatever he'd been doing, he hadn't been happy about it.

He gave me a long contemplative look, his face hard. Raking a hand over his face, he exhaled sharply. "I know you're not going to believe me, but I didn't have time to explain and for you to understand. I took you for your safety."

I snorted, still glaring. "You're *such* an asshole."

He leaned back, but still in the squatting position.

I hated when people could do that. It always looked so cool and so comfortable, and I was not a person who could do that. Angie Papdailier loved doing that in high school. She'd been cheerleader captain, and the sweetest, and all the guys wanted her. So of course she could rest on the back of her heels from a squatting position. Like, way to rub it in how *extra* lucky you are, and the fact Jake was doing that?

Not cool.

I ramped up my glaring wattage.

His lip twitched, reaching up and resting his hands on the bed, the one I was still tied to.

"There's a contract out on me." He was all stonewalled to me, but his jaw clenched again, and his gaze fell to my chest, staring hard at me. I caught movement to the right and saw his hand making a quick fist before smoothing it back out and taking a firm hold of the bed. He pulled on it, standing up, and went over to a chair in the corner.

A contract? A *hit*? "Why do you have a contract out on you? A contract for what?"

I didn't like that he sat down, back in the shadows. I liked having him in front of me. I liked being able to see his face, trying to get a read on him.

It gave me one sense of control, just an iota of it, and that's all I had. I was clinging to it.

His voice went back to monotone, talking to me as if we were discussing our favorite breakfast food. Maybe that was a little exaggeration. There was a terse edge to his tone, but I grunted in frustration because I had no idea how he felt about any of this and since *I* was the kidnapped one, I needed to know the mindset of my kidnapper.

He was saying, "—there are things about me that you don't know."

"No shit, Sherlock. You're a psychopath." I seethed. "What kind of a person are you that'd get a contract put on them?"

He ignored that. "It's for two million, so that means until pictures of my dead body hit the internet and my death's been verified, they're not going to stop coming. Two different shooters in the same day? I was worried if I left you at your cousin's, then whoever was coming at me would take you and try to use you as bait. You'd be collateral." He paused, briefly, his voice grating. "I was right. A picture was taken of us when we were leaving the station and an hour ago, another one was uploaded to the contract file. It showed us leaving the diner."

I . . . What?

I had no idea what he was talking about.

"Who the fuck are you? I don't—none of this makes sense."

His stark expression was telling me that there had been two shooters. He wasn't lying about that, no matter how much I didn't want to believe him.

My heart sank. There was a contract out on me? "Where?"

His chair scraped against the floor as he got up, walking over to me, walking all slow and ominous until he sat on the bed by me. As he did, his face moved into the moonlight, and I could see him again. A part of me sagged in relief. Another part of me froze up because there was nothing on his face. No facial expression. No regret. Nothing.

He was just all-business, all clenched and chiseled jaw.

He leaned down, his elbows on his knees. His hip pressed into my side. "It's a website. We've been trying to get it taken down, but it never works. It pops back up. So now we mostly monitor it. I am so fucking sorry that you got pulled into this."

God.

He meant it. He wasn't showing me anything, but his tone was ragged.

That tore through me, for some reason.

I was tied to a bed. Two guys had been killed in front of me, and now there were pictures of me on some website?

My eyes welled up. A tear rolled down my face.

He watched it go, his jaw clenching again, but his shoulders only rose and held before he let out a soft exhale. He tipped his head up, meeting my gaze. "I have to be blunt with you. You can't leave."

No . . .

I asked, "Where's my phone?"

"You can't call anyone. You can't have *them* call you. Once you've been identified, there are going to be men searching for you as well.

That means tagging your family, intercepting any call they might get from you. Tracing it. Law enforcement can't help, not in this situation. You walk out that door, and they will kill you. They'll kill you because they'll try to use you to get to me, and Sawyer"—he leaned in, his eyes going almost primal—"they're not going to be successful. You got me? I'd like to tell you that I'm a good guy, but the truth is that I'm not. I sold my soul a long fucking time ago, and while I'm not scared about dying, there's a few things I'm going to do before I let that happen. So if you want to stay alive, your best bet is doing what I tell you."

My heart had paused, waiting to hear what he'd said. It fell now, along with letting some fear slither in.

He would let me die to save his own ass.

"The house is on lockdown." He stood, his voice dropping, back to business. "Every door. Every window. We've got seven miles of woods around us so if you run, I'll hear the minute you try leaving. Trust me, I will hunt you down."

My mouth went dry as he loomed over me.

"Do you understand me?"

"I understand you're a selfish prick. I understand that," I spat at him.

I was seething inside.

Fuck this. Fuck him. Fuck everything. "I have stuff to do! Things. Lists. A bucket list that . . ." That I would not be finishing now.

He ignored my glaring and began untying me. "I'm assuming you need the bathroom again."

"Yes. That's on the list too," I snapped at him. As soon as I was free, he scooped me up from the bed. I began squirming to get free. I really *really* had to go, but Jake only held me tighter and walked me into a bathroom that was connected to the bedroom. He lifted the lid, sat me down, and reached for my jeans.

I began hitting him. "Oh no. No way. I'm not that hard-up for sex."

Not anymore.

"I'm trying to help you. Your hands were tied in the same position for hours."

"And who tied them? Fuck you." I shoved at him, trying to get him away from me, ignoring the feeling of needles coursing through my arms and hands.

He stopped, but lifted his head, his face two inches from me, and he scowled. "You want to piss your pants? Have at it." He stalked out of the bathroom, slamming the door behind him.

As soon as he was gone and as soon as there was a barrier between us, I let it down.

There was a wall that I erected inside of me, around my heart. I'd need to keep everything locked up inside if I was going to get out of this alive because no matter how much I thought my life was over before, it was nothing to this situation.

It was almost laughable. To think I'd been so devastated about the two decades I gave to Beck and my best friend.

Funny. That didn't have the same paralyzing pain it had a day ago.

CHAPTER ELEVEN

JAKE

Everything was completely screwed.

I could hear Sawyer crying inside, but fuck. *Fuck!*

Because of my dipshit decision, she was involved. Kidnapping. Jesus Christ. If we survived—no, fuck that. We would. She and I together.

My phone began ringing, and looking at the screen, a hollow laugh ripped out of me. I hit accept and went to the kitchen, pouring myself a stiff drink. A very stiff drink.

"Walden. What gave you the idea I'd want to speak to you again?"

Ashton Walden laughed smoothly on the other end, but I expected nothing less from him. He was the head of the Walden Mafia, one of the two families in control of the city. The other was led by his best friend, and while I had hatred for Ashton's best friend and the best friend's woman, that was on a personal level. The same wasn't so for Ashton himself. There was a sort of past with him that filled me with regret, self-loathing, and the odd mix of fondness. Another life and we might've been friends, but not this life.

Ashton said, "Want to meet up so I can take pictures of your dead body and collect two million?"

I was a dead man walking, on the phone with a Mafia head, and he was joking about my death contract. For some reason, that relaxed me. "Only if you promise to give your wife the money."

He laughed. "I could never tell Molly. She'd be aghast that I might've benefited off your neck."

"How about instead you tell me why there's a hit put out on me? That'd be helpful."

He got quiet. "You don't know?"

I snorted. "About the hit? No. I have no fucking idea who's behind it. My family? Your family? Trace's? This came out of left field. Someone with a vendetta against me as a cop? Think if I put out a memo that I retired, they'll take it down?"

"No, but I can tell you that if I wanted you dead, I'd be doing that torture shit personally. You know me. That's my *thing*."

Indeed it was. It was widely known he enjoyed torture.

I picked up my glass of bourbon and went to the living room. With my back to the wall, I leaned there with a perfect view of the bathroom door and took a drag of the liquor.

I never felt the burn.

I replied, "If you're trying to trace this call, you can't. FYI, Mr. Cybersecurity Expert."

"We already got the location bounced back to us, and you sent a virus into my favorite laptop. I was impressed, Worthing. I didn't know you were capable of that sort of cyber sophistication."

Of course he'd try to trace me. He was Mafia.

I scowled. "You really don't know who put the hit out on me?"

Ashton got serious. I heard a squeak on his end, maybe his chair was pushed back as he stood. "All I know is that it's someone in your own camp. I don't know the name. You need to clean house in your family."

My gut twisted.

Fuck that. Fuck that so much.

Frustration welled up, and I said roughly, "Thanks for the advice. I've been a cop most of my life. You got any other tips on how to not be a cop and go up and murder half of my family because they're all fucking criminals? If so, I'd love to know how to get myself to do that."

Everything I said was the truth. I gritted my teeth.

Ashton was the head of the Walden family. His best friend Assface was head of the West family, and me? According to a call from one of my uncles, my family, who mostly operated out of Maine because it kept them under the radar, said they took a vote and I was the new head of the Worthing Mafia.

Me. The head of any Mafia.

It was a sick joke, and I already knew the hit came from someone on the inside because the second shooter had been one of our guys. He was usually used as a gunrunner, but he was in the city, and he'd tried to kill me.

I was a lone wolf for this. No police friends. No family.

Then again, if I'd been asked my preference, it would've been this way. I might've had resources offered to me, but when it would come down to it, I wasn't a guy who stood in the back and gave orders. I was the one who went to the front line.

I *was* the weapon.

If I was going to order people dead, I was the type who preferred to do it myself. I'd like to say it was because then I knew it was done right, but that wasn't the truth. It was the adrenaline of being in the fray, of being the monster hiding in the shadows. There was a sick fascination of feeling your enemy's blood spilling over your hand. In that moment, when you were the reason someone's life was draining out of them, that was when I felt the most alive.

Ashton replied, "Though, according to the street cameras and how you reacted to the second shooter, you were already aware of that fact. Who's the girl?"

I ignored that. "I'd hoped you would have a name for who's going after me in my family. No one's reached out?"

"I have a cordial relationship with you. I would *not* with anyone else in your family." Ashton's voice cooled significantly. "If you indeed take over your family's business, I may entertain the idea of working with you, but it would only be under those circumstances. You misunderstood me. I meant that you needed to go and clean house in the legal way."

I frowned, considering what he just said. "You want me to arrest my family?" Also, "How very not-Ashton of you. I'd assume you were all for me going in and killing everyone."

"That would be my way, yes. But since your identity is still wrapped up with being law enforcement, I'd assume you would want to do it a way that would let you sleep at night."

A dark churning filled me, and I looked down at my drink, swirling the liquid around.

Ashton didn't know me anymore. Then again, maybe he never had.

He added, "They turned their back on you after Justin was murdered."

I said harshly, "You don't know anything about me and my family."

A pang went through me at the mention of my own brother, but Ashton was right. I'd reached out for help and instead had been led on a goose chase by my cousin, and when I reached out for assistance on reining him in, all four of my uncles laughed in my face.

That was the day I went rogue, going on the path that led me to the truth. The end result was a dead cousin, a multitude of our soldiers dead, and most of my family in denial about how much they fucked up when they appointed Nicolai as the head.

"Why are you calling? You're not being helpful at all." I eyed the bathroom door again. She was taking too long.

Ashton laughed again, softly. "I called to offer assistance. What do you need? I found the girl, by the way. Also, found her family that's concerned because she went to New York to run away from an ex-fiancé. Did you know that her mother sent a text to her aunt about possibly having an intervention when she returns from New York? I found *his* new woman. He did not trade up. I am guessing that's your woman and you're into bondage role-play? Because if not, it looked like you kidnapped a woman, and my guess is that you got her at some safe house you kept for this particular reason. Tell me how wrong I am. Go ahead. I bet you can't."

He was so fucking smug, and I did not need to hear half that shit from him.

"You need to *stop* talking about her. That's what you need to do."

He was quiet. "Jake—"

"Not another word about her. You hear me?" I growled, taking the rest of my drink like it was a shot. Sawyer had been in the bathroom too long by herself, and Ashton was starting to piss me off. "You want to help? Use some of that hacking ability on my family's texts. Find out who I need to take out to get the contract off my head."

"Killing whoever put it out won't get the contract taken down. You need to have them do it or they'll keep coming for you. Money's already loaded for the winner. You know how it works."

I did, and nothing he was saying was helping to take the edge off. "Find me a name, Ashton. I've done a lot of shit for you over the years, saved your ass a few times. Save mine this time."

I didn't wait to hear his response. I ended the call, pocketed the phone, and went over to the door. "Sawyer, we need to talk." I waited for her to reply, but there was nothing. No breathing. No water running. No toilet flushing. It was silent.

I didn't stop to question it.

I reared back and kicked open the door.

She was gone.

CHAPTER TWELVE

SAWYER

Seven miles, my ass.

Jake had been lying. There was no way we were surrounded by seven miles of forest. At first I thought I had this in the bag. I've done half marathons before.

Seven miles? Pfft. Not a problem.

I started hotfooting it. I'd been going a good while before I heard a shout from behind me.

My heart sank as some fear stung me. He finally checked the bathroom and realized a window had been left open, just an inch but it was enough.

Dumbass.

Everything alarmed, my ass.

I went faster, but it was still dark out and the moon only penetrated certain areas of the woods. It was dense so I couldn't run at my full speed, not unless I was willing to risk a rolled or broken ankle. Or some other injury.

It felt like I'd been running for an hour. My breathing was choppy. It had been a few years since my last half marathon, when I really thought about it. My heart was spiking. Where was the road? I heard a road. I knew I did. It didn't sound seven miles away, but the farther I went, I was starting to doubt myself.

Had I misheard?

Had I gone in the wrong direction? Was I—I didn't even know. I had no idea where I was. I could be going into a national park, for all I knew.

Dammit.

I stopped, panting, and immediately bent down to rest my hands on my knees.

My heart was trying to burst its way out of my chest, but I needed to think.

Think. Be rational. Come up with a plan.

I had no plan. Running was my plan, and the only thing I did before seeing if I could get out the window was go to the bathroom.

I was shivering now. That's what happens when you're running during the early-morning hours when it's still chilly. If I made it out of this, I'd probably get pneumonia.

I didn't want to think what Aunt Clara would have to say to that. Or Bess. My mom would just shake her head. She never understood why I ran in the first place. My mom was a bit old-school.

"Are you done?"

I screamed, whirling around.

Jake materialized from behind a tree, and that asshole, he looked smug and all warm and comfortable. Maybe a bit irate, as his smirk transitioned to a glare. Ooh. His eyes flashed at me. He was angry, real angry. He snarled, and I noticed he had stopped to formulate a plan before he went after me. He was dressed all in black. Black coat. Black pants. Black shoes. He was even wearing black gloves, and in one hand was a handgun.

I swallowed. Why did that gun look so much scarier than it had before?

I eased back a step. "I had to try."

"No!" He stalked toward me. "You didn't."

Oh. Oh no! He did *not* just yell at me.

My chest puffed up. I was about to yell back, except—I turned and fled. It was more a reflex because he was hella scary as he was coming for me, but before I could take more than a couple steps, he was on me.

"I don't think so, princess."

"No!" I yelled, battering at him. "And don't call me that."

"I'll call you whatever the fuck I want," he growled, cutting himself off as he swiftly wrapped something around me and lifted me up. I tried kicking at him, but he maneuvered me around so my feet could move, but they couldn't hit anything.

Jesus. Fuck. I hadn't even noticed him carrying anything.

I began wriggling around, turned upside-down and facing away from him.

I had no idea how he was doing this. "Agh! No fair."

"What part of being kidnapped do you think is supposed to be fair? Stop *fucking* fighting."

"No!" I flailed with more oomph, but to no avail. I was hitting air. I didn't even know where his head was at this point. "Put me down! I'm going to vomit. I just ran three miles." I was guessing.

"Whose fault was that? I told you not to run. Told you it was seven miles. And you ran a little over a mile."

I groaned. "Way to rub it in."

He snorted, starting a trek through the woods. He wrapped his arm tighter around my legs, and that's when I realized he had me around his back, like I was some sort of toddler. What—it was kinda genius, and comfortable, but I couldn't move.

"I don't like you."

"I don't give a fuck."

I opened my mouth to argue.

He said, before I could get one word out, "I took you for your safety. I didn't kidnap you for sick pleasure."

"Yeah, right." I snorted. "I'm sure that's what every kidnapper says to themselves when they're doing the kidnapping. It's called trying to justify your habit."

He tensed underneath me, turning to cement. A low rumble started from low in his chest. "I'm not justifying shit. It's the truth."

"Whatever you need to tell yourself so you can keep that pep in your step. You told me yourself that you're not a good guy. Now I'm supposed to believe you? Yeah. Sure. You were tying me up for my own good."

His sarcasm was just as strong. "And look at you, proving me wrong right now. Way to go. You're being super logical."

"If I could bite your ass, I would."

A smothered laugh vibrated against my back. "Why do you think I have you turned that way?"

"I feel like an idiot. You put me in some sort of adult-sized swaddler, backward. Where did you get this? Are there stores for kidnappers? Kidnappers-R-Us?"

A smothered laugh reverberated behind me. He coughed over it. "Just quit bitching until you hear what I have to say. I'll explain everything."

I went still, not that I was moving much. It was completely useless. But the little struggling I was still trying, for my own mental sake, I halted. "You promise? *Everything?*"

"Yes." He cleared the trees, and I saw there was a small road that he'd used, where some kind of cart was parked. Instead of untying me and letting me sit on the seat, he climbed up, sat sideways, and pulled his phone out of his pocket.

He retucked me, pulling me tighter around him so I couldn't move an inch.

I wanted to protest, but . . . I felt kinda snug. Though, hanging down was annoying. I growled until the cart started up. That distracted me because holy shit, it was silent. Like, stealth silent and with no lights. He drove us back like that from his phone.

I was so frustrated.

I had no fighting chance against him. Not when he had toys like this.

"What kind of cop has access to tech like that? Aren't you guys supposed to be poor?"

"Were you not paying attention when my cousin was bitching? Money is not an issue for my family. Any of us."

He sighed. I felt it more than heard it, and after that, I got quiet, feeling just how seriously strong he was. There was no softness on his body. He was pure muscle. Feeling him, remembering that glimpse I got of him earlier when he'd changed clothes and a small section of his very flat stomach showed, I gulped, feeling itchy.

"Stop squirming. Just wait to hear me out. You know I was forced to take you."

"Our definitions of force vary. What dictionary are you using? The criminal one?"

A slight snort sounded from him. "We're almost back."

Oh joy. Almost back to where he'd put me on a chair, tie me to it. It didn't matter if it was reclined or not, I'd be tied down.

I didn't think so. "Promise you won't tie me up." I tried to look at him, but the most I could see was the back of his shoulder.

He went still, his head turning toward me. "Promise you'll hear me out."

I let out a long, frustrated breath of air, but said, "Fine."

"Fine," he clipped out, just as annoyed.

We kept going in the complete dark. "How are you driving this thing? There's no lights."

He didn't reply, only saying, "We're almost back. I'll make you food too."

And with that, my stomach let loose a growl that could've scared off a grizzly bear. Normally I'd be mortified, but we were past that with the whole two dead guys and him kidnapping me. Plus, I'd peed in front of him.

When he pulled up to the house, he stowed the cart in a building, plugging it in. He kept me on his back. How strong was this guy? Seriously? I was a good hundred and forty pounds. I wasn't some lightweight woman, but he was walking around as if I were a backpack that he was too lazy to drop.

I was getting a little sick from the different motions and all the ups and downs before he stepped out and hit another button on his phone. A big door closed, coming from the top like it was a garage door.

As we crossed to the house, I took in the scenery this time. I hadn't been able to before.

He was right. We were surrounded by trees. Trees and trees and trees. A knot formed, thinking how stupid it had been of me to try, but I had to. That was lesson one of being kidnapped. You get a chance, you run.

We'd come up a smaller trail, but there was a driveway jutting out to my left side.

Which would be my right side if I was normal, and not upside-down.

Wait . . . Did I have that wrong?

I was frustrated all over again because this was so confusing.

He was at the back door, putting in a code. The locks were unlocking, and as he stepped inside, he moved around so my head didn't hit the doorframe (so considerate of him) before he punched in another set of codes. The door shut, and he did a whole set of codes after that.

The guy hadn't lied about that security. Fuck. He was either *really* into security or paranoid. Though, the contract out on his life was giving him some credibility. If I believed him. I still wasn't sure about that. I watched *Nightline*. Kidnappers brainwashed their kidnappees.

He didn't turn on the lights, going through the kitchen and moving into the bedroom where he turned with his back to the bed. I heard a swish and I was airborne. "Oooh!" I fell to the bed with a bounce. That was a little jarring. I glared, sitting up. "You could've warned me."

He didn't spare me a look, moving around the room.

There were two of them. They were going in circles.

Now three.

Was I hearing birds?

I lay back down, cursing because I knew better.

He laughed, not trying to hide it. "I could've told you not to sit up. All the blood's at your head."

I rolled so I could watch him, and as he paused at the window, I called his name. "Jake."

He looked.

I held out my middle finger, making a point to turn it around so it was upright. "Fuck you."

He stared at me for another moment, taking me in. There was no glare back, or curse, or even annoyance. His jaw just tightened before he moved to the last window. "This room is secure."

I smirked. "Did you check the bathroom?"

His jaw clenched. "Already done. That won't happen again."

It was dumb of me, but I couldn't help myself. I needed to taunt him. I was helpless so I wanted him to feel an eighth of what I was experiencing, even if it was foolish of me. There was something in me *needing* a reaction out of him. Any sort of reaction.

My tone was mocking. "I thought the whole place was on lockdown. You're like some security guru or something?"

"Just double-checking, now knowing your proclivities for not believing me."

I laughed, giving up on watching him, and closed my eyes because the ceiling was still circling. "I hate you."

"You're not some treat either, princess."

"Shut up with that name or I'll start calling you names too."

He grunted, opening a door and flicking on a light. "You already have."

"I have?" I lifted my head, seeing him standing upside-down in what looked like a doorway to a bathroom. I moaned because there were still two of him. At least the third had gone away. Small blessings. Just the one was enough of an annoyance to me.

"Psychopath? Asshole?"

I muttered under my breath, "Well, you are."

"Lunatic," he shot back.

I winced, raising my hands to start rubbing at my temples. "I think you've cured me of my slight break in my mental health. Funnily enough, if my best friend called me up, I'd answer."

He stopped in his tracks. "That's who he left you for? Your best friend?" His voice went low.

Oh. I hadn't gotten to that part. A knot formed in my throat, but I swallowed it down, not sure why it was there anymore. "Not that it's any of your business, but yes."

"How long was she your best friend?"

I grimaced. "Again, *not* that it's any of your business, but I met her in college. She was my freshman roommate and then we rushed the same sorority together."

"Since college?"

My throat was suddenly dry, so very dry. I said a little quieter, "Yeah. Since college."

"You called her your best friend."

That knot was back, and this time it was a little harder to shove it down. "*Ex*–best friend. Slip of the tongue."

He was quiet again for a moment before walking away. "When you can stand, help yourself to a shower. There's clothes in the closet. Find whatever that'll fit. Come out when you're done. I'll get started on the food."

I yelled as he left, "Are you going to be cooking up an explanation too?"

He shut the door, and said from the other side, his voice muffled, "Wash up. You stink."

"Here's another name for you." I made a face. *"Dick."*

CHAPTER THIRTEEN

SAWYER

After showering and finding some clothes to change into, my stomach was rumbling by the time I left the room. I didn't want to give him any credit; the aromas coming from the kitchen were too much for me to resist. A part of me considered going on a hunger strike, more to just be a pain in the ass than any other reason. I was pissed about all of this. Pissed that we'd been shot at twice. Pissed that he kidnapped me.

Pissed that I ran maybe three miles only to be carried back like I was a giant toddler.

I decided to take a stand that it was three miles, not however long he said. He didn't know what he was talking about. So yeah.

I was *pissed*.

That was the only reason I wanted to join him, so I could piss him off. If I was going to be miserable, so was he.

I watched him for a moment when he wasn't aware of my presence. He was at the stove, his head down as he was staring at his phone, idly stirring whatever was in the pot, and I saw the exhaustion on his face.

Exhaustion and other emotions, ones that made my stomach get all twisty inside as I didn't know if I wanted to try and decipher them, but it was enough of an unguarded moment for me to push away the immaturity of an adult temper tantrum.

He'd changed into sweats and an old-school vintage varsity Henley.

My mouth watered a little bit, seeing how he looked in that shirt. There was a hockey emblem on it, but I didn't recognize the team.

My mouth was watering from whatever he was cooking. I cleared my throat. "What'd you make?"

He put his phone away, stuffing it into his back pocket, and glanced over his shoulder. His eyes ran over me, lingering on my bare feet and calves—I'd pulled up the sweats I found so they were just under my knees—before sweeping back to my face. They narrowed, holding on my lips, where I was biting down on my bottom one, then rose and held my gaze. Hunger flared in him, hot and primal for a moment.

He was attracted to me.

My own arousal flared, which pissed me off all over again.

He didn't deserve that. Whatever the earlier connection had been between us, he killed that. It was destroyed.

It should've been gone.

I clamped down on the throb that was starting between my legs. Not today, you traitorous pussy.

I was definitely ignoring my own body's reaction, and half glared at him. "That is food, right?"

He blinked again, some of the hunger banking. "I made soup. If you don't like soup, tough shit." He glared back, some of his heat morphing into hostility. He gestured to a cupboard. "There's bowls up there. Crackers."

I pulled out two bowls but didn't move from the counter. He was in front of the food. I was not going over there to get it, not with him so close.

He must've sensed my thoughts because he made a grunting sound and reached for the bowls. Our fingers grazed each other as I held one out to him. His eyes jumped back to mine, staring into me. Hard. Searching for . . . I didn't know. I shoved down all of my thoughts. There was no way I was letting him in so he could read me.

He saw the wall slam down and his only reaction was that he tensed, but he said roughly, "Here."

I took it, making sure not to touch him, and went to the table. I was starting to sit, when he stopped me, saying, "Living room. Might as well get comfortable for what I need to tell you."

That sent my stomach into a whole new tizzy, tightening up.

Grabbing a spoon and a napkin that he'd laid out, I stalked to the other room. Curling up in a corner of one of the couches, I glared as he joined me. There were two couches in the room with a television in the corner. The front door was in the opposite corner.

He walked in carrying his soup and two water bottles. He didn't hand it to me or bring it over to me. He sat on the opposite couch. We couldn't have been farther apart unless there were other chairs and one was positioned literally right in front of the door. He tossed one of the bottles so it landed next to me.

I glared. I was going to do all the glaring I wanted because I had a right to be livid.

I stated, "So."

His eyes lifted from his soup, finding me. Darkening.

I folded my legs underneath me, getting more comfortable, holding my soup up in front of me as I lifted the spoon. "Who the hell are you, Jake Worthing?"

The corner of his mouth lifted up, slightly, but it was gone as quick as it appeared. If I hadn't been watching him, I would've missed it. Then he got serious, his face getting scary. "A while ago, my younger brother met and fell in love with a woman. Her name was Kelly. He fell hard and fast, and well, that's the beginning of all of this, or maybe it was the night they were both murdered."

I sucked in some air. "I'm sorry." I hadn't known his brother was murdered, but I'd heard how his body was found.

Damn.

He dropped his gaze, setting his soup on the nearest end table. "I mentioned this earlier, but some of my family are cops and there's another whole section that's pretty much the opposite." He looked up, meeting my eyes. "They're in the Mafia."

My mouth dried up quickly.

My hands began shaking so I put my soup on the end table next to me, then wrapped my arms around both of my knees, hugging them to my chest.

This wasn't good. "Mafia?"

"Yeah," he said quietly, but with a clipped edge. "Justin, that's my brother. He and I weren't close to either side. That was my choice. I moved to the city to get away from both sides of the family. Some of them are up in Maine, some are spread out around the city. But when Justin came with me, it didn't end well for him."

My heart sank for him. "He was murdered?"

"He was murdered," he confirmed. His face was set in a mask of concrete. "I'm supposed to go up to Maine and take over the family business."

"You mean join the force up in Maine?" I leaned forward in my seat. "With the other law-abiding family up there?"

His head lifted again. His eyes were stark, and I had my answer.

I fell back into the couch again. "Not the law-abiding side, huh?" That came out in a soft whisper.

"I'm supposed to be their head."

The head? What did that mean?

My head was swimming.

He kept talking. "The second shooter used to be one of my family's soldiers. *That's* why I grabbed you. Like I explained before, we didn't have time for me to suss it all out and for me to explain it to you or for you to understand it. He had a silencer, but I didn't. That neighborhood, they probably aren't used to the sounds of a gunshot. Someone's going to look. If we stayed, cops would've arrived, and it'd be a whole different ball game from the first shooting. I would've been taken in, questioned. You too. We would've had a whole bunch of eyes on us, including dirty cops. Anyone who was able to send one of my own family's soldiers after us would've easily got to someone in the force to finish the job. There's also the fact that two shooters already saw you with me. He got us outside of your cousin's place. I wasn't followed. He was waiting for us there."

He waited, letting me connect the dots.

They already knew about me.

Holy shit.

They'd looked into my cousin, found his address.

"Is my cousin in danger?"

"He's probably being monitored to see if you show up again. And if you do, I've no doubt that you'll be snatched to try to lure me out."

He'd been right to kidnap me.

I deflated.

"I put in some calls and confirmed the contract on my head, but your pictures were added. You need to stay away from your family, for their safety, at this point."

"Even my mom? My aunts?"

"You have to proceed with caution. Don't contact them."

Aunt Clara and Bess would not be happy about that. Or my mom. "Um, that might backfire."

His jaw clenched. "Sawyer."

I unfolded and leaned forward. He had to hear this. "You don't understand. My mom and my aunts, they're not normal."

He was gripping his bowl so hard.

I shook my head. I had to get through to him. "My mom is old-fashioned. She's a little like the Montana version of a Stepford wife, but my aunts are not. They're so the opposite, but the one thing those three have in common is the lengths they'll go to for me. My aunts didn't have kids. I am their kid. You're not getting one mom. You're getting three. If I don't contact them, they will come here to look for me. They will raise hell until I'm found. Trust me."

He was quiet for a moment. "What'd they think of your ex?"

I almost laughed because I hadn't heard him correctly. "What?"

He was serious.

Oh. I coughed, clearing my throat. "Slight detour there. Uh. About my ex?"

He was waiting, his face all serious.

I shook my head, shrugging a shoulder. "I don't know. My aunts hated him at first sight. They always hated him, but I'm ride-or-die. Unfortunately." I bulged my eyes out at him. "Never wanted to do that literally, but here we are. But, uh. Yeah. My aunts stopped saying things when they realized I wasn't going to leave him. They never asked about marriage. I think they were hoping what happened would happen. My mom . . . I think my mom hoped for me because she thought I loved him."

"You didn't?"

Didn't I?

I loved Beck . . .

Of course I loved him, but being in love with him—I couldn't think about that. Not now. I shook my head. "Can we not . . . do this?" I motioned between us. "I don't open up to you anymore. Remember? You kidnapped me."

But, right. My family.

I began chewing on the inside of my cheek. "Are they in danger? My family? My cousin?"

"They'll be monitored and watched, and as long as you stay away, they'll be safe." He was warning me, his gaze hard on me.

I gritted my teeth.

This whole thing sucked majorly. "I don't like this."

His mouth was so tight. "I'm aware."

I let out a harsh laugh. He didn't care, as long as his neck was safe. That's all he cared about. I was stuck in this situation with another selfish prick. Lovely. "Do you know who put the contract out?"

An emotion flickered in his gaze before he cut it off. "Someone in my family."

Air caught, trapped in my lungs. What kind of family did that to each other?

A Mafia family, that's who. The answer came immediately.

That's the kind of person I was stuck in this entire fucked-up situation with too. A Mafia ex-cop. I rubbed at my forehead, a pounding headache suddenly showed up. "This is such a twisted joke on me. The universe is really laughing at me." Sick laughter rippled up from my sternum. Sick and twisted, and bitter.

He was shutting down, closing off to me.

"I wasted almost *two decades* on a *piece of shit boyfriend* only to get *kidnapped* by you. *You.*" I sneered, that bitter laughter morphing into something sounding unhinged. "A Mafia ex-cop who's in the middle of an identity crisis. Who are you? Really? Are you a cop or are you Mafia? Maybe you need to pick a fucking lane. Arrest people. Kill people. I don't care. Just *do something.*"

His jaw kept getting harder and harder the more I spoke.

I exploded, my fury refusing to be repressed anymore. "Sorry, but I'm kinda for you just killing people if that gets us the best result. I *want my life back*!"

I hadn't realized I started to stand as I was beginning to yell, but as I started across the room to him, he shoved up and caught me, his hands clamping down on my hips.

I officially lost my shit when he did that.

Wrong fucking move, dude.

CHAPTER FOURTEEN

SAWYER

"Sawyer—"

I didn't realize I was across the room, with a hand up in the air, as if I was going to strike him until an ugly look came over Jake's face. He was up in my face, forcing me backward, but if anything, that unleashed more of my fury.

It was alive inside of me. Writhing. Needing an outlet.

Fuck this guy. Goddamn. This guy.

I was snarling because in that moment, I hated him. How fucking dare he involve me in his shit?

Images flashed in my mind.

How he got in my face on the subway train.

How surprised he was at seeing me in the police station.

How he stared at me, coming to stand in front of me as if he wanted to say something to me.

How his cousin threw her arms around me, demanding I come with them, but it was his look that was coming to my memory now.

How he looked pleased at the thought.

Pleased.

Fucking pleased!

A pent-up growl began low in my stomach, and as it rose up, moving through my throat, traveling to my mouth, it was savage and boiling, and when I let it loose, I was seeing things in a whole new light.

He did this. He wanted me to come with them.

This was his fault.

His.

How *dare* he?

I was done. Officially done. I'd reached my limit of taking this bullshit.

A dark warning was in his eyes as his hand closed around my hip. "Don't—"

"*You* don't!"

His eyes went feral, and I reacted, matching it. I was *all about* that. The inferno inside of me was lit up and needing an outlet. He just volunteered as tribute.

He went feral. I went primal.

I lunged at him, and since we were so close, my body hit against his, but instead of both of us going backward, he caught me. His arms wrapped around my body, and I was held imprisoned in the air. Somehow that made it worse, and I screamed, struggling to get free while I hit his shoulder.

"Goddammit," he growled, readjusting his hold.

We were moving.

I kept trying to kick free from him, but then we were falling.

My back hit the bed, and he landed on top of me, but he must've caught his weight somehow. He didn't crush me. I was stunned for a second, and he used that time to lay his entire weight down on top of me.

"Stop." He pinned me down, moving my wrists so they were beside my head.

I couldn't. I, just, couldn't.

I began fighting again. "I hate you. I fucking hate you."

He growled again, a vicious sound ripping from him, as he moved my arms higher. When I tried bucking him off me, he twisted, scissoring my legs open in one smooth move, and he maneuvered himself between them, kicking them out so I couldn't move them except—I wrapped them around his waist, and oooh.

We both paused.

Anger was still boiling in me and I couldn't hit out at him. That made it worse. "Fuck you." My voice broke. My chest was heaving.

He lifted his head higher so he could see me better.

We stared at each other.

He was breathing hard as well.

I didn't think it was from the exertion of fighting me.

Shit.

My fight was changing swiftly, lighting up my arousal.

His eyes darkened, seeing the change.

I was still breathing hard, my chest rising up and down rapidly.

But then he ground against me, purposefully, and held my gaze the whole time.

That felt good.

Dammit.

His head fell to the side, his eyes closing. He did it again, pressing harder into me, holding it there.

We both groaned.

That felt so good. I gasped lightly. The throbbing between my legs was spreading through my body. Racing all the way up, sending sensations through me until my mouth was watering again.

"Fuck," I whispered.

I hadn't thought that through when I got up from the couch.

I ground up against him.

"Sawyer. Wai—" he rasped into my ear, his entire body pressing me down.

I didn't. I lifted my hips up against him again, rotating. I panted. The inferno in me transformed so fast into lust now. Need.

I was aching from a whole different outlet.

I licked my lips because a deep yearning took root inside of me, starting to pulsate at the base of my spine.

I needed this touch. I needed to feel good, for once.

All the pain from the last couple weeks, I wanted it gone. The fear of being shot at. I came to this city despondent. Lost. My spirit had been fractured, but this, here with him—he could make me feel good. He could make me forget. And suddenly, that's the only thing I was desperate for.

I *needed* to forget.

Turning my head, I fused my mouth to his. That taste electrified me, and I groaned, trying to pull my hands free.

I was beyond caring about anything else except the feel of him on top of me.

I gasped into his mouth, "Jake."

"Sawyer." Jake lifted his head, tearing his mouth from me as he gazed down at me, his eyes very alert, very focused. "Wha—" He let go of one of my wrists, running his hand down my arm.

My hand shot to his jaw, and I held him.

His eyes smoldered, and for a moment, we scowled at each other.

Need pulsated through me. I could feel it in the air, the pressure was pushing down on us. Everything else faded away. It was only him. Me. He studied me, until he saw whatever he needed. The searching look cleared, another darker emotion slamming into its place, overriding everything else.

He pushed against me, up and into me, and right there. God. Right there.

Pulling my other hand free, it went to his hip. My fingers dug in as he moved over me.

That's where I needed him.

"Are you sure about this?" he asked, his voice thick and hoarse.

It's what I needed. That's all that mattered to me. I lifted my mouth up to him for my answer. That was enough for Jake. He took over, opening his mouth over mine, demanding entrance.

I granted it, his tongue sliding inside. And I moaned, my toes curling from how good he tasted.

It was like he was eating me from the inside out, in long and slow bites.

My body was buzzing. My blood whirled.

My hand went to his shirt, and I pushed at it.

He shifted, cursing under his breath. "Jesus Christ." He caught his shirt, his gaze taking me in, probably seeing the madness that invaded me. Whatever he saw, it had an effect on him. He whisked his shirt off, his movements going fast. His hand slid under my back, lifting me up off the bed.

I'd never experienced that. A man lifting me as easily as he did, rearranging me so deftly. My mouth parted.

He lifted his head, holding my gaze with an intensity that held me captive. I almost didn't dare to move, afraid to break whatever this new spell was wrapping around us. As I held my breath, waiting, his hand slid down my back, sliding inside my pants. He cupped my ass, yanking me further against him. The pleasure overwhelmed me.

That friction was what I needed. Carnal pleasure rocketing through me.

His hand slid over my hip again and he moved to the side so his free hand began undoing the drawstrings on my pants. He didn't move them down, but there was enough room for him. His hand dipped between my legs, burrowing underneath my panties.

He continued to watch me, burning fiercely as he slid a finger inside of me.

I gasped, arching my back.

He felt so good inside of me, and he thrust in, slowly, stretching me. He went farther into me, going as far as he could. I gasped. Fuck. He felt good in there. A second finger joined, stretching me even more. He rubbed against my walls before pulling them out, only to push them back in.

He started the rhythm.

In and out.

He went faster, building.

Harder.

Holding.

Moving out and then in. He hit the right spot, and just then, his thumb began rubbing over my clit.

"Is this what you wanted?" he demanded, gritty. "What your pussy wanted?"

I opened my eyelids, just barely, watching him from underneath.

He saw me, and a knowing smirk formed over his face, but his eyes were just as heated as I knew mine were.

He kept sliding in and out of me. His thumb's rubbing became more measured. More purposeful. "You're dripping. Is that for me? Hmmm." He leaned down, his nose nuzzling alongside my jaw. He stayed there, his hand playing me like a puppet, pulling my strings exactly how he wanted me to jump and dance. "You were soaked before I touched you. That was all for me. Wasn't it? Because you want this from me. Your cunt is pleading for me. Isn't it?"

I frowned, briefly. The pleasure was overwhelming. I could only hold on to him as he continued plundering inside of me.

"Sawyer," he said briskly, his hand slid out from underneath me, finding my throat. At the same time, he lifted himself up, rising over me, but he didn't move away. He just readjusted so he was looming over me more. He was in a more dominant position, and slowly, as every single one of his muscles was so tight, working so smoothly together, he slowly, almost achingly, pushed me all the way down to the bed. He had both hands on me, one pinning me down at my throat as the other continued moving inside of me with those long and smooth strokes.

I panted, my mouth opening.

I couldn't do anything.

Somehow, at some point, he shifted the dynamic between us where he took on the look of a predator. I was his prey and he was watching me with glittering eyes, so fucking intent on what he was doing to my body.

"Answer me." His voice shook with his restraint.

My eyes widened, but I gasped softly. "Harder."

His eyes narrowed. That wasn't the right thing to say, and he stopped, his fingers still pushed so far in me that I didn't think he could go any deeper. "What did you say?"

"Go. Harder."

His head moved back, his body lifting off me so he was sitting up but straddling me. His knees sank down to the bed on either side of me, his muscled thighs closing me in. He still held me down with a hand to my throat. The other inside of me. His knuckles rubbed against the insides of *my* thighs.

"You don't know this." He lowered his head, his forehead rested on mine, and his breath coated me, warming my mouth. "But I don't take orders, not anymore, and most certainly not in bed from some stranger who wants to escape life for a hot fucking minute."

Stranger. Hot fucking minute.

Anger blasted me.

I narrowed my eyes. *Fuck* him.

He saw it, and a cruel smirk came over him. His thumb lifted, going up to my chin and he tugged down, opening my mouth. "You asked for this. *You* initiated this."

As he began speaking, his fingers inside of me twitched, rubbing.

A moan escaped me, but fuck. I hadn't wanted that to come out.

My teeth sank down on my bottom lip, trying to keep from another slipping free. He held me captive, in multiple ways now, but he didn't need *more* evidence of how complete his hold was on me.

He smirked again. A dark triumphant look shone briefly before he turned his head, his lips brushing against mine. He said in a low tone, almost a warning, "You want this?"

I swallowed against his hand. His grip tightened before relaxing.

I cursed before saying, "Yes." Because, god help me, I did. So much. Afterward I would condemn myself, but right now, I didn't think there was anything I wouldn't say or do to feel him push inside of me. I wanted all of him. I wanted to see how far I would stretch for him, and then I wanted him to fuck me into oblivion.

He brushed a kiss, an almost achingly tender kiss, against the corner of my mouth.

Tingles shot through my entire body.

"Say please, Sawyer."

I—I couldn't. I guess there *was* a line I wouldn't cross. Did he want to humiliate me?

"What are you doing?"

His hand tensed around my throat again, before he released me, only to slowly run his hand down my front. He pushed my shirt as far down as it would go before he switched directions, yanking it up and over my head. My bra was next, and then his hand went back to my chest, and he ran it between my breasts, pausing in the middle. He moved to cup one of them, his thumb tweaking over my nipple. "I'm doing whatever the fuck I want to do. That's what I'm doing." He'd been watching his hand as he played with my breast but lifted his eyes to meet mine again. His fingers continued moving into me. His top lip curled upward, not in a nice way. "You came at me."

"I'm *pissed* at you."

A hard look came into his gaze. His fingers were still holding still inside of me.

The throbbing was compounding me, spreading up through my stomach. I wriggled around, trying to get some relief from it, just a little.

He said flatly, "I apologized."

"I don't care." But I did. I would, just later.

His eyes went flat. "Trust me. If I'd known what would be happening, I never would've met you. But we're both here now, and you're trying to use me to get you off. That is what you're doing, right? You want a quick fuck to escape our shitty reality? I'm supposed to give that to you." His eyes grew colder as he spoke, and when he was done, a third finger shoved in. Rough and fast.

I gasped, my body squirming under his from the penetration, but fuck. I began panting again because that was exactly what my body needed. Pleasure coated the edges of my vision so I closed my eyes. Arching up against him once again, it was a second before I opened my eyes again, seeing his head folded. He was watching us, where his hand was between my legs.

"I don't like being used." His words sounded like an afterthought. "But that's all I've been, all my life. Someone else's fucking puppet." He lifted his head again, still bent over me. I gulped at the blazing determination shining so fiercely in his eyes. He blinked. A starkness replacing it. "*Not* anymore. That ends today."

And with that, he pulled out, clambering off me.

I jerked up, a protest in my throat. "Wha—what are you doing?"

He was gone in a flash.

The bedroom door slammed shut behind him.

I was still on the bed, confused at the sudden change in everything, before the next sound registered.

A lock clicked into place.

What . . .

No.

I jerked off the bed, catching myself before I stumbled, and then crossed the room to the door. I pulled it open, except it didn't.

I jerked on the handle again. "What?"

No, no.

I hit it. "What are you doing?"

He didn't answer except I heard another door slamming shut.

A few seconds passed.

My heart was pounding in my chest. Where was he going?

His headlights turned on outside the cabin, and I could hear his vehicle leaving.

That asshole had left me. *Again.*

CHAPTER FIFTEEN

JAKE

Leaving Sawyer on my bed, panting, begging for it—it took every amount of willpower for me to walk away. Fuck. Fucking fuck. She undid me with just a look and a whimper, and how soaked she'd been for me. I didn't know what I'd be walking into when I got back, but I needed space and I needed my head on straight again.

I needed to head this way anyway because at the end of the day, no matter how fucking hard my dick was, I still needed to find out who ordered the hit.

There was an underground tunnel that led to the basement of my uncle's nightclub, Shivers.

It was a smaller club, but it was exclusive and had the reputation that it catered to any of their customers' desires. When I'd been a cop, I stayed away. Because of that and because of the contract on my head, I was sneaking in through the back way, or the *back* back way. I knew the employees had no idea about this entrance. When I rounded into the basement, I waited, hearing voices coming from somewhere, pulling the door so only an inch was still open, enough where I could hear and they couldn't see me.

It was a secret door.

". . . did he say? We're not supposed to be down here." A girl was saying, hushed, but a breathless excitement in her voice.

"Why not? This place is awesome."

That was a guy with her.

I didn't recognize either of them.

The girl shuddered. "It's a total sex dungeon feel down here."

"Fuck yeah. That'd be awesome if Worthing turned this into that type of club. I bet his dumbass sons would be down for that."

"Oh. Ew. Don't mention either of them when we're down here to do this." The girl snorted, then moaned. "We need to hurry, Rad."

"What do you think I'm doing here? Do me a favor and shut up."

She giggled before it ended in a sigh, a moan quickly following. "You're so good at that."

"Hmmm mmmm, babe."

After that, sounds of groaning, moaning, and thumping went on for another five minutes before he groaned. He cursed, out of breath as she made some sort of hiccupping sound.

I fought against rolling my eyes. A hundred bucks she faked it.

"God, babe. That was amazing."

Another wispy giggle from her. "I know. You're going to call me after this, right?"

"What? Yeah. Sure. We gotta get out of here. We're not supposed to be down here."

Their voices were loud, passing. Footsteps sounded going up the stairs.

She replied, but I couldn't catch it. Small blessings.

Their voices drifted, but I could hear him. "He's not going to be happy, but this place could—" A door opened. The sounds of the club grew loud, then were muffled as the door must've closed.

I slipped out.

They'd left the lights on. I figured that'd get caught so I needed to move fast.

A second later, the door burst open.

I got to the room just beyond the stairway when heavy footsteps pounded down the stairs. "Jesus Christ, what did they d—" He got to the bottom when I moved in behind him, my gun pressed to his neck.

He froze.

I warned, "Don't move."

His hands went up, his entire body tense. At my words, he looked back. "Jake?"

It was Crispin Worthing. Overall douchebag. Meathead. Musclebuilder type that oozed sliminess. I detested him and his brother. Crispin and Penn. They were also my cousins.

Justin had been the fucking happy social butterfly golden boy. He spent time with them, but that'd been just who he was. He was good, and because he was so good, sometimes he only saw the good in others. I never knew why he bothered. I didn't think there was any good in this dumbass or his brother. What Justin didn't know, but I did, was that these two were enforcers for their father. He sent them out to intimidate, beat up, or execute who he said on his orders.

I shoved him forward, barking, "Move."

"What?"

I raised the gun to his head. "I said *move*."

His eyes were wide, staring at me with confusion before he began walking. "What are you doing, man? You have something to talk to the family about? You're the head—"

"Shut the fuck up." I shoved him forward.

"Hey, man. You don't have—" He'd edged farther into the room, but his entire body tightened dramatically as a calculating expression came over his face.

He was going to try something so I reacted first, kicking him out from the back of his knees. "You never did learn how to fight someone who could fight back, did you, Crispin?"

He dropped. "Wha—ooh! What the *fuck*, Jake?"

I rounded on him, delivering a swift kick underneath his chin. It threw him backward, and when he didn't move right away, I knew I'd winded him. I taunted him, "You and Penn. You're both nothing except overgrown bullies. You probably think you're so tough and badass, right? At the top of the food chain, except you've never gone against someone who could actually fight you. Look at you now."

He tried sitting up, only to fall over.

He coughed, shaking his head, but he started to crawl away.

I let him go, enjoying this sight.

If it wasn't him, if it wasn't his brother, or his father, it was someone else in the family who'd sold me out. So yeah. I was going to relish this big hulking cousin of mine crawling to get away from me. The only problem was that I couldn't let him get too far away. Where he went, his almost twin-like brother was sure to follow.

Putting my toe to his shoulder, I tipped him over.

"With the war against Walden and West, how did you and your fuck-buddy survive? Hmmm. You're both beyond stupid." I grunted as I stood over him when he went down. Rearing back, I punched down. Then I used the back of my gun to knock him out. It worked. I wouldn't have long until he regained consciousness so I moved fast, hurrying upstairs to lock the door. My hand was smarting, but that'd been worth it too. I wasn't sure when Penn would come looking for his brother, but I knew that he would.

I needed to move fast.

Searching through the basement, I hauled his ass into a room in the back, then up into a chair.

I cursed, panting a little. He was heavy. By the time I'd finished securing him, the music from upstairs burst down into the basement.

I cursed under my breath.

Someone else was coming down.

Grabbing a towel from my bag, I quickly tied it around his mouth.

Penn called out, "Crispin? Dude. You locked the door when you're down here? What the fuck, man? Where are you? You getting your dick sucked or something? If so, uh . . . why didn't you invite me? I've got like eighty texts from that blonde you bagged last night. She's begging for some attention." He was coming down the stairs as he talked.

I scanned the room. A tarp was rolled up on the side.

"Yo!" he called out again. A door banged open down the hall. A second later, another door banged open. He was going from room to room.

I knelt by the tarp and began to unwrap it. More doors were hit open. He was getting closer.

I used the tarp to cover Crispin on the chair. It wasn't a great trap, but my cousins were not geniuses. It would work for what I had in mind.

I moved behind the door.

"What the *fuck*, man? Where are you?" He was outside this room.

I waited, holding up my gun once more.

A ringing filled the room, and I cursed under my breath. Of course he was going to call him.

"You in there? Huh?"

The ringing came from under the tarp.

He opened the door, letting it swing open. He stepped in, the hallway's light hitting over Crispin before Penn's shadow blocked him. "Dude . . . ?" He came forward another step, then stopped. He breathed deep. "Crisp? That you?"

The phone stopped ringing.

Penn was frozen, just inside the door. He wasn't in far enough for me, and as his gaze was riveted on the tarp, his thumb moved on his phone. He pressed a button.

Crispin's phone started ringing again.

Fuck's sake.

One more step, dickhead.

He sighed, taking that last step. He took more, going all the way to Crispin and reaching for the tarp. "Is that—" He pulled it off. His phone clattered to the ground. He gaped at the sight of his brother all tied up and pretty where I'd left him. "What the fuck?"

I moved behind him, putting my gun to the back of his head. "On your knees."

He tensed a half second before his head whirled around.

Nope. Shit. That wasn't the move I wanted.

He snarled, a vicious look twisting on his face.

He went to lunge at me, but I ducked out of the way, coming up swiftly behind him. I delivered one hard kick to the back of his knee. He grunted as his leg folded underneath him. He went to the ground, but he wasn't going to stay. He was enraged and Penn was like a bull, only seeing red. Or my murder.

As he moved to grab me, I pivoted, raising my hand up. Just as he reached for me, I brought down the back of my gun, using all of my body weight behind my hit. It held enough of a punch to make him see double.

I swore. This cousin wasn't going down.

Sweat rolled down my back, and I cursed again because I didn't have more in my tank for a knockout hit. Eyeing him warily, there was another way, but I didn't want this asshole to bite me or stab me. I also needed to put down my gun for it. Saying a little prayer to my previous wrestling gods that helped me make all-state, I made a move, rolling both of us. It knocked him over, but I went with him, coming out with one of his hands twisted around and my legs wrapped tight around his neck.

He couldn't bite me. And as I began squeezing his neck, he began thrashing around. His legs kicked. I grunted from the force it was taking to keep him in the hold. His free hand tried hitting at me, but it was only landing on my thigh. He began flailing behind him, looking for a weapon.

I cursed, seeing I hadn't left my gun out of reach. I didn't like risking making a move without it, but I also knew he would've grabbed it if it was on me.

God.

He kept fighting.

I squeezed harder.

He landed a few punches before his body went slack.

Finally. Fuck! Breathing hard again, I let him go and his unconscious body slumped out of my hold.

I pressed two fingers to his carotid, and relief went through me. He still had a pulse, so I hadn't killed him. But then there was the dilemma of what to do when he woke up.

I gave the room another scan.

There were no more chairs.

CHAPTER SIXTEEN

SAWYER

I hated Jake. I hated him with every fiber of my being.

He left me needing and panting and begging, and death to Jake. I swore it. Death to him. He locked me in the room, but after he did, the throbbing had been too much. I got myself off as I began plotting my revenge for when Jake would come back.

That was until he stayed gone.

He was gone for hours. Part of that time, I ranted. I planned. There was a time when I calmed down and took a nap because the sunlight was starting to rise outside.

How did I get myself into these situations? Honestly. It was me. Must be me.

Beck and Manda.

Stalking my own cousin.

It was me. I was a magnet for chaos. That's the only thing that made sense to me, but I could hear my phone going off in the next room.

My mom. My aunts. If I didn't check in with them, they *would* send a search party for me. If Jake wasn't careful, he'd be hunted down and taken out by those three women. His Mafia life had nothing on the Matsen women.

I was beyond listening to what he had said. Use caution, my ass.

Was the contract even real? Was all of this an elaborate ruse? His cousin did seem to target me. Was she in on it too?

Maybe I was being paranoid, but I'd been kidnapped. I figured the first thing someone did in that situation was start telling all sorts of lies to make the kidnappee scared of leaving. *That* made sense to me.

I just knew one thing at this point. I *needed* to get out.

I tried picking the lock. That didn't work. I tried wedging it open. That didn't work either. Finally I just started unscrewing everything I could and well, the whole door came off that way. He had a lock bolting it to the doorframe on one side, but not the other. I pulled it open and heaved it to the side, then stood there, panting and sweating. My knees were cramping. My one leg was asleep from how long I had to be in the same position to get that door unscrewed. And my hands were bleeding. I'd cut them a whole bunch and chipped two of my nails. Each time, I'd indulged in screaming. I figured it wouldn't hurt, so I let loose, really throwing my whole gusto into the screams. I would've made any horror movie director proud.

My phone started going again. I hurried across the room, ignoring the pins and needles now zipping up and down my left leg. It was on the table, coming from under a bunch of papers. I rifled through them, finding it and my hand closed around it as I got weepy.

Finally. Something good went my way.

It stopped ringing as soon as I picked it up, but I went through it.

The battery was going to go out soon. I had 5 percent left so I'd need to make it count.

Thirty-nine missed calls.

I grimaced, quickly going to my texts.

There were 184 text alerts. Good gracious.

I started to call my mom, but then paused. What would I tell her? Jake's warning went through my head. I gulped. If I ignored them and he hadn't been lying? I couldn't endanger their lives.

What should I do instead?

Stay here? He'd just lock me up all over again, and I shuddered. I couldn't go through that. I hated that feeling. But what were my options?

A text from an unknown number popped up. I clicked on it, frowning.

> This is Graham, your cousin. I'm not sure what to do here. A detective called me and said he was going to bring you over, but you never showed. Now our aunts are calling me. My mother gave me this number for you. Are you here in the city? I know we've not met, but you are family. If you're here and in trouble, I'll come and get you.

My heart began pounding. He was probably the closest . . . He *was* family . . .

I tried running through the scenarios. If my name was released for this contract? Someone had found us outside my cousin's place so he probably *was* being watched. Could I call from my phone? I didn't know. I just didn't know and panic was rising in me the longer I considered all my options.

Fuck! I just didn't know what to do.

Sandra Bullock in *The Net* would use a computer. Ashley Judd in *Double Jeopardy* was all about the public library. I could do that. Pack up. Head out. Find a local town and contact my cousin that way, give him directions on how to sneak out and find me. Goodness. I needed to warn him that he might be in danger. What a great cousin I was, totally involving him, putting him in danger, and then asking him to come and get me? I was insane.

I blamed Beck for everything.

If he hadn't dumped me, I wouldn't have come to New York. It was all his fault.

I began searching through the drawers. Maybe there was something I could use to help me get out of here.

An old grocery bag was crumpled up. I put some protein bars and a couple bottles of water inside. My purse was on the table, too, so I grabbed that and frantically continued with my search.

I went through the drawers, but there was nothing there. Dammit. I needed—my hand flipped a picture over, and I went still, looking at it. It was Jake. But, wait . . . No. It wasn't. It was too recent. I flipped it over, seeing the date. That *wasn't* Jake. I turned it back, staring at the little boy. He looked five. Dark features. Dark, almost black eyes. A rich head of hair.

Did Jake have a son? He'd never mentioned a son.

A knot formed in my throat.

Jake had a son. It had to be. He looked just like Jake. He had the same eyes. The same cheeks. There was no doubt who he came from, but he was smiling. Such warmth and happiness filled his face. Was that what Jake would've looked like as a child?

That knot slipped down my throat.

I tucked the photo into my pocket, not sure why but also not questioning myself. I needed to get back to my escape.

After patting down some newspaper, I hit a lump. The sound of keys had me freezing for a second before hope burst up in me. I dug through, lifting out a set of keys.

I began smiling.

Oh, *hell* yeah.

CHAPTER SEVENTEEN

JAKE

I'd secured both, tying Crispin to his chair. His feet and hands were bound. Both were gagged. Penn was left on the floor. He could roll around if he wanted, but this room only had barrels of wine in it so there was no danger that I could see. His hands and feet were also bound.

I pulled out Crispin's phone, opening his eyelid and scanning it with his phone so I could get into it. It was after I did that when he woke up. He began shouting through his gag. His eyes were wide, angry. He was rattling around on the chair. That's what woke Penn up, who rolled a little, moaning before he blinked enough to clear whatever fog was in his mind.

Both were shouting as loud as they could, but the sound was muffled.

I'd initially been intending on taking pictures of everything down here, then slipping upstairs and pickpocketing Crispin's phone. He was the smarter one of the two and he would've had any information I needed on his phone. Their dad had put them in charge of running the club after the war with Ashton and Trace's family. He'd left to hide in Maine, not wanting to be around in case either of the two families tried to take him out. Course, he hadn't known then that they'd taken his two sons and held them in a warehouse until the war was over. They let them both go, but Crispin and Penn were useless. There was no way they were actually running this club. Both lived for booze, drugs, pussy, and lifting weights.

And strutting around as if they were badasses.

Four of our uncles made up the board for the business, but I decided there was only one that I needed to talk to for my information.

I shot off a text after I searched his phone.

Crispin: I just heard some shit about a contract on Jake's head. Wtf, dad? Do I need to know something?

Uncle Toby wasn't tech-savvy so I held up my gun and moved back to Crispin, tearing off the tape. I spoke through his howl. "Your dad's going to call you in a moment, and you're going to say whatever the fuck you need to say to find out who put a contract on my head. You got me?"

"You fucking—"

I took the safety off and pressed it harder against his temple. They didn't know the lengths I could go. No, that wasn't correct. They knew the lengths I went to, to protect my brother, but I was thinking they needed a reminder.

He shut up, but his eyes narrowed. Confusion showed.

"I mean it, Crisp. I went through your messages. I know you got a little girlfriend in Jersey and I'm guessing there's a reason you're keeping her a secret. You want to keep her secret, you play ball."

His eyes continued glaring before looking down to where Penn was lying.

Oh. I'd just outed him.

I shrugged. "We'll work something out with him."

He continued seething at me.

I ignored him, saying, "I don't have to time to be fucking diplomatic here. Someone's trying to kill me. You help me find out who that is so that I can put a bullet in their head or you don't. If you choose option two, trust me, I will have no problem taking down every single family member with me. You get me?"

I stared at him, hard. Letting him see just how far I was willing to go, and if that meant putting a bullet in each of my uncles' heads, in each of my cousins' like him, I had no problem doing that. When he stilled, and swallowed, I finished, "Are you in or out? Your dad is going to call any second."

Fury showed before he banked it and slowly nodded. "Yeah, yeah. I'll ask him."

The phone began ringing.

"You do what the fuck you need to get the answers. You got me?"

He nodded again, this time quicker, so I accepted the call, putting him on speaker.

He coughed, clearing his throat. "Hey—"

"What are you playing at? Sending that shit over text? Have you lost your damn mind—"

I moved the gun so it was directed at Penn, who froze when he saw the move.

"Dad—*Dad*! Shut up."

There was a beat of silence, but Uncle Toby was not one that you told to shut up.

"Listen here, you little piece of shit. You—"

"Who's trying to take out Jake?"

Silence again. "Why the fuck do you care about that fucker? He's a traitor. Who the fuck cares—"

Crispin paled, cursing under his breath. *"Dad!"*

There was another moment of silence.

Uncle Toby was the keeper of all the secrets. He knew everything, and since I didn't have time for a trip to Maine right now, his sons were the closest way to get those answers.

"Dad, there's a hit on Jake." Sweat poured down Crispin's face. He needed to blink a few times as some of it went over his eyes. His voice was raspy, strained. "Who put it there? I gotta know. I gotta . . . He's in the city, Dad. Are we in danger? What's going on?"

My cousin truly sucked at being an actor.

"Why?" His dad's voice dipped low. Also hoarse. "The fuck are you asking this shit? What are you playing at? You know we don't give a shit about that kid."

Kid. I stopped being a kid when he put a gun in my hands when I was twelve. When he told me I needed to learn how to kill a man. My dad found out two years later what Uncle Toby had me doing, shooting men for him, but the damage was done. I had already been turned into an executioner by then.

That was when my dad stepped away from the family business. It was the first rift among the brothers.

Maybe that was the beginning of the end for the Worthing Mafia.

". . . he's going to be taken out and you need to just shut your fat fucking mouth until then. You hear me?" He didn't wait, bellowing, "You hear me? You answer me, boy!"

I pulled the phone away from my cousin. The frustration that had been rising in me began to morph into a calmness. It was somewhat nice. Serene. It was a dead feeling of calm.

I continued listening as my uncle confirmed every single one of my suspicions. He was saying, spewing into the phone, "Calling me and asking me about family business. You don't fucking do that. You know better."

I sighed audibly before speaking, in a low voice. "Uncle Toby."

Crispin was bugging out at me, his eyes bulging. I didn't want to hear whatever he was going to say so I shoved tape back over his mouth. He tried yelling through it.

I took the phone and walked away, noting how quiet it was now.

"Who put the contract on me, Uncle Toby?" I went over, bending to pick up a knife that I'd stripped from Penn earlier. I twirled it in my hand. "You can answer me in the next five seconds, but I'll let you know, every minute you waste my time will cost you. I'll start stripping inches of skin off one of your boys."

Crispin went pale again. I didn't think he had any more color in him. As I neared him, he tried jerking the chair away from me. It started to tip back, but I stopped it with my foot and slammed him back down.

"Jacob."

I had to smile. He sounded so cautious now. "This is karmic. Isn't it, Uncle?" I flicked the knife in my hand, letting it spin in circles on my palm. "You were the one who turned me into a killer. Now here I am. Using some of those skills on your own boys. That is, unless you stop wasting my time and give me the name I need. What are you going to do, Uncle Toby?"

I leaned forward, pressing the edge of the blade to Crispin's leg.

He went so still, only barely breathing.

I forgot the power that filled you in these types of interrogations. I forgot the adrenaline. It was addicting.

"You got my son?" he asked, quietly.

"I got both of them. They're alive." I kicked at Crispin's chair, enjoying the wave of fear that rolled from him. "For now."

"What's this he's saying? Someone's trying to kill you?" He tried to sound casual.

I grunted. "Wrong move, Uncle." I tore Crispin's pants, ripping them until there was a good chunk of skin exposed, and I put the knife to it.

My cousin began screaming. It was muffled by the tape, but it was loud.

I moved the phone back to my mouth, speaking as Crispin continued screaming, "You hear that, Uncle? You should be able to guess what comes next, since you're the one who taught me the five main steps of torture."

"Jesus Christ! Stop, Jacob. Stop. Please . . ."

I stared at the phone. That was different. I had never heard my uncle beg.

I liked it. I wanted to hear more.

"You know"—I pulled the knife away, straightening up. Maybe we'd go down this one road first—"I got to thinking about the logistics of when the board appointed me head of the family. You said it yourself. You still think of me as a kid, but you're forgetting what I was before we left. Aren't you? You're forgetting the reason I left in the first place. Justin's gone now."

He was quiet again.

I smiled into the phone, knowing it connected to the emptiness inside of me. "I'm no longer a cop, Uncle. And here I am. Picking up the old trade. It's like riding a bike again. I forgot the rush you get from torture—"

"Jacob, stop! Stop. Please . . . Please. Just. Fucking stop. I'll tell you whatever you want."

I met Crispin's eyes. He was looking at me like he'd never known me, as if I'd sprouted a second head. Then again, maybe he never knew that his father began molding me into being the family's own personal assassin because at the end of the day, that's where I thrived.

"What do you want to know? I'll—what do you want to know, Nephew?"

"Let's start with Nicolai. How did he become appointed the head? Because the last I knew of him, he wasn't on top of the food chain. He was on the bottom, and somehow he shot up to the top spot. Who's *really* calling the shots, Uncle? Is that who put the hit out on me?"

His tone went flat, but he sighed. "I think you know better than to have this conversation over the phone—"

I cut him off, impatient. "Stop fucking with me or I will start cutting. You know if I start, I'll finish. That's how you trained me. Remember? *Stop* with the games. Crispin's phone is encrypted. You have him here to oversee the storage and distribution you use for this nightclub. Saving your boy's life isn't enough incentive? Fine. I'm aware of what you have in this basement. It would be easy for me to drop a tip to the right person. Let them know the drugs, the black-market goods you store here. It's up to you for that one. You want me to call law enforcement? Or Ashton Walden?"

He got quiet, real quiet.

I showed my teeth to his son, who was watching me so warily now. "I'm *pissed* off, and I have nothing left to lose."

"Nephew—"

"Time's up." I aimed the knife, ready to lodge it into Crispin's leg.

Crispin and Penn were both screaming through their tape. Crispin was trying to break free from his chair. Penn was trying to roll at me, but I kicked him away.

"—wait!"

He cursed on his end.

"Too late," I clipped out, raising my hand with the knife.

"We don't know him!" my uncle cried out.

I paused before lowering my hand back to my side. "Explain."

"Why don't you come here? We'll send a plane. It'll be a quick ride. We'll have dinner. The family. We can talk over a nice meal. Be civilized."

I was done. He was still not remembering who I was.

I moved in a flash, lodging the knife in Crispin's thigh.

His scream went up a notch. Bloodcurdling.

"Oh *Christ*. Christ. Jacob—stop! Please."

"Start talking, Uncle, or . . ." I dragged the knife down Crispin's thigh until I got to his knee, then ripped the blade out.

Crispin got silent, and I looked. He'd passed out. I shook my head, tsking into the phone. "Your boy's already out. I've barely started, Uncle."

"Fuck!" he yelled into the phone. "We—he's not one of us."

I paused, hearing an answer. Finally.

"Creighton Lane," Uncle Toby said hurriedly. Frantic. "I don't know if you know of him, but—"

"I know who he is. What does he have to do with the hit on me?"

Creighton Lane ran Cincinnati. He was a self-made mobster who rose from the streets. By the time he was nineteen, he was running everything. I knew people who'd gone after him, and none of them came out alive. As a cop and an organized crime detective, the few times I heard about him, I'd been thankful he never came to my city. We had the West and Walden Mafia families here and they were enough to handle, but Creighton was a loose cannon. He was a whole different sort of animal.

"He's behind the hit."

I stepped away. Blood dripped to the floor from the knife in my hand. "Why?" I'd had no dealings with Lane. None.

My uncle hesitated, then sighed. "Because he's one of us."

I reared back. "One of us?"

"Our family. He's a cousin. He's got Worthing blood in him. I don't know how he found out, but he's one of us."

"He grew up in Cincinnati. He's *from* Cincinnati. He grew up in foster care." No. Fuck that. "He grew up on the streets."

"None of us were aware he was one of ours. Your aunt Taunti, she ran away when she was young. We never knew where she went, but he's hers."

Crispin was starting to wake. He moaned, his head falling backward.

"This is verified?"

"Yeah. All verified."

"How long, Uncle? How long have you known?"

He was quiet again before surrendering, "He reached out two years ago."

"Two years?"

Crispin's groaning hit a high note. His head was rolling from side to side.

Penn grunted from the floor. From the angle he'd ended at after my kick, and from his weight, he couldn't do much except try to flail around.

Creighton Lane was a one-man tsunami. He ran the entire city from the street to the elected officials. They were all under his control, and how he'd managed it wasn't quite known, but he had an iron-tight grip on that city.

"What does he want?" I asked.

"What do you think he wants? He wants to take over."

Understanding was starting to click into place. "He would've come in with demands. Our current head had just died—" Nicolai.

"We—we did what we thought we needed to do. When we heard you were resigning, we thought it was perfect."

"You wanted me to handle this problem for you."

"I mean, you're the organized crime pig. If anyone knows how to take someone out like Creighton Lane, it'd be you. Am I right? I'm right. You're the guy. You're *our* guy."

"I'm your guy?" I echoed, softly. Those were similar words to another time he spoke to me.

You're going to be our executioner, Jake. Our guy. Our little assassin.

Penn was eyeing me warily.

"Yeah. Our guy." My uncle laughed, forcing it. "Right? You can handle him."

A whole storm was stirring inside of me. One where I yearned to reach through the phone to rip my uncle's head off his neck and bathe in his blood. It was angry, churning, and *hungry*. I was one person, offered up on a platter by the people who shared my blood, and they'd put me in the path of a monster like Creighton Lane.

I was seething, until a decision came to me. Instant calmness settled over me, soothing everything out. I knew now what I needed to do.

I must've been quiet for too long because my uncle said, "Jacob?"

I raised the phone up to my mouth and spoke directly into it. "Start packing, Uncle. After I deal with Lane, I'm going to clean house, and I'll start with yours. I'm coming for you."

I put the knife down and picked up the gun, aiming.

"Wait. Wha—"

Crispin began struggling, screaming again, blood draining from his face. Penn was flailing around, shouting. Both of their voices went up a whole octave.

"Run, Uncle Toby. Run."

Bang!

CHAPTER EIGHTEEN

JAKE

I was just stepping out of my car to meet with Ashton Walden when my phone buzzed.

Alert: guest bedroom window open.

Alarm went through me as I clicked over to check the video footage.

I went cold at the sight of seeing Sawyer half running and half hopping across the yard to the garage, then the shed.

My phone buzzed again.

Alert: Garage door opened.

Alert: Shed side door opened.

Alert: Shed main door opened.

I was in disbelief when my old truck drove out of the shed, with Sawyer behind the wheel. I paused the video and zoomed in to see her face. Her eyes were wild, dilated. Her hair was a mess, but her mouth was in a set and determined line. Her face, hands, and arms were caked in blood.

Blood? What the fuck? How had that happened? Alarm spread through me.

No one did that to her. No one found her.

I tried her number, but it went to voicemail.

Where the fuck was she going?

"Do you need to be somewhere else, Worthing?" Walden asked sarcastically. A hard smirk on his face.

I glanced at him, seeing he'd raised an eyebrow toward me. He added, his voice cutting, "Am I keeping you from something else? Someone else?" His other eyebrow rose, taunting. "Maybe a Miss Sawyer Matsen, by any chance?"

I cursed, shoving my phone in my pocket. "I don't have time for your jabs. I'm here because I found out who put the hit out on me, and he's going to be a problem for you as well."

The humor faded from Ashton's face. He got serious. Dark shadows crossed over his face. "Keep going. Don't stop at the best part."

"Creighton Lane."

I knew Ashton and knew when he opened his mouth, he had a sharp retort on the tip of his tongue, but the name I'd just said stopped him in his tracks. He closed his mouth and took a step back before raising an eyebrow once again to me. "Why the fuck are you saying Creighton Lane is going to be an issue for all of us?"

My phone kept fucking buzzing and I knew it was all my territory alerts notifying me of Sawyer's whereabouts. I had a tracker on the truck, but I just didn't know her intended target. I didn't have time to waste here, and said quickly, succinctly, as I began heading back to my vehicle, "Turns out he's the fucking devil, and that my family's a bunch of scared shitheads."

"Is that supposed to make sense to me?"

I got to my truck, opened the door, and looked in Ashton's direction. "He found out he's related to us. Now he wants to take over, and apparently putting a hit out on the current head is his first step."

Ashton's eyebrows lowered as he went very still, an ominous wave starting to rise from him.

I didn't know what kind of relationship I had with Ashton Walden.

I'd done a lot of shitty things in life—being on Ashton's payroll as a detective in the organized crime unit hit pretty high on that list—but there'd been reasons. Ashton was aware that I walked the line. I had still been a cop but, knowing if the Walden and West family businesses fell, they'd be replaced with worse families, I gave them information at times to keep them where they were. I'd gotten a glimpse of who wanted to take over from them and I chose the devil I knew. Trace and Ashton weren't bad men. They just did bad things, and somewhere down the road, Ashton and I became friends. Reluctantly.

I respected him, liked him, but loathed him at the same time.

I also never wanted to see him or talk to him again, but this was the second reach-out we'd had about my current problem. He'd reached out first. I reached out now.

I also couldn't deny those two had happened for a reason, but when it came to his best friend, I hated Trace West. There was a personal history that I would never get over. Ashton was also aware of this, hence why he showed up without his self-indignant asshole of a best friend and business partner.

"Jake," Ashton clipped out. He took a step toward me but stopped. His hands were in fists, pressed at his sides. His jaw clenched. "What are you planning? Lane's a different sort of beast."

I shook my head, a whole new feeling of exhaustion hitting me at the moment. "I don't have one fucking idea. I can't operate with this contract on my head so I'll have to get him to take it down, somehow."

Ashton's eyes were shrewd and I knew I had only three options. I'd either give Lane what he wanted from the family, kill him, or let the contract be fulfilled. He said, "Lane took control of Cincinnati through a cultlike worship of followers. He went after the gang leaders, corrupt politicians, and law enforcement, and rival organized crime organizations, then gave their money to people on the streets. He is protected by a million followers. You won't be able to bribe your way to him."

Fuck. I knew Creighton Lane was different, but hearing this—*fuck*. I raked a hand over my face. "I'm going to have to try, or I don't know what I'm going to do. He's decided he wants my family. He made his demands known to them a while ago."

Ashton's jaw clenched again. "Don't choose the same door your cousin Nicolai chose. Don't open that door."

I knew. I fucking knew I couldn't. "Don't worry, but if you know of a way to get to Lane, I'd appreciate it. Until then, I need to go and track down the current pain in my ass."

"I know of a way you can get his attention."

Ashton had stepped to the door, stopping it before I could close it. A starkness on his face had me pausing, questioning for a slight second if I wanted to know his idea. He didn't seem keen on it himself.

I said lightly, "Why does it look like this idea of yours is probably a suicide mission?"

His eyes flared, but his hand fell away from the door. He moved back, shutting down. "Because it probably is, but it's Lane's only weakness that I'm aware of."

My gut flared, not liking this, wherever it was going, but I couldn't afford not to hear it. "What's his weakness?"

"A girl. He's obsessed with her, but she's not in the life. You want to get his attention, take the girl. I'll send you the information I have on her." He shut the door for me and headed to his own car.

I took off, not happy with how that conversation had gone, but resigned at the same time.

A bitter and harsh laugh rippled up my chest at the thought of how far I'd fallen in this world. My new career as a criminal was already budding.

Now I had to kidnap a different woman.

CHAPTER NINETEEN

SAWYER

I could totally *Gone Girl* my way if I ever needed to. A whole buzz of victory went through me, growing the farther I got. After going through two towns, I pulled into a public library and used their computer to DM my cousin.

> SawyerMatsenNottotallyoriginal1: This is your cousin. I'm hoping you check your messages?? I got your text, but I can't reply on my phone. I need your help. I'll wait to see if you respond before I send more information.

I hit send, then switched to my email, typing one out right away to my mother.

> Mom, I lost my phone. All is good!! I'm so sorry. I'm trying to get a hold of Graham to see if he can help or not. Can you message him and ask him to check his Instagram messages? He might need to check the other folder. Once I get connected with him and get a new phone, I'll give you a call. Don't panic. New

York is amazing. I'm so glad I came here. Let Clara and Bess know that I'm safe. I just lost my phone. That's all. LOVE YOU SO MUCH—Sawyer

My mom was not normally glued to her email, but since I'd gone on the missing train, I had a feeling she would be this time.

An email hit my inbox almost immediately from her.

I clicked on it, holding my breath against what her reaction would be.

Sawyer Kathleen Matsen, you are in so much trouble YOU LOST YOUR PHONE? We called your hotel. You've not been back to check out. They have all your things. You have never, not once, in your life lost your phone. What is going on in that city over there? You have never been late for a checkout either. Your aunts have already booked their flights. They're flying to see your cousin. They were going to start canvassing the city with flyers with your picture on them. WE WERE WORRIED SICK! Beck has been so distraught.

I got hot at reading that. Hot in an angry way.

Beck and Jake. Both were on my shit list.

I yelped before frantically replying, not reading the rest of her email.

DO NOT TELL BECK ANYTHING!

Her reply was just as quick.

I didn't, but Maude did. The three of us stonewalled him so he went to her. He's been calling me ever since.

I growled, typing back, Just block him.

It was as easy as that. What was my mom doing? Yes, she was stonewalling him, but why hadn't she already blocked him? We lived in a small town. I also got that. Beck was there. He ran a business there, and my mom was into the local town's high society, which Beck was also into. But still. Fucking block him. Everyone would understand.

Ding!

I heard the notification and checked the other tab.

> GrahamM.ArchitectGalligFirm: Sawyer! Is this really you? Your mother told me to check my messages here. Yes. I'm here. Where are you? You need a phone?

Nerves fluttered in my belly because how I maneuvered with him, knowing my aunts were on their way to him, would need to be handled with care. What should I say? I couldn't believe I was involving him, but also, I couldn't stay with Jake. He might've been lying about the whole thing. Maybe? I didn't know anymore.

I just knew I couldn't handle being locked in a room again.

My arms were like lead as I lifted them back to the desk, looking out the windows and spotting a cute little café across the road.

> SawyerMatsenNottotallyoriginal1: I'm in a little town north of the city. Could you come and get me? I'll be at Hen Café in Porter, but Graham, you can't come in your car. You can't tell our aunts anything. And you need to have your phone turned off. Trust me on all of this. Also, do you have a gun? If you do and if you're comfortable with it, you might want to bring it with you.

My stomach was a whole twister inside as I clicked send. I closed my eyes, now waiting for whatever fireworks that was going to set off.

GrahamM.ArchitectGalligFirm: WHAT THE FUCK IS GOING ON????

GrahamM.ArchitectGalligFirm: a gun? Why the fuck would I need a gun? I barely know you. Are you insane? I'm honestly asking. Have you had a recent trip to a mental health hospital? I won't judge you, but I need to know what to prepare myself for. My mother told me why you really came to New York. I'm so sorry about your ex-fiancé, but is this about him? Are you planning on doing something? Hurting yourself?

Indignant anger boiled up, but I fought against letting it out as I replied. I was exhaling deep breaths to keep from losing my shit, cousin or no cousin. A few people in the library kept giving me looks. I ignored them.

SawyerMatsenNottotallyoriginal1: No. It's nothing like that. I'm just—look, I was outside your place and then . . . something happened. I'll explain everything to you when you get here, but please just come. Don't tell our aunts or your mother. This is serious. Just come and get me and I mean it, keep your phone turned off. Don't come in your own vehicle. I hope I'm being too cautious, but I'm just not sure right now myself.

GrahamM.ArchitectGalligFirm: That's an hour outside of the city. I'll have Oliver take care of the aunts when they arrive. Give me a little bit to figure out some things on my end. If the café closes before I get there, there's a statue in every town. Hang out by whatever statue Porter has.

Ooh. He was smart.

SawyerMatsenNottotallyoriginal1: I can do that. THANK YOU! I owe you.

CHAPTER TWENTY

JAKE

I couldn't believe what I was watching.

By the time I got to my cabin, I checked the tracker on my truck. It was parked outside of the library a few towns away, but I didn't know how long Sawyer would stay put. Hurrying through the place, I grabbed any essentials we might need, which were mostly weapons for me. When I got to the town where Sawyer had left the truck, it was easy to find her waiting in the local café.

I considered going in there, throwing her over my shoulder and taking off again, except it was obvious she was waiting for someone. That meant she'd already violated my rule of no contact. My guess was she'd reached out to her cousin, so at this point, he had already been exposed. Even if he returned to his place without Sawyer, someone could still be waiting for him.

The best bet now was to sit back, wait, and follow them. Then, infiltrate and wait for the bad guys to come calling.

I parked in an alley on the other side of the café, able to see where Sawyer was sitting.

She was nervous. The hands wringing together was nonstop, along with gnawing her bottom lip off.

I groaned, seeing all of that happen.

I longed to walk in and stop her from biting that lip. It was mine to bite. Mine to kiss. Mine to suck. Mine to taste. Images of us before I'd left flashed in my head. Feeling my fingers slide inside her pussy, how wet and warm she'd been for me. Her cunt was eager for me, sucking me in, and I rewarded it with pumping her. Long and smooth strokes.

I could remember that needy look in her eyes. Like she was surprised herself at how her body was reacting to me, but fuck. I wanted to reach for my pants, relieve some of the pressure.

It took everything in me to walk away from her, but we couldn't go any further. Emotions had been heightened. She wasn't thinking clearly. We both needed time away.

I was regretting my decision.

When I saw the entire door had been taken off its hinges, I could only gape at it. She took that entire thing off, by herself. It'd been pushed to the side. I'd been impressed and proud, and then I spotted the blood on the door and hinges, and I saw red all over again.

I'd seen the blood on the security cameras, but seeing it in person was a different matter. It was live and in person and there was no grainy filter blurring it.

Jesus. That was on me.

I put her there. I put her in the position where she hurt herself in order to escape.

I'd messed up. I'd messed up badly, but I *would* fix it. Somehow.

Until then, I needed to protect her and do what damage control I could.

An hour later, an attractive male walked inside. Asian. Similar age to Sawyer. He looked around six foot, maybe 210 in weight. Fit. He was dressed in jeans and a snug white sweater. I was guessing this was the cousin, as she perked up, her teeth sinking all the way down into her lip. Jesus Christ. I couldn't handle seeing her do that anymore. It was mine to taste, but fuck.

Fuck!

I had to turn away for a moment, get myself under control.

When I looked back, I'd missed watching the first exchange between her and her cousin. They didn't stay long, which I could tell was because of Sawyer's urgings. She looked panicked. Her cousin was more relaxed, except he was giving her some serious questioning looks when she was looking away.

I almost laughed, wondering how that conversation went where she got him to come get her. He thought she was a nutcase. I could read it on his face. I had half a wonder if he was going to take her back to the city, and then take her to a hospital the next day. My guess was that he had reinforcements flying in. Her mom. His mom. Maybe the aunts? One or all of them?

Yeah. He'd wait. Take her back to the city. Wait for whoever else was flying in to arrive, and then they'd have a meeting. It made sense with him coming up so easily to get her.

They went to a nearby flashy car, *not* a vehicle for someone wanting to blend in. Sawyer's shoulders slumped at seeing the car, but they got in.

She was anxious to be on the road, looking around behind them.

I didn't move. I knew she couldn't see me. She'd need to know to look through the café's windows to the other side of the building. Her eyes skipped right over me.

She breathed out, looking like she could relax a little, as they pulled out into the road.

I eased my vehicle after them.

They paused at a stop sign a block away.

After maneuvering so I was two cars behind, I couldn't keep my eyes off Sawyer. She kept looking around. Her hand was tapping on the door beside her, up by the window. I could see it all. The guy's car was built to draw attention.

They went another block before slowing once more.

Sawyer's head whipped over to her cousin, but he flicked on the turn signal and pulled into the gas station.

I grinned, knowing that I could've read Sawyer's mind in that moment. She thought she'd gotten away. Got her getaway driver and *finally* they could hit the road, put some mileage from here, only to need to get gas.

As they pulled into a slot to fill up, I went past that gas station before pulling over.

My vehicle was full and ready to go. Now it was about tailing them all the way back, but I had a good feeling they were going to her cousin's place. Sawyer was forgetting I already knew where he lived.

When they pulled into a space behind his brownstone, I parked a street over.

I waited in the alley behind their place, keeping hidden until I noticed a good opening to slip inside. I got it when a car arrived, and two older women spilled out of their car.

I was guessing that these were the aunts.

They weren't New Yorkers.

She'd said her mom was a Stepford wife look-alike. These two women were not that. One looked like a giant pit bull with almost white hair and a meanness emanating from her. She was decked out looking like she was going on a safari in Africa, complete with a hat and net over her face and a red fanny pack around her waist. The other was dressed in a pink leopard-print sweat suit. A gold chain hung from her neck, and she had a neon-yellow visor, also with a matching neon-yellow fanny pack. She was taller and bigger, like a lineman. Dark and graying hair. They both looked tough, but the darker-haired one seemed like she'd given birth to an entire brood of guys who ate rocks for their meals. She had a look to her that she could handle anyone, and my mom had that same look on her face growing up. And she'd handled plenty.

I grinned, remembering that about her.

The hit was on my head, not Sawyer's. She was only listed as a point of contact. Some of the killers would lie in wait, grab Sawyer, and use her as bait to draw me out. Those were the nice ones. There were others that wouldn't give a fuck. They would wade into that brownstone and kill everyone before grabbing Sawyer and, again, use her as bait for me. Either way, her family would only be safe if I got Sawyer and took her away, which brought me back to my current movements.

I hadn't planned ahead if Sawyer would be able to reach out to anyone. I should've.

I would've asked Ashton to get cameras and listening devices inside their house, but I just hadn't. I'd been on the defensive this entire time except for this moment.

Right now was the shift.

When the aunts arrived, that's when I got my opening into the brownstone.

The husband took a couple trips to bring all their luggage inside, and the door opened once more when the safari-aunt returned to the car for an item. It looked like a pink furry flamingo clutch. The thing was giant. It drew attention.

Everything about these aunts drew attention, but I slipped to the home when she went back inside.

They didn't turn the security system back on. Not right away.

I was able to open a side door on the lower level.

Navigating through the house took time. It'd been easier than it should've been with five people and two dogs, one bigger and one smaller, and I hadn't glimpsed the dogs. I only heard their barks. Everyone stayed on the main level.

They were drinking. Talking loud. Laughing. I heard crying.

The little dog growled, running after me when he caught my scent, but I stepped into a closet just as one of the guys grabbed their dog. "We've already been over this. You're not getting whatever treats are in there. Come on. We need to make sure your auntie Sawyer is okay. Can you help me with that? Give her extra kisses and cuddles? Hmmm?" He whispered to the dog, "Let's make sure everyone is of sound mind, too, while we're at it. Can you help me with that?" He walked away, but that dog would be back, so I hurried out and slipped through the house until I was on the third level.

It was easy to figure out which room was Sawyer's. Both of the aunts had tossed their visor and net-hat on the bed in the second-floor bedroom. Sawyer had left her purse on the dresser in the other room. Her phone was plugged in, charging next to it. The purse was half on top of it, as if she were hiding it.

Her door was open, but I closed it and grabbed her purse, setting it down in front of the door to try and cover some of my scent.

The dog ran up, sniffing outside.

I moved to her closet, and after a few minutes, after he was called back downstairs, he left.

I snuck out, returning her purse to the dresser. After using the attached bathroom, I opened her bedroom door an inch and moved to her closet, leaving that door open an inch as well. I was able to hear their voices, and heard the different trotting from the two dogs. One was slow, barely moving around. I was guessing that it was a bigger dog. Maybe an older dog, which was a slight blessing for me, but neither of these dogs were guard dogs. When the smaller dog didn't return, I settled back and waited.

My phone buzzed silently against my hip. I pulled it out, reading the text.

Ashton: Info on Lane's girl. You're welcome. You owe me.

I rolled my eyes but clicked on the attached file.

An image of a young girl, early twenties, looked back at me. Brown skin. Dark almond eyes. Long black hair. Thin. Tall. It looked like a picture someone told her to stand by the wall for because they needed it for a file. She was holding on to a ragged backpack, the straps nearly torn off. The front pocket had long been pulled off. Some of the strings were still there.

She wasn't smiling. Her eyes were dead. She looked a little malnourished, but she was stunning.

I could see why Lane was obsessed with her, but she was young. I didn't like that part.

I kept scrolling, reading through the rest.

Her name was Blake Green.

She went into the foster system when she was six. She bounced around a bunch of houses until entering one when she was eight. She stayed until she was sixteen, then again bouncing until she aged out of the system.

There was no information where she crossed Lane's path. The rest of the information gave the list of schools she attended. She kept her grades up, so she was smart.

No arrests.

No alcohol or drug history.

There were other pictures of her, but I skimmed over them to the end of the file.

Her latest location was listed in the city, *this* city. She was attending school at one of the city colleges. The file listed her dorm, and a job at—I cursed before texting Ashton.

Me: Are you kidding me with her employment? I just told you about this problem today.

He didn't take long to reply. I could feel his mocking tone.

Ashton: It was a happy coincidence to find a neighbor of hers was already employed at my club.

Me: And you didn't drop her a line to get the girl to apply at your place?

Ashton: There might've been an incentive given, but we can thank you for bringing Creighton Lane to our awareness earlier than we might've otherwise known. Having eyes on his one weakness is smart business. She starts in two days. Would you like her schedule? All this was finalized an hour ago.

I gritted my teeth, hating this. Hating everything about this life, but I replied to him. He moved fast.

Me: Yes, but if I can take her before then, I will.

Ashton: You'll need help setting up the meet with Lane when he reaches out.

I knew he was right. I probably would, but I really wanted to tell him to stick it. There was a smugness Ashton shoved down your throat when he was "helping out." In this situation, the truth was that I was doing him a favor. Lane would more likely kill me for taking his woman, but I had no other options. He was too insulated for any other meet.

Me: Yeah. I'll be in contact.

Ashton: One last thing, your cousin's been showing up in our club lately. She's usually high.

There was only one cousin he could be referring to. Vivianna.

This was also how she and I were both entangled with the West and Walden families.

She knew Ashton from when they were younger. Both were on the modeling circuit for a short time. I wasn't sure when she started hanging out with Trace West's sister, but at some point their paths crossed.

Ashton: Trace kicked her out the last time she came back with his sister. She's becoming a problem. We can handle Remmi, but how do you want your cousin handled?

Me: Already handled. She's in rehab.

Ashton: She's out then, because she was in Katya last night.

I froze, staring at my phone, because there was no fucking way I was reading that right. She was out—but of course she was out. She would've walked in. Waited maybe six hours before signing herself right back out. She did it to avoid a drug charge.

I was going to murder her myself.

Actually. No. I had a better idea. Cousin Viv was officially no longer my problem.

Me: You do whatever you want with her, short of killing her.

Ashton: Are you sure you want to do that?

I knew the twisted delight he was going to take from this gift I was giving him. Just because they might have known each other at some point in their lives, that would not give Vivianna any safety if Ashton deemed someone a problem that needed to be handled.

I almost didn't want to know what he'd do, but I had no doubt my cousin would not be a problem at any point in the future.

Me: Yes. I'm done with her.

Ashton: Now I'm the one thanking you. How did you know my birthday was coming up?

It was probably nowhere close to his birthday, but I didn't reply. A few minutes later, my phone buzzed again. This time it wasn't Ashton.

Uncle Toby: We need to talk in person. It's urgent.

Yeah, right.

Me: The next time I see you, I'll be putting a bullet in your forehead.

Uncle Toby: It's family business. I told you what you wanted to know.

Me: Do not give a fuck.

Uncle Toby: You're considered our Head. Only you can make the decisions we need before moving forward. The longer we wait, the more it'll hurt business.

Me: I'll send a representative. They'll be in contact and they'll pick the time and place for the meet.

Uncle Toby: It has to be someone in the family.

Me: I'll send someone I choose. If you have a problem with who I send, I have no problem coming up early. Who knows. Maybe I'll bring our new cousin with me. We'll clean house together. The family business can be taken over by the women.

He didn't reply so I settled back, listening to Sawyer and her family's voices below again.

It was a long time later when my phone buzzed again.

Uncle Toby: Fine. Who will you be sending?

A very cruel and victorious smirk came over my face because I was going to enjoy this, so very much.

Me: You'll know when they reach out. Do not forget my promise.

Uncle Toby: Fine. What did you do with my sons?

Another faint smile tugged at my face. That meant he hadn't been notified yet. He would.

I wished I could be there when he found out.

Me: No.

I waited, but no more texts came from him and after twenty minutes, I sent another text to Ashton.

Me: My family needs my decisions about some items. I can't go myself. I would like it if you went to represent me.

I fully knew what I was doing with this move. Ashton was the head of a rival Mafia family, and one where my family slaughtered members of his. This was not a favor I was asking of him. This was a *gift* I was giving him. He was helping me with Lane, and this was my thank-you.

I was out. Officially and completely.

Before the contract was put on my head, I had considered going to Maine to sort out what was going on with my family. I wanted to get to the bottom of why they chose me as their new head. That was all done.

The family could burn for all I cared. I just needed to decide how I wanted to make that happen.

Ashton: Happy fucking birthday to me, hmmm.

Me: Don't say you never get a gift from me.

Ashton: When and how?

Me: I have two cousins in Presbyterian. Crispin and Penn. I believe you're familiar with them. Go through them to contact my uncle. You pick the time and place. Uncle Toby knows a representative will be reaching out on my behalf.

Ashton: Your cousins are patients there?

Me: Yes. They were assaulted. Someone decided to beat the shit out of them instead of killing both.

Ashton: Someone?

Me: Just go there, use Crispin's phone. Neither of them have reached out to their father. I don't know the reason for that, but you can get a hold of Uncle Toby for the meet that way.

Ashton: Got it.

Ashton blackmailed me when we first met. It was how I began giving him information.

We'd come a long way since then, but I wasn't kidding myself. There was a very real possibility Ashton and I would stare at each other on the opposite ends of a gun one day.

That day just hadn't come yet.

Another text came through from him, one that I responded to with *no* hesitation.

Ashton: Are you sure about this?

Me: One hundred.

Easiest text I'd sent in a long while.

CHAPTER TWENTY-ONE

JAKE

They were laughing, shouting, or crying through the entire night. And based on hearing all the glasses that were clinking, they were also getting lit downstairs. The doorbell rang at one point, and I moved closer to the door in case it was someone coming for the contract.

It wasn't.

The pizza aroma was the first giveaway. The second was when the husband exclaimed, "It's Napoli's!"

There was a gushing conversation about the place, which led to another conversation about the proper way to eat a slice. Clara was down for the fold. Bess was arguing that it needed to be rolled. I was listening for Sawyer's way of eating it, but she was quiet. Graham was giving Oliver crap about taking the cheese off his slice.

The dogs were barking, asking for their own slices.

I was standing up here like a fucking creeper, knowing there was a legit reason for my stalking, but I had to admit that it was nice to hear these people. They were family. There was a warmth to their entire evening's chatter, with concern tinged underneath it. There were a few awkward silences, but I had to hand it to Sawyer. She said this was why she came to the city. It was a whole deflection so she didn't need to focus on the real loss in her life, but she'd done it. Graham had been brought back into her family, and judging by how her aunts were talking, they weren't letting him go. He was in and there was no option of not being in.

It was now nearing midnight when they began saying good night.

I slipped into Sawyer's bathroom briefly before taking my position once again. If something was going to happen, it would happen now. The guys who were willing to grab Sawyer to kill me would not care if other people were in this house.

Sawyer stumbled to her room twenty minutes later, her gait a little jerky and her foot heavy. She pushed open her door and stopped just inside the doorframe. "Whoa."

"What?"

I pulled the closet door closed and eased farther back in the closet at hearing a male voice. He'd accompanied her.

"Whoa. This is so weird. It smells like . . ."

"What does it smell like?" He drew in an audible breath. "That's probably Oliver. He's been trying new deodorants. He was up here this morning to put fresh sheets on your bed. He must've come up here again to check on your room."

"That makes sense."

No, it didn't. She was smelling me. And she knew it.

She muttered, "You're probably right. I just thought for a second—"

"What?"

"Nothing. It's nothing. This room is amazing. Your whole place is amazing."

"Thanks." He sounded proud. "Oliver . . . Oliver comes from money." His voice hushed at the end.

Sawyer was quiet.

He rushed ahead, his voice rising a little. "Not that his job doesn't do well. He does. He's in real estate. And I do well, too, but we were only able to afford this place because of his family's money. He's not pretentious, though. At all. Thank goodness. I shouldn't have said anything. Please don't tell anyone in the family. My mom doesn't even know—"

He would've kept rambling, but Sawyer cut in, speaking softly. "I won't say anything. Oliver is amazing. You guys seem so happy. How long have you been together?"

"Thanks." He sighed in relief. "We've been together for almost eighteen years."

"Eighteen?" Her voice dipped low.

Jesus. Eighteen. It was the same amount of time she'd been with Douchebag.

"I dated a little when I first came here but met him after a few months. It's been him ever since."

"I'm happy for you."

"Thanks, Sawyer."

A pregnant silence took over them.

Graham said, hesitating, "I know there's a lot to talk about, like real stuff. We didn't get into it tonight, but I have to ask. Can I—you were terrified when I came to get you. It's obvious the aunts don't know about that part, but Sawyer, you thought I might've been followed. I need to know. Are we—are you in any danger? Are we?"

She didn't reply right away. When she did, her voice was low. "I—I don't know, to be honest. My head's been a mess with everything. I've been fucking everything up since I got here."

"What do you mean?"

She was silent again for a few beats. "I think in the beginning, I couldn't handle what my ex did to me. I've done it since I was a kid. If something's happening in my life that I can't cope with, my mind breaks off. I daydream or I think up these things. It's a coping mechanism. Like dissociating a little. I can't answer because I'm not sure myself. Does that make sense?"

That was fucked up. She'd seen two guys try to shoot us. I killed them *in front* of her.

I'd explained everything to her.

But then you locked her in the bedroom when you left, too, a voice spoke up in the back of my head. I ignored that voice. I couldn't afford to wait around and see if she took it seriously. I needed answers. We needed answers. There was no time to hold her hand. Locking her up was the best option for both of us.

She groaned. "I think I just need to sleep. I'm sure things will make sense in the morning."

"Okay. If you're sure?"

"I am. I'm sorry. I'm not intending to keep you in the dark. I just want to make certain that I'm sure about what I'm going to say. There could be ramifications."

He was quiet until he murmured, gently, "If you think that's the right thing to do. I can wait, but tomorrow."

"Tomorrow. Not the aunts. They can't know. God," she exclaimed. "They would lose their shit if they found out."

He said good night after that.

She went to the bathroom, was in there a while, before moving back to the room. The bed creaked. She seemed to be settling to go to sleep when there was a soft knock at her door.

The bed creaked again. She padded to the door, opening it. "Hey?"

One of her aunts was there. "Hey, sweetie. I just wanted to check on you. How are you really doing?"

They eased into the room. The bed protested as someone sat down. "I'm okay."

"No, honey. I mean it. We didn't bring up Beck at all tonight, but that's the whole reason you're here. Your mom's worried. You're not responding to her either."

"I can't. My phone—" She cut herself off.

I waited for her to finish that statement. Her phone had been charging under her purse.

I'd picked up her purse.

I'd put it back in the same place . . . Or was I a few inches off?

Shit. I couldn't remember.

Her aunt didn't notice the slight hitch in Sawyer's voice. "We'll get that fixed in the morning, but I just wanted to check in with you. One on one. Your mom has been blowing up my phone. Did you want to talk about Beck at all? About . . . About him, back home? About Manda?"

"I . . ."

She sounded defeated and tired, so tired. I held back my frustration at needing to stay hidden. Everything in me wanted to tear out of the closet, to take her away from all of these people who were making her talk about topics she clearly didn't want to discuss. Let her deal on her own timetable. I didn't care if she dissociated or deflected. I hated that she was second-guessing herself, hated what part I played in that, but they needed to give her fucking space. Let her talk about it whenever the fuck she wanted to talk about it. She didn't owe them anything.

She finally confessed, "I just really don't want to talk about it."

Exactly.

Her aunt remarked, "Yes, but you need to. Eventually. Call your mom tomorrow. She knows you're fine and she's less worried now that you're with family, but we're all concerned. We have your back. You know that."

"I know. Thank you, Aunt Bess."

Christ. Her voice was soft, as if she were making herself smaller. I gritted my teeth, loathing hearing that. Let her fucking feel what she wanted to feel. Let her think what she wanted to think. Let her be. She'll face her shit when *she* was ready. It was her timetable, not theirs.

"Clara's already made friends with Willy."

"She didn't."

"She did. Willy's pissed at what Beck did to you. He trained his cameras on the house, and he's been sending that footage to Clara on the regular. We know his entire schedule, and say the word, we'll start moving in to fuck him up. You know that Clara also changed her daily walks to go through Manda's neighborhood. She's making connections there, building up a network of spies. We're loading our resources so you have them when you want them. We'll keep compiling all the information you need to know."

Jesus. Her aunt Clara sounded more gruff and abrupt downstairs, but hearing this one speak of their movements, *both* of them thought how Mafia gangsters operated.

Sawyer's voice was strained when she replied, "That's very thoughtful and appreciated, but right now, I kinda just want to go to sleep and wake up tomorrow to enjoy a day with you guys. All of you. I mean, we're in Graham's house. Graham and Oliver." Her voice dropped off to a whisper, thick with emotion. "That's a really big deal, Aunt Bess."

The bed whined again. "Come here." Her voice grew muffled. "One last hug and I'll head off, let you go to sleep."

Sawyer's voice was also muffled, a bit teary as she sniffled. "I love you."

"I love you too, Sawsaw." There was a kissing smack before the bed groaned once more. The floor creaked. The door sounded as it was swung open. "You sleep good. If you can't, you can sneak in with us. That bed is giant. Did you see how big their bed is? Five people could fit in there."

Sawyer snorted, holding back a laugh. "I think it's more so they have enough room for them and the dogs."

"Right. The dogs. We might need to get you a German shepherd when we get back. Or a Doberman."

"I don't need a Do—" She stopped to rethink. "I'll think about it. Night, Aunt Bess."

"Night, sweetie. Love you."

The door shut.

She went to her bathroom and I could hear the water turned on.

I waited for her to finish in there.

Except the closet door swung open.

Sawyer wasn't in the bathroom.

She was staring right at me.

CHAPTER TWENTY-TWO

SAWYER

Oh my god!

There was a man in my closet.

I opened my mouth to scream. He got to me first, his hand clamping over my mouth, and he jerked us around so I was pushed up against the wall. From the movement, we went fast, but he wrapped his other arm around my neck to cushion the impact. My head didn't smash up against the wall, but his body pinned me in place.

That's when rational thinking returned, and I sagged in relief because it was only Jake.

My eyes went wide.

Only. *Jake.*

I tensed all over again. *Jake found me!*

He had been waiting, his head cocked, his eyes narrowed. "Are you going to scream?"

I bit down on the inside of his hand, and when he barely reacted, I growled, shoving him off me. "Asshole."

Holy. I pressed a hand to my chest, feeling my heart pumping like crazy. It needed to slow down.

Jake moved back another step, folding his arms as he watched me try to calm myself down from a fucking panic attack. He raised an eyebrow, smirking. "Surprised to see me?"

I glared at him, panting. "If I knew fifty different languages, I'd be cursing you in all of them. What were you thinking? Hiding in my closet! It's the first place someone hides."

"You'd rather I hid under your bed?"

"Maybe," I growled back. "Then I could've jumped real hard on the mattress and hopefully squashed you."

His eyes flashed, getting hard, and he was in my space once again. I was pushed back to the wall, and he was leaning over me.

I wanted to shove him back, but I figured if I touched him, he'd grab my arms and pull some twisty half-ninja move and somehow I'd just regret it. I huffed, my shoulders slumping down.

"Why did you open the closet door if you were going to be scared by someone being in there?"

"Because I didn't think it was true! I didn't really think someone was in my closet. Just like when you're a kid, you're pretty sure there isn't a monster under your bed so you get up and turn the light on, and then look. And they're never there. Same thought process. But you were in there! I just lost five years of my life." I raised my hands, only to press against his chest, and they stayed there.

Fuck.

He was so warm.

And strong.

And solid.

And not a killer waiting to slit my throat. Or I didn't think.

I eyed him. "Are you going to kidnap me again?"

His gaze turned fierce and he leaned in again. "Princess—"

I gulped. "Don't call me that."

"Lunatic," he clipped out.

I huffed. "That's better."

His hand slid around to the back of my neck, cupping me. He angled my head up to his, and closed the distance between us, his chest pressing to mine. "If you ever think a killer is in your closet, you run, you scream, or you get me. I'd prefer you run and scream first."

Oh, god.

Also, he wasn't answering my question.

I drew in some air, and my chest rose against his.

He felt so good there.

His power, his strength, that I knew he would and could kill, that he was here. A part of me relaxed, knowing I was safe, and I hated registering that part of me. Because I had to admit that the same part of me had been on edge, knowing I was away from him, fearing for my life and my family's.

I was in such trouble.

I half muttered, freaking out more that a part of me trusted him, "And if you're not available?"

His hand tightened on me as he leaned down until there was an inch separating our lips. He drawled, "If you can't run. If you can't scream. If I'm not available, and you have to open that door, you get a gun. You hear me?"

My heart skipped a beat.

He was against me, every inch of him.

I felt a bulge between my legs, and my body was remembering the last time we'd been in the same room. The feel of his fingers pumping inside of me, and the need to feel the rest of him filling me up.

Arousal began spreading through me, making my breathing grow more shallow. My pulse sped up. My mouth started salivating.

"Gun," I croaked. "Got it."

I eyed him, tension edging in.

He saw the switch and angled his head back so he could see me better. His mouth went flat. "What?"

Another part of me twisted because if my body was already trusting that it was him, that he made me feel safe, then that meant the kidnapping had been what he actually said. I was still muddled up, but I whispered, "You really did kidnap me for my safety, didn't you?"

His eyes and mouth immediately softened. He brushed a hand over my forehead in a gentle graze. "Yeah, babe."

Babe.

My heart fluttered. That felt right.

Oh, boy. I was in so much trouble here.

"You were hoping you'd imagined the whole thing?"

The final ring of truth from him was the final nail in my coffin. God. It was all true. Tears immediately came to my eyes, with terror swiftly behind them. Oh, god. Oh, god. Oh, gooooood. My family. I had called my cousin. My aunts. They were all here and so was I.

"Hey, hey." Jake pulled me away from the wall, going to the bed, and he tugged me onto his lap. "Hey." He caught my face, tilting up my chin so I was looking directly at him. He said, firmly, "Stop."

I did. I stopped thinking. I stopped feeling.

In that break, he cupped both sides of my face, his thumbs rubbing under my ears on my neck. "I fucked up here. I'm sorry I took you in the way I did in the first place, and I'm sorry for locking you in the room. I—that's on me."

I closed my eyes, my heart squeezing. Jesus. It was all true. Resting my head against his, I breathed out, in a whimper, "My family is here. They're like moms to me. I *just* met Graham, and he's the sweetest. Oliver too."

His hand moved to my leg, and he pulled me tighter against him, making me brush over his bulge. His hand tightened on my leg, but he said in a low voice back, "I know. I won't let anything happen to them."

I wanted to believe him. I did, but the truth was more terrifying than the other option that he was just a regular run-of-the-mill kidnapper. "You can't promise that."

He tilted his head back, so I raised mine.

We shared a look.

His eyes flashed. A momentary glimpse of regret showed before they softened again. He moved me over his bulge again. "I'll fucking try my best. How does that sound, my little lunatic?"

I really liked hearing that, and he grinned at me, lazily, as he felt my body's reaction.

He drawled once more, "You like that name, huh?" His eyes grew determined and his head began to bend down to mine. "Is it the name Lunatic or that I called you my little lunatic? Which one was it?" He spread his hand on my neck, his thumb resting over my carotid.

I began panting, my hips rolling over him, pressing down over his dick. "It was the last." I grinned, peeking at him from underneath heavy eyelids. "Though, I liked when you called me Lunatic too."

He grunted, his gaze becoming molten, but he continued to guide me over him.

Back and forth.

I shifted on his lap, straddling him, and I began pressing down at the same time.

He was starting to breathe hard, and groaned. "Fuck. This isn't a good idea."

I looked at him, waiting to see what was going to happen next because he was back with me, and his hands were on me, and my pussy was throbbing, and while I hated how he left me the last time, a deep part of me was choosing to bring that battle up later.

Because that same deep part of me wanted this to happen, this being him and me, and as a primal hunger rose up in me, that's when my brain decided to stop thinking.

His mouth slammed down on mine.

CHAPTER TWENTY-THREE

JAKE

My hand touched her hip, sliding to her front, and she began quivering.

A moan slipped out from her, and I gave in. I didn't think she knew she even let that little whimper out, or how there was a plea in her eyes. That sound right there, she broke down my last will of resistance.

I was done. I was going in.

There was no walking away this time.

That sound meant she was mine. *Mine.*

My mouth demanded for her to open to me, and when she did so automatically, I slid inside to taste what was mine. Because she was. This mouth. Her lips. Her throat. Her cunt would be mine. I was going to imprint myself on her so thoroughly that she'd be able to still feel me tomorrow if she only breathed.

"You want this?" I asked, quietly, bending down so she'd feel my breath on her neck.

She shivered, pausing before she nodded once, her head jerking in the slight motion. She breathed out, "Yes."

Her body was trembling over me.

Dark triumph went through me.

She was mine.

I could do with her what I wanted.

Fuck. Jesus.

This feeling was incredible. Liberating.

She awakened something dark inside of me, a beast, and I wasn't sure if I would ever be able to put him back in his cage. Either way, he was loose now. He wanted to rise to the surface and take over.

He wanted to feast.

I slid my hands down her stomach, rubbed her clit. She sagged against my chest, moving her hips over me, and I heard another whine slipping out from her throat. Sliding two of my fingers around her wetness, I slipped them inside. She was so incredibly soaked.

Her knees began to shake next to me. I shifted, wrapping an arm around her, and turned to lay her on the bed. I came down on top of her, giving her enough space so she could breathe, but I slipped down between her legs. I pulled her little fucking shorts farther down so I could get a better look at how pretty and pink her pussy was for me.

"Jake," she moaned, her hands sliding through my hair.

I went to taste her again, my mouth finding hers before I let myself start to explore her. Every fucking inch. And I was going to take my time and savor every inch.

I licked her throat.

She groaned, goose bumps breaking out over her skin. "Jake," she sighed.

"That's it." I was murmuring to her, praising her. "You feel so good around my fingers." I pushed up into her, moving them in and out. "So tight, baby."

She clutched at the back of my arms, her fingers digging in. I heard the slight hitch from her. She liked those little names. Baby. Babe. Lunatic.

That was good to know.

I moved my fingers faster, going deeper with each stroke until I couldn't go any deeper.

I was going to fuck this woman. I'd shove my dick all the way to the hilt. I'd pound into her. I'd do it rough and I'd do it dirty. And we would both love it, but not yet. Not this time. This time was for her because she'd given me a gift. She hadn't meant to. She had no idea she had, but there was something about feeling her trembling beneath me, aching for me, that broke open a cage inside of me.

I needed to thank her for that, and that's what I was doing.

I pressed a kiss to her jawline, feeling her shuddering all over again.

"Jake," she whimpered.

Three fingers.

She moaned again, one that came from her belly. I felt its vibrations as she was starting to thrash in my arms. She was digging into my arms, her nails were going to break my skin.

I kept fucking going, flatting my palm against her clit, rubbing against her.

She started to scream, but I covered her mouth with my hand. She moaned into it and she came apart, surging up in my arms as I felt her climax rip through her entire body.

I watched, mesmerized, as she was still shaking. The wave still crashed through her until eventually she quieted. My fingers were still inside her, held deep. I moved my palm away from her clit and waited until she opened her eyes, looking up.

My other hand fell away from her mouth.

She held my gaze, and I was looking deep, real deep into her, not giving a fuck what she was seeing inside of me. We held still. I might've lost track of time, but somewhere I ceased thinking in the back of my mind.

I just needed to feel more of her.

I wanted to feel her exploding around me again, and again, and again.

I moved up, stretching her legs wide for me.

Her hands fell to my jeans and her fingers went to my buckle, at the same time I began tugging her shorts more out of the way.

I needed to get my dick wet. That's all I was thinking—an alert sounded from downstairs.

CHAPTER TWENTY-FOUR

SAWYER

He froze, his head turning to the side.

My heart began thudding in my chest. Why was he stopping? I wanted this too. He couldn't leave, not like the last time. I opened my mouth, but his hand clamped over mine.

"Someone's in the house."

That's all he needed to say and I froze up again. Fuck. I'd forgotten where we were.

Terror lined inside of me.

He was off the bed in the next instant, and tugged me after him. A strong arm banded around my back, catching me before my feet would've hit the ground hard. I was held up against his chest, his very strong and cement-like chest, as he said quietly in my ear, "We can't make any sound."

I nodded, just a slight tilt of my chin so he knew I understood.

He released me slowly and my feet touched the floor without making a sound. My knees were starting to shake and sweat ran down my spine as his words registered for a second time.

Someone was in the house. A creak sounded from the stairs followed by someone else saying, "Shhhh. She ain't on these floors."

That was definitely not anyone I knew.

My feet locked up. I was so scared of making a sound, if the floor would creak under my feet, but Jake muffled a curse and moved me in his arms. He did something with the bedding before carrying me into the closet.

Closing the door, he stopped it before it clicked, and just then another sound came from the hallway. They were on my floor.

Jake moved me around him, but I began shaking my head. I didn't want to move away from him. I'd run from him and now I clung to him. The irony wasn't lost on me. I'd made a mistake.

That mistake brought these people here, putting people I love in danger.

There was another scuffle sound from outside my door.

I fisted Jake's shirt from behind, pressing my forehead to his back. His muscles were taut, bunched together. Sliding one arm back, he cupped my hip, giving me a slight squeeze. He removed it when my bedroom door opened.

Jake's arm moved again, leaning forward to the closet door.

"She's in the bed," a guy said in such a quiet murmur.

I don't know if I would've woken if I'd been in bed.

Three quiet pops were heard. I gasped, moving so my mouth was pressed against Jake's back so no sound came from me. Those were the same sounds from the other shooter, the one who used a silencer.

"Fuck." That same voice was savage, growling. Two heavy footsteps thudded on the floor. "She ain't here."

"What?" A second voice, also male. More footsteps.

They went to the bathroom. The light was turned on.

"Her bed's still warm." The first voice. "She was just here."

"Check the closet." That was a third voice.

More footsteps came our way.

Jake shoved me to the side and right before they would've opened it, he shot through it.

Bang! Bang!

He shoved open the door and at the same time, a body hit the floor.

"Fuck!" That was them.

All that happened at the same time.

Just as Jake was through the closet door, he turned, and two more gunshots went off.

Another deep thud was heard.

"Stay there," Jake growled at me before stalking forward.

Another gunshot.

I closed my eyes, my whole body shaking.

He walked to the bathroom and there was a last gunshot.

How many shooters were there? Three?

There was a ringing in my ears and the edges of my vision clouded in, giving me tunnel vision. I couldn't hear so well anymore. A deep, rhythmic pounding was overloading my hearing, but then Jake was in front of me, motioning for me to come to him. He was speaking, but I couldn't make out what he was saying anymore. I was underwater, and he was trying to talk to me through the water.

I stepped out, my knees shaking.

"Shit," Jake cursed, still muffled, and bent behind me. His arms swept me up, lifting me against his chest. He was carrying me like I was a baby, but he didn't turn around so I could see the rest of the room. He kept me tucked against him, lifting me so I was folded down. I could only see him, only feel him, only smell him.

There were other voices.

Dogs were barking.

Jake said, gruffly, still muffled, "She's in shock."

My heartbeat pounded.

He moved through the room, stepping into the hallway. Other people were there. Fingers brushed at my forehead. Jake ignored them, taking me downstairs until he got to the main level. More footsteps joined us. More people.

He was speaking to someone else, asking a question. I couldn't make it out anymore.

"—this way."

Jake was following someone down a small hallway. A door opened. The room was dark, blissfully dark. He started to let me down, but I reached for him. "No!"

I heard the voice. A part of me knew it was from me, but that didn't sound like me. That sounded animalistic.

Another part of my brain switched on so I was watching everything from a safe distance. I was outside of my body, witnessing as Jake soothed me, calming me down enough so he could place me on a couch. Graham was there, but he moved out when Oliver took his place. Aunt Bess was also beside me. They were talking to me. Bess was smoothing my hair from my forehead.

Jake was grim, his face like concrete with blood splattered over his neck and jawline. He was conversing with Graham. Aunt Clara was in the background, overhearing. All of them looked shaken, pale.

The dogs were barking in the background.

Graham was saying, "—no, you will not!"

I came back to my body abruptly, jerking upright. Oliver's hand was on my shoulder. Aunt Bess was touching my foot, as if they were both trying to keep me grounded. Their eyes widened at my sudden change. I blinked once, reality slamming down on me, unwelcome, but it was what it was.

Jake was standing sideways, his face and body so tense, but he kept a firm hold on his gun, pressed to his side. "More could be coming here. I need to take her away so none of you are in danger. Sawyer would want that."

Graham leaned in, hissing, "Maybe, but I've a feeling you're the reason she had me driving north of the city to get her and why she was so terrified we were being followed—"

Aunt Clara barked, joining in, "Followed?"

Bess said, "Followed by who?"

Graham didn't see I was cognizant again. No one did. They thought I was still in shock, except Jake, who holstered his gun. His eyes were trained on me, inspecting me. He ran his gaze down my body, darkening, before lifting to meet my eyes once more.

Graham's arm swept in the air, cutting through it. "She wouldn't tell me, but she asked me to pick her up in someone else's car. She was scared of her own shadow when I got there. Who are you?"

"What?" Clara screeched. "Why is this the first we're hearing about this? She's my niece."

"Mine too," Bess huffed, her mouth twisting as she went back to patting my foot.

Oliver cursed under his breath, standing up. "I'm calling the police."

"No police," Jake ordered, his voice sharp, silencing everyone. Even the dogs stopped barking.

It lasted a second.

He asked me, quieting, "Are you okay?"

Oliver drew in air, blinking at me.

Bess, Clara, and Graham all fixed me with stares.

"Oh, baby." Bess's hand gripped my foot.

Clara started to push into the room.

Graham took a step forward.

All of them crowded around me.

Their concern and panic pounded at me from all sides, mixing with my own, but I forced it down. "I'm fine." I cringed. That came out like a squeak.

Jake's eyes narrowed, a dark emotion flashing there before it was banked. His jawline clenched and he came toward me, standing over me. I tilted back, still holding his gaze. He lifted a finger to touch under my chin, running along the length of my jawline before he moved it over my forehead, his mouth turning down at whatever he saw there. He tucked some hair behind my ear, tracing down the rest of my face before ending again under my chin. He tilted me back a little farther, his next words coming out softly, "You were only a person of interest, but an hour ago, a price was put on you too. You're listed as a secondary bonus."

All of my insides took a nosedive to the floor. That wasn't good.

I whispered, "Did you find out who's behind it?"

His eyes went dead, his mouth flattening. "I did. That's why I left, to find out."

That was good. That meant he could fix this.

"Sawyer, honey." Bess's voice dipped. She was fighting back tears. Her hand squeezed my foot. "Who is this man? *What* is going on?"

Oliver suddenly stood up. "We need to call the police. Those were gunshots. Our neighbors would've heard."

I looked to Jake for those answers, seeing he was barely restraining himself. "They won't know which fucking house it came from. Your curtains are drawn. No lights are visible. The police will send a squad car to drive through your neighborhood. They won't find a disturbance unless you create one, and I already said no fucking police."

"Fuck this," Graham muttered, pulling out his phone.

Jake was across the room in the next second, ripping it away.

"Hey!"

Jake ignored him, pulling his gun again.

Bess gasped, shrinking in next to me.

"Jake!" I snapped a reprimand.

He ignored me.

Blood drained from Graham's face.

Oliver fell back against the wall, clutching his chest.

Clara's eyes narrowed, getting that look she got before she was about to rip into whatever mess was ahead of her. It always reminded me of when a bull lowered his head before charging. Clara just needed to huff out some steam and the image would be complete.

"None of you know what the fuck you're doing. You call the cops, that forces us to run. If we don't, if we get taken in, we're dead."

Jake didn't raise his gun, but his hand gripped it tight. He swung his dark gaze over everyone, pinning everyone in place. "Do you hear me? No. Cops."

"What do you mean?" Clara's voice was low, but calm. Strong. She jutted out her chin. "You're saying someone could get to my niece if she goes to a police station? What if they come here and question her?"

He fixed her with an impenetrable stare. "Same *fucking* thing. A case gets opened. That gives these killers more ways to get to her. This shit won't get fixed by them, not in fucking time to save our asses. Mine and your girl's." He motioned to me with the gun.

Bess sagged farther into the couch.

I winced from the movement.

Seeing that, Jake cursed again, but shoved the gun back in his holster. He focused on me, anger and his tightly wound control on edge. "Are you going to run again?"

I swung my gaze up, starting to get pissed.

He ignored that look from me. "Cut it out. I have to ask. Are you in this with me or not? There's a price on your head too, princess."

"Don't fucking call me that name."

"Are you with me or not, Lunatic?"

I relaxed, a slight grin curling at my mouth.

Clara growled. "You don't call her that either."

He ignored her, only talking to me. "I've already explained to you what's going on, so I'm going to step out and call in a crew to help with the cleanup. While I do that, educate your posse here. It's up to you what you want to say, but just so you and me are copacetic, you *will* be leaving with me. These people *will not* say one word of this to anyone." He raised an eyebrow. His next words were a warning. "They do, they will be dead within the week. We clear?"

Every word he said felt like a slap across my face.

He was right, but I didn't like how it was delivered. *"Crystal."*

CHAPTER TWENTY-FIVE

SAWYER

I lied.

I made up a story about how I was being robbed, how Jake happened to be there and stepped in to save me, and how the guy who was trying to rob us was now sending people after us.

It made no sense, but my family did not live a life where they saw crime happening in front of them.

They bought it.

Clara was grumbling, "You need to find the name of this fucker and we can do a background search. I've got friends who are online detectives. We call ourselves Cyber Sleuths. You might've heard about us. We've been featured in documentaries. I bet we could unearth all his dark secrets and blackmail him, get him off your backs that way."

Graham was still frowning, sitting on the edge of a chair with Oliver. "*Why* can't we call the police? That doesn't make sense to me. Robbers don't get all vengeance like this."

So they weren't totally buying it.

I said quickly, "Uh, it wasn't just the robber guy. It was his family. They sent two other guys after us. When Jake stepped in, he really messed him up."

Bess mumbled, "That sounds like the O'Malleys in Bridger. If one gets crossed, they're all crossed."

Clara was nodding. "Your friend must've put him in the hospital or a coma for them to still be sending people after you." She breathed in almost awe. "That sounds like some Mafia shit. Didn't he say a price was on your head? That *is* like the Mafia."

Oh, fuck.

"The Mafia?" Graham fell backward, but Oliver was there to rub a hand down his back, steadying him.

Voices were heard suddenly from the other side of the door, along with footsteps and more commotion.

Oliver crossed the room.

Everyone followed, huddling up behind him as he opened the door an inch. We jostled so we could see. Clara knelt down. Bess pushed her head farther down so she could take Clara's place, and Graham moved up on the chair beside us, angling to see from a higher point of view. I nudged Oliver to the side so we could share the same space.

"Oh, Lordie. Who is *that*?" Bess oohed. "Your man is fine, but so are all of those men. I like the real big one."

Clara snorted softly. "Get in line. Or I'll take the other big one with the dark brown skin. He looks like he could handle a roll with Miss Clara here. He could eat me for breakfast, which I would find delightful."

Oliver stifled a laugh.

Graham snickered before he whispered sharply, "Who is *that*?"

Oliver agreed. "Mmmmm mmmm."

I angled my head a little more so I could see better. Jake moved to the side and two beast-like men came into the room. He motioned and they went upstairs, but another man stepped in behind them. This man was almost startlingly handsome, looking as if he'd stepped out of a boardroom where he was a CEO of a top 100 company that Forbes would cover in their magazine. Caucasian. Square jawline. He was the same height as Jake, with a smoothness that Jake didn't have. This guy came off smooth and sleek with an aura of danger too.

"I didn't call for you." Jake's tone was pitched low.

Jake *did not* like him.

The other guy shrugged before lifting his head to look up the stairs. "I was the closer option. Ashton felt speed was more important than made-up grudges—"

"Fuck made-up." Jake took a step toward him, his voice rising.

The other guy registered all of that, his gaze glancing to Jake before doing another longer sweep around the first floor, finding our closed door and holding.

We all went still.

He pulled his gaze away, but shifted on his feet so we could see his face. His eyebrows arched. "Do you want to hash out facts from how your brother died or do you want to move forward? Ashton's kept me abreast. I'm the one who compiled that nice little file you received earlier on our *mutual* threat."

"Oh, fuck off, West," Jake growled, pulling his gun again. He didn't raise it, but the gesture was noted by the other man, who grew still. Jake added, "My brother wouldn't have died if he never met your woman's fr—"

"I am *done* with you blaming Jess for what your cousin did—"

Jake pushed back, not fazed. His words were savage. "Justin would've handled it differently if he hadn't been with her. She's the reason he was considered a threat."

"Your family killed your brother, and they're the reason why your little girlfriend is locked up in that room over there. Stop putting the blame on other houses and start looking within your own." The other guy was like ice.

"Trust me. I *am*." Jake's tone sent a shiver down my spine. The tightly held promise of violence and bloodshed. I suppressed a second shiver, feeling the heat from his anger.

Clara and Bess were both panting.

Oliver noticed and snorted, trying to smother it but failing.

Graham glanced his way and Oliver gestured toward my aunts.

Some drool was happening.

A grin cracked on Graham's face, his laughing eyes finding mine and for a moment, the stifling threat of violence and hatred from the other room dissipated, lifting off my chest.

I couldn't hold back a chuckle, but then squeaked and clapped a hand over my own mouth.

"What?" Clara was looking between all of us.

Bess was chewing on her bottom lip, trying not to laugh too. Her forehead dipped toward the door. "I can't help it. They are both *fine*. I don't know who your new boyfriend is, but Beck is going to shit his pants when he sees him. He walks and breathes violence." She shared a look with her sister, dropping her voice. "I bet he fucks violence too."

"Aunt Bess!"

Aunt Bess only grinned at me, not admonished one bit.

"Hmmm mmm." Clara's head bopped along, agreeing. "The other one looks like he's from a *GQ* magazine. They're both top shelf."

Graham's hand went to his husband's shoulder. "You aren't seeing us arguing."

"Oh, god. Another one came in."

We all looked at Bess's groan.

Those four were now enjoying all of this. They weren't realizing the real danger that was lingering and falling down over me like a fire blanket. I didn't know who those other men were. A part of me didn't want to know. They belonged to that world. No police badges were being flashed.

That other guy came into the brownstone. Two more men followed him, going upstairs like they'd been told ahead of time where to go.

Clara and Bess were oohing and aahing over this latest addition, and I could see the appeal. He was a little leaner than the Forbes Magazine guy, but he was no less dangerous. He held the same authority and power the other did, but his eyes had a darker and meaner glint in them, matching the smirk on his face. He clasped hands with Jake, whose shoulders relaxed an inch.

This guy was who Jake had called. He was the one Jake wanted to be here.

He walked around to stand in front of Jake and Forbes, his eyes zeroing in on us and staying. He shouldn't be able to see us. The door was barely open. His smirk went up another notch before his shoulders lowered. He faced the other two, his back now to us and blocking our view. All three of their heads folded together, their voices as well. We couldn't hear a thing.

"Fuddruckers." Clara's mouth twisted in a pout.

Graham closed the door with a sigh.

Oliver asked, when we all moved to the couches, "What do you think they're doing out there?"

"Cleaning up those bodies."

Graham turned Clara's way. "How long does that take? You pick up the bodies and carry them outside, right?"

She wrinkled her nose, leaning forward on her seat. Both of my aunts were in their sleep kimonos and slippers. Bess was wearing jersey cow slippers with the cow head on top of her feet. Clara was wearing fuzzy flamingo slippers.

She tugged up her kimono end so it draped just above her knees, where she rested her elbows. She looked very take-charge, that fierce expression on her face. "Not if they're cleaning it like pros. Those out there, they look like pros."

"What do you mean, pros?" Graham leaned closer.

Her eyes got big, real big, and she made a point of closing her mouth, but she sent me a meaningful look.

Everyone followed, their gazes landing on me. My stomach rolled, but I sat up higher. "What?"

Maybe they hadn't bought my story. Maybe I should just tell them those guys were Mafia, but if I said that word, that would set my aunts off in a whole different way. Thinking it was a family with a grudge was different than a real-life, official, organized-crime villain.

Just then, the door opened with Jake appearing as Bear and Pooh darted in, running to their dads.

"Oh, Bear!" Oliver opened his arms and Bear jumped up with a big woof. He caught the giant black Lab, falling backward on the couch as Bear began licking all over his face, his tail wagging and hitting Bess in the face.

Pooh did the same to Graham, making it up in one dainty jump, and her excitement was more controlled. She leaned up, one paw to his chest, licking his jaw before jumping down and starting her way over all of our laps. She got to me, giving me one quick lick before Jake moved her, putting her on the next person's lap. He grabbed my hand, tugging me up with him, and dragged me from the room.

The other two were waiting in the kitchen, both keenly watching me.

"Wait a minute. Where are you taking—" Bess cried out, but all of them clambered to follow us.

Jake stopped them, an arm hitting the doorway and blocking them. "I need to talk to her. You"—he looked at all of them—"stay."

Clara growled, her head down, and I recognized the look in her eye. She did not like what Jake was putting down, and she sure as shit was about to throw it right back in his face. Only, Jake wouldn't react in the way Clara was accustomed. She was used to guys from home backing down from her. She was older than them, sometimes bigger, and she had sass. It was known in Bear Creek, Montana, not to mess with Aunt Clara.

Jake came from a different world. He was living in the world Clara sometimes thought she was living in, and the difference between reality and fantasy was sobering. Clara hadn't learned that.

She wouldn't, not if I had a say in the matter.

I hurried to get between them, pushing Jake backward as I walked in reverse. I brought my hands together and made a pleading look to everyone. "Give us a minute. Okay?" I didn't wait for their permission, hurrying forward to shut the door. When it inched open again, I glared at them. "For real, a minute."

Someone grumbled on the other side and someone laughed.

The door closed that last inch.

I had no doubt they had their ears to the door, listening as much as they could, and knowing that, I whipped back around.

Jake and the other two were watching to see what I'd do.

I didn't want to talk to them. They were powerful and dangerous and I was suddenly so exhausted from everything that had happened over the course of the week. I dropped my gaze, focusing on Jake. Moving a little closer to him, I didn't look up. "Can we go somewhere private?"

A strange stillness came over him. He reached forward, took my hand and led me outside. He threaded our fingers as we went down the back stairs.

I stopped after we went a few more steps. "This is good."

Jake considered me as he stepped close to me, his jeans brushing against mine. He moved our hands to the side, his thumb rubbing over mine. "They're still cleaning upstairs. We can talk in my truck."

I shook my head, stepping back. "No. My family will freak, thinking I left again. We can talk here. We just have to be quiet."

A resigned look came over him as his eyes flicked over my shoulder. "Right."

There was movement behind me.

I started to look, but Jake held me firm.

What? My eyes went wide. Panicked.

Jake met my eyes, his face grim. He leaned in as I felt a pinch in the back of my neck, and he whispered, "I'm sorry, Sawyer. I really am, but I know there's no way your family will let you go. We don't have time."

Not again.

Everything went black.

CHAPTER TWENTY-SIX

SAWYER

I came to with a *vengeance.*

The asshole drugged me.

And kidnapped me. *A-fucking-gain.*

I was going to murder him.

I was going to find a shovel. Find him. Hit him in the back of his head with the shovel, and when he passed out, I was going to tie the asshole up!

Let's fucking see how he liked it.

I wasn't tied up or blindfolded anymore so I tore off the bed, going first to the bathroom. I winced when I looked in the mirror. A mess. A total mess. My hair was in disarray. There were red marks all over my face, neck, arms, shoulders. They looked like indents, like I slept too long on them. Bags under my eyes.

I groaned, not even remembering when I last got decent sleep. It was almost sad to say, but my life in Bear Creek had been boring, but it was just that. Boring. It was stable. Steady. Yeah, maybe my relationship with Beck had been stalled for the last few years, but there was something nice in the predictability of knowing. I knew when I'd wake up. Knew what I'd eat for breakfast. Knew who would make me laugh at work, who'd make me roll my eyes, who'd annoy me. I knew the patients. I knew my colleagues.

Yes, they annoyed me. Always asking when I was going to get married.

When I was going to have kids.

Then at some point, the looks turned pitying. They started thinking it wasn't going to happen.

They'd been correct, but I wasn't feeling that specific heartache right now.

I was missing the familiarity of my life. I knew what to expect. It felt safe.

Wednesday night was martini night at the new bar that everyone in Bear Creek said was so hoity-toity.

I loved the hoity-toitiness of it all.

It made me feel sophisticated. Classy. Like I was going somewhere. Like my life wasn't always going to be the same and I was the hamster never getting off the same wheel.

Beck made fun of me for going to martini night, because who was I to think I belonged in a classy bar like that, drinking martinis like I was some city-folk socialite. It burned at the time because he was right.

It burned worse now because he was wrong.

I belonged anywhere I decided that I belonged. Maybe it was all the kidnappings, or the running, or the people either shooting at me or near me, but all of the little comments Beck used to make about me didn't matter. None of it did.

I could do what I wanted. If I survived this, I was going to do whatever I wanted.

I'd taken on the role of being a supportive and loving partner. That defined me. A job never did. I don't know if I wanted it to define me in the future, but I knew that moving forward, I was going to make moves for me. What was in the best interest for me.

And for damn sure, I was going to go back to Bear Creek and I was going to slam all the martinis that I wanted. After that, I'd figure things out, because I'd woken up with a brand-new fucking lease on life.

Forget my tourist bucket list. I was doing a real bucket list.

Become fluent in Spanish. I was going to do it. Take a cruise to the Bahamas, fuck yes. Backpack through Europe . . . Maybe I'd hire someone to help me with that, but I was down. Whatever invisible strings or handcuffs that kept me chained to Beck or to the role of being Beck's loving and supportive partner—that wasn't going to be me anymore.

I would not ever love and support someone to the detriment of myself. That wasn't a real partnership. I would never have that again, where I gave all of myself and they barely gave me 10 percent back.

I just needed to commit murder first.

I washed up the best I could and smoothed back my hair, cleaned my teeth with a toothbrush that had still been in its packaging and some toothpaste, then I went for the bedroom door. There were no sounds on the other side. The room was unfamiliar, so I didn't think Jake had brought us back to his cabin.

There was a knot in my stomach as I reached for the handle. If it was locked, I was going to burn the place down.

My fingers touched the cool metal and turned. It clicked open.

Relief spread through me, which then ticked me off because I shouldn't have to be relieved that I wasn't being locked up yet *again*.

I found him.

Stopping abruptly, just inside the kitchen door, I saw him in a chair by the table. Sitting back. Eyes closed. Shirtless. Totally and completely asleep.

I already knew Jake had a good physique, but seeing his chest naked now—I trailed down the sleekness of him. All smooth muscles. There were some scars on the side, which had tattoos interweaved with them so they looked like some cool Celtic symbol.

Screw him.

My mouth watered, but I pressed my lips together.

I hated that he could affect me like this.

He deserved nothing from me, certainly no appreciation of his body.

But I couldn't tear my eyes away. He wasn't lean, not totally, but nor was he a bulky bodybuilder. He was solid. Perfect. His chest was hard like cement. His stomach muscles moved as he breathed. They were corded into a valley of dips and mountains.

There was no softness on him anywhere, and I was raking my gaze over every inch of him.

Jake was ripped.

Another tattoo wrapped around his entire right side, taking up the whole length. A scale with a sword in the middle. There was more scrawling over the sword, but I couldn't see the rest from how he was sitting.

My heart hiccupped because a tenderness came over me. He was the reason I was involved in all of this, but he looked vulnerable and soft. And tired.

Really, really tired.

I thought back over the days and wondered if Jake had slept at all.

A gun was on the table beside his phone, wallet, and keys. The coffee machine was brewing behind him, and there was some food opened on the counter. Eggs. Some bread. The toaster was pulled out. A container of butter.

He was making breakfast, sat down, and fell asleep?

More of my anger slid away. Maybe I wouldn't kill him.

I would only maim him. Permanently.

The toaster went off. Two slices of bread popped up.

Jake jerked awake.

His hand picked up his gun. At the same time, he was out of the chair, across the room, and had a hand to my throat as he pinned me to the wall to the side. All of that happened within a second, not even two. I gasped from how fast he moved.

He wasn't letting go.

"Jake," I said, cautious. "It's me."

His eyes weren't focused. He was still half-asleep.

I pressed a hand to his chest, spreading my fingers out so he could feel as much of my palm as possible. I wasn't sure what I was doing. I was going by instinct, but I said softly, "Jake. It's me. Sawyer."

His hand tightened before the sleep cleared from his eyes, leaving him looking haggard and rough.

I had another moment to relax just as his hand fell away to drop the gun to the seat behind him. His arms were around me, picking me up in the next moment.

"Jak—"

His mouth slammed over mine.

I was engulfed in flames.

Panting, a need that demanded to be filled was pounding between my legs, but fuck him right now. Not the literal way. I gasped, "Jake. Stop."

He gripped my hair and tugged my head back, lifting his eyes, glaring at me. "Don't," he growled, but it wasn't what he said that quieted me. It was the absolute *need* in his gaze. He was stripped down, all the way, so I was seeing the deepest darkest part of him. And that part of him demanded this from me.

I gulped.

Damn.

I could hear the walls falling down around me.

I was such a weak sauce, but getting that look from him made something in me have to respond. My heart pounded once before my last bit of resistance crumbled.

I just gave in.

He saw the surrender in my eyes and a raw groan ripped from deep in his chest as he arched over me. His hands cupped the side of my face, and his mouth lowered back to mine.

I wish I could've fought him more. Do a little maiming at least, but I folded. I was done for. This man. This touch from him. How gently and tenderly he was kissing me, and the world swept out from underneath me.

I was falling for this psychopath.

As his kiss grew more insistent, more demanding, his hands fell away from my face to slide down my ass. He cupped both cheeks, getting a good strong and sturdy hold of them. Then he lifted me, stepping between my legs.

It felt so good, all of it.

The sweep of his tongue inside of me, as he was tasting me, claiming me too.

A helpless shudder worked its way up my spine, going backward, and by the time it got to my neck, I'd ceased thinking all together. My arms clung to him as my legs wrapped around his waist.

He carried me to a bedroom, kicking the door shut, and he turned, pressing me against it. His hand went to my thigh, gripping me tightly.

His mouth fell to my throat, tasting me. His other hand went to my shirt, shoving it aside as he grasped my breast, palming it. His finger and thumb rubbed over my nipple, playing with it. He was almost callous in his touching. There wasn't a smoothness there, but that felt right.

I was writhing against him, just needing more. More touch. More of him.

I went to his jeans, unbuckling them. I yanked at the zipper at the same time his other hand dipped between my legs. My pajama shorts were useless. They were no barrier, and Jake easily moved them down, slipping like silk so I could part for him.

He found my clit, and I paused.

"Jake," I gasped again, my head falling back to the wall.

The pleasure was overwhelming.

This attraction had always been there, unbidden and unwanted. The circumstances rose up, demanding we were brought together again and again, and now this. It was an explosion needing to go off.

So let us both explode.

Let us pick up the pieces after, because *then* we would be able to think again. We would have coherent thoughts and we could choose what we wanted to do, how to do it. But this way, there were no thoughts. Just feelings of want and need. It was ferocious and brazen, and I was blind to anything except the feel of Jake between my legs.

He slid a finger between my folds.

A moan escaped me.

"You *ran.*" He lifted his head, his eyes furious, but with a bloodthirst in them too. His finger shoved inside of me.

A moan slipped past my lips.

"You ran from me." A second finger shoved inside. His thumb rubbed over my clit at the same time he pulled those fingers out, only to slide back inside. "You don't fucking run again. Not from me. You hear me? You don't run, *ever.*" He snarled, his fingers almost punishing now, and he bent forward, grazing his teeth over my throat.

Another shiver went through my whole body.

I could only hold on to Jake. The pleasure was accosting me. He felt so good. My legs tightened around him, and when his teeth teased on my skin, I squeezed him so tight that he gasped. I raised myself up.

His head lifted, a warning in his eyes.

I didn't give a fuck.

Closing my eyes, my head fell back, and I rolled my hips, riding his hand.

"You think I should let you come on my fingers?" As he asked, they twitched deep inside of me.

I snarled. "You don't take those fingers out of me."

It wasn't right how good that felt, that it was him who gave me this. Why couldn't it be someone else? Anyone else? But it wasn't. Just this asshole who plucked me out of my midlife identity crisis and yanked me into his world, where violence and death and ruthlessness reigned.

Fuck him for doing that, for changing everything in my world.

He stilled, just slightly.

I didn't, still riding his hand, as I added, almost taunting, "And then when I'm done, you're going to shove your dick inside of me and you're going to fuck me all over again, making me come again and again and again—" I was panting as I was now in a rolling and seamless movement. Jake caught me under my hip, his hand splayed out and urging me on, helping me. "Because you're going to fuck this need out of us."

A savage roar burst out of him as his hand went to my neck, snatching my chin.

I stopped talking, frozen for a second from the promise of violence in that sound and touch, but he only held me. A primal sound slowly rumbled from him. "You think you can tell me what to do?"

"Fuck yeah, I do."

I went back to moving over his hand, slowly to test his reaction, but when he only stabbed back inside of me, I began moving faster. A delicious pressure started pooling, rising.

I was nearing the edge.

I rasped back to Jake, "Tides have turned, asshole. When I give you an order—" I screamed as I was flung over the cliff. Pleasure pulsated inside of me, detonating everywhere, liquefying me.

The waves bombarded me as he eased me to the floor.

I dipped forward, my legs shaking and trembling, but he held me against the wall with his hips as he was making quick work between us. My underwear and shorts were whisked off. His jeans were shoved farther down, then I was picked up once more, and I only came back to the present, the last of my climax still lingering, when he lined up at my entrance.

I reached for his shoulder, my hand starting to sink in. I was going to tell him to wait because my god, that thing was *huge*.

He shoved inside of me, impaling me.

Oooh.

Full.

I was so full.

He groaned next to my ear, "You're so tight. Tight and wet. And mine. You're fucking mine, Sawyer." His hand slid down my stomach, sliding to my clit, and he began rubbing it as he started thrusting in me. "You don't give me orders. You *really* don't tell me that I'm going to fuck this need out of us because, baby—" He'd been holding the back of my hip, half of my ass, as he started his own rhythm, but I was clinging to him enough again. He didn't need to hold me in place, so that other hand caught my jaw again. His finger dipped inside of my mouth.

I didn't think about it. I automatically sucked long and hard on him, tasting the mix of both of us.

His eyelids shuttered, his eyes going so black, as a vein stuck out from his neck. He was slamming into me, that other hand never stopping on my clit. He finished, darkly, "We're just getting started, my little lunatic."

I moaned again, a new whine rising up my throat.

He yanked us from the wall, spinning, and we fell to the bed.

He caught himself so his weight didn't crush me, but he never pulled out of me, and once we were on the bed, he clambered up, curling over me. He began thrusting deep all over again.

This was insane. All of it. Ludicrous.

But I couldn't deny what was happening. This link between us was an invisible string, pulling us tighter when I tried fighting it. It only grew stronger, more taut, and we were going at it, both feral, but we were feeding that connection. We couldn't not. It had a hold on us and it wasn't letting go.

As Jake pounded into me, another release was building in me, pulling me back under until it snapped, making all of my nerve endings flood with ardent bliss.

Jake came not long after, surging inside of me. He held still as he swelled before releasing. My insides clamped down on him, milking his climax, which made him groan. Sweat poured down both of our bodies and there was so much wetness where we were connected, but I savored this moment.

There was nothing beautiful about what we just did. It was rough, harsh, and a little ugly.

An emotion fluttered inside me.

I wanted to do it again.

CHAPTER TWENTY-SEVEN

JAKE

She shoved me off and ran for the bathroom. The door slammed shut, the lock clicked.

Christ.

I rolled to my back and smoothed a hand over my chest. I was still breathing hard. Waiting until my heart rate slowed, I lay there, needing to get myself under control. What the fuck had that just been? It wasn't sex. That was for damn sure. It was more like a rutting. Like we were animals needing to breed, which fuck, fuck, fuck.

I had a day to grab our mark. One day. And we were here, fucking like animals. And even now, she was in that bathroom and my dick was stirring all over again.

I wanted another round. I wanted more than another round. I didn't want to stop.

This was a problem.

I cursed, sitting up, and ran a hand over my face. I'd barely slept in a week. I couldn't remember the last time I had an actual meal, and we had tonight to do this, but I looked down at my cock.

Hard.

Fuck's sake.

And . . . Was that crying I heard?

CHAPTER TWENTY-EIGHT

SAWYER

I needed to get away from him, just for a short reprieve, but as soon as the bathroom door closed, I lost it.

Tears slipped out, but those tears were from the last week. For the love of Aunt Clara, I'd earned a good cry session.

But it wasn't just the tears. It was more.

I couldn't. I just couldn't.

All those years with Beck. College. My twenties. Most of my thirties. It'd never been like that with Beck. *Ever.*

How stupid had I been?

My stomach was rioting. Pressing a hand against it, I slid down the wall until I was on the floor, and that's when the first laugh came out.

Oh. My. God.

I wanted to call a friend and cry and laugh it out with her. That would've been Manda, but he took her.

I'd not been processing the loss of that friendship, but right now, in the bathroom, after having fucking *explosive* sex—she was supposed to be here.

Another laugh gurgled up, and then I couldn't stop.

Jesus fucking Christ. Fucking Manda.

She was who I should've called, but I was also realizing that friendship had been stale too. For too long. We were friends because of why? Out of obligation? Habit? I couldn't remember the last time I needed to call her and only she could say something to make me feel better. I went to my mom. Clara and Bess. I went to them. They were my best friends. Not Manda.

Shit. When had that stopped?

A whole new set of layers was falling from my view. I was seeing the world differently, day by day.

I missed Manda, but also . . . I didn't at the same time.

She never liked martini nights either. She and Beck were perfect for each other. Holy shit.

How had I been so clueless about everything?

Why did I stay with him? Why, why, why?

Had I been brainwashed? Was that it? Or just . . . Had I just never been shown differently? I didn't know what made my heart soar. Now I only wanted to do things that made my heart soar, and fucking Jake was one of those things. Christ. He made everything in me soar. I was on a high right now. Fevered.

My most exciting date with Beck was glow-in-the-dark mini golf, and he wanted to go because he had a fetish about getting a blow job behind the Eiffel Tower.

I was trying not to go and fuck Jake right now because I needed to stay mad at him, chew his ass because he had me drugged to take me away from my family.

There was no comparison. I was fully fucking awake. Life—I wanted it badly. I wanted everything about it.

More laughter poured out.

My sides were hurting, and I gasped, holding on to them, but that made me laugh even harder. I wasn't a good laugher. I couldn't breathe, and somehow that made me cough, and then that could lead me to throwing up. Crying was similar, except if I cried too hard, I'd get clogged up and then I couldn't breathe either. My body didn't want me swinging either way too much.

"Sawyer?" Jake was on the other side of the door. "Are you crying?"

God. Just that, that question. Beck would've been annoyed if he needed to take time out to come and check on me.

Christ. He never had.

That stunned me, because he really never checked on me.

How was I *just* realizing *that*?

My family loved me. They rallied around me. It wasn't that I grew up thinking I wasn't worthy of love, but I'd stayed. That's what I grieved the most. That I stayed.

That I accepted something less for myself than I should've.

Never again. I was never settling again. I would only accept what made my heart race.

I couldn't answer Jake. I couldn't move either. I was wheezing so bad that my nose was starting to get clogged up.

The doorknob started to turn, but stopped. I'd locked it without thinking.

"Babe. Let me in."

I didn't move except to lie down, my arms wrapped tight around my sides.

All those years wasted.

Thud!

He pounded on the door. "Sawyer." His voice went low in a warning. "If you don't open this door, I will break it down."

Another peal of laughter streamed out of me.

Bang!

The door cracked off the hinges in the top corner.

I jumped at the violence. If that fell, I'd need to scoot back past the counter so it wouldn't fall on me, but before it could fall any farther, Jake reached around and hauled it up with another strong heave. It came completely off. He pulled it toward him, letting it fall in the bedroom. Taking its place in the doorway, his hands went to his side, fisting. There was a wildness in his eyes.

Then, all the hard lines on him relaxed. His eyes closed for a second. "You're laughing."

"I'm sorry—" I was trying to control myself, but a few hiccups came next.

He looked adorable now that he knew I was fine. His dark hair was tousled a bit on the top. He'd not shaven in a couple days, so he had a good scruff on his face, giving him an even edgier appeal which contrasted almost beautifully against the soft lines around his eyes and mouth. Looking all sleepy again, with that nicely muscled and smooth chest, and his tats. His one arm was a total sleeve of intricate lines.

He reached over to idly scratch at his chest.

It gave me a better view of the tat that took up his entire right side. The set of justice scales had a sword that ran down the middle of the tattoo and his side. A skull was at the top with blood dripping down from the handle. There were other details on it, words and more, but he was moving again.

He padded over to me barefoot. Bending down, his arms plucked me up from the floor. We went back to his bed, where he laid me down and climbed in behind me. He grabbed me again, turning and situating me so I was on his lap, half resting with my head against his chest.

His hand smoothed down my hair and he bent down, his lips grazing over my shoulder.

A warm tingle seared through me.

He asked, his lips grazing over my skin, "What were you laughing about?"

His arms shifted, pulling me closer against him, and he moved up, nuzzling my hair. All of that was giving me the flutters.

"About this actually." A sigh left me as I began tracing his tattoo on his arm.

"My tat?"

"No." I hid a grin, lifting my chin to meet his gaze. "This, whatever this is between you and me. What we just did . . ." How could I explain to him that one time with him blew an almost two-decade relationship out of the water? I needed to stop comparing, but I was on this whole awakening journey at the same time. I was healing while I was with him.

Fuck me. I never saw that coming when I hoped Jake would belt out show tunes on the subway.

He tensed underneath me.

"I was with Beck since college—"

A growl vibrated from his chest. "Not enjoying hearing his name."

My heart leaped, and I looked again at him.

His eyes were fixed on me in a very possessive way.

More flutters skipped through me, making my body vibrate underneath my skin. I said, slowly, "I was with my *ex*"—his eyes flashed in approval and I kept on, a small smile coming to my face—"for so long and now I'm feeling all sorts of stupidity for being with him. I wasn't living."

I wanted to live.

I wanted to live so bad.

"You want to live now?" His eyes grew soft. He brushed some hair back from my forehead, being so tender about it. "Fucking me made you think of your ex? I'm not sure how I feel about that."

I shook my head slightly, giving him another small grin. "No. It's like living inside a closet, thinking a flashlight hanging from the ceiling was sunshine. Then you came along. You opened the door. You walked me outside and you showed me the real sun. You gave me real sunshine. It's like that." I winced. "Don't get a big head."

He began to grin. "So you're saying that I am like the sun to you—"

I growled before getting serious again.

I wanted to tell him the rest, because I needed to face it. This link with him was the reason we were in this mess. It'd been there from the beginning.

"He didn't leave me because he'd been cheating on me. He left me because she was pregnant."

He went still, still holding me.

My head rested against his chest. "The sex with you woke me up. A month earlier, I'd be calling Manda and dishing out the details. She'd rush over. We'd have wine and gossip all about it. I would do that because that's what I thought I was supposed to do, but I wouldn't have liked it. It would've felt empty to me. It did feel empty with me. Me and her. For so long. She'd tell me what's going on with her life and though we wouldn't be solving world peace, we'd be feeling on top of the world. Or that's what I would feel that we should've been feeling. That's what a good friend does for you. I don't have that." This was the hard truth to admit. "I don't think I ever did."

His hand went to my thigh, giving it a soft squeeze. "I'm sorry about that."

"The last week's put a lot of things into perspective. I'm realizing how empty my life was regarding them. The real thing I gotta grieve is the time I gave them. Both of them. They didn't deserve it. And that . . . I think that'll take some time. That is, if we get out of this whole thing alive."

He tensed all over again underneath me. His hand slid to the inside of my thigh before he turned me around. I went with him until I was straddling him.

Back to business.

His eyes were shadowed, his face hard.

My chin rose, and I told him, "You fucked up."

His eyes narrowed. "I—"

"You shouldn't have taken me how you did. You drugged me."

He let out a ragged breath, some of the fight leaving him. "That was Ashton."

I leaned closer to him, seething. "I don't care who it was. I'm yours. That means it happened on your watch."

His eyes started glittering at me, a new intensity sweeping in there and taking hold.

"I'm going to get you back."

He tensed all over again.

I smirked down at him, resting my hands on his chest. His very strong and cement-like chest that was suddenly so still under my touch. "Payback is going to come. It won't be when you expect it, but it will come. Promise you. But until then"—I smiled, but my own breath hitched at seeing that intense look from him—"I told them a story about a family feud that was going on. My family. They bought it."

"They didn't buy it."

"Yes, they did."

"Your Aunt Clara tried calling 911."

I started to argue until his words registered. "Wait. What?"

"I had a cell jammer turned on so no calls could go through, but it was logged."

"Aren't you full of surprises, with your spy toys."

He snorted, his hands returning to my thighs, starting to mold over them. His eyes lidded, but never moved away from mine. "I worked in organized crime. We were current on a lot of fancy tech. Most departments aren't. Also, so you know, your cousin's husband—his family's connected."

I frowned. "I don't know what that means."

"They're loaded in a way that my family is also loaded."

"Oliver's family is Mafia?"

"They're connected. They have Mafia ties. He recognized the others with me."

I sat even farther back, regarding him. "What?" Replaying the conversation that happened in the study when we'd been eavesdropping on who Jake's friends were, I didn't remember any hint at that. "Are you sure?"

"He tried calling his father right away. That call was also logged."

Some dread trickled in. "What did your friends do after we left?"

"They stayed back to finish cleaning up, and after, they laid out a blunt version of what could happen to your family. Including Oliver."

I swallowed, hard. "What do you mean by that?" I'd gone to the lengths of concocting a whole story. "I wished they would've told me to save my breath."

"They were told the truth."

Ice speared me. "What? Ho-how did they . . . ? Everything?"

"Everything." His mouth went flat. "They're too far in not to know what is going on. There were three shooters. I killed three men in front of them. They needed to be told the ramifications of what would happen if they tried to contact any more family or the police."

I didn't want to hear how they took it.

Jake ran a hand down the side of my face, his whole face softening at whatever he saw from me. He told me, "Your family did not react very well."

My heart sank. There it was. "What exactly was said in the threat to my aunts? You don't know them. If they think I'm in danger, *no one* is going to stop them. They'll call in everyone in our family. I mean it. I've got a cousin in Alaska from my dad's side. They'll call him in. He's stationed there with the coast guard. I wouldn't be surprised if my mom's not already on a plane heading here because I was supposed to call her today, and that didn't happen." I shuddered at the thought of more of my family getting involved.

"She's not."

"You don't know that." I grabbed his pants in frustration, balling the waistline up. "You don't know my family. You can't threaten them to be quiet. They aren't made that way. My uncle says it's because we have some Irish in us, but we did a DNA thing and we don't have any Irish in us. Whatever our ethnicity, one of them down the line was a rebel. Threats don't quiet us. They just make us go a different route. They'll go to the police and if the police won't work, they'll go to the press. If that doesn't work, they'll go to a rival Mafia family. Are you getting my drift here? I had a story concocted."

"Three men broke into your cousin's brownstone and tried to kill you. I left three bodies behind. They weren't going to buy any story other than the truth."

"They bought it—"

His hands rested over mine. "Your aunt didn't try to call the cops one time. She tried fourteen times, and eight of those were when you were in the room with her. You weren't paying attention."

"What?" I'd been in the room?

"And as for the rest, it's been handled."

"You don't understand—"

"I do. They're handled. Everything's handled. This is not the first time for Walden and West."

"Who?"

He cursed under his breath. "The two guys with me. They took care of it. And before you can ask, your aunt was instructed to have a specific phone call with your mother. She was told you were fine, that everything was fine, but you needed some time to get a phone. Your aunts are going to play tourist and when you could get away to have a private call, you would."

I shook my head. "That won't work."

"It already did." He tugged on my hands to jerk me against him. "Your aunts are safe. They're in a secure place, but they are being watched over by some of Ashton's men."

More ice lined my insides. Did he realize how crazy this sounded? "They're being held *captive* by the Mafia? Is kidnapping the answer for everything in this world? Have you lost your mind?"

His mouth flattened. "They're going to be entertained the entire time. They're safe. They'll be fine. It'll be like they're staying with a family friend, except with guards around them for their protection. Your aunts are fine. By the time this is all done and you show up, they'll have barely noticed you were missing."

What family did he come from? "You are severely *so wrong*, and everything is going to blow up in our faces."

"It doesn't change anything because while they're being guarded, we got tonight to do something."

"What are you talking about?"

"We have to go to a meet. This person will open a communication channel to the person behind our hit."

"Why didn't you lead with that this whole time?" I scrambled off him, my heart racing as I looked around for my clothes.

That's when I noticed where we were.

There were feminine touches all over. Candles. Warm and pastel-colored blankets tossed over a couch, a chair, all to look trendy. Pink. There was a lot of pink. Doilies on the wall.

"Jake."

"Hmm?"

"Where are we—" I asked right as I saw a picture frame on the dresser in the corner. Moving toward it, hot burning jealousy rolled through me. Jake was in the picture with his arm around a woman, whose head was resting on his shoulder. Both were smiling wide for the camera. It'd been taken in a bar, and Jake's other hand was holding up a beer.

She was gorgeous. Sleek black hair. Dark brown eyes. Light brown skin. Her mouth was perfect, stretched into a serene smile.

And I remembered her from the police station.

I rounded on him. "Are you serious? You brought us to your *girlfriend's* place?"

CHAPTER TWENTY-NINE

SAWYER

I was still stewing in his truck three hours later as we were parked down in an alley.

He said Detective Laila Whatever-Her-Last-Name-Was wasn't his girlfriend, but I saw her. I saw how she looked at him, how she stood next to him, how she touched him.

Not his girlfriend, my ass. She wanted to be.

But he said she left for Europe on a family trip, and *we* needed a neutral place for us to hunker down for a bit. That's right, Miss Laila Who Wants My Man. We. As in me and Jake. We needed a neutral place to hide out in.

He added, "We're running out of options for places to stay. I can't go to my apartment or my brother's. Because of the meet we gotta take, I can't use any of Ashton or Trace's buildings either. Your aunts are a different matter, but you and me, we're on our own essentially."

I didn't understand any of what he was saying except that he hadn't closed up his brother's place. The one that died?

Also, when was the not-girlfriend coming back? Laila. That was her name.

What kind of name was Laila? According to Google, it had Arabic and Finnish roots, but I didn't like it. Lay-la. Lay-Me-Please-Jake-La.

Maybe my stewing wasn't altogether being productive. I needed to chill. She tried to help his cousin, but I didn't like her. I didn't need to like her to stay in her place.

"Okay. Let's go."

Jake pulled me out of my ruminating thoughts, leaning over me to open the dashboard compartment. He pulled out two handguns.

I hissed, "How many guns do you need?"

He smirked at me, shoving one in his side holster, which was covered by a plaid flannel. When he'd left his not-girlfriend's place, I'd been drooling. I couldn't help myself. Jeans that were snug and worn and fitted over him exactly perfectly, that hung low on his lean hips, with a T-shirt underneath his flannel. He looked good. Add in the tats I was aware of now, how he'd shaved a little but not enough so he still had a good scruff on his face, and the guns on him, I was a walking, throbbing mess.

Christ.

Jake was like my sex-nip. One look, one whiff, and I wanted to jump on his dick and scratch away, rubbing all over him.

His eyes grew lidded as he was watching me watch him. "We got one night. When this is done, I'm going to fuck you all over one of my places."

I almost flooded at that promise, sending a shiver up my spine. Then my eyes bugged out. "One of your places? How many do you have?"

He just continued to grin at me, staring for another moment before groaning, ripping his gaze away. "You need to follow my lead in there. Don't fight me on anything. I say do something, you do it." He hesitated. "This meet is . . . It's going to be a little tricky."

Tricky? That didn't sound good. I asked, "Do you want me to have a gun too?"

He'd started to reach for his door, but paused and raised an eyebrow. "You know how to shoot a gun?"

"I'm from a small town in Montana. Gun safety is like a rite of passage for some."

His head angled back a little, reassessing me. "Are you comfortable with a gun?"

I hesitated. "Not quite. I never learned for hunting. My dad wanted me to learn for safety reasons."

"What are you saying?"

I thrust out my hand. "I'm saying I don't have a permit to carry. I don't know the specific rules here, but I also don't care. Getting arrested for that is the least of our problems."

"Sawyer," he warned, growing impatient.

"Give me a fucking gun, Jake."

Surprise flared before a wariness edged it out as he pulled one of the guns off him and held it to me, handle first. He was studying me intently when I took it, checking the safety was on.

I stuffed it in my purse. "Ready."

He didn't move, taking me in before demanding, "Take it out."

I froze. "Why?"

"Take out the gun. I want to see how you handle it. Check the chamber. Check the safety."

I glared at him, but fine. Whatever. I huffed as I did what he said. The chamber was checked, falling down, and I put it back in place. The bullets were there. I took the safety off before turning it back on. I flipped the gun around a little, showing him that I knew a bit more than how to aim and pull the trigger.

"Good enough? You don't trust me?"

He palmed the back of my head and pulled me to him. He pressed a swift kiss to my forehead. "Trust has nothing to do with it. I just need to know you'll be safe with your own weapon."

We were so close. A few inches separated us. His eyes tracked over my face, falling to my mouth, staying, before his hold on me gentled. His hand slid down to my arm and around to my back, urging me even closer. "You don't pull that out unless I'm unconscious and you're about to be killed. Okay? If someone has you and I have the shot, I'll take the shot. I'm good at this shit. I was trained for this before I became a cop. I'm not going to let anything happen to you."

He was trained for this before he became a cop?

What did he mean by that? Trained for what?

New shivers seared me. Fear and arousal.

I eyed him back and finally said, "If you're not going to fuck me or kiss me, let's get this over with so you *can*."

He gave me a rakish grin before his hand grabbed the back of my neck. He yanked me to him again, his mouth fused with mine. A thrill went through me, sending my pulse speeding. He added pressure, his lips demanding me to open for him, and as I did, lust swept through me. The inferno was switched on once again.

The kiss was over too quickly.

He pulled back, giving me a last heated look before opening his door. "Let's go."

Whoa.

Okay.

Let me just steady my knees and then I'll be ready for a potential shoot-out.

CHAPTER THIRTY

SAWYER

The inside of the pub was busier than it looked from the outside. Long tables lined out from the walls, filled to the brim with people. There were some my age, but the majority were younger, in their twenties. I caught sight of the college shirts on multiple groups and learned that this was a college bar.

This meet was taking place here?

Jake wove through the crowd with an easy deftness. He was right. This sort of stuff was where he excelled. He looked comfortable and at ease, relaxed while my legs were still knocking into each other. The whole comment that he'd been trained for this still nagged at me. I was looking at him with new eyes, looking for that earlier training.

I didn't like the thought that he'd gone through some type of killer training before he was a cop. When was that? Who trained him?

I kept close to him, reaching out and holding on to the back of his flannel at one point.

The crowd was a lot. The press of people had to be violating eighteen different fire codes.

When he felt my touch, he reached back to my hip and yanked me close to him. I was almost hugging him from behind, but he only transferred my hand from his shirt to the side of his pants, tucking my hand into his jeans.

The backs of my fingers rubbed against his warm skin.

I grinned faintly. That felt nice.

It felt . . . It felt right. Like we should've been doing this all our life, and why were we only starting now?

As we kept going, one of his arms returned to the back of my hip, keeping me to him. When he switched directions, he pulled me with him, making it all happen so smoothly.

I had a brief wonder of how he was as a dancer. I bet he was good at it.

More than a few heads turned our way when we first got into the pub. Those eyes were on Jake. I saw the notice in some women's gazes, more than a few showing blatant interest, but the crush of the people took us away from them. However, as we kept moving through the first section of the building and into a back section, more women caught sight of Jake.

A few blinked widely as we passed in front of them.

A few reached out to touch him, but he paid them no attention.

I snuck a peek from the side. Jake was laser-focused ahead, scanning every face with a professional efficiency that he must've perfected as a cop.

Or that training, a small voice whispered in the back of my mind.

That was going to bother me for a while. I wanted to know what all happened to him before he joined the police force.

But that way he was surveying everyone, it was with hawklike precision.

When he caught sight of his target, everything changed. His body tensed. He was locked on. Laser focused.

He moved us to the edge of a group and pulled me in front of him, angling us so my back was to a group behind me. We rested our shoulders against the wall. He was in front of me, his chest to mine. His hand slid up my thigh, around my ass, and he slipped it under my shirt, holding me against him.

That felt nice too.

He dipped his head down to my neck, breathing me in as he was watching behind me.

I shivered, unable to hold back anymore.

Being with him, feeling how he maneuvered me, and now as we were standing like this as a cover to watch for someone, the blanket of lust was too heavy on me. He doused me in him. His touch. His heat. The aroma that was uniquely him. Pinewood and leather.

I pressed against him, sliding my arms around him. He felt so good. The rub against him.

I was breathing him in.

He pulled back enough to look down at me. His eyes found mine, but whatever he saw, he blinked before his hand went to the back of my head. He pressed me closer against him and said into my ear, "Go ahead. I'll keep watch."

A full haze fell over me.

His words only penetrated enough so I understood he was telling me not to hold back. I could get lost in him all I wanted.

I lifted my mouth, my lips found his for one long, drawn-out kiss before he pulled back, switching us so my back was completely against the wall. One of his hands stayed in my hair. The other was holding the wall behind me. He pinned me in place, but his mouth fell to my shoulder before he turned, watching to the side.

That was fine.

With the press of other people around us, the shadows in the pub, no one could see what we were doing unless they were immediately next to us, and those people weren't focused on us at all. Within that crowded pub, we had a relative moment of privacy.

I indulged.

As I lifted my leg up, Jake's hand fell to it, raising it over his hip, and I closed my eyes, enjoying feeling him hit between my legs. His hand tightened over my leg. He closed any last distance there was between us.

I rolled my hip, moving over him, rubbing against him, and it felt fucking amazing.

Sensation soared through me, spreading. It took me over.

I was grinding on him, and I kept going.

The pleasure was building. Rising.

I moved faster, harder. Rolling my hips and pressing down over his bulge. He was hitting me exactly where I needed him.

Jake breathed heavily into my ear, his mouth falling to taste my neck. His hand gripped higher on my leg, closer to my ass. He urged me to go faster.

I couldn't quite hit the right way, not fully, but with a slight growl in my ear, Jake moved and he got the exact right angle.

I bit down on my lip, trying to smother my groan.

"No," he said sharply. His lips moved over mine, not letting me bite down. He sucked where my teeth had just been, and I felt like I was going to combust because that felt so good too.

Too soon, the pressure exploded. The waves throbbed through me. I rested my forehead on his shoulder, riding them out.

His dick was still hard, the bulge pressed up and into me through our clothes, but he didn't make any move to relieve himself. He continued holding me until I drifted back to reality, raising my head back and blinking past the haze.

He was watching me, his eyes heated.

Oh . . .

We were in public and I—embarrassment flooded me until Jake's mouth was on mine again. Hard. Demanding. He clipped out, "Whatever you're fucking thinking, stop. That was the best goddamn thing to experience." He gave me another kiss before turning and looking to the side. He cursed. "Can you move? Are you steady?"

I nodded, still reeling from what I'd just done and where.

"Good," he grunted, giving me a firm kiss on the forehead. "We need to move."

He stepped back, easing me down until I was standing on my feet. When I was solid enough, I gave him a nod. He took my hand, threading our fingers together, and led the way through the pub once again.

We were moving to the back.

"Baby." A drunk guy grabbed my arm. His beer breath accosted me as he pressed up against me. "How about you and me take a trip to the bathr—" He choked off his words because in the next instant, Jake took his arm and shoved him back, going with him until he was slammed into the nearest wall. A bunch of people scattered, jumping out of the way. They weren't happy. Some were shaking off their drinks that had been spilled.

Jake didn't pay them attention. He was all in that guy's space, bending down, leaning over him. His shirt was pulled taut over his back, showing just how rigid he was.

I blinked, all of it happened so fast, but I took a step to the side and blanched.

The guy's eyes were wide, panicked. I saw why.

Jake had his gun out, pressed underneath the guy's jawline.

Whatever he was saying, it had an effect. The guy swallowed nervously, his eyes darting from Jake to where he could feel the gun. He began nodding, his eyes begging, until Jake shoved him back.

I moved in, instinct telling me to touch him.

As I did, saying his name, he turned for me.

I almost took a step back at seeing his expression. Jake was stone cold.

In that moment, he was every bit of the killer that I knew he could be.

I didn't think this was his police academy training. A premonition fell over me, like a shadow that coated me. I knew, somehow, maybe it was a gut feeling, but I just knew that this was the face of the training he mentioned from his childhood.

What had happened to him?

CHAPTER THIRTY-ONE

JAKE

When that guy touched Sawyer, blind rage took over. I would've killed him. *Mine.* He touched what was mine, and that was not going to stand. But, fuck, feeling the guy shaking in my hold, I remembered where we were.

I'd slipped back to the past. My uncle's voice was in my head. Different targets my uncle had me kill flashed in my mind, one after the other.

Fuck. I thought all that was buried deep in me.

"Jake." That was Sawyer. Her hands took one of mine, threading our fingers.

The touch helped me right myself.

The past was shoved back down, and I returned to the present.

I looked at Sawyer, and was rocked.

She was mine. Christ. She truly was.

I was looking at my future.

That thought sealed everything inside of me. I was no longer doing this for me. The first third of my life, I'd lived underneath my uncle's orders. The second third, I'd been existing for my brother. But now, the next third would be for her.

This woman had power over me.

She was in my blood.

When all of this was done, I was taking her away with me and I was going to fuck her in a thousand different positions, different ways, and I was going to make her cry out from pleasure until I couldn't move anymore. It was my own dark promise to myself. I was taking her whether she wanted to go or not.

She was mine. It was that simple.

My captive. My cross to bear. My woman. Mine. Just fucking mine.

But first, we needed to deal with this problem standing in the way.

My target was just ahead. Ashton had helped set this up and his other employee was with her. She was going to lead her to a particular spot for us, and I hurried my pace because we needed to be in the perfect position when it happened.

There were cameras in the pub. They'd be combed through later. Ashton promised that he'd hack in and wipe them, but I'd brought Sawyer with me as added cover. A couple together would make sense. Eyes would more easily skim over us.

I moved the last of the way, getting to the back door, and looked over. Ashton's employee was checking her phone. Lane's girl, Blake Green, had her back to us. She was in the exact place that Ashton said she would be.

We pushed out the door, stepping out into the alley.

The cold night air was a welcome relief. The crush of people inside with the loud music had been a heated pressure cooker. The quietness of the alley and street traffic was also a nice reprieve. Ashton's employee was supposed to be bringing Green out the same door, just minutes behind us. There was a blind spot in the street cameras. I was parked in that blind spot.

I held Sawyer's hand, clipping forward to where we'd parked, when the door opened behind us.

It was go time. I pulled Sawyer close to me. "I need you to do something for me. Don't ask me questions until later. Okay? I'll explain everything."

She was a little confused, which I understood. We were there to talk to the girl. That's what she thought.

"Can you do that for me?"

She jerked her head in a nod. "Yeah." Her eyes were clouded over, her eyebrows pinched together.

We were nearing my truck. I let go of Sawyer's hand and reached into my pocket. Unlocking my truck, I also pulled out the second needle Ashton had given me.

Sawyer's eyes fell to it, horror starting to come over her face.

I reached for the back door and paused, angling us so Sawyer's back was to the alley. I was in front of her as two girls were taking their time following us to the street that was just behind me.

I kissed Sawyer's neck, my eyes on the girls approaching. "Two girls are coming up to us. One is going to come with me in the truck, and I need you to fall in line, take her place, and keep walking with the other to the street."

She tensed. "What?"

My hand found her hip and I pulled her closer to me. "Go to the street, turn right, and walk to the subway. The other girl will go down to the train. You keep moving forward until you see my truck. Okay? Can you do that for me?"

"Jake." Her body shuddered against me. "I don't know—"

"I won't hurt the girl. I promise, but this is the *only* way to get the contract off us. I promise."

She angled her head to meet my eyes, studying me as she sucked her top lip down between her teeth. She was unsure. I got that, but I was finding out there were no limits to what I was willing to do to keep her safe.

Her, I thought as I was staring at Sawyer.

She was the reason my past was being unearthed inside of me, because I was willing to set the world on fire if it meant she would be unscathed by it. Skills I'd needed to be primal and ruthless were being set free, because I needed them for her.

But, fuck. I didn't give a damn. I would embrace whatever I needed for her. I'd do it all for her.

I cupped the back of her head and rested my forehead to hers, even if that meant becoming a man she'd be horrified by. I'd become that man if it meant she was alive, including doing what I was about to do.

We had seconds to go.

The two girls' voices began drifting over to us.

I whispered, fiercely, "Trust me."

It was the right thing to say. I saw the capitulation before she nodded, just slightly.

I breathed out in relief because it was time.

I let go of Sawyer, saying, "Now."

The two girls were almost to us. Green was closest to us, which was the plan. She looked my way, just for a second, before alarm came over her. Her mouth opened to scream, but I took two steps, wrapped my arm around her neck, my hand covering her mouth at the same time I brought the needle to her neck. She started to struggle, but I stuck her and pushed the drug into her that would put her into an immediate deep sleep.

It was over within seconds, her body slumping in my arms.

Sawyer and the other girl both froze, eyes wide and scared.

I caught Green's body in my arms and pulled off her sweatshirt.

The other girl took it from me, putting it on Sawyer with jerking movements.

When both still stayed behind, I barked out, "Go!"

"Wait a minute. Ashton didn't say—" his employee started to say.

She knew there'd be a switch-up. She knew to bring a sweatshirt for Green to wear, and to get Green to wear it when they left the bar with the hood up.

She stopped when I glared at her. "Your boss is in the Mafia. Don't be stupid." I moved to put Green in the back, laying her down. Closing the door, neither had moved. I said again, harshly, "Go! She'll be fine. Jesus Christ."

Ashton's employee jumped, but hurried ahead.

Sawyer lingered.

"Go." I gentled my tone, reaching over and lifting the hood up to cover Sawyer. "The girl's safe. I promise. Catch up with her. Keep your head down."

She blinked a few times before the hesitation cleared, hurrying after the girl.

The street cameras would be blurry at this time of night, but Lane would get a hold of it. He'd have his people comb through every second of it, but I knew what the cameras would see.

They would see a couple stepping into the blind spot.

They would show Green and her friend leaving the bar in the same alley.

They would show a truck leaving with the same couple. The alley would be too dark to get concise features so we would not be identified.

And lastly, the camera on the street would show Green with her friend leaving that alley.

The friend would go on the subway, and Green would walk ahead, into another blind spot where she would disappear.

The license plate on my truck would eventually be run through the system. It'd lead them to a real person with a real address, and it wouldn't be flagged as fake.

By the time anything would be figured out, Lane would get my correspondence.

He wanted to threaten *my* girl. He could learn how it felt.

CHAPTER THIRTY-TWO

SAWYER

"What. The. Fuck?" I was whisper-screaming like a freaking banshee as soon as I got in Jake's truck.

His face was grim, but he shot off into traffic the second my door was closed. "Keep it down. She's out for now."

"What the *fuck*, Jake?" I repeated, facing him. I was not okay with this. "You kidnapped another girl? Is this becoming your next career? This is getting out of hand."

He shot me a dark look, his mouth flat as he kept driving.

"Talk to me." A storm was twisting inside me, making me nauseous and furious and so many other emotions. They were all circling together in a funnel in my stomach. "You want me to keep my cool, you start telling me everything. And I mean *everything*. No more of this bullshit where I only know so much."

He shot me an incredulous look, merging onto the interstate. "We've been over this—"

"No, Jake. You told me *one time* while I was still the kidnapped person that part of your family is in the mob. One conversation isn't enough. It doesn't suffice. You start explaining and you start explaining *now* or I'm going to begin screaming my head off when we get wherever the fuck you're taking us, because, and I cannot believe I have to utter these words, kidnapping girls *is not okay*."

"I'll tell you everything when we get back."

I gritted my teeth. "Do you promise?"

"Yes." His grip tightened over the steering wheel.

"Promise me."

He jerked his gaze to mine again.

I raised an eyebrow.

"Fucking fine. I *promise*."

This whole thing didn't sit right with me, but then again, nothing had felt right since meeting Jake except touching Jake himself. Everything else was a hard pass.

Still.

I glanced over my shoulder at the girl. I'd hear him out. If I didn't like what I heard or if it made no sense to me, I was pulling the plug. I didn't care what that meant for me. Kidnapping and terrorizing an innocent girl was not something I could overcome. It was my line.

The girl was gorgeous. Young. I'd guess early twenties.

Even though her face was turned to the side and some of her hair covered her face, her beauty was striking. Smooth light brown skin. Lips that no makeup could enhance. They were perfect. Plump and pink. Long dark eyelashes. Her hair was smooth and straight, and sleek. She wasn't wearing makeup, but she didn't need it. Her natural beauty was stunning.

Her nail polish was chipped.

Her jeans looked worn, frayed on the edges and not in a trendy way.

Her sneakers were almost falling apart. One of the shoelaces had been woven through some sort of jewel trinket. I squinted, trying to get a better look, but couldn't in the dark. It looked like an infinity symbol?

Jake's phone started ringing. He pulled it out, checked the screen, and cursed. Handing it over, he asked, gruffly, "Can you answer and tell him we got her? I'll call him back once we're situated."

"Who is it?" The screen didn't give me the answer. *Walden Wiseass* scrolled over it.

Jake's lips thinned. "It's one of the Mafia guys."

The one he liked or the one he detested?

I accepted the call and repeated Jake's instructions.

The guy was quiet on his end before drawling, "I was calling to let him know we have a window that we hadn't counted on, but considering that's not dire information, I'd much rather talk to you. Sawyer Matsen, tell me about yourself. How does my boy compare to that ex-fiancé of yours?"

I stiffened, holding the phone tightly. "Wha—how do you know about that?"

"This is my city. Jake has become a friend of mine. Though he doesn't like admitting that. He still operates as if we're enemies half the time. You don't think I'm not going to do a thorough search on the woman he's trying to defy gravity for?"

My neck flushed, but one thing stood out. "What do you mean he's trying to defy gravity for me?"

Jake bit out a curse, yanking the phone from me. "Stop fucking with her. What do you want? I'm driving. Some of us don't have fancy drivers and bodyguards."

There was a smooth reply back, which had Jake relaxing, just a tiny bit.

I gave him the side-eye. They talked a bit more and by the end, the corner of Jake's mouth curved in a half grin.

Was Jake friends with that guy? One of the Mafia heads. He would've been the second one that arrived at Graham's house. The one who looked as if he had a sharp retort and a cruel smirk for everything, while enjoying that there were dead bodies upstairs.

I hunched down in my seat, a little uneasy about who was watching my family.

The call ended, but we didn't talk the rest of the drive.

Once we got back to Detective Booty-Call's place, Jake carried the girl up through the back door and into one of the bedrooms. I followed him, waiting in the doorway as he checked the windows and glanced around the room.

"What are you looking for?"

"Weapons." His answer was curt.

Jesus. Weapons.

Because again, she'd been kidnapped. By us.

I was going to hell.

Appeased, he motioned for me to follow him. He waited until I was comfortable on the couch before he started. He told me about Creighton Lane. About his demands to take over Jake's family business. He told me what he knew about Lane, his rise to power in Cincinnati, how untouchable he was, how he knew other law enforcement had tried to take him down and everything failed. Every single time.

"Is he more dangerous than your Mafia buddies?"

Jake hesitated before shrugging. "The West and Walden families run the city. There's other criminal organizations under them, gangs et cetera, but everyone pays Trace and Ashton a percentage. Don't be mistaken. Ashton's helping me, and there's a certain level of respect between us, but he does bad things. His best friend too. If people don't pay the percentage, they're dealt with. Sometimes that means they're killed. In some ways, since Trace and Ashton took over, they're more dangerous than their families were before. There's no boards either of them have to go through. It's them now, just those two making the decisions, and they're a well-oiled team. They've been best friends most of their life. Ashton's first business was cybersecurity. West was a Wall Street analyst. Ashton *enjoys* torturing. He *enjoys* being cruel. West can go ice cold. Those two are formidable, but Lane is a different beast himself. He inspires cultlike followers. It's how he took over Cincinnati by the time he was nineteen. He ran the politicians by the time he was twenty-two. I've never read a profile on Lane that felt right, so I don't totally know how to handle him. That said, he's got one weakness." He indicated the guest bedroom. "She's his one weakness. He's obsessed with her, and from the information I have on her, she doesn't want to be in this lifestyle."

A feeling of doom settled in my stomach. None of this was making that lessen.

He stopped to study the closed door, his forehead furrowing. "The reason we needed to take her tonight was because she's usually protected by a small army of men. She wasn't tonight. According to new information that Ashton got, the reason she didn't have Lane's small army following her is because he doesn't know she was here. That won't last. He will find her, except this way, he'll have to go through me."

I rocked back in my seat. That meant he was her stalker. I shot to my feet. "We are not going to hand her over."

Jake went back to pacing. "I need to think."

"No, Jake! No. He's her stalker. She was here hiding from him. You can't do that. *We* can't do that."

Jake folded his head down, his hands on his hips, and he shook his head slowly from side to side. "This is the only way I can get to him."

"That you know of," I retorted.

He spun to me, his face tight. Furious. "That I *know. I* know. I was an organized crime detective. I know how this world works from both ends."

"This is wrong—"

He thundered, "I don't give a fuck."

My body wavered backward. His anger was palpable.

He choked out, "If it means you're safe? If it means you're alive? I don't give a fuck. If it means you or her?" His eyes grew so fierce. "It's *you*, Sawyer."

CHAPTER THIRTY-THREE

SAWYER

I shuddered.

So many emotions and thoughts were spinning inside of me, but I had to know about the girl because that might be his choice. It wasn't mine. I had some responsibility for that girl and she was not going to be harmed because of us. She was innocent. I wasn't. If it came down to a question of keeping her safe or me, my choice would be her.

"What are you planning to do with her?"

Some of the harshness from him faded. He drew in a sharp breath before answering, cupping the back of my head, his fingers threading through my hair. "When I'm ready, I'll reach out to Lane."

I tipped my chin up.

He touched underneath it, running a thumb over the corner of my mouth, lingering over my cheek, cupping the side of my face in his palm. His eyes held mine.

"She needs to be kept safe."

He was reading something in my eyes I didn't want him to know, something I didn't want anyone to know, but whatever he saw, he didn't comment on it. He only nodded before stepping away, his arms falling to his sides. "She'll be kept safe."

Good. Relief filled my chest. Good.

I glanced at the door behind him. "I should check on her."

He caught my arm, stopping me. "This *is* the only way for us to get to him."

I frowned, pulling away from him, and moved to the door.

Right as I touched the doorknob, his words stopped me again. "Sawyer."

I looked over my shoulder.

His gaze was soft, but there was a lethal promise lurking in them just under the surface. The memories of how easily and quickly he'd killed five men flashed in my mind. How easy it had been for him to kidnap her, how smooth the operation was handled. How he'd threatened that drunk guy who grabbed me. How he held a gun as if it were the most natural thing in the world to him.

What happened to him in his childhood?

I needed to acknowledge another truth about Jake to myself, one I couldn't forget. Jake Worthing might not be a Mafia head boss and he might not want to be a Mafia head boss, but he was every bit as dangerous as they were.

He might be worse.

He added, "You or her, it's you. You or me, it's you. You or your aunts, it's you. Your cousin or you, it's you. *Anyone* or you, it's you. I don't care who the other choice is. It's always going to be you."

Why did those words feel like a looming warning?

And why did that make me feel things that I never thought I'd feel in my life?

I was falling in love with him. I just didn't know what to do with that now.

I turned the doorknob, took a step inside, and it took a beat before I cleared my mind of my muddled thoughts and registered the empty bed that I was seeing.

I gasped. "She's gone!"

Jake tore into the room but stopped as soon as he saw the window open. He looked down, cursed, and sprinted out the door. His gun was out and in his hand. He held it pointing down at his side, but it molded to him like another appendage. It was a part of him.

It was his skin.

He yelled over his shoulder, "Stay here. Lock the door."

"Where are you going?" My heart was in my throat.

"Lock the door, Sawyer," he commanded again.

The door shut and I flicked the lock, but he wasn't gone long. Ten minutes later, I jumped as someone pounded on the door.

"It's me."

Jake.

"That was fast." I fumbled for the lock, throwing open the door.

He came in, carrying the girl. She was struggling, her feet kicking in the air, and he grunted as he shifted his weight so she was higher in the air.

"Let me go!" she screamed.

"Lock the door," he said, gruffly, as he dumped her on the couch.

"You assfuck pubic hair on a grandpa's balls." She tried crawling away, but Jake pinned her down.

She screamed again, twisting around, and she went to scratch his face.

He hissed, jerking his head out of the way, and grabbed her wrist. "Stop it," he growled. She tried with the other and he caught that one too. As he yanked both arms back, her scream went up a whole octave and I gritted my teeth, my eardrums bleeding. He let go of her arms enough that he could grab them from a different angle.

"Sawyer, my cuffs."

"Huh?"

She was still bucking, and he grunted, keeping her in place. He indicated his wallet. "On the table, over there. There's a pair in a drawer."

Cuffs? At his *girlfriend's* house? I sneered, forgetting what was happening in front of me for a whole thirty seconds because I was forgetting his ex was also a cop. My mind went to a dirtier reason those cuffs were here.

Now I was nauseous and rageful.

"Fuck you both," the girl spat out. "You are so fucked. You *really* messed up. You have no clue—"

That brought me back to the present. I grimaced as I picked up the handcuffs using only my pinkie and walked them over.

Jake took them, an exasperated expression on his face. "Are you kidding me?"

The girl was still yelling threats, but I tuned her out. "I don't know where those have been."

"I put them there last night. Jesus Christ." He snapped them in place on her wrists. She stopped bucking and began muttering variations of the same threat over and over under her breath, her face pressed into the couch cushions.

We were going to die.

My spine was going to be yanked out through the skin.

My eyeballs would be fed to Jake and his dick would be cut off and forced down my throat. After the pubic hair comment, these were less colorful, but once the cuffs were in place, she stopped physically fighting.

Jake stood up and hauled her up. Her face had lines from the cushions and some of her hair fell over her eyes, but she blew out an angry puff of air. If looks could kill, we'd be in hell by now. "You guys have no clue—"

"Actually, we do." Jake waited until she was steady on her feet. Once she was, he marched her back into the bedroom, letting her sit on the edge of the bed as he went back to checking the room once more. Déjà vu. The window was relocked, and the rest of the room passed his search. Joining me at the door, he leaned against the wall, his arms crossed over his chest.

She continued to scowl as she moved around to face us. "What do you want?"

I searched her, but there was no fear. There should've been fear. "You're not scared of him."

Her eyes flickered. "What?"

"I thought—"

Jake moved, his arm grazed against mine.

I shut up and moved back. "Never mind."

Her eyebrows drew together. "You both will be killed for taking me. Whenever you're done with whatever freaky shit you're into, no matter what you do to me, he will kill you."

I glanced Jake's way. His eyes were intent on her.

"*He* will hunt you down like you're prey, and he will relish it. After that, he'll torture you for weeks. Months, maybe." She met Jake's gaze and motioned to me with her chin. The ends of her mouth curved down. "He'll let his men rape her in front of you. When she's begging to be put out of her misery, you don't want to know how he'll prolong her torture. You, he'll remove every piece of your body one by one. He'll take your organs out while you're breathing and he'll keep you alive until the very last one. He'll dig your heart out with a toothpick, and he'll do it fucking humming to some sick song that's only in his head." She slumped down on the bed. "You dug your graves by doing this."

Jake didn't blink. "You done?"

Her eyebrows pinched together. "I'm not lying. You don't even know who I'm talking—"

"Creighton Lane."

His words stopped her and her head lifted again. "You know about him?"

"Yeah," Jake taunted, softly. "He's the *reason* we took you."

A shadow crossed over her face for a second. "What's wrong with you people? I'm telling you what's going to happen. Your best shot, if you want to make it out of this alive, is to let me go. I'll give you the time it takes me to get to my apartment before I call him. You'll have that time for a head start out of here."

A cruel smirk tugged at the corner of his mouth. "Thank you."

I frowned.

So did she. "Huh?"

Jake stalked toward her. "You just told me how to contact him."

She shrank down an inch, her frown deepening. "He has men on me all the time. There's no getting away from him."

"He has men on you *usually*. Tonight he didn't."

She flinched.

Jake added, "And he didn't because he doesn't know you're here. You're hiding from him."

She shut down, a wall coming down over her.

Jake sighed. "Well, if you're done talking, I'm off to grab your second phone."

Her eyes shot to his again.

His smirk returned. Ruthless. "You fucked up. The phone he tracks, the phone you use to contact him, is at your place. You just told me." His head cocked to the side. "Don't worry. I'll make sure to erase any tracking apps he has on it before using it. Now scoot back so I can put the handcuffs around the bedpost."

He leaned behind her, but she sprang. A feral edge on her face. The handcuffs dropped to the bed as she was suddenly free of them. She'd been using the time while they were talking to get herself out of them. She swiped Jake's gun all at the same time. A millisecond later, she threw herself backward and rolled to her feet, all in one smooth motion. The gun was trained on Jake.

My heart slowed.

No.

I wouldn't let this happen.

Her eyes turned off. A coldness seeped over her.

There'd be no threats. I knew it in my gut. This girl was going to kill him. She aimed for his chest, but her eyes flickered. Just once before they hardened.

She raised her hands.

The gun barrel was a few feet from his head. She took the safety off right before she said, "Sorr—"

No! I lunged for her.

"*Sawyer*, no—" Jake shouted.

Too late.

I tackled her from the side.

The gun went off.

CHAPTER THIRTY-FOUR

JAKE

I was starting to think Sawyer was going to get me killed, just by being in my life.

The bullet went wide, but I lost years of my life watching her throw herself at Green. She might as well have stepped in front of the bullet. She had no fighting skill, whereas it was easy to see that the other girl did. If I hadn't known from the file I read, I would've learned the second I caught her and dragged her back to the apartment that she knew how to fight. She knew street fighting, which meant that if it came to her versus Sawyer, my girl would've been the one with the bullet in the brain.

A shudder went through me.

That would *never* happen.

After swiping the gun back and fighting with Green all over again, I ordered Sawyer to walk.

She hesitated.

I growled, "Not a suggestion. Walk. Chill the fuck out."

A muffled scream ripped from her closed mouth, and she gave me a nasty look, but she spun on her heels and stalked off.

When Green tried swiping my feet out from under me, I perched her on my hip and threw her down on the bed. She was fighting against me again, but I knew some of her tricks this time. The first time, she'd crawled down an entire story until I caught up to her. This time, she'd picked the handcuffs, and I had to wonder how long she'd been waiting to make her move.

She was tough. I gave her that.

"Your woman's got a screw loose," she grumbled after I finished tying her down.

I huffed. "Don't I know it."

I stepped back from the bed. I'd taken zip ties to her wrists, stretching them to each side of the bed. And judging from her past escape attempts, I tied both of her ankles down, her legs spread out as well. She couldn't do a thing to get away now, not unless she could dislocate her shoulder and somehow get an arm free, but even that might not help her.

"What?" I asked before affirming to myself she wouldn't be able to get free.

"Your woman. She nuts?" A grudging look of respect was in her gaze, along with frustration and, if I wasn't mistaken, some desperation too.

"No." I chuckled. "She's solid except if she lets herself slip away into a delusion, but who wouldn't want a Broadway play to start performing on the metro?"

Green's head twisted around. "Say what?"

I laughed again before getting back to business, dropping the amused tone. "Listen. I know who you are. I know who Lane is. You did a good job trying to get underneath our skin, but I knew what you were doing. Sawyer didn't." All civilities were dropped. I drew my gun. I was all the way cold now, and letting her see it. I said, a very real warning, "You will walk free from here. We don't have plans to kill you, but that will change the *second* you might get an idea to turn that gun on Sawyer.

She saw the same look in your eyes that I did. You were going to shoot me. You would've turned the gun on her right after."

I kept the safety on, but put the barrel to her forehead.

It was a different feeling when a gun touched you.

A cold feeling. Slight. Almost like it was nothing, except the knowledge of what it could do.

A chill worked its way through Green before she suppressed it, swallowing tightly.

I leaned closer, meaning every fucking word I said. "You *ever* point a gun at Sawyer, I will end you." She was weighing my words, seeing into me. She saw I meant it, no matter the monster that was obsessed with her.

She slunk down in the bed. "You look just like him," she whispered, more to herself than me.

I frowned before putting my gun away. "Who?"

She blinked a couple times, realizing she'd said those words aloud. "Creighton. There's a look in his eyes sometimes. I've never seen it on anyone else before." She swallowed again, her throat moving rapidly, and she let out a calming breath before she was more composed. She jerked her chin up to me. "You had that same look in your eyes."

I straightened up, my shoulders rolling back and relaxing. I could work with that. "Get comfortable. Sleep if you can. I've got things to attend to before I call my cousin."

I shut the door, but not before I heard a gasp. "Wait. Your *what*?"

CHAPTER THIRTY-FIVE

SAWYER

I was zoned out in the shower when a warm hand slid from my back to my front, and I was hauled against a very hard chest. Jake breathed out next to my ear, a low baritone that buzzed over my skin, "You think you're going to put yourself in danger for me? If someone has a gun on me, you don't throw yourself at them."

Anger was vibrating out of him, and god, I closed my eyes, giving in. He was *pissed*.

I was exhausted from all the tension, the drama, the ups and downs, the uncertainties, and he was holding me to him, and I just gave in. Every bone in me melted.

I responded, breathless, "So you can do it, but I can't?" I turned in his arms, put my arms around his shoulders, and I jumped.

Surprise flashed in his eyes, but he responded quickly. He caught me, and moved me against the wall, resting both of us there a moment. The water sliced down over us, but it was just us in that shower, that room, the building, the city. Everything else faded away. It was only us, and a shiver went through me at feeling myself in his arms, feeling him holding me. He'd put me in danger, but he yanked me right out. He'd killed for me.

I lifted my head, letting it rest against the shower tiles to look at him.

He held my gaze.

"You've kidnapped me twice."

He winced.

I touched his chin, my hand cupping his jawline. "Just so you know, this . . ." I touched his chest, then mine. "This goes both ways."

His eyes began sparking, almost glittering.

I squeezed my legs around him. His hands slid to my ass, and one of his fingers grazed down my center. Another shiver wound its way through me. This one was delicious. It coated pleasure in its trail.

"What goes both ways, hmmm?" He began nuzzling into my neck, peppering soft kisses under my jawline and throat.

I closed my eyes, giving in to the sensations. "Yeah. Cause that's the kind of girl I am. I'm not the kind that sits on the sidelines and whines or waits. I see an opening to help, I'm throwing myself in."

His finger moved between my legs, his thumb pressing over my clit.

I trembled, my limbs starting to lose the ability to hold on to him.

His mouth clamped down on my throat.

I gasped, but he didn't bite down. He just used his lips to mark me. Hard. His tongue swirled over his touch, before he growled, lifting his head. His finger slid inside of me as he spoke. "You've wound this spell over me, tying your life to mine, so, babe, if you get in the way between me and a bullet with my name on it, you stay back. You hear me?"

I was hearing him. A cocky little smirk tugged at my mouth because the question he should've been asking was if I would do what he said.

His eyes flashed, seeing my smirk. His other hand moved up, wrapping around my throat. "Oh. You think you're funny, hmmm?"

So slowly, he applied pressure, pinning me in place, as he switched between my legs, and as his finger slid out, his cock thrust in.

I was almost purring. That felt so good.

His hand tightened, his finger moving so it was over my carotid. He was feeling the effect he was having as he began to fuck me. He felt how fast he could make my heartbeat race. He could feel when he began going harder, when he became rougher, how that was like putting a firework to my blood. It made me lose my shit for a second. I was mewling and writhing against him, needing more and more and more.

He was completely keeping me in place by that hand to my throat, but I could still breathe. It was a fucking possessive hold, and knowing he would kill for me made all of my organs and bones liquefy. He had that power over me. One touch, one look, and this need for him pumped so deep inside of me that it was carnal. He could strip me raw, and I'd just shiver, desperate for more.

He thrust up, jarring me against the tiles. His other hand wrapped around my hip, using that touch to anchor me so he could pound up into me at a deeper angle.

I groaned. "That's so good."

His hand squeezed before loosening. He dipped his mouth to my lips, grazing them. "You like when I fuck you?"

I sank my fingers into his shoulders.

"Yeah." His mouth closed over mine, his tongue sliding inside. His hips were hitting against mine. Hard. He ripped his mouth back, his voice guttural. "You like when I fuck you."

I squeezed him with my legs, rolling my hips with his.

We were both breathing hard. He curved over me, his forehead almost resting on my shoulder as he looked down to where we were coming together. His hand moved over, closer, his fingers splayed out. "Look at us, Sawyer. Look at how hot this is." He moaned, moving faster inside of me. His breath caught, but he wasn't looking away from us.

Me, I couldn't tear my eyes away from him.

When he looked up to me, there was a wildness in his eyes, making them unfocused, and then they flashed before he stopped all the sudden moving in me. I reached for him, pulling him back to me. "Don't stop."

He blinked away that haze, focusing, and a lazy grin tugged at his mouth. His hand inched further down, finding my clit again, and he began rubbing it. As he did, he started moving in rhythm, with slow and purposeful strokes.

Fuck. Jesus.

It was building, waiting.

Rising.

He bucked up against me harder, jostling against the wall. His eyes were heated, watching me as he was going to make me come apart under his touch. "Jake," I groaned, raking my nails down his chest.

"Are you going to put yourself between me and a gun next time?"

He paused in his ministrations.

Oh. Oh! I saw what he was doing. I moved my hips harder over him, working us all by myself.

He growled, his hand dropping from my throat to my other hip, and he tried to hold me in place.

I moved under his hands.

"Sawyer," he snarled, but his eyes glazed over. He bit back another moan.

"What?" I gasped, going harder, raising my entire bottom half of my body so I was fucking him instead.

His eyes fluttered because I knew how good it was feeling. It was going to send me soaring in a minute.

Another growl erupted from him, and he pulled out of me.

"What—" I yelped, but he turned me again, my front was pressed against the wall, and he kicked my legs apart, making me almost vulnerable to him. But I felt him press against my opening, and he slid inside, one of his arms wrapped around my front, hugging me to him. As he began thrusting up, power rippling from him, he began tasting my throat, over his mark, and he was deepening it. His other hand splayed out again over my stomach, sliding down, and he began rubbing me.

I wasn't going to be able to hold out. My body was already shaking from the onslaught of sensations.

"Jake," I panted, my head resting against his shoulder.

"Don't do that again for me, babe. I couldn't handle it if you got hurt."

I was never going to agree to that, and when he slowed in his thrusts, he could sense the resistance in me. "Fuck," he cursed, but then he rested his forehead under my shoulder blades. His hands moved to hold me on both sides of my hips, and he thundered into me.

My release crashed inside of me, exploding, and I screamed from the power of it. It ripped me in half, making even my toes curl. My entire body lifted up from its ferocity. Then, as I was a shaking mess, all the strength in me gave out from my climax. The aftershocks continued to wash over me in waves. Jake gave in himself, fucking me fast and hard, holding me in place for himself.

I squeezed him, and he erupted inside of me. A roar came from him. He lifted me in place, pressing both of us against the wall, and he kept moving in me, drawing out the last of both of our releases.

I was out of breath, and my mind was scrambled, but that was some of the best sex I would ever have in my life.

I wanted to do it again.

Jake slowly eased out of me and my knees buckled. I slid down the shower wall, but his arm held me in place, still wrapped around my waist. He picked me up, carrying me to the bed.

"Jake, the bed. I'll soak it."

"I don't care." He laid me down but disappeared, going back into the bathroom and returning with some towels. Spreading them out on the mattress, he moved me over them, joining me. As soon as he did, he tugged me into his arms.

His head lifted, nuzzling into my neck before he breathed me in. "You smell like cupcakes."

I grinned against his chest, loving *this*. "That must be my natural scent because your girlfriend's shampoo was some tea-smelling stuff."

His arms tightened around me. "She's not my girlfriend."

I propped my chin on his chest, stretching languidly over him. "Then what is she to you?"

"Laila was a hookup that I kept going back to because she was convenient." He tilted my chin up. "She's the past." A different expression switched over his face, tightening in regret. "But you do need to know that I am divorced."

I tensed. He'd been *married*?

He frowned, feeling that. "What's going on in your head?"

I shook my head. "You were married?" I hesitated, then saw where my nails had cut into him. I smoothed a hand over them. They were my mark, just as he had marked me. A satisfied feeling of possessiveness rose in me. *Good.* I liked seeing my mark on him.

He ran his thumb over his mark on me as well, but he was frowning, and I knew his mind had slipped away to what he needed to tell me.

"I—"

His eyes fell to mine, growing clear again. "What?"

"I found a picture." I bit down on my bottom lip. What if I shouldn't bring that up? What if I was opening a door to a vault that should've been left locked up? But he told me that he was divorced . . .

"Stop that." He touched my lip, making me release my lip. "I told you. If someone bites you, it's me. It's only me." He leaned down, his mouth fusing with mine.

I breathed him in, and breathed in the kiss. If we could be like this forever? I wanted that. Except not with the kidnapped girl. Let's work toward not kidnapping people.

He nipped me one last time before lifting his head. "You found a picture?"

My heart speared, but I just asked him. "Do you have kids?"

His eyes held mine a moment before he nodded. "I have a boy."

"You have a son?" He was his son. I'd been right. My mouth went soft, remembering the picture I found. "How old?"

"He's seventeen."

I pushed up. "How old were you when you had him?"

"We were eighteen. Young."

I did the math in my head, and I wasn't a math person. My eyes got big, so big. "You're thirty-five?"

His eyes narrowed. "Yeah . . ."

I was a cougar. A total cougar. "I'm older than you."

I'd never been the older woman.

I was now the older woman.

I didn't know how I felt about this. "I'm like your sugar mama."

A grin tugged at the corner of his mouth. "You're a year older than me. And this is not a sugar-mama situation."

Okay. We were back to being serious. I told my inner cougar to take a nap. Scooting to his side, I moved so I was facing him, my legs crossed in front of me. It gave me some breathing room, but Jake sat up and pulled me onto his lap, straddling him. His back was against the headboard, and his hands fell to my thighs, tracing up and down.

He didn't just have a son. I noted, "You have a young adult."

"Tab and I were high school sweethearts. We tried. Or I tried. We got married at the courthouse, but it was over almost before it ever got started. Her family was pissed about the marriage. They didn't approve of my family."

"They knew about your family's business?"

His mouth tugged up in a half-hearted grin. With the lines under his eyes and the shadows in them, the half grin looked sad. "Everyone did where we lived. My family likes to operate out of Maine because it's easy to be remote up there. They don't use the usual protection tax, stuff like that. The locals are left alone and in return they leave us alone. My family specializes in transportation and storage. Some of our warehouses have things a lot of governments would love to get their hands on, but it's kept under wraps."

"What sort of things?" I traced my hands down his chest, lingering on his stomach. His muscles shifted under my touch, but he didn't seem to notice. He was frowning at my shoulder, lost in thought.

"Things I don't want to tell you. Things used in wars. Other things." The shadows doubled in his gaze.

My stomach dipped.

He smoothed a hand back up the side of my thigh, his fingers sinking into my skin. "Tab was . . ." He hesitated, a shadow flitting over his face. "Tab was my escape. I was still—Jesus. I have to tell you all of it to make you understand."

The air grew thick. Tense.

I quieted, knowing this was important. I reached for his hand.

He didn't look at me, instead focusing on our hands. "First time I killed someone, I was twelve."

Pain sliced through me.

He continued, his voice hoarse, "My dad found out when I was fourteen, and he didn't agree with the direction my uncles wanted me to go with the business."

"The Mafia business?"

His eyes lifted, haunted. "I was being trained to be their personal assassin. Not just their assassin, but one that they could sell my services for others."

My heart shattered.

"When my dad found out, he left the family business." He was so rigid. "I didn't, though."

"What? How?"

"With my family leaving the business, they were pissed. They exiled them, effectively cutting them off from everything. I could see it was hurting my mom not to be able to talk to my other aunts. Some of them were close. So I went to my uncle and struck a deal. I'd continue my services if they'd ease up on some of the restrictions."

"Your dad didn't know?"

"No. It got better, a little bit. But I needed a cover for why I was leaving the house all the time. Tab and I started dating early in high school. She didn't know what was going on. She just knew I did something for my family off the books and thought it was cool. We *were* dating, but I mostly used her as a cover in the beginning. After a bit, it grew more real. She became my escape in a lot of ways. I hated lying to my parents. I hated doing what my uncles were making me do, but my mom was happy. Then . . . Tab got pregnant and I did what I had to do."

"What happened?"

"Tab's dad had political ambitions. He was a judge back then. He's also a piece of shit as a husband, father, and person. He found out and went crazy. He forced her to divorce me after EJ was born."

"Did you fight it? Did you want the marriage?"

His eyes lifted to mine, a stark expression in them. "No." He sighed again. "I didn't want to be married, to be honest. We'd been together for three years in high school."

"Your family was against the marriage too?"

He nodded, his gaze falling back to my chest, slowly descending. "My parents were okay with it. They wanted to support me, do what they could, but Tab's father went to my uncles and promised to use all his resources to go after the family if they didn't make me go through with the divorce. They . . . forced my hand. Said they would tell my parents what I'd been doing for them. I . . . I think my uncles were picking their battles, and I guess I did too. I didn't love her enough to go against my family, or hers. When Tab realized I wasn't going to fight it, she took off to California. Took EJ with her."

"She took your son from you? Did you follow her?"

His hand ran to the back of my thigh, pulling me tighter against him. "At first, yeah. I moved into a place down the block and got a job. My uncles left me alone, and things were okay. I enjoyed having the freedom, but then my parents were in a car accident."

"Jake," I murmured, my palm against his chest again.

"They didn't make it, and there was Justin. He was still a teenager. My uncles offered to take him in, but fuck if I was going to let them brainwash him to be like them. I knew what they would do to him, so I went back to raise him. Tab refused to come with me. That was when her father asked for a meeting. He was powerful by then, and he threatened me. Said he could make my family's life hell if I didn't agree to leave Tab and my son alone. I didn't believe him, told him to fuck off. Nothing and no one was going to come between my son and me, you know? I was young and pissed. My parents *just* died. I'd already divorced her, but there was no way I was going to give up being a part of my son's life. I didn't give a fuck what he said. The family didn't rally around us after my parents' death. They died while they were exiled so the family didn't see it any other way. Even in death, they were still exiled.

"My mental state wasn't too stable, I guess you could say. I didn't care whatever Tab's dad had on my family, until he showed me a file. At first I thought he knew about what *I'd* done for them, but it was a lot of circumstantial evidence on my uncles. Nothing that they couldn't have fought against themselves, but then he pulled out a photo of a young girl."

I waited for him to keep going. He didn't, too lost in the past.

"Who was the girl?"

His gaze jerked up to me, the same haunted expression floated in and took hold. "My dad had an affair. He'd been financially supporting the woman and the little girl. My dad's daughter. Tab's father had everything. Who the mother was. Where they lived. The money trail."

"You have a sister?"

His eyes darkened. "I took over the payments. The mother doesn't know my dad is dead. She just knows the money shows up in her account every month and she seems okay with it."

"That's why you stayed away from your son? Tabitha's dad blackmailed you?"

"No. There's more." He pulled me further against him, both of his hands gripping behind me, beginning to roll me over him. Back and forth. "Tab was there. I didn't know that. She'd left EJ in California with her aunt, and came because she knew her dad was going to make this play. I told her dad to go to hell, but when he was threatening to expose my sister, Justin showed up." He stopped, swallowing thickly.

Those shadows seemed to flit across his face. He was tormented. One of his hands shook on my hip before clamping down once more. "Justin was not in a good mindset either. He knew about the mob business, but Justin, he—he wasn't like me or the rest. He was good. He was always good. Popular. Athletic. He was the definition of a golden boy, but he came to the house and overheard the last part. He lost it when he heard Tabitha's dad threaten to expose our sister to the rest of the family. We would've been fine with her. We would've loved her. I do love her, but exposing her would've put her on our uncles' radar. Justin knew what would happen if that occurred. They would've forced her and her mother into our family. Girls in the Mafia are sometimes married off for an alliance. My uncles back then liked to still do that. Her life would've been ruined. Justin, he—" He stopped again, his chest rising sharply. "Justin killed him."

"What?" I froze.

"Tab was there, saw the whole thing."

I was starting to put the pieces together with a sinking feeling. "Tab's father didn't blackmail you to stay away from your son because—"

His eyes held mine, so tortured, so lost. "Tab did. She threatened to expose our sister and Justin."

"It was her dad. Wasn't she—I mean—"

"Wasn't she grief-stricken?" An ugly laugh came from him. "No. Like I said, her dad was a piece of shit, but Tab capitalized on what happened." His hands held me firm, yanking me to him, crushing my chest to his, but his gaze was focused behind me. I didn't think he was still in this room. He was back there, in his past. "She had video footage. She threatened to expose Justin for what he did, and expose our sister if I didn't stay away from her and EJ until he turned eighteen. I started to tell her to go fuck herself, but then I got a good look at Justin. He wasn't there. There was an unhinged look in his eyes, and he took off after that. I had to go after him. I didn't know what he was going to do."

He had to choose between his brother and sister, or his son.

He began kneading my thighs, moving me over him again. I wasn't sure if he was aware of his ministrations.

"Jake," I murmured softly.

I wished I could've been there. I wished I could've done something for him, reason with Tabitha, help watch over Justin. Anything. "What happened after all of that?"

"Justin's good. Every part of his DNA is, just, good. What he did, on top of the grief from losing our parents . . . By the time I found him, he'd snapped. His mind broke. He didn't remember what he did. He didn't remember anything, not even hearing about our new sister."

"He had no idea what he'd done?"

He shook his head, his head angling so he could see me better. His hand lifted, cupping the side of my face. His thumb smoothed over my cheek. "I took it as a sign. If this was the sort of shit that could happen to my brother, maybe Tab was right? I *should* stay away from EJ so this wouldn't happen to him either."

I sank back on his legs, catching his hands and holding them in mine. He looked down at them.

I stated, "So you stayed out of your son's life."

"I took care of Justin."

Right. His brother and sister, or his son. "I'm so sorry, Jake."

"I took Justin away from there. By that time, my uncles were starting to circle us. They wanted me back killing for them, and if I didn't, they were going to take Justin away too. That's when I had enough. We moved to the city, and I enrolled in the police academy. We had other family down here. Some were cops. They helped take care of Justin."

"Did he ever remember anything of what he did?"

He shook his head. "If he did, he never said."

"And your Mafia family? They left you alone?"

Another harsh-sounding laugh sounded from him. His gaze was fixated on my lips, and he raised a thumb, tracing it over my bottom lip. "No. They wouldn't totally let us go. I had my mother's inheritance now and her shares in our family's business. It's a front for the business, but my uncles wanted those shares. I wasn't about to give them up. I had to give them something so they felt like they could control us."

"What do you mean?"

"That's when I became a dirty cop."

My heart paused, stricken.

He was waiting for my reaction. His hand fell from my mouth.

God. My chest ached at seeing everything that was haunting him. Too many ghosts surrounded him.

He frowned, slightly. "Aren't you going to say something? Condemn me? Tell me what a piece of shit I am?"

Wordlessly, I shook my head. I saw how he condemned himself. He did it enough for both of us. Reaching for his hand, I took it in mine and held it between both of my hands.

His eyes fell to watch what I was doing.

Softly, gently, I said, "You were between so many walls. Justin. Your sister. Your parents. Your uncles. Tabitha. Your son. It kept squeezing you and squeezing you. You were alone?"

The side of his mouth dipped down. "I had Justin."

"No. You were caring for, supporting, and protecting Justin. Who was protecting you?"

He swallowed starkly, his Adam's apple jutting up and down sharply.

This man who was underneath me, who sat between my legs—he'd been just a boy when his world fell apart. He had monsters trying to take away who he loved on all sides. So he reached for what he could to protect himself.

He got a badge.

He rasped out, in a rough confession, "I started taking bribes from Ashton Walden as a way to help protect Justin and myself from my own family. His family was powerful enough to go against mine. Ashton got enjoyment out of taunting my uncles, that he now had me and they didn't."

"Wouldn't it—" I didn't even like thinking this way, but . . . "Why didn't they have you killed?"

He laughed, softly. "They tried a few times. It never worked, and by then, I was too insulated. By law enforcement and with Ashton's family. Enough people knew that if something happened to me, who it would've been."

Another piece fit together.

"I just cared that they left Justin alone, which they finally did."

"He never knew, did he?"

"No." His eyes were so dark, almost black, when he added, "I'm done staying away from my son. I stayed away because of Justin and my sister. Then I stayed to find Justin's killer. When this contract is gone, there's nothing keeping me away anymore."

"What about your sister?"

"Tab and I will have a conversation about that. I'm not going to let that happen, either, but that alone isn't going to keep me away any longer." He caught my chin and pulled me to him. His eyes studied my face. I didn't know what he was searching for, but I held my hand over his.

"We just need to get rid of the contract first."

"Damn straight," he said softly.

"How are you going to do that?"

"I'm going to let the world burn."

CHAPTER THIRTY-SIX

JAKE

"Why the fuck does your family gravitate toward this club?" Ashton griped, sliding in next to where I was sitting in one of the back VIP booths. We were set back on a raised floor with enough space in front of us so we could have our own dance floor if we wanted, or if others wanted. There were other booths lining the wall. They were bigger, more private, and each booth got its own bottle service.

That's not why I was there at Octavia, a nightclub run by the Mauricio family.

I flashed Ashton a dry grin, picking up my bourbon. "Because it's not one of yours, and since I don't own a nightclub, it was either this or a cop bar." I raised an eyebrow at him, enjoying his automatic sneer. "Next time I'll pick a cop bar. We could do the one where Trace's woman has roots. Bear's not there anymore, but I'm sure you'd be welcome now that you and his woman are friends. Right?"

His eyes promised me death as a server came over, sliding his drink in front of him. "Mr. Walden." She gave him a coy and seductive smile before slinking away.

I couldn't help but laugh. "Are you friendly with Cole Mauricio? Why am I not surprised." He was the nightclub owner.

Ashton picked up the glass, sniffing at it before he put it down without taking a sip. The drink was ignored as he leaned back against the booth. "We're not friendly, but Trace and I have businesses in the city he runs, and he has this one in our city. We have an agreement."

"In Chicago."

"What? Yes." He turned his gaze back to the nightclub, measuring and analyzing each person.

I watched him do his thing for a moment.

"Are you going to tell me why you wanted this meet? You're still alive. Lane must not know you took his obsession." Ashton was done cataloging the people around us.

"You brought up my ex-wife and kids last year."

He stilled, just slightly. I knew him well enough to read him. He was wary.

I liked that he was wary of me. He should be.

"What about it?"

"How'd you know about Tabitha and my son?"

His eyes widened slightly before a cool mask slid back in place. "Cybersecurity is one of my expertises. A marriage certificate came up when I ran you one time. I found her online and saw the kids."

That made sense, but I didn't like it. "Why were you looking me up?"

Ignoring his glass, he plucked mine up and took a swallow of the drink. "It came up the first time I ran you before I began paying you. Why are you bringing it up now?" He frowned at me. "You said you had kids. Plural. As in more than one son."

"I have a son and he has two half sisters." I added, "They are not mine."

Ashton was still considering me. "I was needling you last year. The divorce certificate hadn't come up on the first search, but her name did. And that she was related to a judge." He took another drag from my bourbon before putting the glass on the table again, sliding it away. "I looked into the possibility if I could use him for anything, but saw he was dead. Is there a reason your son has no idea who you are?"

I gritted my teeth, but that was why I'd called him here.

I said, "It's none of your fucking business, but I need a favor."

He laughed, his smirk morphing into a genuine grin before he shook his head. "This oughta be good. Let me guess, you want me to make all that information I was able to unearth not be unearthable?"

"I want it to go away."

"You haven't made contact with Lane yet, have you?"

"Before I declare open war on Lane, I want to make sure EJ and his family are safe."

"Why does your son think another man is his father?"

I countered, "What do you want from me in order to make that go away?"

He went still before expelling a ragged breath. "You're kidding, right? Your divorce certificate was never put in the system. Why is that?"

I gave him a hard grin. "Because I still have it."

One of his eyebrows shot up.

"It was one of my fail-safes against Tabitha if I'd ever need it."

"She married."

My grin widened. I liked hearing that, liked knowing that I had the power to fuck up her world if I ever needed to. Tabitha liked following the law. She was a rule abider.

She would never recognize me now. I was so far from the boy she knew.

I said, "I know."

Ashton's eyes narrowed.

If I wasn't sure he was too sick and twisted inside, I could've sworn there was a flare of respect that flitted over his face before he masked it.

"I know you have the skills to make anything and anyone disappear online. I'm sure Lane would've done a perfunctory search on all the members in my family, but there's a shit ton of us. He couldn't have done deep searches on every single one of us. He might not have found my marriage certificate."

"No, he wouldn't have."

I went rigid, hearing how smooth Ashton just said that.

His mouth lifted up, a cocky glint in his eyes. "Especially because I hid it years ago."

"Why the fuck would you have done that?"

"Because you were my employee. I took it on the off chance I would need it to use against you one day. I got a good enough file on you to know that you hated your family almost as much as I did, or more, in fact. You were quite a good little asset that fell into my hands. I sent your uncle a thank-you card when it happened. He didn't enjoy the card."

"Which uncle?"

"All of them."

And this was a part of the reason I felt like Ashton and I were friends sometimes, or could've been friends in another life. I wasn't foolish enough to call anyone in this world a friend. You had alliances, connections, pawns, or enemies.

I grunted. "Good."

I felt his surprise more than I saw it. No one else would've noticed a reaction at all.

He leaned back. "There's nothing that can be found in an online search that connects you to your ex-wife or your son. I found the marriage certificate. You know what I did with that, and the other pieces were some high school items linking your name to hers. I can take care of those, but according to the records, she's only married to one man. Your name was not put on any of the children's birth certificates. The other man's name is on the two girls', but not your son's. At the moment, I didn't give it a thought, but the boy is yours. If Lane isn't directed to her, he won't look close enough to see the resemblance."

Good. That was all good.

I admitted, "I don't know what kind of monster I'm unleashing when I let him know about Green."

Ashton didn't reply, a calculating expression coming over his face. There was the mask of the monster I knew resided inside of him, the one that enjoyed coming out to torture people.

I wasn't going to defeat Lane. I already knew that. I'd done more research on him since finding out his role in my life, and I couldn't get a bead on him. Studying Ashton, I had a feeling he couldn't either. And if he couldn't, then neither could his best friend. Ashton wasn't smug and if he hadn't felt wary of Lane, he would've been all up in my face taunting me about my long-lost cousin.

He wasn't saying a word.

He was worried.

Was I all sorts of fucked here? Yes.

Did I have any other choice? No.

"I'll take care of making any connection between you and your son disappear."

"What do you want in return?"

"Nothing." He chuckled, wryly, at seeing my reaction. "I'm aware of what we're about to do. This is my city. Lane's not allowed in it."

"The Worthings were still in Maine when he made his demands. He might just stick to Maine."

Ashton shared a look with me, a mocking curve tugging at his mouth. "You've not been aware of this, but while your family was declaring war with us, Lane was also on the move. He has strongholds in Cincinnati, Buffalo, Pittsburgh, Ocean City, Providence, and Albany. He doesn't give a fuck about Maine. He wants your family's soldiers. Why do you think that is?"

I was placing all the cities in my head, and holy fuck. "He's surrounding the city."

"*My* city is in his sights. Trace and I are aware of this. The war isn't between *you* and Lane. It's between us and Lane. I'll do my part, but you need to do yours."

A lot of people were about to die.

"Is that an order?"

Ashton didn't catch the warning in my tone. "If you need that. Yes, Jake. Consider it a last order from me. Now do your boss a favor and fucking declare war on this motherfucker."

Everything inside of me turned to ice too. It spread. "I'm not one of your soldiers anymore."

He rolled his eyes again, shoving up, and he tossed some cash on the table. "Did you ever actually stop? Call Lane tonight. I'd like to finish this war before Lane even fucking knows it's here. We'll all be better off when this piece of shit is dead."

My eyes narrowed when he stood. They turned to slits watching him leave.

Ashton just made a mistake with me. I'd meant what I said to Sawyer.

I was done with taking orders.

CHAPTER THIRTY-SEVEN

SAWYER

"You know you're totally fucking up here, right?"

It was the next day and our captive wouldn't shut up. She'd been let free to use the bathroom. Jake stood by the bedroom door to give her privacy, but I stood within eyesight while she did her business. She'd proven to be a little escape artist, so we weren't taking any chances.

Jake woke me up with his mouth between my legs. I hadn't lasted long. He brought me to explode fast, and I wasn't sure if that was something I should've been proud of or embarrassed about, but Jake's dick soon followed. He'd been smug, but took us on a rough round that left me fully sated and my chest heaving to catch my breath.

That didn't last long, either, before Jake rolled me to my stomach and slid inside from behind. He held me pinned down, pounding inside of me for what felt like forever.

Not that I was complaining.

I came four times by the time morning peaked and I could still feel him inside of me. So when our captive said that to me, I got a little look on my face because yes, that seemed to be our theme lately.

Fucking.

I loved it.

I was trying to give her some breakfast, but she caught my look. "Are you aware that you're a loud lay?"

I startled back to the present, to the kitchen table, and almost dropped the fork in my hands.

"What?" My face flushed. "I am not."

"Nothing wrong with that. Some guys like a screecher. Most guys find it annoying. If you want to keep him, I'd advise learning how to shut your mouth, though."

"Shut up." She was trying to get a rise out of me, and what was annoying was that it was working.

She seemed to know that too. Her smirk became mocking. "Then again, Creighton will just kill you both when he finds out what you did. So maybe enjoy it while you can. He does sound like a good one in bed. Rode you long, hard, and dirty, huh?" Her eyes were knowing. "That's how it sounded."

I hadn't even considered her last night, that she could've heard us. That was embarrassing.

I shoved back from the table and began gathering everything up. "Breakfast is done."

She began laughing. "You're blushing. Where did he find you? Cause I know he wouldn't give two shits if I heard you too. If you'd been more of a bitch, I would've found it disgusting. Since you're kinda nice, it was a turn-on. Nothing to be embarrassed about."

God. So mortifying. I hissed, "If you don't shut up, I'll gag you."

That made her laugh harder.

I frowned her way. "You're not acting like someone who's been kidnapped."

"How am I supposed to act?" Her face grew tight. "This isn't my first rodeo."

That got my attention. "You've been kidnapped before?"

Her eyes grew hard before cutting away. "Eight has a lot of enemies."

"Eight?" I felt a little bad for her.

Her eyes got big, inhaling swiftly. "Creighton. He's the biggest and baddest where I'm from, and every now and then some punk gets ambitious, starts thinking of ways to bring Creight to his knees. Lane doesn't go to his knees for anyone." She glanced my way, adding with an edge, "They all eventually learn."

I did feel bad for her, considering what she must've gone through. "I'm sorry."

Her eyes flared. Heated. "Fuck off. How about that? You're going to be dead soon anyways."

I wasn't sure on the protocol of being the kidnapper versus being the kidnapped. I'd only recently switched roles. "For what it's worth, we were already running for our lives." More like hiding for our lives, but semantics.

She tilted her head. "What?"

"There was a contract put out on Jake's head. I happened to be with him when the first guy tried to kill him and somehow my name got added to it. I guess we're really not doing anything to make our situation worse. You don't have to keep threatening us. This is a last-ditch effort to try and save our necks."

She was looking at me as if I'd grown two heads. "You really are not from this world."

I shrugged. "I'm from Montana. I came here to get away because my ex-fiancé called off our wedding because he knocked up my best friend."

"You're joking."

I shook my head. "They'd been having a relationship behind my back for years."

"How long?"

I wrinkled my nose. "He told me three years, but I think he was lying. Isn't there a rule about liars? The number they give you, multiply it by three? It doesn't matter really. Not anymore."

"Men suck."

I peeked at her, wondering . . . I hadn't told Jake this part, but my aunts had let it slip. "We were supposed to get married a little over a week ago, and he went through with it. With her."

"No way." Her eyebrows shot up. "He married her *instead*?"

I nodded.

"At *your* wedding?"

She didn't even know the worst part of it. "He's also my boss, so I'm out of a job."

"Dick."

"And I think he's still in my house."

She choked again. "*Your* house?"

I nodded again. "I'd been with him since college. Almost two decades. I think this is my midlife crisis, if I survive it."

She went back to watching me warily. "For a midlife crisis, you went extreme. I mean, you went all out. Some people get a fancy new sports car. You committed a felony." The side of her mouth lifted in a wry grin. "I kinda hope you survive now."

I flinched at hearing that. She was right. There was a chance I might not. And if I was about to die, I needed to call my family. I needed to tell them how much I loved them, one last time.

I stood up. "I need to—"

The door opened and Jake walked through, his phone in his hand.

He put his phone on the table and pulled out his gun. "Time to call your boyfriend."

Ice ran down my spine. I wasn't ready for this, because what then? Seriously. What then? Did Jake have a plan? What were we doing here?

He was supposed to tell me these things now. We were in this together.

I opened my mouth to say something, anything—too late.

He pressed the call button at the same time he moved her gag back in place.

The call was picked up on the other end, but he didn't say anything for a moment. "I don't know this number, but I know you got *this* number from someone I care about. I'd advise you to tell me who you are before I send my team to identify you. One would be less bloody."

Jake said, "Hello, Cousin. It seems you have lost something of yours."

"Jake Worthing." Lane's voice didn't warm. "I was hoping to receive a call letting me know you were dead. What do I owe this pleasure of hearing from you personally?"

This was the guy behind our contracts? *This* guy?

He sounded annoyed more than murderous, despite his words.

Jake was like cement, but I glanced in Blake's direction. She froze when his voice first spoke through the phone. Now she was blinking rapidly as sweat began to pour down her face. She looked terrified.

My heart ached again.

She'd been hiding from him for a reason.

I missed my family. I wished they were here with me. Clara, Bess, and my mom would have had it figured out within a few minutes. Their plan might not have been logical, but I would've felt comforted knowing they were with me. They wouldn't have helped kidnap someone only to turn around and offer that person to their stalker. Well . . . they would've helped kidnap someone. They'd do that in a heartbeat. It would be giving the person up where they would draw the line.

Jake said to trust him, but he also told me that if it came down to anyone or me, he would choose me. He'd give Blake up in a heartbeat if it meant I'd live.

I couldn't let that happen. I just couldn't.

A plan started to form.

It was a bad plan. A totally illogical and reckless plan, but when I looked at Blake again, a single tear slid down her face. She was blinking again, trying to stop that tear from slipping out, but it was too late.

Her eyes met mine. I saw the anguish there.

I couldn't do it.

I *wouldn't* do it.

Seeing something in me, she straightened suddenly, pushing up in her seat.

Jake and Creighton were talking, but in that moment, Blake and I were having our own.

I mouthed to her, hoping she could read my words. "I will help you."

Her eyes narrowed before relief blazed in them, quickly masked as she began blinking again. She schooled her face back to a mask.

How was I going to do this?

Phone. I needed my phone.

And my aunts. They would help.

I risked a look at Jake.

Oh, Jake.

I was going to betray him.

My throat tightened.

He'd be okay. He'd have to be okay.

Once everything was set, I'd figure out how to help Blake *and* help Jake and myself.

There needed to be a way. Some way.

Maybe a miracle? It was time to start praying.

I came back to the present when I heard Lane ask, "Is she there?"

Jake tugged down her gag. "Speak."

"Blake?" Lane said through the phone.

She shifted on the seat, wincing. Her voice came out husky and soft. "Hey, Eight."

He was quiet for a beat before asking, his voice low, "Are you okay, my little quokka?"

Blake huffed. "Oh, fuck you." Some of the terror had fled when we'd had our understanding, but I was able to see through her now. A little bit. She was putting on a good front that this wasn't bothering her, but I saw it now. She was quaking inside at whatever this man was to her.

More shame rose in me. I'd helped put her in this position.

"Have your hosts been treating you well?"

Her jaw clenched. "Fuck's sake, Eight. I was kidnapped. They're not my hosts. We're not having Sunday brunch here."

A low and smooth chuckle slid through the phone from his end. "I'll see what I can do."

If her hands hadn't been tied to the chair, I had a feeling she would've been giving the phone a middle finger. She retorted, "Yeah. You do that."

"Worthing." His voice dipped, showing some of his anger.

There it was. It was a brief glimpse, but there was the monster everyone had been talking about. In just that word, I could hear how he was capable of ordering our deaths even though he had no clue who one of those people was.

Jake met my gaze, frowning, before he took the phone off speaker and took it into the other room. I heard before he closed the door, "Let's talk."

"Don't let it fool you," Blake said.

All the stress lines in her face, the bags under her eyes, the shadows and ghosts, all of it suddenly was on full display. She wasn't hiding from me at all. Her shoulders sagged and her head fell down. She didn't have the energy to keep her mask up.

She added, grimacing, "He's being all smooth now because he doesn't want your man to know how pissed he is, but trust me. When you see him, he'll let you see the evil inside of him. He is furious. I know what you said, but let it go. I'll survive. I always do. You need to focus on yourself. Run. Right now." She nodded to the door. "Your man did this. I'll cover for you, tell Creighton you tried to help me. He'll take you off the contract, but it's over for your man. Creighton won't forget this. No matter what, your man is toast. Glad you got dicked down good last night because you need to save yourself."

That impending doom just exploded inside of me.

CHAPTER THIRTY-EIGHT

JAKE

"You have my attention, Worthing. What do you want?"

"Done with the niceties?"

"You have something of mine. I want it back."

It.

I smirked. "A nice way to think of your girl."

"She's mine. What *the fuck* do you want, Jacob?"

Fine. He was showing his cards. I would too. "I want my name and Sawyer's off your website. I want the contract dissolved." He was quiet on his end and I laughed over it, harshly. "Yeah. I'm fully fucking aware that you own that website and your team runs the operations. Get my name off that list, and Sawyer's. Then we'll talk when you get your '*it*.'"

"Sawyer's your woman now?"

I stilled, not liking the smugness coming from him. "She's a civilian. She was in the wrong place at the wrong time. She got caught up in all of this and none of this is her doing. You kill innocent people? All the hype about you and that was one thing I hadn't heard about you, you and your fucking modern-day Robin Hood type of reputation? It's all bullshit. That's nice to hear. You let her go down with a bullet and I will make it my last mission in life to destroy your ass. I have a feeling there's a whole cult following that might rethink their brainwashed beliefs about you. I won't get through to all of them, but I'll make a dent. I'm sure of it."

He said her name and I went red. The rage took over.

Of course he knew her. Of course he knew her name. But Sawyer was mine.

I said briskly, "Our names are off the list with a promise to *keep* them off the list and I'll hand your girl over to you. It's as simple as that."

"Except it's not."

Fuck.

He was too smooth in his retort. Too smooth. Too confident.

My hand tightened around the phone. This wasn't going to be good, whatever he was going to say.

"I have no problem removing your Sawyer's name from the list. In fact, it's done. You can check yourself. I won't add her name again, but what I'll do instead is wipe out her family. Every single one of them. All her aunts. All her cousins. Every last person she calls family, including the new cousin she met on her romp around the city. Even the fiancé who dumped her, the best friend who married him in her place, and the child in that woman's belly. I have a policy where innocents are left out of my business, but the second you took your woman from that police station, you brought her into this world. You made her my business. She's your weakness and if you don't bring Blake to me, I will burn the world down around your woman and let her live in its ashes. It's your choice."

I glanced at the closed door before turning away, my gut shifting.

When I spoke, I didn't hesitate and I didn't let emotion slip through because my cousin was a ruthless fucker.

Got it. I was too. "Do it."

Apparently it was genetic.

He went quiet.

"You think I give a shit about her family? I *don't*. Her or them, it's *her*. Kill every single one of them. I'll give you the address where Tristian West is hiding three of those family members. I'll give them on a platter to you, but here's my counteroffer. You wipe out her family, you think of putting her name back on that list, and I will butcher your woman. I will cut her up into pieces and ship every single piece to you, one by one. Gift-wrapped."

He was breathing hard on his end.

I added, "You fucked up, Lane. You think you know me? You have no fucking clue who I actually am. I'm not the rest of *our* pathetic family and I am *done* taking orders. I am done taking threats. I care about two people in my life and one of them is dead. I'm not a good guy. I've never been a good guy. So go ahead and wipe out Sawyer's family. I don't give one fuck about them. You want your woman? You do what I say and only what I say because I think at the end of this negotiation, your obsession with Blake Green is more than whatever feelings you think I have about my woman's family. Call me when you're done, because if you do what you're threatening, you can put your toy back together by connecting all her body parts."

I ended the call, my heart fucking racing.

Goddamn.

Goddamn.

A choked sob had me whirling around.

My heart splintered.

Sawyer was in the doorway.

She'd opened it a crack. Now pale. Horror in her eyes. Her bottom lip was trembling. She was pressing a hand to her mouth. It curled into a fist and she kept pressing it harder and harder.

Fuck.

"Sawyer." I took a step toward her.

She jumped back as if I'd slapped her, holding out a hand. *"No."*

Her voice cracked, sounding like a wounded animal.

I flinched. Shit.

"No." She said it again, savagely, a wildness coming over her. Her eyes grew panicked. Her mouth strained at the ends. She began looking around her, a desperate frenzy seeping into the air.

"It's not what you think," I grated out. Low. Rough. I'd messed up. I thought the door was closed. "I didn't mean what you heard—"

"You said it!" she raged at me, her motion reversing. She flew at me instead, one arm in the air as if to strike me.

I braced, my hands lifting to catch her, but my phone rang. It stopped everything.

She froze, a choked gurgle slipping out as she saw Creighton's name on the screen. Her eyes closed. Her body wavered on her feet.

Grim, so fucking grim, I accepted the call and put him on speaker. "Did you make a decision?"

His tone was like ice. "Your names have been removed from the list. Bring Blake to the coordinates I send in one hour and your names will remain off that list."

No emotion. I couldn't think anything. I couldn't feel anything. This was how this fucking world worked. Collateral. Trades. Negotiations. Deals. These types of cruel arrangements. It was a dirty business, but it's what I'd endured all my life. I survived it, walking the line between two sides of the same coin. Law and crime. I walked away from a bloodbath only needing to keep returning to one, over and over again.

This was it. This was the end.

I was done after this.

Sawyer was watching me, a plea in her eyes. There was a softness in her, one I couldn't indulge and one I shouldn't be around. I'd make it worse.

I made her like me.

She had a light in her. It'd been there, only dulled, when I met her on that subway train. Every day it grew, no matter the threat against her. It was still there. Getting bigger. Bolder. Healthier. Life had come back to her cheeks, giving her color. It made her glow until she overheard this call. I'd snuffed it out so easily.

It'd been a bluff, but it didn't matter because if he called my bluff, I would be the reason her world shattered.

Me. I did that.

I was a curse to her.

I said swiftly, coldly, "Deal."

Sawyer flinched this time, her face wincing, and she took a step away from me.

It wasn't a good move, that I was letting him choose the location and time of the meeting, but a part of me stopped caring. As long as Sawyer was alive. As long as my son remained hidden from all of this.

It would soon be done.

"You can't do this."

She hated me. I saw it in her, the loathing of me. I shut down. She could return to Montana because she didn't belong in this world.

But she'd be alive.

She'd be alive.

I turned my back to her, grabbed my gun, and shoved it in my holster. "We leave in ten."

The door shut behind me. I faltered now, slipping to sit on the edge of the bed, my blood roaring in my ears.

I'd give her ten minutes.

CHAPTER THIRTY-NINE

SAWYER

My heart was pounding.

Everything was coming apart inside of me. So many emotions. Panic. Terror. I wanted to fall to the floor, fold in a ball, and disappear, but I couldn't do that. Ten minutes. I almost started laughing at the absurdity of it. Ten whole minutes. Only ten fucking minutes.

I flicked on the bathroom fan, slammed that door shut, and ran for Blake's room. Jake would think I was in the bathroom. Jesus. I hoped he'd stay in the bedroom. I didn't know when he'd come out, but I flung Blake's door open.

She jerked around, shoving to her feet. I hadn't tied her back on the bed, which Jake would've assumed I had done at gunpoint. I motioned to her. "We have to go." I spoke low. Urgent. "Now. He's giving you back."

Her face shuttered closed, a wall coming over her expression, and she dipped her head in a brisk nod. She merely came with me, ready. She bypassed me, seeing the closed bedroom door next to us. "Follow me."

She led the way out of the apartment, grabbing keys, a phone, a gun on the way. She took them all with deft hands, and I wanted to sprint once we got to the hallway, but not her. Cool, calm, and collected. She walked—*walked*—to the elevator. Hit the button.

I was gaping at her. "What are you doing?" I hissed.

She gave me a once-over, briskly, assessing me. "Do you have a gun?"

"No." I thrust a hand out at the one she'd shoved in her back pocket. "But you do."

The elevator arrived and she stepped on, still so fucking smooth. Who *was* this girl? It was like the second I opened the door, she turned into someone who could live in a *Mission: Impossible* movie.

She hit the first-floor button and was doing something with the phone.

"What are you doing?"

"Disabling the tracking. Give me your phone. Though I'm sure your man already did the same with it. Unless he wanted to track you himself?"

I dug it out, handed it over. "I don't know. He doesn't seem to have a problem finding me."

She checked it over before handing it back. "It's off. Contact your family the fastest way you can."

"They're being guarded."

Her nostrils flared at my words. She didn't ask who was guarding them. "Tell them to get away if they can and give us a location where to meet them. As you do that, tell me what you overheard on that phone call."

"What?"

She repeated the question, still acting so fucking calm. I was losing it and she was acting like we were going to church. As I messaged Graham on his social media, the same way I'd messaged him before, I told her what I'd overheard. Lane threatening my family and Jake's response.

She didn't react, just nodded to herself. We got to the first floor and she stepped out, tucking her shirt to cover the gun. We bypassed the front desk, ignored the clerk who was watching us with narrowed eyes, and stepped out onto the street.

"You took his keys. His truck is parked over here."

"No." She tossed them in a garbage can as we passed it. "He would have trackers on all his vehicles. I'm just slowing him down."

I nodded. That made sense. Total spy sort of sense, but it made sense.

We went one block and she began jogging, turning down an alley. I went with her as she said, "If I know Creighton, he already knew I was gone and knew who took me. He was waiting to be contacted. He knew who you were, knew about your family. What he said wasn't his move and he wouldn't have upheld his end when your man handed me over. I meant it. Jake took me. You took me. You both have to die for that, no matter what. It's how Creighton operates. I was stood up by a guy for a date and Creighton cut his tongue out."

"That's . . . confusing." I thought he wanted her in *that* way?

We came to a car. She went to the driver's side window and paused to tell me, "I was sixteen."

I frowned.

"He was pissed that the guy hurt my feelings." She rammed the back of her elbow into the window, shattering it.

No alarm pierced the air.

She reached in, making sure not to get cut by the glass, and undid the lock. Opening the door, she hit the unlock for the rest. I hurried around to the passenger side. She was hot-wiring the car and by the time I slipped inside, my door shut, she had the engine going.

So totally spy-like.

"Seriously. Who *are* you?" I was all focused on her right now and not in any way focusing on how Jake had betrayed me, at how emotionless he'd been offering up my family to this killer. He hadn't blinked. He hadn't cared. The man who held me in his arms at night was a stranger to me in that moment.

But I wasn't focusing on that because if I were, I'd be a slobbering, blubbering, brokenhearted idiot and I could not be that person right now.

I needed to stay in this reality and not slip off to Broadway daydream land. (That would come later.)

Blake knew what she was doing. Follow her lead.

That was easy enough for me. I didn't have to think or feel. I could just let her run the show.

She pulled out of the alley at the same time Jake was exiting the building.

Blake cursed softly.

He saw us, his mouth tight, but his eyes widened when he saw who was in the driver's seat and who wasn't. Our eyes met as we passed him. There was a moment between us.

He'd lied about everything he said. To keep me safe. That I was his. If he gave up my family, he gave me up, and he knew that. I was a package deal with them. He *knew* that. I told him how close my family was. They were my best friends. Not Manda like I'd thought. My aunts. My mom. *My family.*

Okay, so for a split second, just one, a crack ran down the length of my wall. Some of the hurt slipped through, bowling me over, and I had to bite down on my lip to keep from letting more spill through, but he saw it.

He blanched, briefly, and then drew his gun.

"He's going to shoot us."

"No." Her voice was strained. "He won't. He won't risk hitting you."

She kept driving and as I felt that crack splintering down the entire length inside of me, she was right. He lowered the gun after a few seconds. He ran to his truck, his phone to his mouth.

She sighed, switching lanes and turning. "He'll be calling in his associates. Whoever they are." Her eyes slid sideways to me, a question in them. "He was a cop? Did I get that right? Will he use those resources to find us? Because if so, we need to move a whole lot faster."

I shook my head, pushing the hurt aside. I needed to be numb. I couldn't let myself feel anything. "No. He's probably calling his Mafia friends. I think Ashton—"

"Walden?" she asked, sharply.

I frowned. "Yeah. And the other guy."

"Tristian West. Your boyfriend is connected to them?"

I was bitter as I said, "He's not my boyfriend, but yes. It's confusing. He doesn't like the West guy. I know that much."

She sucked in some air, cursing. "West is the more logical one of them. Walden is a loose cannon."

"I think Walden's the one guarding my family." I eyed her as she kept turning onto different roads. "How do you know about them?"

Her eyes went flat. "I've known Creighton for fourteen years. I grew up in this world. Trust me. When I decided to come to New York, I did my research. If Creighton found me, he wouldn't be able to take over so easily. I started planning to come here two years ago."

Fourteen years? "How old are you?"

I didn't remember Jake telling me, but the bar we'd gone to was a college bar. She looked young then. She didn't look young now. She looked as if we'd switched ages. She was the thirty-six-year-old adult, all capable and shit, and I was the floundering college student, all wide-eyed and gaping mouth on the floor, one thought away from falling into a sobbing paralysis.

"I'm twenty-two."

I sucked in some air. "You're still a baby. Cut off four years and you could've been my baby."

Her mouth tightened and her gaze grew haunted, an emptiness coming over her face at the same time.

I stopped asking questions. She had survived this world, and I wouldn't.

I didn't know why my comments gave her that look, but I felt bad about it.

My phone beeped ten minutes later, and I cried out when I read the text. Finally something good had happened. "Graham got back to me. They got away."

She laughed, surprised. "How? But—no. Never mind. We need to get to them. Ask them where they are."

We were able to get away from Jake. My family got away, too, and that was another lucky break.

I had a feeling it wouldn't last, though. Our luck was going to run out, because I felt it.

We were two dead girls driving in this car.

Death was coming for us.

I looked back, as if I could see it behind me.

A shiver pooled in the small of my back.

It was there. Taunting. Mocking. Promising.

So be it.

If death was coming for me, it would have to wait in line.

My family came first.

CHAPTER FORTY

JAKE

She left me. Sawyer left me.

Fuck her.

I gritted my teeth. Grabbing a car. They'd taken the keys. Smart move on their part if they'd been my keys and not Laila's. My phone was ringing when I got inside my truck. I tossed it on the passenger seat, and Ashton's voice answered through my dashboard. "What is it?"

I shook my head at his hardened voice. He knew shit was going to go down. He helped set all this up, and he was going to come on the phone like that?

"They bolted."

A second. "What?"

I was trying to catch them, but Green—who was at the wheel, how did that happen?—kept turning. I was going to lose them in the traffic. I told him, "You said West would have Sawyer's family. Where are they?"

"Why?"

"Fucking—just do what I say for one goddamn time, Walden! They bolted. Both of them. Why the fuck do you think I'm asking? I need Green for the handoff and I'm running out of time to make that happen. They'll be going for Sawyer's family. Where are they?"

"Green's free?"

"Yes! Catch the fuck up. Aren't you watching this all happen somewhere through your fucking hacking laptop? They're gone. Lane's expecting me to hand over his woman and I don't have her. She took my woman with her."

A snicker sounded. "They're running together?"

I was going to kill him. The second I saw him, I was putting a bullet in his forehead. "*Catch up.* Where is West keeping Sawyer's family?"

"Who cares. Green's going to ditch her the second she can. You need Green, not your woman."

"She should, yes, but she's not. They took off *together*. Green was at the wheel. Not Sawyer. Again, she took Sawyer *with* her. You're not comprehending this."

"Why would she do that?"

"I don't fucking know! But if I can't catch Green, I need to get Sawyer and get the fuck out of the city. She's not safe on her own. Lane will kill her. He'll do it just to spite me."

There was a beep on his end, and he cursed. "Uh, you're not going to like this."

"What?" My jaw clenched. What next?

"We were keeping her family at Jess's mom's house with her and the brother. It's normal. Civilians. Jess argued they shouldn't feel they were being imprisoned, but, uh . . . they're gone."

"Why *the fuck* does West's woman have any input on my woman's family?"

This could not be happening.

Wait. "What did you say? They're gone?"

"Trace just got an alert. They left three minutes ago."

"Where were their guards?"

He swore under his breath. "They were never told they were being held captive so the guards stayed at a distance. Jess argued hard for that. You know Trace's woman. Still a PO in her heart, trying to do good.

Trace just got a call. That was the notice I got. His men are down. All of them."

"I killed three people in her cousin's house. What the fuck did they think was happening?"

"Jess didn't want to terrify them. She gave them a version of the truth, told them a cop had already taken care of it."

"What? Who?"

"You, dumbass."

"I'm not a cop."

"Jess was a PO. I'm sure she flashed badges or showed them pictures. I don't know. She's the one who told them you were an undercover detective and everything was being handled. She thought it was the best way to keep them contained. Trace agreed. I was overruled. Your woman's family were told that Sawyer was needed to testify against the bad guys. You took her into protective custody."

I'd had enough with people being in danger because *they didn't know they were in danger*.

I needed to count down from ten because I wasn't hearing this bullshit. Because if I was, if anything happened to Sawyer, I would return to the skills I learned from my childhood.

I'd only stick around to count the bodies to see if I'd missed anyone.

"Where the fuck are they?"

Another beep on his end.

"Good news, we know what vehicle they took."

"What's the bad news?"

"The bad news is that Jess's mom gave them her minivan. Handed over the keys. Helped them put their suitcases in the back."

"Why would she do that?"

"Jess's mom probably became friends with the aunts, sent them off with a hug and baked goods."

I wasn't going to ask any more questions. The more I did, the more my grasp on my control slipped. I was becoming like Sawyer, except she went into show-tunes-land and I went into the land where I needed to spill blood.

"Tell me you have a tracker on that minivan. Tell me you're able to hack into traffic cameras and can find them. Tell me that, Ashton, because if you don't, you did not hold up your end of our bargain. You were supposed to handle the aunts. You didn't."

His tone hardened. "Don't forget who you're talking to, Worthing."

My jaw clenched. "Honestly? I think it's time you learn who *you're* talking to."

"What the fuck does that mean?"

I didn't respond and he didn't push it.

I could hear tapping on his end.

"There's no tracker on her minivan. I think it'd be a better move for me to track Green."

"No." I hated this. My knuckles were white from gripping the steering wheel so hard. "Green's in the wind. Sawyer's with her. Green wasn't expecting to be taken, but she knows now. She's gone. It'll take longer to find her than the aunts. The aunts are the weak link."

"Hold on."

I heard a beep in the background.

He said, "I just got a notice from a traffic cam. Found the minivan that you want so badly, but you're going to be too late."

My blood chilled. "Where are they?"

He told me, and I looked at the time. He was right. I couldn't get to them, get Sawyer, and take Green to Lane. There was only enough time to grab Sawyer and run.

"Get your girl and get the fuck out of my city."

"Gladly."

CHAPTER FORTY-ONE

SAWYER

"They might not be there." That was my fear.

"They'll be there."

"What if they're not?" I glanced in Blake's direction, my voice all high and matching the anxiety that was tunneling in my chest.

She sighed and not for the first time, taking one of the last turns to where we were supposed to meet my family. "They'll be there. They said they would."

"What if they're not?" And I was on repeat, not for the first time either.

If they weren't there, I didn't know what I was going to do. Find them? Hunt them? I'd have to go back to Jake, and that would not be a happy reunion. I was sure I'd get some punishing sex out of the deal, which—*shiver* in a good way. But I ran for a reason. And speaking of . . . I looked in Blake's direction. She played the cool and calm secret agent spy role the whole drive. It'd been her idea where to meet. Well, hers and my cousin's, since Graham knew New York the best, but she proved to be adept at reading maps and shit. I was useless, which . . . not surprising. I was a tourist.

Which, sigh. I missed the old days when I just wanted to be the best tourist I could be. Gone were those lists. Gone was the real-life bucket list. Now I had one main objective: survive.

Blake didn't respond to me, but it didn't matter. We pulled into a parking lot, and they were there.

I cried out in relief.

"Is that them?"

A minivan was parked in the back corner, but I could see Graham in the driver's seat. Oliver was in the front passenger seat. There were others in the back. In fact, there were more than two more heads and two dogs.

"Who is with them?" My voice cracked. All the tightness in my chest exploded to happy flutters.

She drove over to them. Parked.

I was reaching for the door, bursting to physically be near my family again, when Blake's hand caught my arm. "Wait," she barked.

Tension fell over us.

She was watching the street, her eyes trained on a car that was driving past the lot at a slow pace. She kept scanning. A bunch of abandoned and broken-down homes were across the road. A lot of vehicles were parked up and down also, but ironically, not a lot of people.

She let go of my arm. "We're good."

I could tell she was going to wait in the car.

"Come with me." I caught her hand.

She blinked at me. "Uh . . ."

"Meet my family. Fair warning, they'll try to adopt you." I shoved out of the car. I hadn't missed how she blinked rapidly, like I'd blinded her, but then I was running for the minivan.

The side door swished open and my family spilled out from inside.

Bess winced, stepping down. Her hand went to her knee.

Clara shoved at her from behind. "Scoot, woman. You're holding me up from hugging my niece."

Two dogs jumped out, hurrying around both of them.

The older Lab ran up to me, bouncing awkwardly with his mouth wide open, smiling. His big tongue hung lopsided out. He loped around me, dodging my hand, and he kept doing circles. Pooh, their little white rescue, ran up to me and expected me to pick her up, so I did just that, swooping her up and cradling her against my chest.

By that time, Bess had moved to the side, still grimacing from her leg.

Clara was almost to me, her arms up, when I saw who else had stumbled out of the minivan.

"Mom!"

And then, "Aunt *Maude*?"

Clara pffted, her nose wrinkling before she yanked me to her. "Come here, you. We were starting to get worried. We couldn't get a hold of you yesterday."

I glanced back, seeing that Blake had gotten out of the car and come around to my side, but held back. We shared a look because they were *starting* to get worried? They hadn't already been worried?

Clara gave me a last squeeze, muttering into my ear, "We tried keeping the Fourth from coming with us, but we couldn't shake her. She and your mom hopped a plane yesterday without telling us. It was a whole big awkward surprise when they called from the airport because they didn't know where to go. Also, why is that car's window busted?"

My mom was trying to hold back her tears, standing just behind Clara, and she was failing. Maude moved to the other side, overhearing what Clara said. She spoke up, griping, "Why wouldn't I have come? He's my son, after all. Of course I'm coming to see my son. I won't let you start acting like you were the one who wiped his ass and changed his diapers like you do with Phyllis's daughter here. My son is mine, not yours."

"Maude!"

"Mom!" Graham was not happy.

Clara had stepped aside, but froze at hearing what her sister just said.

My mom froze too, horrified. She snapped, adding, "Take that back. That's a horrible thing to say. We're *family*."

Clara glared, retorting, "She's my godchild. Can you say that much?"

The back of my neck grew heated. The verbal sparring had begun.

Maude rolled her eyes, moving stiffly to me. She was the shortest of the sisters, around five feet and one inch. Clara was a few inches taller, but the roundest of them. Maude was shaped more like a box, with a few extra layers of skin. She didn't have the curves like Clara and Bess did, but she was bulky. Her brown and graying hair was pulled up in a bun, a bunch of stray hairs falling free where half her hair was a mess. The bun almost seemed like a joke. She didn't seem to care, blowing out some air and grabbing me, jerking me to her for a brusque hug. I felt like I was hugging a stiff cardboard box. I wasn't sure what to do, so I patted her on the arms before she let me go.

I said, "Hi, Aunt Maude. Welcome to New York." I tried to grin, but it failed miserably.

Bess joined the group, on the outskirts. Graham was next to her, giving me a tired look.

I caught movement from behind them on the other side of the minivan. Oliver was trying to wrangle the two dogs. Pooh was in his arms but struggling to jump out.

I looked down, distracted, seeing that the dog had escaped my arms at some point.

"Honey." My mom's voice broke.

I went straight to her, no longer waiting.

She stepped into my chest, her forehead meeting just under my neck, and she was already sobbing before my arms closed around her. "Oh, honey." Her hands fisted my shirt from behind me.

I was at a loss.

My mom cried. Sure, this happened. A good movie. A sad movie. Animal rescue commercials. A neighbor telling a story about their kid coming home for a weekend. These things made her cry, but it was also a few tears shed. Not this. She was sobbing.

"Mom." I tightened my hold on her.

She burrowed even more into me. "It's nothing. It's everything. The wedding. You left. We couldn't get a hold of you. Then you were gone again. I couldn't stay home. Your dad kept reassuring me you were fine, but it's a mother's intuition. You weren't. I could just feel it. But you're here." She was squeezing me so hard.

My breasts were going to pop, but also, oh no. A mother's intuition was correct. I shared a look with Blake, even though I knew she couldn't have heard my mom.

"I'm fine, Mom. We're all fine."

Bess was tsking her from behind, pushing her way to me. "It's my turn. Always the last, I'm telling you."

My mom refused to let go, but it made no difference to Bess. She towered over my mom, who was barely taller than Maude, but my mom was the skinniest. She was too skinny. Bess wrapped her arms around us both. It was as if my mom was barely there.

"It's good to see you again, Sawsaw."

"Sawsaw," Clara snickered, now holding Pooh, who was licking her face and her little tail wagging. "Always makes me want to cut down a tree with a real saw."

Oliver looked slightly horrified and confused, but seeing me looking his way, that expression cleared. A warm smile took its place, and once Bess stepped back, and my mom loosened her hold, I stepped toward the outskirts of the group.

Oliver met me halfway, giving me a tight hug, which surprised me. He murmured into my ear, "I've not said anything, but Graham and I are a bit more in the know, and we know there are other factors here. We can talk about that later, but for right now, are you safe?" He stepped back, his face still leaning close. "Are we safe?"

My throat suddenly swelled.

Graham joined us and my eyes went sideways to him.

Oliver read my expression, his hands falling back from my arms. He stilled.

"Oliver?" Graham was watching his husband.

Oliver patted his arm, his gaze trained on me. "We need to go. Right?"

I nodded, slowly.

Graham heaved a deep sigh, his gaze trailing behind me. "It's honestly like herding a bunch of stray feral cats who think they're chickens. I swear I heard Clara clucking in the van. Then she was hissing at my mother. Hissing. At my mother. Who barked back. Bear and Pooh joined in. Is this normal for them?"

I cringed. "I'd like to say no, but . . ."

He huffed. "Gracious. Thank you for coming here. I already love you. I'm looking forward to continuing this relationship, but take them home. *Please.*"

Oliver was softly laughing beside us, his shoulders shaking.

"Who are you?" Clara barked over the group, staring at Blake, who was still leaning by the car.

Everyone looked her way.

"This is . . . uh—" In the distance, there was a screech. Some honking. I wasn't paying it attention, instead concentrating on how to introduce Blake. "Um—" I had no idea.

Blake's eyes widened. She stepped forward. Her hands were pressed together, in front of her. Her shoulders were hunched. "I met Sawyer through—"

My head went higher. "Yes. Right. Through Jake—"

"Through that undercover cop?" Clara supplied, her voice gravelly.

I frowned, but no one was reacting to those words. "Undercover what?"

"Yeah. Detective Worthing. Chelsea and her daughter told us all about him, said he was undercover and that's why you never called the police to Graham's with those bodies. Jess Montell filled us in."

A choked sound came from Blake, who'd gone back to blinking rapidly.

I had no idea who Chelsea and Jess Montell were.

Blake moved to my side, her frown deepening. "Jess Montell? Engaged to Tristian West?"

"Oh yes! That hottie. He was there that night Detective Drool-Worthy took Sawyer because he needed her help identifying men for the case he's working on." My mother was beaming, so proud that she could contribute to the conversation though she'd never been there. She added, "Chelsea told us there's a bun in the oven too. It's still a secret."

Bun? What bun?

In the oven?

They'd been baking this whole time?

My mind was too scattered to make sense of what she was saying.

She winked at me, but her smile faltered at seeing my face. "Oh, Sawyer. I'm sorry. I didn't mean—" She started for me again.

I wasn't sure about the change of her thoughts, but Oliver cut in. "Yes. Not so we get off track, but *yes*. We were told lots of things at their new friend's house. That we stayed in because the cops needed to go through our brownstone. Secretly. Because the whole operation was undercover." He stared hard at me first, then at Blake.

My mom and my aunts were all beaming. Except Maude. She looked disgruntled.

That was her resting face.

Oliver added, "Maybe we could have this conversation somewhere else?" His eyebrows were raised.

"Yes. An eatery. I'm famished." Clara was nodding along.

Bess's smile brightened. "Food's always good when the family gets together." Her gaze caught on Maude, and her smile went rigid. "Or most family."

Maude sneered at her. "That attitude right there. Why do you think my boy moved away and my girls—"

"Mom!" Graham interrupted this time, his tone sharp. He and Oliver both looked strained and his voice had an edge to it. His patience was thin. "Stop talking on my behalf in the future. Also, everyone back into the minivan. Sawyer, do you and your friend, here, uh—"

"Her name is Blake, and yes. She'll come with us." I'd decided.

Blake hadn't, though. "Uh. What?"

My smile was forced but had an extra meaning in it. "Yes. You're coming with us."

Blake tentatively took a step backward.

My eyes flashed. Sorry, but I knew the card to pull. I turned to all of my aunts who had moved back to the minivan. "She grew up in the foster system, and she recently moved to the city here. She has no family."

Blake was horrified. So were Graham and Oliver.

My aunts were not.

My mom's reaction was instant. *"She has no one?"*

Clara grumbled, scowling, "Not anymore, you don't. You hear me?"

Bess chimed in, "You are never alone anymore."

They swarmed her. Even Maude went with them, blinking back tears.

"Come here."

"You'll come with us."

"A good family sit-down is what we need."

"You'll tell us all about yourself, Blake. First, though, what's your favorite kind of food? Do you have a certain kind of pie you like?"

"Did you grow up eating casserole? A good Tater Tot hotdish has to be experienced. Did you go to a potluck with any of your foster houses?"

My aunts were speaking over one another as they pulled Blake into the minivan with them.

Bess looked her over, frowning. "Where's your car keys, hun? We can put them behind one of the tires and call a mechanic to come get your vehicle. That'll need to be fixed. Clara's got Triple A. She can call for you."

"Oh. Uh . . ." Blake cast me one last look before she was tugged into the back seat.

Maude crawled in first. My mom went after Blake. Clara and Bess took the two middle seats. Bear jumped up inside, his tail wagging so hard he was hitting Clara and Bess while his nose was turned toward the back end.

Pooh clambered up so she was standing on top of Bess's thigh, panting, and waiting for her dads.

Oliver remarked under his breath to Graham, "I'm pretty sure that car was stolen."

Another screech of brakes sounded from the street, this time closer.

An engine revved loudly.

I turned toward it. That sounded just around the corner.

"Honey, get in the car." Graham was talking to Oliver, who stiffly hurried around the side of the minivan.

I started to go with them, but another screeching sound made me turn around.

That sound was now so close.

A vehicle careened around the corner, fishtailing so it could turn into the same parking lot that we were in. It didn't make it, braking suddenly, and reversing.

My feet were already moving before my brain was catching up that I *needed to move.*

The SUV was barreling at me, bearing down at a fast pace.

Time slowed because I saw what was going to happen. They were here for us.

I was too far away.

It was too late for me. It was not too late for my family.

I began yelling at Graham. "Go! Now! They're here."

"Who is that?"

Oliver was yelling.

My aunts were shouting.

The dogs were barking.

Graham started the engine, giving me an agonizing expression, but I made a decision. I'd made my decision long ago. Me or my family? My family every goddamn time.

They needed more time to get away, so when the doors of the SUV opened, I ran toward them. I could still hear the minivan behind me, but I screamed, the sound curdling my blood, "*Go! Please!*"

One of the men reached out to me to catch me, but I evaded his touch. The man behind him caught me, but I grabbed for his holstered gun and ripped out of his arms, using a sudden burst of momentum that he wasn't expecting.

I moved back, his gun in my hand.

All their attention was suddenly on me.

My heart was pounding.

Terror raced through me, but my family had to live.

They were still fucking here.

"*Go! Fucking go!*" I screamed with everything in me.

They peeled out of there, right as the men closed in on me.

I could hear my family screaming, but just before they were out of sight, I looked up.

Blake was in the back, with the door open, and our eyes met. She gave me a nod.

I didn't know what that meant, but the gun was ripped out of my hands. They grabbed me.

This time, my kidnapping was real.

CHAPTER FORTY-TWO

JAKE

The coordinates he sent were for a warehouse. The door was left wide open so I drove right in.

Lane wouldn't be alone. He'd have men, a multitude of men with him. I was a good shot, but I wouldn't be able to get all of his men before one of them got me. I'd have to make my shots count, but it was really only one bullet I needed. Just one.

Two of his men opened my door for me and jerked me out of it.

"Hands up," one growled.

I knew the deal.

He was searching for that gun on me.

I lifted my hands in the air, spread my legs, and he patted me down. Ignoring him and his buddy, who had an assault rifle pointed at me, I glared across the warehouse to where Lane was standing.

I had a file on him. I'd read everything compiled from my previous colleagues already. Read the file that Ashton sent me too. His was more in depth, but I called in a favor and the file from the unit that was assigned to Lane solely was better. How he moved, how he operated were the actions of an older man. Not the twenty-eight years that his file said he was.

He was seven years younger than me.

Dressed in a black Henley, black jeans, black boots, he looked nothing like the criminal mastermind he was. His face was one my previous colleagues would've laughed about. He was too pretty to be who he was. Short black hair, a little more on top that looked like he ran his hand through it often. I wondered if that was a tell of his. I'd look out for it, but I cataloged the rest of him. Gray eyes. Tan skin. Caucasian. No distinguishable tattoos, which I had to assume was by design because a guy in his life, they were covered with them. It's how stories were told on their bodies. It's how they were identified, how their rank was known, what they've done in their service to whichever family they vowed their life to. If the police raided this warehouse right now, he could simply walk out with a backpack on him and a baseball cap. He would've looked like a normal college kid. He was tall, with broad shoulders, and had a lean build. Maybe a preppy college kid, but he would've blended.

That was done by design.

There was no backpack, though. No baseball cap. Instead, he had men with guns and that, no matter how young his face looked, those eyes gave him away. Always had to look in the eyes. That's where you'd find anything you needed to know about someone. Eyes could be masked, yeah, but at some point, the mask would fall and you'd get the window you needed.

My cousin had my mother's eyes.

I fucking hated that. "I never knew your mother."

His two men finished searching me and shoved me forward. One held back, looking into my truck. "Blake's not here."

His man used her first name and Lane barely paid him attention. His focus was on me. That also told me his men were familiar with her, familiar enough to be comfortable using her first name.

Lane gave a slight nod and his other man started walking me toward him. I caught him by surprise with what I'd said. He hadn't been expecting it.

How much did he wonder about his family? Did he at all?

I was jerked to a stop a few yards away and lowered my hands, my one hand itching to grab my gun and get this done. I'd be killed, but it wouldn't matter. Sawyer would be safe. EJ would be safe. I'd be with my brother.

It was a win, win, win.

Justin . . .

"What do you remember about your mom?" A part of me wanted to know. He *was* my cousin. "Your mom ran away when she was a teenager, from what I grew up knowing about her. They never talked about her." My gut shifted. There would've been a reason. A reason why she left, a reason they didn't talk about her, a reason why no one went after her.

I frowned, thinking about that now as an adult.

Lane's eyes narrowed, but he was letting me talk. His face was blank. He wasn't letting me read him. There was no flicker of life in those eyes of his.

Justin's same eyes.

"She was a whore, used up by the Santorinis. They hooked her on drugs and sold her body every night. I was taken away from her in the hospital, maybe the one good decision she made when she gave birth."

He was right. If she'd had him in a hotel room or on the street, he would've either been tossed in a dumpster or sold.

"The Santorinis are no longer in business, from what I know."

"They shouldn't be. I killed them all." There was still no emotion shown from him. Murdering an entire family was like taking out the trash to him. It was just something he did so the stink wouldn't build up. "It was the least I could do for what they did to my mother. Don't you agree?"

That last question was a test. He was looking for something in me now.

If someone did that to my mother? To Sawyer? Would I wipe out an entire family?

The answer was swift inside of me. I would have no problem killing the ones who had a hand in hurting either of them, but extending that to others who had no part in it? No. I wouldn't kill anyone who was innocent, but I knew that absolutely no Santorini existed anymore. Even second cousins and third cousins had been executed no matter where they lived. One was in Singapore and had no idea of his relations, and he'd been killed. It was a mystery that cops talked about because no one had a clue.

"I'm not like you in that regard."

He raised his chin up. "Not a killer?"

"Not a mass murderer." But that was a lie. It's the first job I'd been trained for in my life.

He smirked, the first emotion showing from him. "That'd be the cop inside you. Once a cop, always a cop."

"Yeah, sure."

He tilted his head to the side, sizing me up again, as if looking for something he hadn't looked for before. "You've always been the lone wolf too. Except you had a cub with you." He paused. That smirk only deepened. "Your brother. Justin." He was so fucking smug, indicating his eyes. "I saw the pictures. I share these with him. It's the one family trait I noticed. Your mother. Your brother. My mother. There's a few others in the family with the same eyes. Do you miss him? Your brother. You dedicated so much of your life to protecting him. *Coddling* him."

My blood started to heat. "I didn't coddle him."

"You did." His voice was even, casual. "If you hadn't sheltered him so much, he would've had a different reaction when he found out who your cousin was working for. That's the real reason he's dead, isn't it?"

My blood was fast on its way to boiling. "You don't know shit about that."

His eyes went back to looking like death. The smirk disappeared, his mouth returning to being flat. A flat affect, it's a term used to categorize someone who didn't show emotions. Some people had resting bitch face. Creighton had a non-emotive face. It was his default setting.

The corner of his mouth lifted up, a rareness. There'd never been a picture of my cousin grinning or smiling. I saw it now and it was surprising, but none of it reached his eyes.

He was gone. There was no redemption for Creighton Lane. He was a crime lord and he had no soul. He would never care about anyone. He would never feel guilt or shame. He was a corpse that walked around with a ruthless brain.

I pitied Blake Green.

"Your strength is also your weakness. You're a lone wolf. That makes you dangerous. Those men couldn't kill you because of how good you are at being the lone wolf, but it made you weak today. Out of everyone in this game we're playing, you have the most power, and you never once thought to wield it. You could've used our shared family, called in some of the Worthing men to back you up. You were police. You could've called in favors, used those resources. It's the biggest gang, after all. Or the other two kings of this city. Why are they not here having your back? Why are you alone, like you always are? Being a lone wolf was reckless, but that's your nature. I wondered what you would do, but a part of me knew you wouldn't go against your nature. So very few actually do. It's who you are. What other options do you have except to be who you are? Still, though. I hoped you would surprise me today, but you didn't. There's no cavalry coming for you. It's *just* you. I'm disappointed."

I was done with the formalities. "Don't you want to know where your woman is?"

His eyes sharpened, but he blinked lazily. "There have been a few changes since our initial agreement."

The hairs on the back of my neck stood on end. "What changes?"

"Well, the first one is that I'm aware you don't have my toy. You, in fact, don't have her at all." He motioned to his men, and a far door opened.

I shifted, my hand reaching for my gun. There was a flap on my vest, which his men would've skipped over, not questioning it. They wouldn't have felt for the small compartment where my gun was hidden. It was designed to mold against my body so their hands shifted over it, just assuming it had a rough extra layer.

I began tugging at the flap, pulling the Velcro off slowly.

More of his men stepped through the door. They were dragging two people with them.

No.

Everything stopped for me.

My body went cold.

No. No. No . . .

"I mentioned a cub earlier." Lane's smirk was back. "I wasn't only talking about your brother. I was talking about your son."

They were dragging Sawyer *and EJ* into the warehouse.

My knees almost buckled.

They dropped both of them on the ground between us. His men went to each, grabbing a hold of their hair, and yanked them up so they were kneeling on the cement ground. His men took position. Two behind each of them. Two guns pointed at their heads.

Both had been worked over with bruises already showing. Their faces were swollen. Their hands were taped together, the tape so tight their hands were turning white. The same duct tape was over their mouths. Fresh and dried blood covered their faces.

EJ's eyes weren't focused. They'd tortured him.

Jesus. EJ.

His sweatshirt was torn. His jeans roughed up. Bloodied. He had no shoes. His feet were bare.

Sawyer was alert, but pained.

She met my gaze, an apology flaring brightly in her eyes.

Rage swept through me. It wasn't fast, how I might've assumed it would be. It was slow, blanketing over every organ, every limb, every cell, every tendon.

It was shutting everything off inside of me.

"Like I was saying earlier, you don't have my toy, but you know how to find her. My men informed me that Blake went with your woman's family. So because of that, I'll give you a choice. You go and get my toy for me, bring her back to me, and I'll reward you. You can choose who lives. Your woman or your son."

He wasn't going to do this.

I had no choice. I had no options, just the one I came here to do.

"You should've done your homework better on me, cousin." I didn't recognize myself. That voice that came out of me belonged to someone else, someone who was at his end. I sounded like Lane, and so be it. "I didn't call on our family because they would've come, but you would've killed them. You're smarter than any of them. I'm aware of this. I'm sure you're smarter than me, but in the end, you would've killed the rest of our family and in the process, I would've gotten you." My voice cracked, thinking about a possible shoot-out with Sawyer in the middle, with EJ in the middle, and hardened again. "Maybe I could've called in favors from some police buddies. But you would've been alerted by that too. You have men on your payroll, I'm sure of it. You would've known before we even showed up. And as for Ashton and Trace, you're wrong about them." My hand moved away from my flap. My gun would need to stay where it was. "I'm done with taking orders. I'm done with receiving ultimatums. That means I'm also done being used as a pawn. You want your woman? Too bad. She doesn't want you."

There was no way out of this for me, for Sawyer, for EJ now.

I said, "I'll give *you* one option."

Something flickered in his eyes. Interest. "What?"

"My life for theirs."

Whatever it was flickered right out of his eyes. They returned to being flat. I momentarily interested him, but just as quickly bored him. "That's nothing new. You're going to die no matter what. You were always going to die. You've just been very good at evading it until today. You are a dead man standing right now. That's all you are." His eyes turned mean. "I don't care enough about you to kill you myself. This is the only choice you will get today, and I'm being gracious in giving this to you. You can save the life of one of these two. Your woman or your son. You failed to bring me my toy, so one of them will die because of that, but the other I'll set free. Your life will take their place."

I shook my head, a part of me disassociating with myself.

My soul was leaving my body, stepping away because of what I would need to do, what I'd been trained to become.

His men took the safety off their guns.

Creighton said, "*Choose*."

I did. "My son."

CHAPTER FORTY-THREE

SAWYER

Jake looked ready to collapse as soon as he chose. My heart ached for him.

When they brought me in, I tried to let him know. I was sorry for running. I was sorry for not trusting him. I wasn't sorry for helping Blake, but I was sorry I got caught. I was sorry for not thinking anything through, but there were other things I wanted to tell him.

I wanted to tell him all the things that I wasn't sorry about. Meeting him. Kissing him. Falling in love with him. But it was almost over. The fight had started to drain from him and as soon as he said those words, an order was given.

EJ was dragged out of there.

That voice spoke, so emotionless behind me, "Take him to Presbyterian. Dump him in front of the ER, then wait for more orders."

"Yes, boss."

I hadn't looked behind me. I'd only gotten a glimpse of some men in the warehouse before I saw Jake, and I hadn't looked away from him. He was staring at me, his shoulders drooping in defeat. He'd had a plan.

I saw it. There'd been something he was going to do, but the second he saw us, it changed. I watched it drain out of him.

I wished he would see that so many of the men were leaving. If we could do something, it would be now. EJ was safe, or would be safe. We could fight back.

Dammit. I had a bucket list. I was determined to go to the Aloha Festival in Hawaii. According to Google, it was famous. Him and me. We could still go.

We could do something, anything, and we could live. That's what we did. We survived and then we did stupid things in bed together. I wanted to do that again. I wanted to be stupid with him. *Let's be stupid together, Jake.*

I was silently pleading, but he shook his head, just slightly.

He was done.

All the hope left me. It'd been EJ. The sight of him stopped everything. Lane knew about his son. He would always know about his son.

He'd always be able to get to his son. That's what Jake was thinking.

A swell of frustration and helplessness burst inside of me because we could kill him now. Then EJ would be safe.

I tried to look behind me. I wanted to see what this fucking monster looked like, but there was still one man behind me, and he growled, "Eyes front, bitch." He used his gun to hit my face, sending me sprawling on the ground in front of him.

A savage growl erupted behind me. A body launched himself over me, and I heard fighting sounds. Grunts. Fists connecting.

Bang! "Enough. Stop this." That was Lane. A body hit the ground at an angle, and my heart froze because was that Jake? Had he shot Jake? I knew by how hard that body hit and how that body wasn't moving, they were dead. Whoever they were.

My jaw and cheek were throbbing from where the guy kicked me, and tears rushed to my eyes, but I held them back. I looked, rolling over a little bit to see who had been shot behind me.

I was staring into the dead eyes of someone I didn't know. It wasn't Jake.

Relief coursed through me, and a sob broke out.

I looked, searching. He was breathing hard, but he was still on his feet. We weren't all the way gone. There was still hope. As long as one of us was standing, there was hope.

I didn't want to die today.

So many stupid regrets flew through my mind. All of it was there in a flash. Stupid Beck. I didn't love him. I didn't think I ever had. Maybe I had. I must've at some point, but that died long ago. I hadn't known. I didn't care anymore. There was so much more in life. I wanted to do it all. Experience it all. Achieve it all. I had a bucket list of accomplishments I wanted to check off, but settling down in Bear Creek with Beck as my husband should've never been on that list. I was thankful for Manda now. I wanted to send them a gift basket, wish them well, and congratulate them on their coming baby.

I would never have to have kids with Beck. Thank you, Jesus.

I wanted those things with Jake.

I wanted to go whale watching with Jake.

Go to an elephant sanctuary.

See if zebras truly were mean or just misunderstood.

I wanted a *home* with Jake.

I wanted a career, whatever that would be. I wanted to find it, with Jake at my side.

I wanted *all of it* with Jake.

I wanted to have kids with him. We still had time. I was only one year his cougar. I wanted to have sex all day and all night long. I wanted to do it for a week. A fuck week. Go to Tahiti and never leave the hotel room because of all the fucking yummy delicious sex. *With Jake.*

I wanted to see my family again. Hug my mom. Laugh with Graham. I even wanted to give Maude a hug. It wasn't her fault she was so grouchy, I didn't think. I wanted to find out either way, but I couldn't do any of that if we didn't fight. I still wanted to get to the bottom of the family rift. I hadn't mended it.

Let's fight, Jake. Go out in a blaze of glory. I'd be down for that, as long as it was with him.

But to do that, he needed to fight. *We* needed to fight.

We could do anything together.

I was trying to relay all of this with my eyes, and he was reading it all, but there was nothing looking back at me. He was lying down for Lane.

Then he winked at me.

I gasped, and regretted it. Stupid duct tape.

But he winked. I saw it. He *winked.*

Okay, okay. I was wiggling around, trying to throw myself up on my knees. I was doing a hell of an impersonation of a turtle flipped on its shell. My limbs somewhat flailing around.

I was ferocious.

"Get her up."

I manifested that, just not quite this way. Two rough sets of hands took my arms and hauled me to my feet. I was jerked around, this time facing Jake and Lane.

Ugh. I could see which one was him right away. Short. Grotesque. No wonder Blake was running from him. He had a belly on him and he was sweating profusely. He was so dirty inside. I could tell. He had a gun in his hand too, but it was pointed at the floor. He wasn't man enough to handle us without a gun, huh? All his men he paid weren't enough for him? Or he was going to shoot us instead—

He spoke. "Take the tape off her. You can both have a moment. Say goodbye. It's the least I could do for family."

That little sweaty guy was not Lane.

It was the kid next to him. The kid! What the hell? He was a kid. How old was he? Then again, Blake was young too, but this guy? Really? He looked like any other young twenty-year-old. He could've still been in college. I mean, he was good looking in an "I'm dead inside and don't care about putting a bullet in your forehead" kind of way, but him? *Him?*

He didn't even have a gun. And he was half standing, as if bored by the whole fiasco. He looked more ready to pop on some headphones and take a stroll outside listening to music on his way to some party. Maybe I was exaggerating how young he looked, but he didn't look old enough to be the evil and heartless monster that he was.

Rough hands grasped my head. I had one second's notice and the tape was ripped off.

"Aghhhhhyoufuckingpieceofohmygodthatfuckinghurt," I screeched, sputtered, and whined, bending over to breathe out through my nose. I was going to kill Lane. I was going to kill the dude who took that tape off. I was going to kill the guy who kicked me, oh—he was already dead. I was going to kill everyone, and I glared around the warehouse to let them all know.

They were so terrified of me they didn't dare let it show. Good. Right. Don't let me see how much I unnerve you. I was still going to kill them all.

Just needed a fucking plan to do it.

"I hope she kills you one day," I hissed. It hurt to talk.

Lane turned that lifeless gaze my way.

I flinched because it was eerie to have that stare on me.

"I changed my mind." He raised his gun swiftly—*Where did that gun come from?*

"No!" Jake got in his way, stepping between us. His back to me. "Jesus Christ, Lane! She's going to die. Of course she's going to try and say something. She doesn't go down easily."

Lane sighed. "This has taken too much time already. Say your goodbyes."

"I want to hug her."

"You want to *hug* her?"

Jake was firm. "Yes." He'd stepped back, close enough to touch me. I didn't look at Lane again. I didn't want to see that zombie-looking pretty face anymore. Jake was all that mattered. He stepped farther into me, and brushed the back of—what was I feeling?

I mean, his vest was rubbing over my breasts and he was kinda getting them excited.

Vest. He was wearing a vest. The lightbulb clicked on.

This was Jake's plan.

We could get out of this.

He was bargaining to get my hands freed. I was only half listening, because he was rubbing against me in the slightest movements. They were tiny and he was trying not to draw attention to it, but he was being purposeful about it.

What was this extra bulge I was feeling? It was pressing under my sternum. That's what he was rubbing over me. He wanted my attention drawn there.

Was that . . . My hands were still tied together. No matter what, I couldn't do anything until they were freed.

"Fine. Fuck's sake. Cut her hands free. Let them hug. Then kill them while they're embracing. I want to get on with this and find my toy."

A man approached, grabbed my arms, and jerked me to the side. He took a knife, cutting through the tape. I released a breath of air when I had feeling in my hands again, which then were immediately filled with pins and needles as the blood drained back down. I hissed again, wiggling my fingers.

Jake turned to face me, his eyes intent on me. He spoke low under his breath, "Back flap."

I frowned, whispering, "What?"

His face cleared. "My back flap."

Where he'd been rubbing against me. A flap.

Holy Gods of Everything Against Mafia. He had a gun there. Or a weapon. I was hoping it wasn't a knife because we were screwed if that was the case. I had no knife-throwing skills.

"Hug, fucking hell." Lane's patience was done.

Jake stepped into me, his eyes going over my shoulder.

He had something else planned, but I knew my mission.

Our chests touched, my hand slipped under his shirt, found the flap, yanked it open and shoved inside. As soon as my hand closed around the end of a gun, Jake growled in my ear, "Now!"

He reached behind me, grabbing the guy that was there as I stepped to the side, his gun coming out of his vest and in my hands. I aimed it right at Lane, who didn't move except his eyes widened only a little bit. A spark lit.

There was a slight scuffle behind me, but another body hit the ground. I heard the safety being taken off a gun. Crap. Right. I needed to do that too. I'd forgotten.

Jake yelled, as the rest of the men in the warehouse drew their guns on us, "No one fucking move!" Then he shot three times. Three thuds sounded right after. He moved to block me. "We have one gun on your boss and I've got the rest of you in my sights. Don't fucking move."

No one moved, but I was betting those three thuds were guys that had moved.

My heart was soaring. This plan was awesome. We were going down fighting.

"I'd appreciate it if you'd *stop* killing my men, cousin. Though, maybe you're weeding my infrastructure, making it more sturdy? In that case, thanks." Lane flashed his teeth, biting out that word before the corner of his mouth turned down. He studied us. "What do you think is going to happen here?"

Jake expelled a harsh sound. "I think we're going to walk out of here and we'll continue this fight another day. That's what I think is going to happen."

"I still have your son, Jake." Lane's face still never showed any emotion, but that spark was there. Faintly. But no other emotions. No fear. No surprise. If anything, he seemed a little befuddled, but that was it. He wasn't perturbed. His face was still flat.

"When he's dropped off at the ER, when your men get back, we'll walk out of here."

"I'll send them after him again."

"Then Sawyer walks out of here *now*."

Lane's mouth lifted in a smile. It was startling. "Yes. You'll let your woman get a running chance, won't you? And you'll stay here, holding my men off because, as you're aware, I've done my research. You think I didn't know what our family first trained you to become, but I do. I'm glad that you've decided to show it to me." He sounded genuine.

Jake's eyebrows bunched together, momentarily. "I can see the antisocial diagnosis, but were you also diagnosed as a sociopath?"

Lane grunted. "Not quite."

Jake made a noncommittal sound, his lips pressed together. "Psychopath. Good to know."

I was bouncing between them. What did this all mean?

Jake went back to being Mr. Killer Man, but the random question got Lane's attention. His gaze lingered on my man, a different look starting to edge into his gaze. I couldn't place it. I wasn't sure I wanted to even try, but he kept studying Jake.

"This was supposed to be a suicide mission, wasn't it?" Lane could not look away from Jake. It was as if he were a new puzzle to him. "Killing me was the only way to ensure those you love would live."

Jake didn't reply. I could feel the tension and anger rolling off him in waves. It was filling the warehouse up, adding and doubling when it was meeting the tension from the rest of the men. All the men. All with guns. All pointed at us, and we were holding off certain death with Jake's shooting skills.

If we got out of this, the first thing we were doing was booking our trip to Tahiti. I *really* wanted to fuck my man right now. And then we'd talk about this fucking asinine suicide mission, because *what the fuck*? I was finally living my life, and he was going to end his?

I don't fucking think so.

He couldn't give me the sun and *take it back*.

Everything stopped in the next breath because Lane said, "I'm going to call your bluff." He began to raise his gun.

My stomach dropped.

Then two things happened at once.

A minivan roared into the warehouse, and I pulled the trigger.

CHAPTER FORTY-FOUR

JAKE

Sawyer shot Lane.

Holy shit.

He stepped to the side as the minivan burst inside the warehouse, at the same exact time Sawyer pulled her trigger so her bullet grazed him.

Holy fuck.

Holy fuck.

She almost shot him. She did shoot him. She could've killed him.

He didn't even wince as the bullet skimmed the side of his arm. He just stopped in his tracks and fixed Sawyer with an impenetrable darkness. Murder. He was going to kill her.

No.

No, he would not.

But as the three of us were holding in our death-off, the door for the minivan opened. The cast of *Goonies* spilled out of the minivan. It wasn't the actual cast, but it was the same effect, as two dogs, four women who were pushing slightly older than middle age, two guys, and Blake Green flooded from the vehicle.

Later I would contemplate how all of them fit in there. Now, I wasn't the only one caught off-guard. The four older women all had different weapons in their hands and they ran right toward Lane's men. One was throwing out nunchucks. What the—I couldn't even finish that thought.

Lane's gaze zeroed in on Sawyer.

He began to raise his gun again.

So did I, and I was moving before he could pull the trigger. My feet took me to stand in front of Sawyer. I wanted to pull the trigger. My finger was itching to do it. It'd be so easy. I'd done it before. My blood was pumping fast through my body.

At the same time, Blake's voice yelled over everyone. "Don't! Don't shoot. *Stop.*" She screamed, making her voice break. She looked as if she were trying to literally stop the bullets from passing through air, as if she had that power.

Lane's reaction was swift, his eyes widening, jerking straight to her like she was a magnet for him.

Lane's men turned their guns on her, except for the two defending themselves against Clara and Bess. I didn't know the other two, but judging by the resemblance of the petite woman, I was guessing that was Sawyer's mom. Her and the last woman weren't doing anything. Clara was trying to karate chop a guy with her hands. Her knee rose up in a *Karate Kid* rendition while Bess was swinging the nunchucks. She had no idea how to use them so they were mostly banging up her arms as she was dodging them herself. Sawyer's mom jumped in to give the guy's shin a kick.

The fourth still wasn't doing anything, except when one of them men turned a gun on the other women, a mean glint gleamed in her eyes and she charged him. She was using her body like a bowling ball. That was . . . That was a different fighting technique. He didn't see her coming and she took him down. She was turning to repeat the process on another guy when Lane's voice cleared the room. "Stop. *Now.*"

It was low but filled with authority. Everyone froze, adhering to his order.

Lane stalked forward, snarling at his men, "No guns pointed at her. Point them down. *Now.*" Anger was brimming over his face, the first real emotion I had seen on him. Most of his men realized their mistakes and corrected themselves, but two weren't so fast.

Lane growled, shooting both in the head.

Their bodies fell to the ground.

The rest of his men scrambled, dropping their guns in their haste.

Also, fuck, he was a good shot too.

"Oh no." Sawyer began crying. These weren't soft or simple tears. They were soul-encumbered, big and fat tears that were rolling down her face. "My family."

She started to go for them, but I caught her arm. "Give me your gun, babe."

She shuddered, and I pulled her into my arms. Pressing her forehead into the crook of my neck and shoulder. I felt her push the gun into my hand and without letting her go, I put the safety back on and stuffed it inside my back pocket. Sawyer's hands grazed mine as she helped put the flap back over it, then tugged my shirt on top. After that, she wrapped both her arms tight around me.

We were taking a moment.

"Round them up. Now!" Lane barked.

His men began going for Sawyer's family, but they stopped when Green spoke up. "No."

I moved Sawyer out of the way, easing her toward her aunts. As I did, I could see Green and Lane embroiled in an intense stare-off, not that different from the murder-off the three of us had been in a few seconds earlier.

His eyes narrowed, holding hers.

Her order had been just that, an order. She didn't say it with a hitch in her voice. There was no uncertainty in her. She wasn't scared. She said it as if they *would* do as she said. Confidence rolled off her. She cocked her chin up, her eyes flashing a challenge as she continued to hold Lane's gaze.

She added, her voice dipping low, "I said no, Creight."

His face went cold. "Quo—"

"Do not fucking call me that, and I'm firm on this. Let. Them. *Go.*" She drew her chin up even higher, defiance sparking from her gaze. Her hands went into her pockets, an almost contradiction of her assertiveness, but it didn't make her seem as if she were challenging him. She was outright commanding him.

Who was this girl to my psychopathic cousin?

"Let them go, Creighton. I won't say it again."

The rest of us were forgotten. Seeing that, knowing that, I kept edging backward. Lane couldn't look away from Green anymore and that needed to be capitalized on.

He countered, taking a step toward her, "Them for you."

She sucked in a ragged breath, her eyes bleak. *"No."*

"Quokka—"

She threw a hand in the air, palm toward him. "I will lose my shit if you say that name one more time." She tucked her chin now, losing some of that assertiveness.

Seeing her switch, Lane put his gun away. He gentled his tone. "Blake. I want you—"

Her chin jerked back up, and she snapped, "I don't give a shit what you want. They all go free, and I mean it. Not one of them will be harmed. The people each of them love will not be harmed. This fight with Sawyer, with your own cousin, will end now."

"He took you from me."

She threw back, just as quickly, "You only knew where I was because of him."

His eyes narrowed to slits. "I would've found you."

"Yes, you would've, but not as fast. You should be thanking him." Her nostrils flared as she spoke, and she moved closer to him. "I'm not coming back home, but I also won't run."

"Come home—"

She cut him off. "You have my terms." She took another step, close enough to touch him if she chose. Her hands were still in her pockets. She tilted her head up to stare into his eyes and she breathed out, "*Choose.*"

A look flared over him. I didn't recognize it, but it was gone quickly. I wasn't going to wait around and decide what he was going to say. He was a fucking psychopath. I pivoted around, hauling Sawyer with me, and I herded her to the minivan. The husbands were holding their dogs back, right by the doors. I motioned to them. "Get in. Everyone, get the fuck in. Now."

Urged on by my voice, the steel in it, the guys hopped in, but Graham took hold of Sawyer. He pulled her with him, and I got a glimpse at the set of his face. She was nonnegotiable to him. I gave him a small nod, and he caught it, his mouth parting, just slightly. The aunts were all chattering, hurrying inside. As soon as the last one was in, Sawyer moved to the seat beside me. She leaned out, but not one, two, or three hands grabbed for her. Four hands took hold of her, as if they were scared she'd slip out of their hold.

She wasn't going anywhere.

She leaned toward me. "Come with us."

I looked over my shoulder.

Lane and Green were both watching us.

My cousin met my gaze and we shared a look. We both understood each other at that moment. I didn't know how, but a clarity came over me suddenly. He was going to choose to let all of us live, but I caught a shroud of darkness at his edges, and I said to Green, "Make him promise to let them live their fullest and happiest lives. That means sans torture or interference from him *in any way.*"

That darkness flashed bright, hot, before it slunk away. He would've let them live, but barely. It was his work-around.

Green's eyes filled with outrage and she rounded on him. "You will leave them the fuck alone. They live, all of them, and they live to their happiest ability and everything he just said."

There was no change from him.

She dropped her voice, but it was loud enough for me to hear. "They took me in, Eight. They cared about me in the span of knowing me for only a second."

He switched his murderous gaze from me to her, and they gentled. The shift was so fast, it was like flipping the lights on. Poof and the shadows were gone. They were lit up, but that was her effect on him.

I saw the capitulation in him, and rounded. Fusing my mouth with Sawyer, I breathed against her lips, "I love you."

I felt and heard her gasp but then I ripped myself away, slammed shut the door, and pounded on it once. "Go!"

It shot out of there.

CHAPTER FORTY-FIVE

SAWYER

"What the ever-loving fuck just happened?"

We drove straight to Graham and Oliver's place, and as soon as we stumbled inside, that was what Aunt Bess exclaimed. She stopped in the middle of the living room, just a few feet from the front door, and her head was tipped as if that question was for the Almighty above.

Graham and Oliver carried Bear and Pooh into the house, immediately easing both to the floor so the two dogs could go crazy all by themselves.

Everyone else spilled inside.

I stepped to the side, dazed.

We left Jake behind. We left him behind. And Blake.

I hugged myself, wanting to ward off some of the cold that I'd been feeling since the minivan peeled out of there. We left them behind.

That wasn't going to stop repeating in my head. It was wrong, all wrong.

Aunt Clara began moving around the brownstone, looking in the drawers and not finding whatever she needed so she moved on to the next drawer.

My mom stopped a few feet from me, her eyes worried.

The dogs were barking. Their tails wagging. They kept circling everyone.

Graham and Oliver both beelined for the liquor cabinet. They were pulling out every single bottle they had, along with the mixers. Oliver began cutting limes. Graham took a shot and grabbed some of the lime that wasn't cut, sinking his teeth into it. He nodded emphatically, giving his husband a thumbs-up that he was cutting more slices. He made a sound, but it was muffled around the lime.

Aunt Maude came in last and stopped just inside the door. She took us all in, and shook her head, harrumphing loudly. Everyone paused in what they were doing to look her way, but she ignored us, trudging to the back door in her yellow clogs, and opened the door for the dogs. Bear and Pooh happily darted outside to do their business.

She returned, taking us all in again and shook her head again. The judgment was just rolling off her.

I snapped, fed up, "What the fuck is your problem?"

Aunt Clara and Bess both whirled my way.

My mom hissed, "Sawyer."

Oliver and Graham paused in their drinks ministrations. A lime fell out of Graham's mouth, plopping down on the counter.

I was done dealing with this. "Honestly. I want to know. What the fuck is your problem?" I motioned to the door. "Coming in here, having an opinion that everyone is stressed about what we just left? Who the fuck are you to judge how we should react?" She didn't reply, but she wanted to. I saw the heat in her eyes. When she only kept that mouth shut, I rolled my eyes. "Of course you're not going to say a thing. Why would you? It's easier for you to be passive aggressive and say shit behind everyone else's backs."

She sucked in some air and shifted on her feet, her beady eyes somehow becoming beadier. "You need to watch what you say—"

That unleashed something inside of me. I didn't even know there was still something I was holding back, but at her lecture or whatever it was, I could hear the latch being broken. The gate swung open and I was going to let frustration I held at the entire family loose on her, and I was going to enjoy it.

I opened my mouth, drew in a breath—and Graham stole the show.

He said, "She's not wrong, Mom."

Aunt Maude shuffled to take her son in better. "You agree with her?"

His eyes flared briefly, a shine of tears there as he grabbed an uncut lime and began to squeeze it in his hand. "She came here to meet me. Because of the rift between all of you. She wanted my help to mend this, but the way you talk to each other, it's horrible. She didn't know anything about me except what she learned from social media. Why is that, Mom? Is it that you don't talk about me or that you just don't talk to your sisters? Is it me?" He glanced at Oliver, who touched his arm, rubbing it in support. "Is it because I'm gay?"

"I—" Aunt Maude couldn't talk. She gurgled that word out, paling.

Oliver shared a sad smile with me before looking away.

No. No!

"It had better not be because of that! Is it?"

Aunt Clara made a gargling sound before she drew upright. "It better fucking not be because of that." She swung accusing eyes around to her sister, pinning her in place. "I mostly like women."

Maude's eyes were so heated. The anger was rising.

I held my breath, wanting it to keep rising. Please, please, please. She was a pressure cooker and I wanted to see her blow. Or, hell, if I were being honest, I wanted someone to blow because I had some stress. I was going to join in. A good family brawl where everything came out was the best sort of stress release. We were due. The last good one we had was the Christmas family event of 2013. That one had been a doozy.

"It's not about—" Maude just kept rising. Her chest was red. Her neck. Her jaw. She sputtered a bit more. "I—it has nothing to do with who's fucking who!"

She blew.

It was a glorious sight.

The red went to her forehead.

Aunt Bess griped, "Then what's it got to do with? We don't know our nephew. We felt like it was wrong to reach out to him, and that's on you. You don't want us in your life, in your kids' lives. You never see us. You never come on holidays. The few times we do see you, it's like talking to a damned rock trying to find out anything about you, about your boy, about your girls. I've not seen my other two nieces in twelve years."

"No." Clara corrected her, shaking her head. "We went shopping that one time in Missoula."

"That's right. It's been four years since I saw your girls and another eight before that. You're their mother. You set the tone. I've been asking for the last three years for their addresses so I could send a Christmas card their way. You always 'forget.'" She harrumphed. "Bullshit. You just don't want us to be a part of our nieces' and nephew's lives."

"It's—" Maude kept shaking her head, her eyes shining again. She looked like she was struggling to speak.

I felt a little bad. I felt part of this was my fault.

She choked out, "You're all adults. You can—" She waved a hand around the room, really trying to hold back her tears, but they trickled down.

There was a scraping sound at the back door, and a bark that followed.

My mom crossed the room to let Bear and Pooh inside. They scampered around, saying their hellos to everyone before going to the water bowl.

Oliver moved to the kitchen and a rustling sound was soon heard. The crinkle of dog food being poured into a bowl. He put the dog food away before returning to Graham's side, taking his hand in his and gripping it tightly.

Maude drew in a sharp breath, saying so tightly, her voice strained, "I've never meant to keep anyone away from each other. I swear. It's . . ."

"What?" Aunt Bess moved her way, her voice sharp. "It's what?"

"It's . . ." Aunt Maude stopped trying to fight the tears from falling. She let them fall, her eyes opening wide, and she motioned around the room. "It's you guys."

The sisters all shared a look.

"It's Mom and Dad." Her voice broke. "It was Mom and Dad."

I lowered my head, and then felt a glass of something being pushed into my hand. A warm arm slid over my shoulders as another warm body pressed up on my other side. Graham and Oliver had come to stand beside me as Oliver had made me a drink.

I whispered, "Thanks." It was pink and green and looked like a real-life watermelon, just liquid and in a glass. "It's real pretty."

Graham snorted.

Oliver snickered, leaning into my other side. "I tripled the booze."

I said it again, breathless, "*Thank you.*"

Both laughed quietly.

I took a sip, and almost moaned because it was sooo good, but all four sisters were finally talking. To each other. (To clarify.)

My mom said, "What do you mean by that? It was Mom and Dad? They've been gone for years."

Maude sighed, blinking back tears. Her whole chest deflated. "Mom—she told me to go. Said for me not to come back. I . . . I took that literally. I was hurting. My pride—I was so stubborn. I was wrong to be so stubborn." Her eyes held to her son, misery and guilt shining.

"What did you fight about?" Bess's voice quieted, calming down. A twinge of pity crossed her face. "Mom and Dad weren't perfect, but I can't imagine Mom would kick you out."

"She did. She, uh, she didn't want to hear something I had to say."

Oh no. A new bad feeling was sneaking into my gut, settling there.

"What did you tell her?" Clara rasped out, demanding. A bit rough.

"I told her . . ." More tears trickled down Aunt Maude's face. "I told her a teacher touched me—"

My mom gasped.

"Oh, no," Bess said under her breath.

Maude finished, faintly, "—Mom didn't want to hear it. She told me I was lying, but I would not go back to that school."

"That's when you dropped out." My mom again, softly. "You moved after that."

Maude hung her head, not looking at anyone. "I'm fine with, you know. What he did, it wasn't that bad, but it would have gotten worse. Mom didn't want to deal with it. She wanted me to apologize to him for making up that lie. I wasn't lying. I—I vowed then and there I was done with the family. I'm sorry."

My heart broke. For her. For the years of separation that started from that day on.

Graham whispered to me, "I never met Grandma and Grandpa. What were they like?"

Graham knew. This, what his mom just shared, it wasn't a secret to him.

I said back, "You knew?"

"Our grandparents?"

"No. What she just said."

"Oh." A shadow crossed his face before he blinked it away, some wetness appearing in its wake. "Yes. She's always advocated that we respect our boundaries around people. She explained the reasons why. It broke my heart knowing what happened to her, but I didn't know the part about Grandma. I didn't know it was the reason for all of this. I . . ." His voice grew hoarse. "Were they like that? Grandma and Grandpa?"

I met my mom's gaze. She'd overheard us, and she drew in a sad smile. She said for me, "They were, yes."

Graham and Oliver looked her way. The rest quieted.

My mom added, "I don't like to speak ill of the dead, but they weren't understanding. I had no idea something happened to my sister, but I knew I didn't quite trust my little girl around them. We kept away to protect Sawyer. Then they passed and I didn't see a reason to talk about that, about them." She glanced in Maude's direction. "I regret that now. I wished I'd known, Maude."

"It's not . . . It's not just that. I'm okay. I really am. I healed from what that teacher did. Got counseling, but Mom and Dad have been gone. I could've come back. I—just—" Maude spoke again. "I'm not like the three of you. I don't fit in. I never have been—"

Phyllis murmured, "Oh, Maude. I'm so sorry—"

"Don't sorry her!" Clara's voice hitched high. "I'm sorry for what happened to you. I am. And I'm going to want his name, but if I'd known back then, I would've done something. To the teacher, to Mom. It wouldn't have flown if I'd known, but they've been gone for years. You stayed away. We're all different. I mean, look at me, for one. I'm not supposed to fit in. That's what the rest of the world tells me. Kumbay-fucking-yah. You think most people look at me and think, 'Yeah, her. I'm going to only include her.' News flash: None of us are those types of people."

Aunt Bess was nodding with everything Clara was saying. "You decided to stay away."

"If anyone doesn't fit in, it's Phyllis." Clara gestured to my mom, her voice rising. "Look at her. She's churchy and pretty and she cares what people think of her. She's the one that fits in with the world, but shouldn't fit in with us."

My mom was nodding also, blinking back tears until that. "Wait. What? Are you saying I don't fit in? That's—I fit in. I—I—that's my problem, I fit in so much. I'm trying not to fit in so much." A sheen of sweat formed on her forehead.

This whole mending conversation was going sideways. I cocked my head, wondering if I should say something, steer it back.

Clara puffed up her chest. "I love you, Phyll, but get over it. You fit in with society. I don't." She motioned toward Maude and Bess. "We don't. We don't uphold society's beauty standards. That's just one of the ways. I'm loud. I want my opinion heard. No one's going to tell me to be quiet. I'm a big woman."

Bess spoke up. "You're curvy. Like me."

Clara threw her a look. "I'm tough. That's what I care about. I don't give a fuck if my arms aren't twigs. I got personality. I got a good sense of don't fuck with me. And I can take care of shit. No one messes with me. That's what I like. And I like me. The world looks at me and tells me that I'm not supposed to like me, but fuck 'em. I do. It's my life. I live it how I want to. No one else does. I'm good with that."

"Me too." Bess shared a smile with Clara. "I think I might want to marry again. I tried it once, but he wasn't the one for me. I've been eyeing that Joe fellow."

Clara raised her chin up. "The one who runs the farming equipment store in town?"

"That's the one. He has coffee down at Bear Paws Coffee. I see him every morning. We've started sitting together and doing crossword puzzles. I like him. I let him fing—"

"Oh! No. Please, Aunt Bess." Graham's hold on me tightened. He looked a little green around his mouth. "Can we—" He coughed, clearing his throat.

I spoke up, letting myself enjoy this. "I don't think we need to hear the details, but good for you, Aunt Bess." I gave her a thumbs-up.

Clara started laughing. "Anyways. We're all weird. It's how we are. I don't give a fuck. You shouldn't either, Maude. You can't keep away from us. Not anymore." She motioned to where I stood with Graham and Oliver. "We met your boy and his husband. The cousins have teamed up together. It's only a matter of time before Sawyer gets back and hunts down your other girls—"

"And Blake," Maude interjected.

Blake. My heart took a dip.

We'd left her behind. Left Jake behind.

But he'd be okay. I was trying to tell myself that.

He knew what he was doing.

I needed to trust him . . .

This time right now was precious. It was one of the reasons I came.

"That girl will be fine." My mom was trying to reassure me, eyeing me.

I tried to give her a smile, but it fell.

"We'll give it some time and look her up. We'll reach out. Everything will be fine, honey. I know things have been stressful, but honey, we'll make a list. Write down everything that needs to be done. Cross it out as we accomplish it. Okay?"

"That's a great idea, Aunt Phyllis."

She gave Graham a warm smile. "Thank you, honey. You have no idea how stressful the wedding's been with Beck—" She stopped talking, remembering all of a sudden the reason that set all of this off. "Oh, honey. I'm so sorry."

I was good with letting it go. I wanted to see what happened.

I leaned heavily against Oliver and Graham, giving her a wave. "No problem, Mom. I'm all good about that situation. When we get back, I'll need to hand in my resignation, if Beck hasn't officially fired me. And kick him out of my house. Though, I'm hoping he's living with Manda now since I guess they got married."

All other conversations stopped.

Their attention swung my way.

I held up my watermelon drink. It was almost all gone.

"House?" My mom's voice cracked, but it was sharp. Correction, it was pissed off. My mom was pissed off. "*House?* That's your house?"

Oh . . . I forgot. "Yeah." I gave them a weak smile. "Oops. We never told anyone because of Beck's ego and all, but yeah. It's my house. I bought it."

Someone sucked in some air.

"Is it in your name?" Oliver asked me, still hugging me.

I nodded, some pride filling my chest. "Beck was ticked about that, but I bought it. The mortgage is in my name. The title is in my name. It's all mine. None of it is his."

A new calculating gleam came over Oliver and he shared a secretive smile over my head. He squeezed me to his chest. "Please, Sawyer. Please let me help you with this. I would love nothing more than to help draft a letter that you can give to your ex. He will be packed and out of that house within half a day. I love doing this sort of thing." He waited, brimming with excited energy.

Graham whispered in my ear, "He had an ex before me that was a freeloader. This is his thing. He's helped some of our other friends in similar situations."

"I—" I gave Oliver a smile. "Sure. I mean, why not. I'd love the help."

His eyes got so big, delighted. "I'm going to start now."

"Wait." I caught him before he rushed off and held out my now-empty glass. "Can you make another? Before you go and do your thing?"

"Oh." He laughed, taking the glass. "Of course." He went over to the liquor cabinet, the back of his ears a little red.

Without Oliver on my other side, Graham pulled me so my front was into his side, as if he were happy to have me all to himself. He spoke over my head, his breath teasing my forehead. "So have the four of you figured your shit out? Because, Mom, I've not pushed getting to know my family. I did that mostly because it was exhausting to ask you how my aunts and my cousin were doing. You never wanted to talk about them so I let it go. When I moved out here, I was all about my life being here and then I was all about Oliver. When I got older, with the distance it was easier to let it go, but not anymore. Sawyer came here for me. My aunts have all come here. Stayed at my house. I love you, Mom, but the separation ends here. No matter what is resolved, or if you decide to fall back on old habits, I'm going to have a relationship with them."

She returned, "I would never ask you not to have a relationship with them. I never did."

Graham said, a little more tender, "But you're my mom. You set the tone. I was doing what I thought you wanted. I didn't want to open old wounds."

She was blinking back some tears. "I never meant to be a block between you or my girls and the rest of the family. It's been me. It's just how I am. I've always struggled letting people in. I learned not to open up to people. Mostly they don't want to hear what you have to say unless it goes along with the status quo. Whatever's convenient, but I'm not convenient. I know this about me. But I never wanted that to affect you or your sisters. I'm sorry for that. I really am. I—it just felt safer to stay away." She lowered her head, her shoulders pulling in. "I need to work on that."

No one said anything at first.

The sisters all shared a look except for Bess. She was staring right at Maude's bent head and after she pressed her lips together in a flat line, she said loudly, "You damn well will work on that."

Maude's head jerked up.

Bess motioned to herself and Clara. "Tough shit if you think we're going to let you stay away now. Bad habit is what your son said, but our habit is to get involved. We're not great with boundaries. We'll work on that, but knowing now what happened to you, good luck keeping us away. We bulldoze over the ones we love with our love." She paused, frowning. "That doesn't sound right. You know what I mean."

Clara said to Graham, "You don't need to worry about your mom staying away. She's a few hours away. We'll make it a weekly thing, just show up at her house with our suitcases. I have good people skills. I'll make friends with her neighbors, have them report to me how she's doing if she stops taking my calls. I ain't above using trackers on vehicles. We got your mom."

Graham's arm tightened around me. His chest rose. "I love hearing everything about that."

Bess was just as sharp, saying, "You shouldn't, because we're nosy. Said it once, but it bears saying again."

"Yep." Clara nodded.

"You're in the fold now, Graham. You and Oliver." Bess wasn't done. "You're going to look back on these past years with fondness because you'll miss the lovely boundaries and privacy you had. We don't operate like that."

"Not one bit." Clara had gotten a drink somehow and held her glass up.

"And we do it because we love you, but—uh—we're going to smother you with our aunt love."

"Prepare for that shit." Clara tipped her head back and guzzled half her drink.

Oliver's eyes went so wide. "No—I—oh dear."

My mom burst into tears, and she headed right for me. "You did this." She burrowed into me. I wrapped my arms around her, and Graham put a hand on her back. She choked out, "Thank you for coming here and doing this and bringing Graham back into the family, and my sister. I—"

She couldn't breathe. She was crying so hard.

It's where I got that too. I patted her back, saying, "Pull back some of those emotions, Mom. You can't breathe and cry. The universe wanted you to pick a lane and keep with it." And since we always needed to breathe, the decision was forced. I was giving the universe a side-eye. Just a little one, because I still needed some help from it.

My mom softened on her sniffles, but stayed burrowing into my chest.

I looked around the room.

Maude was smiling, faintly. She'd migrated closer to Clara and Bess.

I wasn't so worried about the family anymore.

"Sawsaw."

I glanced in Bess's direction.

"When your man shows up, you'll need to get that Blake girl's information. The sooner she realizes she's been unofficially adopted into the family, the better. We're not letting that one go, despite the lunatic attached to her hip. If she's worried about him, we'll handle him just fine. He can't push his way around Bear Creek."

Lunatic. Jake. Blake.

I pulled Mom back to me and tightened my hold. This time, I burrowed my head into her neck.

Please, Universe. Bring me back my man, breathing and all in one piece.

I needed to tell him that I loved him too.

CHAPTER FORTY-SIX

SAWYER

He never showed. There were no calls. No texts.

That was when I realized I'd never had his number in the first place. That was a sobering realization. I felt like I'd lost him all over again.

We flew back a few days later.

We couldn't stay in New York forever. At some point, we needed to return home. I wanted to hold off, but I couldn't. There was a mess in Montana that I still needed to sort through, including kicking Beck out of my house, which was so satisfying.

I also turned in my resignation, not that anyone thought I was going to continue working for my ex. When I dropped it off, I meant to sneak in, slip it under the door, but the office was already open. It was early, but one of the patient assistants was already there. We talked a little and I found out half Beck's employees quit the day he married Manda in my place.

That warmed my heart because a small town meant a small pool to replace good employees with new ones. Plus, the gossip was brutal. If so many employees left him, that said a lot about where the town had placed their loyalty. With me. I wouldn't be surprised if Beck was going to lose patients and would need to set up in a different town.

Time would tell.

Time would tell for me as well because I ached for Jake.

Every day and every night. I couldn't sleep because I wanted him. I lost my appetite, finally losing some of that weight my mother once mentioned to me, but she broke down crying one day, saying, "I was wrong. It doesn't matter. The stupid weight. It doesn't matter. I want you to shine, and you're not shining."

I understood what she was saying, but I couldn't make myself shine without Jake in my life.

A month passed.

Then another one. No call. No texts. No emails.

My things were mailed a week later. They were the items that I'd left behind when Blake and I ran for it. At first I thought that meant he was alive. He sent them, until I found a note that they were mailed to my address at the request from Jake.

It was in a woman's handwriting. No name was attached, so did that mean Laila sent them? I was half tempted to call her. I knew where I could get a hold of her, but another part of me knew that I would shatter if I found out he was with her. He said they'd only had a benefits-type situationship and it wasn't serious, but he had a key to her place.

I wanted to murder him. I wanted to yell at him, throw things at him, maybe stab him with a trident. Anything to hear from him. I never maimed him. That'd been my promise to myself the second time he kidnapped me. It was the only way I gave up my anger at him so fast, but I know now that I melted for him so quickly because I'd already fallen for him.

I loved him.

This was Jake's effect.

I was different and as the days went by, I was changing more and more.

The color left.

The world had been washed-out colors, the barest of neutral colors before him. Then Jake entered my world and boom, before I knew it was happening, despite if I wanted it to happen, everything became yellow, orange, neon. The brightest purple. The prettiest pink. Even black and white had texture.

Jake gave me color. Then he took it away.

The sun went away again.

"Honey, are you ready?" My mom came into the room, dressed in a fancy white sweater tank top. Underneath were skinny jeans and sparkly pink shoes that peeked out over her toes. I whistled, taking in all her gloriousness, complete with the low-hanging pendant necklace and the clutch that matched her shoes.

"Mom."

She blushed. "What?"

"You look hot. Beautiful, but hot." I teased her, cocking my head to the side. "Are you and Dad okay? Are you having problems? Does he know you're hoping to pick someone up at this barbecue?"

Her blush doubled. She waved a hand at me before turning for the door. "Oh, you. You're always teasing lately. Come on. We're already a bit late."

We'd been waiting for Dad this whole time. I'd been ready for the last hour, waiting, thinking, and knowing I shouldn't be thinking. Like she said, I was always teasing. That was me lately.

Teasing. Smiling. Faking.

My heart had been ripped out all over again.

I didn't know when it happened, or even how, but at some point, Jake became mine too. Mine back. He gave me the sun. How fucking dare he take it back? This was worse than Beck, than Manda. That'd been nothing compared to this and I couldn't do a thing to fix it.

Jake was gone.

My chest ached, but this was the moment when I felt like breaking down and when I wanted to crawl in bed and never leave again—this was when I covered it up with a joke. No one could see the cracks. If they did, they'd realize how close I was to having the entire wall fall down. It was already collapsing. I was barely holding the weight up, but my knees were buckling.

I wanted to fall down, but fuck no. Jake wouldn't have done that. So I'd keep waiting. That's all I *could* do.

So I did that. I waited for Jake.

CHAPTER FORTY-SEVEN

SAWYER

The bed depressing under someone's weight woke me up at the same time I heard Jake's mocking voice. "I've not had to keep quiet because of parents for a long fucking time." He was climbing into my bed. My childhood bed. Taking the corner of my blanket, he flung it off me.

"What?" I surged upright in my bed.

I was seeing things.

Jake was here.

Jake was in Montana.

"Jake?"

"Hi," he whispered, still laughing under his breath. He leaned over me and nipped at my mouth before resting his forehead to mine. "I've missed you."

"You're here?" I grasped both of his arms, not wanting to let him go.

"Yeah. I'm here. I couldn't stay away any longer." He moved to the side and slid under my blanket.

The reality of our location hit me. "This is my parents' house."

"I know." He settled on my side, his gaze raking me up and down. Dark approval was in those eyes of his. I could see enough from a little light plugged in the room's corner. "I'm liking what you're wearing." His hand ran to the end of my shirt. Correction, his shirt.

"How the fuck did you get this?" he asked.

"I stuffed it in my purse when I ran. I wasn't sure if I'd get more clothes. I was on the run." When I pulled it out, I burst into tears.

His smirk fell away, and he grew somber. "You're not anymore." His hand slid to the back of my head, his fingers sliding through my hair. He tipped me up to see him better and he angled himself so he was almost gazing down into my soul. Almost directly above me. "I made a deal." His voice grew hoarse.

My heart faltered. My hand rose to press against his chest. "What kind of deal? What about Blake? Is Blake okay?" My voice rose. "And why are you just now finding me? It's been two months. Two months! You asshole."

He gave me a resigned smile, laying his head down, still watching me. "She's fine. And I had to stay away because I needed to make sure EJ was safe. I'm sorry, baby."

I might've swooned at that name, but still gave him a look.

He snorted out a laugh. "My lunatic."

I grinned. "Better." I reached for his hand, entwining our fingers. I lay down, too, in shock. He was here. I needed to ask more about Blake, but later. Right now, I couldn't stop focusing on Jake. I flattened my hand against him and slid it upward, my palm flat against his skin. It went to his neck, where I could still feel his pulse. I closed my eyes because in that moment, all the fear I'd been holding over the last two months flooded me.

I choked out, "I've been so scared you were dead."

"Sawyer," he rasped out, curling me up to him as he moved both of us so he was lying down and I was tucked into his side. He pulled my legs over him, continuing to move me gently until I was curled in a ball on top of him. His head lifted up, touching against mine, and I let out a sob. He soothed, "I'm okay. I'm alive."

I fisted his shirt in my hands. "But are you going to stay alive?" The fear was so strong inside of me.

One of his hands ran down my back, sliding up under his shirt and tucking into the back of my panties. "I'm safe. I will be safe. We're okay."

Another shudder wracked through me, but I looked up at him. I needed to see his eyes when I asked this next question. "What was included in the deal? I need to know all of it."

"You." His other hand touched my bottom lip, pulling it down a little. "Me. EJ. Anyone you love. Anyone EJ loves. That was the deal."

I let that sink in before I sat up, now fully straddling him. He adjusted with me, moving so he was sitting against my bed's headboard. My legs sank down on either side of him, and his hands went to them, anchoring me against him. I closed my eyes, giving in for a moment, savoring the feel of him between my legs. I rocked forward.

His hands tightened on me, pulling me to him as he groaned.

God. That felt good. So fucking good.

I paused, opening my eyes to see him watching me. His own serious. Dark with lust. My chest rose up and down in a slow breath. "I thought Blake already made that deal?"

He nodded, his hands running up my legs. "She did, but she disappeared almost right away. Lane would've used that as a loophole. So I made a deal with him myself."

"She disappeared?"

"Yeah, but she's okay. She didn't disappear because of him or to go back on not making sure you guys are all safe. It was a sort of inevitable thing she needed to do, but it's all good. I helped her sort it out too. I was doing that before I came here."

"What about EJ?"

"He's good. That's where I was the last month. I went to California and introduced myself to EJ's half sisters and Tab's husband."

I wanted to hear more about that situation, but the Lane part was nagging at me. "What'd you have to do to get Lane to agree with upholding letting all of us be alive and torture-free?" Or worse. "What'd you give up so he'd agree with that deal?"

He shook his head, leaning toward me. His hand returned to the back of my head, cupping me. "Nothing that you need to worry about."

I braced a hand to his chest. "Jake." His heartbeat pounded through his chest, into my hand. It distracted me momentarily. "I need to know what kind of deal you made."

His lips twisted down. "I gave him something that he's been wanting the whole time. That's all. I'm not trying to keep it from you, but I need to tell someone else first."

"Who?"

"One of the guys from the city."

I frowned. "One of the Mafia guys?"

He nodded, silent.

"The one you like?"

His lips twisted again, finding that amusing. "Walden and I have always had a weird dynamic. We're friends. We're enemies. We're going to be more enemies than friends from now on."

My frown deepened.

His hand began rubbing over my leg, tugging me to ride over him. He added, "But that was his doing. Not mine. Not yours. He did that, so the deal I made with Lane closes a door to us. That's it. The only consequence is that we can't go to the city again."

My lips parted. "Ever?"

"Not for a long while." He blew out a ragged breath. "Is that okay? I know you just met your cousin. And you had that list of tourist things you wanted to do. We can't go back there. Not for a while. It won't be safe. I'm sorry about that, about taking away that city from you."

"Stop." I pushed up against his chest again, climbing higher on his lap. "I don't care about that right now."

"But you can't visit your cousin."

I waved that off. "Graham can come here. He is coming here."

"You never saw a Broadway show."

"I can watch something on television and pretend I'm there. Have you met me? I have a good imagination. Plus, there's no line for the bathroom here. Or there isn't usually. Snacks are significantly cheaper too. If I get drunk, I don't need to worry about my safety on the subway or if I should cab it home."

"I still feel bad."

I rolled my eyes. "Like my aunts won't figure out some way to get into that city? They've been antsy, waiting to reach out to Blake. Maude's the worst. It'll be fine." I laid my hand to his face, cupping it. "You told me you love me. Don't think for a second I'm ignoring that."

He snorted, his head resting back as he shook it from side to side. Slowly. "I do love you. And I don't know what the fuck goes on in your head sometimes, but no. I didn't come all this way, driving through the goddamn mountains to say goodbye, if that's what you're thinking." He suddenly jerked forward, stopping two inches from me. His next words came out fierce. "I came to get you."

My mouth parted even more. My chest began pounding. "What . . ." I licked my lips. "What does that mean?"

He pulled me forward, his hand fisting tightly in my hair. He growled, possessively. Primal. "That means you're *mine*. A war was already brewing, but for you, I lit a match and dropped it. I'm going to let the whole city burn for you."

I didn't know what that meant, but he came for me. Not to say goodbye to me. Not to leave me again. My body sagged forward. He caught me, easing me down gently. My head went to his neck and he cradled me against his chest. His lips grazed my forehead before he whispered, "I love you. I have no clue when it happened. If it was already in that subway train when I made up an excuse to talk to you, or when I saw you at the police station, or when I tasted you for the first time. I don't know, but it happened and I'm never letting you go. *I love you.*"

Warmth burst through me.

So I started crying.

Of course.

I lifted my head again, finding him watching me. So serious.

A new tenderness shone from his eyes. "I've always walked the line between the two worlds. I was half-Mafia. Half-cop. I had to be both. For me. For Justin. I didn't know how far over the edge I was willing to go. A part of me was scared to find out because if I did, then who was I going to hurt because of it? I was already trying to protect Justin, my sister, and EJ. My life was fucked, Sawyer. It wasn't mine. I was living in the gray and I couldn't find my footing. All that changed when I got you. Everything suddenly made sense. I know exactly how far I'd go to keep you safe. I'm still walking that line, but I'm doing that for me. Right here, right now, there's no one else pulling my strings except *me*. I'm both. I'm bad and I'm good. I've got no problem doing what I need to do to protect the people I love. That's you. You and EJ. You are mine. There's nothing I won't do to keep you alive. You formed the foundation under my feet and I finally know who I am, all the parts of me. You help meld it all together. You make everything make sense. You gave me that clarity. You gave me freedom."

I caught both sides of his face in my hands, more tears sliding down my face. "Jake," I whispered.

"Are you happy here?"

"What?" I blinked away some of the tears.

He wiped them away from my cheeks, repeating, "Are you happy here?"

"I . . ." I didn't know what to say until the truth hit me hard. "I'm happy *with you*." I touched his chest and his hand covered mine, keeping it there. His heartbeat picked up, thumping even stronger.

"My life is done on the East Coast. I can't guarantee no one will come after me, but as it stands now, I don't think they will. EJ knows about me. Tab knows what happened. She's not happy, but I don't give a fuck anymore. I cleared everything so if you wanted, we could go to

California. Unless you're happy here? Your family is here. I'll go back and forth to see EJ, but I won't stay away any longer."

"What are you actually asking me?" My head was swimming.

He moved both hands to mine, keeping it anchored to him. He stared hard at me. "I want you with me for the rest of my life. That's what I want. I want you as my woman forever. I want a partner. I want you as my family. That's what I want, but I'll go where you are. If it's here, I'll move here. If you want to go to California, I'm sure EJ would like that as well. But you and me. That's what I want." He caught my bottom lip again, his eyes searching inside of me. "Is that something you'd be okay with? I want you. I want all of you. Forever."

Love filled me. Happiness. Peace. I leaned forward, my forehead returning to its spot against his, and I breathed into him, "Yes. I want all of that. I love you."

His mouth found mine, and I let myself get swept up in everything that was Jake Worthing.

The kiss was rough, demanding, and soon it was desperate. It'd been too long since we'd been together.

He picked me up, turning, and laid me underneath him. His hands found mine, pinning them above me. "How quiet can you be?"

"What?" I surged up against him, grinding against him. He felt so good. I began panting.

"We're in your childhood bed, and babe, I want to do some dirty things to you here. I'll ask again. How quiet can you be?"

I gasped. "My parents are here." But as I said that, I wound my legs around him and arched up into him. He wasn't moving, so I'd move for both of us. I kept rubbing against him. Pleasure began building. I moved faster, harder against him. The ache was back, starting to throb between my legs. I wanted him inside of me.

"I'm aware. So are you going to be quiet, like a good little girl?" he teased before nipping at my lips, then slid one possessive hand down my body, slid his shirt up and off me. His hand quickly found my breast, circling it. His thumb ran over my nipple.

I moaned. "Jake." That felt so good.

"I'm going to fuck you."

I moaned again as his lips found my throat, tasting me.

"But you need to keep it down or your parents are going to catch us, because once I'm inside of you, I'm not leaving. You got that?" His hand continued its slow descent, sliding down my stomach, over my hip, dipping between my legs. His finger circled my clit, rubbing over it, and my body shivered.

"Jake." I reached for his shoulders, trying to yank him up to me.

"No. Not yet." He ignored my hold, moving farther down. He pulled my panties off, then he was back between my legs.

His tongue circled me, and I arched, the hunger erupting inside of me. I needed him. I needed him now.

He slid inside of me, thrusting deep with his tongue.

My legs wrapped around his head.

He groaned, eating me up. "You taste so good. Always so sweet."

He kept tasting me, his tongue sliding in and out as he built the pressure inside of me. When he sucked on my clit, long and hard, he slid two fingers deep into me at the same time, and it was enough. I went over the edge, soaring over it and almost frantically. I yanked myself up off the bed, using him as leverage with my legs clasped so tightly around his head. He lapped everything from me, continuing to lick me and then soothe me through my release until my body lowered back down to the bed.

My legs fell to the side, now feeling boneless. My whole body seemed to melt into the bed, but Jake growled, his teeth grazing the inside of my thigh before he lifted, then positioned himself at my entrance. I felt his cock nudge my opening. "I'm still safe."

I nodded, pulling him into me. "Me too."

He slid inside of me, bare. Pushing all the way, both of us went still at the feel of him. I was so full.

He groaned. "Fuck. You feel good. Tight." He began moving, moving out. Pushing back in.

Carnal desire *inflamed* me.

He picked up the pace, thrusting almost wildly. Rough. Hard.

I loved it so much.

I loved him so much so I told him, whispering, "I was tossed out like the trash when you met me."

He tensed, raising himself up to see me, but he kept moving inside of me, just slowing.

What he was doing to me, showing me, was a beautiful thing. He needed to know this about me. "He made me feel like I was the garbage, and I ran away."

He laid a hand against the side of my face, thrusting in again.

Another tear slid free. I ignored it, saying, "He broke me down, Jake. It's the only reason I stayed with him for so long. He was using me, and a part of me knew it. I let him use me because at some point, he made me think I couldn't get anything better. That I didn't deserve anything better. He conditioned me so that I accepted the crumbs he was giving me, and I stayed. I wasn't happy. I wasn't in love. But I stayed and I couldn't understand why I stayed, but then I met you." I pulled my wrist out from his hold, reaching up and framing his face as he continued sliding inside of me. My legs were wrapped around him, moving with him. The pleasure was bursting out of me. The love. The sun. He gave that to me. He had to know. "I ran to you. I just didn't know I was running to you until you caught me. You fought for me. You protected me. You saved me. You did it because you love me. I never got that from him. It's *all* I've gotten from you because that's who you are as a man. You make me feel beautiful. You make me feel priceless. You are ruthless. You are reckless at times. You can be calculating and brash. Blunt. Rude. But I love every part of you because when I met you, I found me again."

Another moan left him as he bent over me, grabbing the headboard. He began fucking me harder. Deeper.

I closed my eyes, my head falling down as I let the sensations ride over me.

"*Fuck*, Sawyer." His head fell down, his body blanketing me, but he continued to pound me. A new frenzy came over both of us. He turned so he could see me, his hand reaching for my mouth, hooking my head so I could see him too.

We were both breathing hard.

Our bodies clambered to get even closer to each other, if it was even possible.

"I love you," I whispered, my eyes wetting.

"Christ." He raised his head up to find me, his mouth covering me, and he breathed into me. He pounded into me, holding deep as the pressure sped through me. My release spread through my entire body, making me tremble from the aftershocks. He shoved an arm underneath me and held me up against him in a firm grip. Then his teeth raked over my shoulder as he thrust a few more times until I felt him swell inside of me. I grasped onto him, holding him to me this time as he released inside of me.

He collapsed on top of me.

A moment later, he rolled to the side, grabbing my face. "I'm *never* fucking letting you go now. Not that I would've before, but all that shit you just said. You cemented your fate to me. Never leaving you. Never letting you go."

That made my heart soar. "Promise?" I raised up my pinkie.

His eyes turned molten before he wrapped his with mine. "Promise."

There. Forever.

Someone knocked on my bedroom door.

My mom called through it, "Sawyer? Are you awake in there?"

We both tensed, before falling into quiet laughter.

Jake grinned at me, smoothing some of my hair behind my ear. "You should've been more quiet."

I grinned back, shaking my head. "No." Because it was perfect.

All of it was, just, perfect.

Wait. Not totally perfect.

I held a hand to his chest, stopping him from kissing me again. "One second."

Jake lifted up, giving me space.

I rolled over and reached for my nightstand. I pulled open the drawer and grabbed the knife inside.

He had a careful measured look in his eyes as he watched me lie on my back again. "Sawyer." His voice went low. "What are you doing with that?"

I smiled at him, letting him see all the love I had for him. He relaxed into my touch. "Told you that you wouldn't see it coming. I'm keeping a promise to myself." While he was busy staring into my eyes, his muscles continuing to relax, I flipped the knife around and then impaled it on his leg.

There.

A strangled cry left him before he quickly tried to muffle it. "What? Why?" He was breathing through the pain, the force of it making him lose some of his color.

I gave him a soft peck on the lips. "Payback. Stay here. I'll grab some first aid for you. I don't think you'll need the hospital." I climbed out of the bed and padded barefoot into the bathroom.

Turns out, he did need the hospital for a few stitches.

Now it was perfect.

EPILOGUE

SAWYER

My parents met him that morning when I brought him back from the hospital. My mom already knew him, but there'd been no bonding moments. Her glimpses were of him shooting people and yelling at us to leave. Not a super great first impression.

They'd warm to him. I knew it.

The rest of the family came over that afternoon. Clara and Bess officially met him too. Of course they'd seen him longer, but their impression was the same as my mom's. Just more. More shooting and more yelling. Clara asked if he knew any snipers and if she could get lessons. Bess was excited to parade him through Bear Creek, specifically in front of Beck's chiropractor clinic.

I wasn't sure what Jake thought of them, but he only told me later, "Some families are great and supportive. They circle the wagons for each other. Some don't. You got one that circles. I'll love 'em for that fact alone."

We stayed in Bear Creek, figuring out my house. I'd been staying with my parents because the thought of being in there alone . . . Well. All the shooting had an effect.

I decided to put it on the market, and three weeks later, when we were in California, my Realtor called with an offer that was asking price. I accepted, getting off the phone to let Jake know the good news. We were at a house that he'd bought a block over from his ex. It was close enough for EJ to easily come and go as he liked, which was the new arrangement between Jake and his ex-wife. It'd been touch and go at first, especially with his ex and her husband. Both feared Jake, with good reason, but EJ was coming around every so often to see his dad. He had one more year in high school before college.

I knew Jake wanted to wait and see where EJ would go for college. After that, we'd make a final decision on where we would find a permanent home. In the meantime, we went back often to visit my family, but we kept returning to California.

I was good with that arrangement. It felt like the best of both worlds.

Also, Jake's cousin hadn't been lying. Jake's family was wealthy, really wealthy. Which he explained was through a trust from the oil business family members. Neither of us needed to work again, but that wasn't who Jake was, or me. While we were going back and forth between my family and EJ, Jake started buying real estate. That began his new career. In the future, he would flip houses, then move on to flipping mansions, but some of his buildings would have renters. As for myself, I was never going to work for someone unless it was something I truly enjoyed. I just didn't know what I wanted to do.

So I was taking my time.

If that meant going back to college, then that's what I would do. I wasn't sure yet.

There was no rush.

But I also had a real-life bucket list to start crossing off.

I was excited because Jake was all in. Turns out that he had another cousin in Hawaii, and we met them when we went for the Aloha Festival. I was also currently learning Spanish, but it was coming along slow. Very slow. Muy lentamente.

As for New York City, we'd be going back. I just hadn't told Jake yet.

He told me about the deal he struck with his cousin, and I mentioned what I could to my aunts and mom.

A plan was forming.

My mom was in charge of that list.

JAKE

I'd been putting this last call off for so long. Too long. It was time. In fact, it might've been too late, but I needed to call him. I'd finally told Sawyer what I bargained for our safety.

I stepped outside, breathed in the night air, and hit call on my phone.

The other line rang. A moment later, it was answered.

Ashton's voice was abrupt. "It's been a minute since we've had a call. I'll admit, a part of me is excited while a part of me is disappointed. I thought we were done with this. I thought our last correspondence *was* our last correspondence."

There'd been a time in my life when I considered him my only friend. It was when the world was dark, when no one helped and only my supposed enemy extended a helping hand. We had years together where I'd been an ally of sorts. I was a loyal man. I only betrayed those who betrayed me first.

That was the reason for this call. Because Ashton betrayed me.

I drew in a breath before saying, "I'm not calling to catch up."

Ashton grew quiet on his end. "I wouldn't think you would. What's the reason for this call, Worthing? What did you do, Jake?"

I murmured, "It's more what you did, Ashton. You fucked up."

He was quiet again before saying, "I fucked up? Okay. Tell me how I fucked up. Tell me the reason you're shifting blame for whatever the fuck you did. I'd love to hear this."

It was so simple really. I didn't understand how he couldn't realize it. I told him, "I asked you for help with saving my woman's life. You said no." I cringed, hearing the laughter that came from him that day. "You laughed at me."

"I did not," he returned, so smoothly.

"You did." It was the day I didn't know if I could save Sawyer's life. I would never forget that day. "You should've helped me that day."

Ashton was quiet again before he exploded, "I already had! What are you talking about? I'd done too much. I couldn't do any more without risking a full-blown war between us and your cousin."

There it was. The truth.

I noted, softly, "There was already a war, remember? You'd already been waging it against my cousin, but you wouldn't help me that day because I was your first wave. Wasn't I?" I figured it out later. If Creighton had known, then there was no reason Ashton hadn't also. "You knew what my family trained me to become, didn't you?"

There was silence for a bit. And that was my answer.

"Jake," he started. "You were a cop—"

"There's a difference between what my family had me doing and what I did for the force. A major difference and you know it. That's what you were banking on. You knew he had Sawyer. You knew the lengths I'd go to save her. I was the first wave. You were hoping I'd kill my cousin. And if I went with him, if that was the only way I could kill him, then that just meant I was collateral. Right? That was your plan?"

My chest filled with anger and bitterness. Ashton had power and control. I came from a position of no power.

"I asked for your help against Lane. You told me no."

"You were asking for too much—"

"I wasn't. He had my woman. He had my *son*."

"I didn't know."

I didn't believe him and it didn't matter anymore. "You fucked up, Ashton. You lost sight of what was in front of you. You were my family's enemy and I chose your side."

"You used my side to keep yours in check. Do not change the script on what fucking happened in the past."

It didn't matter. Not anymore. "I struck a deal with my cousin. I'm calling to give you notice."

"With Lane?"

Here was the kicker, the real part that Ashton never considered and what he should've.

I said into the phone, "You're under the impression that my family's operation is solely in Maine and that my cousin only tried to push his way into the city. You think we didn't have any hold already in the city. You're wrong to make that assumption."

He was quiet again before asking, "What are you talking about?"

"We have assets set up throughout the entire city. Manhattan. Brooklyn. Tribeca. Soho. Red Hook. Queens. Harlem. The Bronx. We have a distribution pipeline that's used for transport of all goods. We have trucks in the city. We have men in the city. We have nightclubs that we use as camouflage for our other operations. We have businesses that we use to clean money for clients. My family is a lot bigger, a lot more powerful, and a lot more dangerous than you think. When our families went to war, you did not wipe us out. You only made a dent."

Ashton went quiet. "What the fuck did you do?"

"You knew my cousin would have too many men. You knew I wouldn't be able to take all of them out, but I just needed the one shot. Right? Just the one." If only he had helped . . . But he hadn't.

"What. Did. You. Do?"

"The deal was for my life. My woman's life. My son's. Everyone that Sawyer loves and everyone my son loves. That's what I bargained with Lane for our lives."

He'd grown quiet. Waiting.

"I stepped aside, Ashton."

"What?" he asked, curtly.

"This call was a courtesy. Through the years, your family's name gave Justin the ability to be normal for a while. Because of that, I'm giving you a heads-up of what's coming your way."

"You still haven't said what the fuck you did—"

"I gave him my family."

Ashton stopped talking, abruptly.

This was it. This was what I did. "I stepped aside and I gave him the keys to my family's business. He knows the locations. He knows the passcodes. I gave him every piece of information he would need to move in and seize control of my family. My uncles have already either been killed or they've been immobilized. I don't care. He needed a stronghold in the city, and I'm the one that gave it to him."

"You fucking piece of shit—" Ashton cut himself off, but I heard the swift curses falling from him. "And if I send men after you? You opened a goddamn back door to my city, you fuck. You're my enemy now. I know your weaknesses because that's the kind of enemy I am. I could send men to execute that pretty little delusional woman of yours."

I waited for him to finish.

"One call and your son is dead. His entire family. His sisters. His mother. You'd have to walk through their blood as you'd be the one who would discover their bodies. You want me to do that? Because that's who I am, Worthing. You are forgetting who I am in this world."

"You won't. Because when you calm down, you'll remember that I know more about your business than you think I do. And I know your woman. I know West's woman. I know about your new compound. I know your businesses, the ones you don't want anyone to know. And I know that in the back of your mind, you'll think about everything that I knew about my family that I never told you. You'll start wondering what else I know about your businesses. So, Ashton. It's your move. You send men after me and mine, I'll come for you and yours."

"I *despise* you."

I shook my head, holding my phone so tightly, but I knew the truth. I heard through the anger from him, saying, "Maybe. But I also helped give you your sunshine and I know what that's like now. The war's at your doorstep. I just opened the door for him to come in."

"*Fuck* you, Worthing."

I ended the call.

Glancing over my shoulder to where Sawyer was laughing at the table with EJ, I was looking at my new life. I meant what I said. He stood by as my lifelines could've been taken from me. There was no forgiving that.

This new life was just beginning.

Seeing me through the door, Sawyer smiled and waved at me. "Are you coming? Your beer's getting warm. What are you doing?"

I grinned at her, sliding my hand inside my front pocket.

EJ gave me a knowing look and stood up, coming my way. He stepped through the door and lowered his voice. "You ready for this, old man?"

He was teasing, already knowing what I had planned when I walked inside.

It'd been hard between us.

Hard for him to accept that his mom never mentioned me. Hard for him to accept the reasons why I stayed away. He learned everything. I was done with keeping secrets. When he found out about Justin, he cried in my arms. "I wish I'd known him."

I hugged him and shed my own tears. My voice was thick as I rasped, "He would've adored you. He did adore you, what he remembered about you."

"So he knew about me?"

I hesitated. "He forgot a lot from that night. I think it was on purpose, but he never brought you up again. I decided to let it rest. I'm sorry."

He shook his head, pushing away and raking his hands through his hair. "I'm furious with Mom. Like, I'm so fucking furious, but when I was taken and when you walked into that warehouse, things began to make sense. Things clicked that never clicked before. You were my dad. I could see that right away. I don't totally remember everything that happened in that warehouse, but I remember that you loved me. That you were going to fight for me. That you did fight for me. I knew that much. That's what stayed with me until I woke up in the hospital. I looked over and you were in the chair next to me. Everything, just, felt—I don't know. My chest felt easier. Like I could breathe better. I had this feeling things were going to get better now. Things would make sense." He looked my way, my jawline, my nose, my face, my hair all looking back at me. He had Justin's eyes. But he was my son. "You know what I mean?"

I had a hard time getting a word out. "I know what you mean."

Goddamn. I loved my kid.

I always loved him, but now I got to love him, and that was for the rest of my life.

It's the type of love that brings a man to his knees. My son brought me to my knees and I knew there'd be more moments in the future.

I couldn't wait.

He nudged my hand now. "Do you have a plan on how to do this?" He grinned, teasing, "Need to make a fucking list? Like Sawyer's obsessed with. That's what you have to look forward to. Lists and then lists upon lists and even lists for those lists."

"Shut up." I was grinning.

He was funny and teasing me.

I was happy, and I knew in a moment, I'd be even happier.

"My plan is to go in there. You start recording and I'll take a knee."

"This should be good. I'm shocked her family's not here for it."

I held back my grimace because he didn't know they were waiting not far from here. They'd taken it upon themselves to arrive early, and they went to Tab's house to introduce themselves to EJ's mom and two sisters. Tab didn't know, but she'd never follow through with her threat against my sister. If she did, I was going to let loose Clara on her. Clara and Maude, because the two had bonded. Sawyer said there was retribution against a retired teacher. She wouldn't tell me the details, just saying it was better if I didn't know. I left it alone.

Feeling some nerves kick up inside of me, I opened the door and stepped through.

EJ moved around me, saying under his breath, "Lists, Dad. Lists."

I suppressed my laugh until I met Sawyer's eyes.

She was taking in EJ as he pulled out his phone and began recording, aiming at her.

She started to say, "What—"

I knelt before her, pulling out a small box in my hand.

Her eyes widened. She gasped, breathless, as I opened the box and held up my mother's ring. If she didn't like it, I'd get a different one. I didn't care, but it felt right to do this with a part of my mom with me. With us.

I held it up. "Will you marry me?"

ABOUT THE AUTHOR

Tijan is a *New York Times* bestselling author who writes suspenseful and unpredictable novels. Her characters are strong, intense, and gut-wrenchingly real with a little bit of sass on the side. Tijan began writing after college, and once she started, she was hooked. She's written multiple bestsellers including the Fallen Crest series, *Ryan's Bed, Enemies*, and others.

Tijan is currently writing many new books and series with an English cocker spaniel whom she adores. Connect with the author on her website (www.TijansBooks.com), on Facebook (www.facebook.com/tijansbooks), and on X (@TijansBooks). You can also check out her Instagram at www.instagram.com/tijansbooks. Tijan is managed by Park, Fine, & Brower Literary Management.